Magical Midlife Alliance

ALSO BY K.F. BREENE

LEVELING UP

Magical Midlife Madness
Magical Midlife Dating
Magical Midlife Invasion
Magical Midlife Love
Magical Midlife Meeting
Magical Midlife Challenge
Magical Midlife Alliance

DELICIOUSLY DARK FAIRYTALES

A Ruin of Roses
A Throne of Ruin
A Kingdom of Ruin
A Queen of Ruin

DEMIGODS OF SAN FRANCISCO

Sin & Chocolate
Sin & Magic
Sin & Salvation
Sin & Spirit
Sin & Lightning
Sin & Surrender

DEMON DAYS VAMPIRE NIGHTS WORLD

Born in Fire
Raised in Fire
Fused in Fire
Natural Witch
Natural Mage
Natural Dual-Mage
Warrior Fae Trapped
Warrior Fae Princess
Revealed in Fire
Mentored in Fire
Battle with Fire

Magical Midlife Alliance

By K.F. Breene

Contact info:
www.kfbreene.com
books@kfbreene.com

CHAPTER 1

JESSIE

"RISE AND SHINE, miss." Mr. Tom set my coffee on the nightstand. "It's time to get schooled by a very pushy garhette."

Garhette was the term they used for female gargoyles who didn't shift. He could only mean Patty, Ulric's mom. She'd promised to help me go through the connection requests that the gargoyle cairn leaders had sent. I was the new kid on the block and the only living female gargoyle that could shift and do magic. They were curious.

Hopefully that curiosity would turn into a desire to form an alliance. To help Kingsley, we needed numbers. The basajaunak had turned us down, and so now the gargoyles were our only hope.

Mr. Tom laid a white T-shirt across the bed over my midsection.

I wiped the sleep out of my eyes and checked the

clock on the nightstand. Ten a.m. About normal for my wake-up time.

"Is she ready to get to the connection requests?" I asked, sitting up.

"Yes. She's moved them all to the largest sitting room in the back of the house and organized them yet again. She has also tramped through the town and heard any and all gossip she possibly could. Very nosey, that woman. She's in everyone's business all the time."

"That's what makes her great at networking. It's why she's here."

He sniffed, not able to argue with that.

Patty had been on a one-woman mission to learn every inch of the territory. In just a few days of being here she seemed to be intimate friends with a great many residents, both magical and not, and knew by name absolutely everyone who frequented Austin's bar. Even crazier, I'd heard that she'd somehow organized a dinner at Broken Sue's house that *she* would be hosting. The woman was a manipulative powerhouse, but you wouldn't know it with all her pleasant smiles and seemingly innocuous chitchat.

"Here we go." He patted the white T-shirt, which could only be Austin's. "This one isn't fresh, but it should still suffice. Austin Steele needs to come back and spend some time here so I can grab more of his discarded laundry."

I should really tell Mr. Tom to stop stealing Austin's clothes, but I loved being wrapped up in his smell. People said the yearning for each other usually waned after the first week of mating, but that hadn't happened in our case. If anything, it kept getting stronger. Hence the stolen, dirty clothes of my mate that I wore in the mornings, especially after a night when he hadn't made it over. Unfortunately, last night was one of them.

"He's been busy," I said as I reached for the shirt. "I wish there was something more I could do to help."

"We can help right now, miss. Here we go." Mr. Tom picked up my coffee mug and held it out to me. "Let's get some coffee in us, and then we will be ready for the day."

A knock sounded at the door as I checked in with Austin through our links. He seemed distracted, frustrated, annoyed, and determined. Also fatigued. Very fatigued.

I quickly got to work healing him as Mr. Tom crossed to the door. Before he got there, it swung open and Ulric poked his head in. His blue and pink hair caught the light, newly dyed and very bright.

"Oh good, you're up." He pushed the door open a little farther as Mr. Tom stopped in front of him, blocking his way.

"She is not *up*, as you can plainly see. She is *awake*," Mr. Tom said in a snooty tone. "She understands that your mother is ready to get started, thank you very much. She will take her breakfast as usual and be down when she is able. The mistress of Ivy House is not to be rushed. It's time you learned this."

I frowned at Mr. Tom. He was *literally* just rushing me.

"It's fine." I slipped the shirt on before pushing the covers away and swinging my feet over the edge of the mattress. I held my hand out for the coffee mug Mr. Tom still held. "I'm good. I was just up late last night looking over the spell books Sebastian wants me to learn."

"A good use of your time." Mr. Tom turned with a stiff back and delivered my coffee. Instead of leaving to grab my breakfast, though, he stood off to the side and glared at Ulric.

Ulric barely suppressed a grin as he stepped a little farther into the room. The grin pulled into a smile as he gave me a sweeping bow. "Good morning, miss. I trust you slept well?"

"What do you need, Ulric?" I stood and took a sip of the coffee as I made my way across the room. I looked out the windows at the beautiful day. Green grass stretched across the backyard and a doll with a billy club trudged its length. "Why…"

Another doll, down the way, stomped through Edgar's flowers with a machete. Yet another, deeper in the trees, held a large knife in one hand and tapped the end against its other hand.

"What's going on with the dolls?" I asked, immediately feeling around for the others. For this reason, and this reason alone, I was grateful I could detect them through my connection to the house. Some were in their room, but most were wandering the grounds.

"Oh, that." Mr. Tom headed into my closet. "It seems the garhette only spooked the gnomes. She didn't entirely chase them away. They are currently in the woods, hidden from detection by Ivy House, and an elaborately violent game of hide-and-seek is underway."

I grimaced and backed away from the window. "Who is playing this game? Just the dolls and the gnomes?"

"It's hard to say. So far it seems anyone who ventures too far into the woods is playing the game. That is, if Edgar's shouts and screams are any indication. The dolls are on the case, but the gnomes are proving wily. There is a war brewing, I think."

"Why is Ivy House hiding the location of the gnomes?" Ulric asked, edging closer to the window and looking out.

"It is anyone's guess," Mr. Tom said, bringing out a pair of jeans and a black, flowy blouse. "It's best to just ride these things out. Ulric, make your point and leave the miss to wake up. She has to deal with your mother all day. She needs to prepare."

"She's not that bad," Ulric muttered. "I just wanted to say, Jessie, that if my mom gets to be too much, or she is a little too pushy, or if she won't listen to you, just let me know. I'll try to run interference. She might not shift, but she has a lot of the more…robust gargoyle characteristics."

"What does that mean?" I asked.

"It means she is incredibly stubborn and hard to manage," Mr. Tom said. "She thinks she knows everything and attempts to assume control of that which is none of her business."

It was like he'd forgotten that he, too, was a gargoyle and shared a lot of those traits…

"Got it," I said, finishing my first cup of coffee. "I think I can handle it. Mr. Tom, can you grab me another cup of coffee? I'm going to jump in the shower."

A HALF-HOUR LATER, I was dressed, fed, and ready to wade through the connection requests. Part of me was excited to see what the cairns had sent! Most had sent their invitations with gifts, and I'd been assured I could keep everything without guilt because this was how things were done in the gargoyle world.

The other part of me knew what was on the line. This wasn't fun and games. I'd need to choose whom to invite wisely and be quick about it. Time was ticking.

"Here we are." Mr. Tom led me to the door of the largest sitting room, opened it up, and stepped aside with a flourish. "Good luck, miss. We're all counting on you."

"Thanks," I muttered, stepping through.

My eyes widened at the sight that awaited me in the room.

Boxes. Boxes everywhere! Some with bows, some wrapped, some just a plain color, like white or pink. A few baskets sat among the boxes, and a couple of trunks. It was like the most elaborate Christmas morning setup I'd ever seen.

A sound like *heh* escaped my lips as I took one more step forward, scanning the bounty. Patty had definitely organized everything. There seemed to be sections, all the packages grouped together in clusters around the room. Within the sections, each package was given its own space so that nothing was crowded.

No wonder she'd set this up in the big room.

Sebastian and Nessa sat on one of the couches, each

looking up with bright, excited eyes. They obviously wanted to see what was in all of the packages. Jasper and Nathanial stood at the back of the room, waiting patiently to be of some use. Niamh sat in a chair at the side, sipping out of a teacup. It was anyone's guess if that cup contained tea or whiskey. Patty loitered on the outskirts of one of the smaller clusters, her manicured finger out, muttering to herself.

"What about the rest of our crew?" I asked, noticing the absence of Cyra, Hollace, and Edgar. Through the Ivy House link, I could feel them in the distance, what felt like a town away or more.

"They went on a seed-buying expedition with Edgar," Mr. Tom said. "There is some sort of flower show on the horizon that he's very excited for."

It was then I felt the front door open and registered the footsteps that had entered Ivy House's property.

Austin.

Butterflies fluttered through my belly, and I instantly stopped and turned toward the door.

He came through it a moment later, his steps hurried until he saw me. Then he slowed, his cobalt gaze lingering on mine before sweeping down my front. I'd changed into real clothes, thankfully, and wasn't still wearing his old T-shirt. Not that he would have minded.

"Hey, baby," he said, not glancing around or acknowledging anyone else in the room. This was his way of showing the world that I was the most important thing to him, and anyone else had better be prepared to wait until he was done greeting me.

The sentiment made me swoon every time.

"Hey," I said with what I knew was a dopey grin. "We're about to start going through the connection requests. Do you have time to hang out for a while?"

He ran his thumb along my bottom lip. "Always."

Shivers coated my skin, and my eyes fluttered as he leaned down to kiss me, his lips grazing mine until they pressed more firmly. I opened my mouth to him, rewarded by his intoxicating taste and a thrill of electricity.

"I missed you," he whispered when we came up for air. "I plan on staying tonight."

"Will you be going home to freshen up a bit first?" Mr. Tom asked from beside the door. "Or maybe you'd like to shower quickly right now, put on some house sweats, and meet us back here. I doubt we'll be very far along with the way Mrs. Sunauk chatters on."

"Manners, Mr. Tom," I chastised him, slipping my hand into Austin's.

Austin's brow furrowed as he attempted to process what Mr. Tom had said.

"Come on, the show is about to begin." I tugged him along.

"Is he saying I stink?" Austin asked as he allowed me to pull him to the couch. He bent his head, clearly trying to get a whiff of himself. "I haven't done much fighting or sweating today. I should be good."

I laughed as we sat down. "Never mind him. You smell good. Spicy and masculine."

"No gorilla trailing along behind you, huh?" Nessa mock-pouted. "And here I wore my *good* ponytail holder."

Sebastian spat out a laugh. "That's as much as you try anymore, huh?"

"Like you can talk, rocking your sweatpants."

"These are sports sweats. They count as pants."

"I don't think you're going to thaw that gorilla," Ulric said as he opened his laptop and sat down on the couch behind his mom. "He's got a lot of baggage that he seems to want to hang on to."

"He can hang on to his baggage," Nessa responded, "just as long as he drops his pants."

Ulric laughed delightedly. "A-men, sister. Happy hunting."

"Mr. Steele." Mr. Tom half bowed to Austin. "Might I offer you something to eat or drink? A sandwich, perhaps?"

"Yeah, that would be great," Austin said, leaning back and getting comfortable.

"Can I have a sandwich, too?" Jasper called after him.

Ulric raised his hand. "I can always eat."

"Isn't that the truth," Patty grumbled before clapping to get everyone's attention. "Every gargoyle leader put his best foot forward and now awaits Jessie's judgment on whether or not his cairn will get an audience. Shall we begin?"

"I'm about to pee myself, I'm so excited," Nessa said, leaning forward on the couch.

Patty bustled to the far right corner. "Okay, now, Jessie. A few things—"

"Oh my God, she is great at dangling the bait." Nessa puffed out a breath, still leaning forward in anticipation.

"Ulric has a spreadsheet open." Patty gestured to where her son sat. "On that spreadsheet I have listed all the cairns, those who sent gifts and those who did not. I will stop myself here and mention that those who did not send anything, in this instance, likely didn't think they had anything to offer. Almost anyone of relevance did send a gift. So we are in very good shape going into this. Let's have a round of applause for a great start…"

Patty clapped animatedly. Nessa joined in, shoving

Sebastian with her elbow to make him clap too. Jasper and Ulric looked around in confusion with their hands poised.

"I have the cairns and their statuses pre-entered." Patty nodded at the laptop. "Ulric will enter what you've received today. A *summary*, Ulric. We just need to refresh our memories later on."

"I'm very good at vague thank-you cards," I said, feeling the anticipation burn through me.

"Oh my no, Jessie. No, no." Patty shook her head, her blond curls dancing. "No, dear. There will be no thank-you cards. You will either send a delicate rejection letter—I can craft that, if you'd like—or an invitation to meet. If you decide to issue an invitation, you will provide three dates—only *three*, mind. They will need to make one of those dates work."

"But what if I want to meet them and they don't have the space on their schedule?"

Patty stared at me for a long beat. "Dear, you are the only living female gargoyle in existence. The only one who has existed for some time. The gargoyle world at large was starting to think shifting females were a myth, that they'd gone extinct and would never come back. All these gargoyles"—she gestured around the room at the packages—"are desperate to meet you. They might not want to be led by you just yet, since that's another ball of wax, but if you turn out to be the genuine article within the community, their status will increase merely because you've given them an invitation. They will move heaven and earth to get here. Providing three dates is generous."

"Elaborate on them not wanting to be led by her," Austin said.

"Well, to put it simply, she'll need to prove herself. They'll want to know she can lead, and that she can protect both her people and theirs."

"Even if she proves herself," Nathanial said, "large cairn leaders are used to giving orders, not taking them. It will take a lot for that to change. I think for now we want to make a good impression, prove our territory is more than capable, and try to attract a host of guardians. That'll help us with the battle in Kingsley's territory, and we can work on our overall status in due time."

"Yes, fantastic point, Nathanial." Patty beamed. "But let's keep our status in mind, yes? We want to show well so that our status rises in the gargoyle community. The large cairn leaders will help with that. A lot to think about. Baby steps. Step one…here, Jessie, open the first gift."

CHAPTER 2

JESSIE

"OH, WAIT." PATTY held up a hand, stopping Jasper from picking up the package she'd indicated. "Let me just quickly go over how everything is organized."

"She did it again!" Nessa slapped her thighs, laughing. "Are we ever going to be able to open anything?"

Patty laughed also, clearly enjoying Nessa's lightheartedness. "We can open while I explain," she relented, motioning to Jasper and Nathanial. "Grab a few boxes from just over here, boys."

"*Finally*," Nessa said, her eyes hungry.

"This is the collection of gifts from some lower-status and rather poor cairns," Patty said, watching Jasper lift a medium-sized, pale pink box.

"Is there space on that spreadsheet that lists cairn size?" Austin asked. "Battle power, strongest members, things like that? We'll need location, as well. They might not get invited for a visit, but if we are traveling for other reasons, we can always stop in to meet them."

"I have a very rough estimate," Patty responded, "but unfortunately, a lot of that information is kept private. Cairns tend to keep their poker hands close to the chest, as it were."

"They must keep that information somewhere, though, right?" Nessa asked. "Surely large cairns keep records of their people. Even just payroll."

"Well, I know ours has a very robust network, yes," Patty said slowly. "But it has a lot of cybersecurity, and none of those *in the know* are at all prone to gossip. I have tried until I'm blue in the face. But I do have a lot of anecdotal information—"

"Nessa, here…grab…" Sebastian held his hand out toward Ulric and opened and closed his fingers.

"Words, Sebastian," I said. "Use your words."

Nathanial knelt beside me with a smallish white box wrapped in a pink bow, leaving Jasper to wait for a moment.

"Miss," he said softly, a smile lightly curling his lips. "This is just the beginning. I can't wait to witness your continued climb to greatness."

"That's a little much," I murmured, but couldn't help my grin as I took the box. I felt like royalty.

"I got it." Nessa hopped up, grabbing the laptop out

of Ulric's lap. "I'll just take over here, if you don't mind."

She bounded back to Sebastian, sitting and holding the computer out a little so they could both see.

"Here, Ulric," Niamh called. "Go get me Mr. Tom's laptop, would ya? It's the cleanest in the house. He doesn't seem to know porn exists. Nessa, slap that spreadsheet onto Google Drive so we can all access it."

"Uh…yup, okay." Ulric bounced up and jogged from the room.

Patty looked around at everyone with raised eyebrows.

"She already knows what we're thinking, Sabby," Nessa murmured, pointing at something on the screen. "Very clever, our Irishwoman."

"Well, it's no great mystery," Niamh replied. "Any great fool knows that network security is only as good as the people who set it up. A few taps, and we'll have all the information we please. Jasper, text that scruffy lad in town with the spiky hair and missing pinky. The ferret. I don't think there is a system he can't hack into. We'll lift up these cairns' kilts and give their balls a wee tickle."

"Pay?" Jasper asked, looking down at his phone.

"Ye really ought to recruit that gobshite into yer pack, Austin Steele," Niamh grumbled. "Then I wouldn't have to haggle with the bollocks. Tell him I'll sort him out, Jasper. We might as well set up a fortified network here while we have him, I suppose. We don't want those cairns to return the favor and pull down our knickers."

"Lots of metaphors involving private parts in cyber-security, it seems," Nessa murmured.

Patty nodded. "Yes, that sounds great. Let's give our team a round of applause." Everyone looked around in confusion this time. "Now, Jessie, each cairn name is written on the bottom of the box or package. Go ahead and open it, have a genuine reaction, and then we can check out the name of the cairn."

"I'm not sure this step is really necessary," Nathanial said. "She doesn't know one cairn from the other. She won't be swayed by names."

Patty hesitated. "This is true. Well…we might as well tell her anyway. These cairns are mostly well established, though still low status. They haven't been able to rise in the ranks. If you were a betting woman, you'd bet they'd remain as they are: unworthy of a second glance."

"Harsh," Jasper said with a grin as I lifted the lid and peered inside.

"Oh." Trying not to show my disappointment, I pulled out a chipped beige pot containing a couple of succulents. The rocks and much of the dirt had escaped the pot in transit and ended up at the bottom. "That's…nice. Edgar will be able to do something with that."

Nathanial frowned at it. "Like throw it away."

"Yes, well…" Patty walked over and took the box, checking the label at the bottom. "Ah. *Them.* I've heard that the leader has been through three mates so far. All of them have packed up and left the cairn, seemingly without notice. He has no stability. Definitely not someone to waste our time with." She handed the box off to Nessa, presumably so she could write down the name. "What's next?"

Nathanial handed over another box, this one a bit larger. Maybe one foot high and two feet wide. White Styrofoam sat snugly within it.

I worked my fingers in the sides only to have Nathanial put down the box Jasper had just handed him and reach for the one I held.

"Allow me, alpha," he murmured, taking the box and working out the contents. That done, he handed it back for me to do the final reveal.

"Okay, here we go, Austin Steele." Mr. Tom bustled in with a large plate piled high with two cheeseburgers with all the fixings and homemade fries. "I felt this might go over a bit better than a sandwich. Also, I ran out of lunchmeat—Good gracious, what *is* that ghastly thing?"

I held a little metal gargoyle with large, outstretched wings made in purple and blue stained glass.

"This is nice," I said, turning it to inspect the back. "The body isn't very detailed, but the wings are pretty. Look! It has little claws. How cute."

"Pretty? No. Reject that cairn immediately," Mr. Tom said with distaste. "What a horrid caricature of our great species. Have they no class?"

"It seems Mr. Tom feels strongly about this one, Captain," Sebastian told Nessa. "I think the alliance potential has been significantly lowered."

"Yes, indeed," she responded, typing the gift into the spreadsheet as Patty handed them the box with the name on the bottom. "A mockery of the great gargoyle. Such things cannot be tolerated."

"Here we go, miss." Nathanial took the gargoyle and handed me the next box, saying the name for Nessa as he did so.

"Give that statue thing here, Nathanial," Niamh called with outstretched hands. "I'll take it. It reminds me of Mr. Tom."

"How dare you!" Mr. Tom braced his fists on his hips before shaking his head as he left the room.

"We have a lot to get through," Patty said, taking a

seat. "We might want to expedite the process of opening these smaller packages."

"Oh!" Sebastian held out his hands. "I'll open some. I never get presents."

"How *dare* you!" Nessa mimicked Mr. Tom. "I get you presents twice a year."

"You're too lazy to wrap them, though," he returned as Jasper handed him a couple of boxes.

"And now we know how fussy you are," Nessa responded, her eyes glued to the box I'd positioned on my lap. This one was smaller than the last, only about a hand length wide and not much taller. "All this time you've gushed and swooned, and really you were just wishing for a little wrapping paper."

"Yes, well…" Sebastian ripped into the paper covering the long and shallow box he held. "The truth eventually finds us all."

I opened the dull brown shipping box I held and peered inside at a collection of T-shirts.

"Huh." Sebastian lifted out a knitted sweater with large wooden toggles for buttons. "Who do they actually want an alliance with? Jessie or Edgar?"

"Edgar, obviously," Nessa said as she entered the newest present.

"Yes, that is…disappointing." Patty pursed her lips. "And Jessie, what is that? Oh…no." The first shirt read

Reras in large letters with some sort of twisted rope for an insignia. "I'd heard that they'd gone and branded themselves, but I had no idea they'd done such a terrible job at it."

"Should we have expected better from these cairns?" Sebastian asked, ripping into the next box. A silver bow went flying.

"Not…really," Patty said, watching him dig through packing paper.

The next I opened held an assortment of bath bombs with the best smells.

Patty gasped, her face closing down in rage. "Strike them off the list," she yelled at Nessa.

"Oh my God—" Nessa flared her fingers, looking hard at the screen. "I will, I will! Quick, who are they?"

"Oh." I paused in pulling a face mask out from under the bath bombs. "What's wrong with these? They're actually kind of nice."

"That is a present for a Jane, not a gargoyle," she said, bracing her fists on her hips. "A gargoyle would *never* send that to a garhette, let alone a female gargoyle. That cairn is clearly calling you out for your past. What an insult!"

"What'd I miss?" Ulric asked, jogging back in with Mr. Tom's laptop.

"The Zakun cairn sent her bath bombs." Patty tsked

and shook her head. "They should be invited just so I can give them a piece of my mind. Everyone—and I mean *everyone*—is going to hear about this. The disrespect! The sheer disrespect in a gift like that… I'm at a loss for words. I simply have nothing to say about this flagrant disrespect."

"At…a…loss…for…words," Nessa typed. "Absolutely…invited…here. Can't…wait…for…fallout." She smacked the enter key. "While we're on the subject, though…" Nessa looked up and put out her hand. "Can I have them if you don't want them? Because I love taking baths. I'll use them."

"This face mask is good, too." I put it to the side before giving an excited little yelp at the fuzzy bathrobe beneath. "I mean…I'll share, but I am absolutely using this. Why don't garhettes get bath stuff as presents?"

Before Patty could answer, Sebastian craned his neck as he peered into the next box and said, "May I interest you in chocolate on a stick? It looks like you can dip it in coffee? Or milk, I guess. Or your mouth, maybe? There's a few pictures here, along with a box of chocolates. Also…what looks like some sort of candy—Oh, peanut brittle. Duh. It's peanut brittle. Essentially, this is a box of sugar."

"Yum!" Nessa said, making notes.

"Another distasteful gift." Patty went to look at the

boxes in the next grouping. "This is like a poke in her eye."

"They may have been attempting to send personalized gifts," Nathanial said, giving me the last box in that grouping. "She's a woman and a past Jane. They clearly looked up what that type of person might like and sent that. It seems they were correct. Let's not apply a slight where one might not have been intended."

"But let's find out, one way or another," Sebastian said, putting his box to the side. "If they *did* intend to deliver a slight, invite them here so we can watch Austin Steele lose his mind when they disrespect her."

"Um…" I pulled out the contents of the last box. "Something like a Brillo pad, a full-strength nail clipper, a…whisker trimmer…" I looked up at Patty with a crinkled nose. "Do female gargoyles usually have beards and hard-to-manage fingernails?"

She tsked again. "I swear, do none of these cairns *think*? That is an insignificant gift for a male gargoyle."

"It's like a Dick getting a tie for his birthday," Ulric said. "Pretty lame."

"Wouldn't *that* be a slight?" Nessa pointed at the box. "Could they not have looked you up online and seen your whisker-free face and dainty nails? Or is that kit for when you're in gargoyle form?"

"Here we go." Mr. Tom walked in with a fresh tray

full of sandwiches. "I found some chicken hiding in the back of the fridge. It should suffice. You guys heal quickly, at any rate, in case the chicken has been there too long. I'll bring some chips and fruit in a moment. Refreshments, anyone? Who is thirsty—No, I am not asking *you*." He scowled at Niamh's raised hand. "Unless you would like water. You need to drink more water."

"Beer is basically water. I'll take one of those," she replied.

"Do you think we can expect anything good?" Nessa asked over their conversation. "Because so far this has been a buzzkill."

"Let's hope so," Patty replied. "Boys, you can pile all the opened things to the side. We'll distribute them or throw them away later, as needed."

She waited for everyone's attention before beaming at the room at large.

The feeling of one familiar and two unfamiliar presences entered the Ivy House woods way on the other side, toward the mountains. The basajaun—Dave—was returning from his home lands and had two visitors in tow. Given their stride length, they were obviously basajaunak.

I glanced at Austin with wide eyes. A tiny smile curved his lush lips as the rest of my crew reacted to the news. Other than Sebastian and Nessa, who didn't have official places in the crew, they could all feel presences on Ivy House land as well as I could.

"Is that…?" Ulric looked at Jasper. "Dave was only going to bring *one* basandere to stay with us, right?"

"Did he convince someone else to come along?" Jasper asked.

"It could be one of her parents coming to check things out." I raised my eyebrows.

"They could just be visiting, yes," Niamh said, looking down at the laptop Ulric had given her. "Then they might have a wee nibble of Edgar's tasty flowers, or wander through this new wood, or scare hikers on the mountain. Who knows what they might get up to? And maybe, just maybe, they'll *both* decide to stay on awhile."

Ulric grinned and held up his hand to show his crossed fingers.

"What am I missing?" Patty asked, looking around. "What's happening?"

"Nothing, Mom, it's fine." Ulric wandered in her direction, ready to grab the next set of boxes. "What's this group?"

She stared at him for a beat, and it was obvious she was debating whether to press the issue.

"I'll explain later," he said. "Let's just get these requests done."

After another silent beat, she glanced back at me. "This grouping have only marginally higher status than the cairns whose gifts we just opened. But, and here is the huge difference, they are worth much more."

Confusion bled through the link from Austin as Patty walked around to stand behind a large trunk that reached up past her knee.

"These are from the production cairns." She spread her arms, looking down at the packages around the trunk. "They specialize in a few products that they sell for profit. It could be woodwork"—she bent to touch the top of the trunk—"or textiles or dairy. Maybe they mine gold. Maybe they make jewelry. What they don't do, however, is have the ability to protect what they create. They are weak in battle."

"And that's why their status is low?" Nessa asked.

"Yes..." Patty tilted her head from side to side. "Kinda. You see, when a production cairn shows that it is stable and profitable, it will look for an alliance with a larger cairn. That cairn will offer them protection in exchange for a cut of their profits. The production cairn will then inherit the status of the larger cairn."

"And...so..." Nessa leaned forward over the laptop.

"These cairns mostly do not have an affiliation. You see..." Patty puffed out a breath, looking upward to think. "I didn't realize how hard it would be to explain all of this."

"Production cairns will only submit their products if they are actively looking for an affiliation," Nathanial offered.

"Yes, exactly. Thank you, Nathanial." She gave him a thumbs-up. "Very well put."

"Can the bigger cairns ally with more than one production cairn?" Austin asked.

"Yes," Nathanial responded. "They can take on as many alliances as they can handle. The protectors will usually send a host of guardians to the production cairn for protection. But a cairn only has so many guardians to protect itself and others from raids."

"What kind of raids?" I asked.

"Cairns take goods from each other," Nathanial continued. "It's not like Jane stealing, because there are rules. The more experienced cairns will take something with meaning. A battle item or a relic. The item is almost always kept under maximum protection, so taking it proves that they have a stronger force. It gives them status. A lesser cairn will take anything of value. Lesser still, and it's anything they can grab."

"Rules?" Austin asked. "What kind of rules?"

"For it to not count as stealing, which would *reduce* status, the attacking party must allow the defending cairn time to prepare. That's one type of raid. The second is to destroy goods."

"Why?" I blurted.

"They do that to wipe out their competition," he said. "If they can also destroy the equipment that creates the goods, even better. Gargoyles try to keep their trading within the species, so if you wipe out anyone else who makes your product, you can get a monopoly."

"Sounds fun," I said darkly. Because the last thing I wanted was anyone else trying to raid us.

Once Nathanial finished, Patty continued. "So *these* cairns are either newer, or they aren't profitable or established enough to have attracted an affiliate cairn. They're trying their hand with you."

I leaned back into the couch as Nessa tapped the keys a mile a minute.

"That all makes sense, but…" I hesitated, trying to process everything.

"It's a lot of information, I know," Patty said. "I *know*! I keep forgetting how new you are to all of this."

"She learns quick," Niamh said, making her own notes.

"I got it, Jessie, don't you worry." Nessa stalled for a moment to give me a thumbs-up. "I'm writing it all down. We're learning right along with you. We'll get this, no problem."

"It's not that different from the power structure of shifter packs." Austin rubbed my back.

"When in doubt, open presents." Patty reached down and grabbed the nearest box. "I *do* love opening presents. Here we go, Jessie, this is a good one. I can feel it. No whisker trimmers in this one."

"What sort of protection do the cairns need?" Austin asked as Patty delivered the box and squeezed in beside me.

I opened a few boxes as Nathanial explained some common threats, like bears or encroaching humans. The goods in the boxes were from established production cairns, and none of them were great. I got why no one had picked them up.

"Raids are really the main threat," he started before Patty cut him off.

"Oh yeah, here we go," she said in a loud voice, her excitement rising. "I have heard *amazing* things about the leader of this cairn." She clearly remembered which cairn it was from despite having hidden the name. The excitement in her eyes dulled as she glanced at Austin. "Well. I guess that doesn't really matter for you. But Nessa, this might interest *you*. The leader was a bit wild in his younger years, but he's smoothed out in all the right ways. I hear he is a real looker with a very big…"

She paused before clearing her throat.

"Fun factory," Nessa supplied.

I opened the box to find a patterned piece of fabric in soft pink and brown. Pulling it out, I realized it was a cashmere scarf.

"Fun factory, yes." Patty took the scarf from me as I checked out what was beneath it. "Oh my goodness, it's so soft. And look at the pattern. Very *chic*."

Next was a snow-white sweater in the same material, fantastically soft and exactly my size. I said as much, rubbing it along my cheek.

All typing stopped. Eyes found me. Tumultuous emotion filtered through the bond.

"What?" I asked, pausing.

"It could be a coincidence," Jasper said slowly. "It's not like her size is uncommon."

I pulled out the next sweater, this one a deep blue green with a slightly popped collar. Spreading it out, I realized it wasn't meant for me.

I handed it off to Austin.

Having finished his burgers, he'd put the plate on the coffee table. Even so, he wiped his hands a second time before reaching for the sweater. A moment later he pulled it over his head and stood—the fit was absolutely perfect, which was not easy with his wide shoulders and trim waist.

"Maybe not a coincidence," Jasper mumbled.

CHAPTER 3

JESSIE

"MR. TOM, YOU order various articles of clothing for the house," Sebastian said. "Do you keep a list of sizes?"

"Well, of course I do," Mr. Tom replied. "I write them all down in my ledger."

"And then I enter them into a spreadsheet that is backed up to the house cloud," Ulric said, scratching his chest.

Niamh looked across the space at Sebastian, who was looking at Nessa.

"I'm going to need access to everything on that cloud," Sebastian said. "I need to know what other people might know. Jessie, do you keep financial information anywhere online?"

"N-no," I said, alarmed. "Mr. Tom has me write it in a big book—"

"A financial ledger," Mr. Tom supplied.

“I’ve been meaning to do some sort of online bookkeeping—I don’t even know who our accountant is—but I haven’t had a chance.”

“She has personal account information online, I reckon,” Niamh said. “The house’s bank accounts are online in various countries.”

Sebastian nodded, lightly tapping his fingers on his knees. “It’ll be interesting to see how far they might’ve gotten. It takes a damn good hacker to get into a bank’s system.”

“Why are we worried?” I asked, clutching the edges of the now-empty box. “We don’t have anything to hide.”

Sebastian swung his gaze my way, the wheels in his brain clearly turning. “The game is to know more about your opponent than they know about you,” he said, taking out his phone and starting to tap on it. “We want them guessing about you and this house. About your crew. What they *do* know needs to be used against them, if at all possible. Meanwhile, we can leverage what we know about them. It’s a dance, Jessie. An elaborate dance. There is very little room for error.”

“Niamh,” Nessa said. “I hope you are checking into their social media accounts. That’s the low-hanging fruit that can help us shape our strategies.”

“O’ course I am,” Niamh replied. “Do I look like an

amateur?"

"This just got very intense." Patty looked around at each of us with wide eyes. "I can help, of course. Any information you need spread, you just look to me. Misinformation, I mean. Things that will confuse them. I know how gossip works. Just a kernel of truth, and you have a believable story."

Nessa didn't look up from her computer as she pointed at Patty. "Ace in the hole, right there. Excellent skill, Patty. We will absolutely use it. I've tried for something similar in the past and no one believed me."

Patty beamed. "Well, anyway. Venavin, that's the cairn name. The leader, Pierce, was trained in Aadath, Nikken's production cairn—"

"Whoa, whoa, whoa." Nessa put out her hands. "That's a lot of names flying at me."

"Pierce was trained in one of the most affluent production cairns," Patty summed up. "Now…there are some rumors as to why he left, but no grievances have been filed by either the affiliate cairn or production cairn. I don't know the real story, but he's the most eligible bachelor of the new guys, and he knows it."

"Jasper, help me with this trunk," Ulric said. They hauled it over.

"This is a woodworking cairn *and* a textile cairn," Patty whispered as she ran her fingers over the top of the trunk. "Very well made, this trunk. Their leader is new to the job. He left his birth cairn, a middle-class production cairn specializing in smelly perfumes. I am not a fan of them. Stinky stuff, popular with people suffering from body odor. Wise move, walking away from that. I've heard he is very odd, but he seems stable enough. Smart."

Austin looked over with interest as I pinched the heavy bronze clasp on the trunk to pop the lock free.

"That part is well made," I said.

"Hmm. Maybe they have some good metal workers, too," Patty said. "I'll have to check…"

After lifting the lid, I peered at a beautifully patterned…*something*…in an explosion of muted colors that all seemed to work together. It was the kind of thing that could probably blend into any area and accent any color palette. Then again, I wasn't great at interior design. Honestly, I wasn't sure I liked the thing. But I didn't hate it, either…

"I'm not sure if I like it or hate it," Patty said, echoing my unspoken sentiments.

After taking it out, I found it to be a finely crafted rug that seemed durable but expensive. In my experience, that wasn't a common combination.

"I'm liking it more and more," Patty said, taking it from me with a furrowed brow. "Or am I? Well, the seam work is *very* good, I know that much."

Austin leaned back and draped his arm across the back of the couch. "Understood."

"Still not sure how I feel about this rug!" Patty said in annoyance.

The next group had more status, and the groups after had more still. Most items weren't personal, and those that were tended to be only vaguely so. Only a couple of the gifts set off Sebastian and Niamh's warning bells, resulting in another flurry of note taking, probably to jot down security ideas. Patty was set off by different items, mainly those that hinted at or outright acknowledged my past Jane status. We still didn't know if that was an intended slight.

Finally, we came to the big dogs—the cairns that had wealth and power and the ability to splash both around.

"I thought you said there were four big cairns." I surveyed the solitary, smallish white box sitting in front of me on the coffee table.

"Four cairns to rule them all," Nessa murmured softly, once again tapping on the keyboard.

"Four, yes." Patty sat beside me, back from reorganizing the opened packages. "The rest of the gifts were too big to bring inside. Now, these four have it all, including exceptional leadership and generations-long stability. Each has several townships within their territory, like the situation Austin Steele is starting to create. They work with anywhere between none to four or so production cairns who make exceptional products. In short, they are the cream. For now, we are aiming to get just one of these cairns on your side. We can build from there." She wiped her brow with her middle finger. "If you can keep them in line, of course."

"We can keep them in line," Austin growled.

Patty didn't comment. I doubted she believed him. But then, she hadn't seen Austin in action.

"Right." I sat forward and waited while Nathanial lifted the box and moved it closer to me. "Let's see what the best of the best thought to send."

I pulled off the lid to find a black velvet case on the inside.

"Jewelry," Nessa said, eyes on the prize. "I bet it's jewelry."

I turned the box over to free the velvet case, and the name of the cairn flashed up at me from the bottom.

"Gimerel," I said as the black box shimmied out onto my palm.

"Got it," Nessa said, squinting at her screen, probably to get the cairn's stats.

The length of the box suggested a bracelet, and the delicately rounded corners and little gold hinges indicated it was a good one.

"Here goes nothin'." I tipped the cover back.

"Oh my word," Patty said quietly, her hand drifting to her chest. "Is that what I think it is?"

"What? What do you think it is?" Nessa stood to get a better look, nearly dumping the laptop onto the floor. Sebastian quickly grabbed it from her. "I can't see!"

Light danced off the multi-gem bracelet delicately strapped within the velvet. Rubies, emeralds, and sapphires, all different cuts and set seemingly at random, ran along its length. Round-cut diamonds pooled around the gems like a stream, and the bracelet was a robust inch wide.

"It's beautiful," I said, looking a little closer. "But it's nothing compared to what Ivy House has lying around. Monetary-wise, I mean. Assuming they are going for a flagrant display of wealth."

"How do you mean?" Sebastian asked, at the helm with the computer now, braced to take notes.

I'd never given him a real tour of the place. Some of the wealth randomly stored in nooks and crannies boggled the mind. I said as much.

"I'll need to see everything you have." His fingers flowed over the keyboard. "I need an itemized list of everything that can be worn or otherwise shown off."

"Why?" Mr. Tom asked, still perched by the door

after the latest food delivery. "Are you planning to resurrect your thieving ways and rob us blind?"

Sebastian didn't even look up at the slight. Instead, he grinned. "Ivy House would kill me before I made it to the front door."

"That gift is not about the worth of the bracelet," Nathanial said, bending closer to look. "Gimerel has a production cairn with a mine rich in rubies and sapphires. Another of their production cairns handcrafts exquisite jewelry. Their work is heavily sought after. This is a perfect marriage of both, and a display of the cairn's wealth and status. The Gimerel leader was very proud of that bracelet. Almost immediately after he first showed it off, another large cairn raided Gimerel to try to get it. They failed, and since then, all three of the other most prestigious cairns have tried to take it. A couple of the lesser cairns even joined forces to attempt a raid. In all that time, Gimerel protected their prize. No one could get close. That bracelet is a testimony to their battle strength. I greatly hoped that one day I'd have enough status for an invitation to see it."

I blinked at it, then lowered my eyebrows. "And he's just giving it to me? I don't get to try my hand at a raid? That's lame. I bet we could have taken it."

Ulric and Jasper started to laugh. "She's definitely a gargoyle," Ulric said.

"Be that as it may," Nathanial said, his eyes glued to the bracelet, "giving you that is a huge honor. It's the pride of their cairn."

"He's showing off," Nessa said, now leaning back as Sebastian continued to tap on the keyboard. "He's showing you how big his dick is. It isn't a present for *you*—it is a display of how powerful *he* is. It's a testimony to what he's worth."

"It's a challenge, is what it is," Niamh said.

"Yeah, agree." Nessa nodded. "He's just shown you the bar. You'll have to top it for him to give you the time of day."

"That was always going to be the case," Patty said. "Always. That's what we're up against."

"It's also a gorgeous piece of jewelry," Ulric said. "Even if she didn't know the full history, she has an authentic piece of jewelry, worth a pretty penny, that displays the talents of his cairn. You have to hand it to the guy, it's the perfect gift."

"No argument there," Nessa said. "He's good."

"We'll have our hands full with him," Austin said. He'd been mostly quiet up until this point, which added weight to the sentiment.

Silence filtered through the room for a moment. I handed the bracelet to Nathanial, who handled it like the priceless relic he clearly considered it to be. The other gargoyles came closer and bent to look, their eyes full of reverence.

"Right," I said to break the silence. "What's next?"

I grabbed a glass of water while checking on the basajaunak. They were meandering around the wood, probably checking out the basandere's new home. Edgar, Cyra, and Hollace were heading home from the other direction, moving fast. In the car, obviously. I wondered if Edgar had felt the basajaunak and was now rushing back to protect his flowers. He'd want to go over the rules with the new additions.

"Yes, let's move this along." Patty gazed at the bracelet a little longer—Nathanial had passed it to her—before gingerly setting it on the coffee table. "Should we…pop that into a safe, perhaps? Secure it in some way?"

"No one is going to steal that trinket," Mr. Tom said, lifting his chin. "Ivy House has many more authentic pieces of jewelry worth much more, I assure you. They were bathed in the blood of empires, ripped from—"

"Okay, okay, settle down." I put out a hand to placate Mr. Tom as I stood. "Let's respect the gifts of *today*, shall we?"

"If we must." Mr. Tom's wings rustled.

"I mean, not to toot my own horn," Sebastian said,

standing, "but the red diamond I gave Jessie when in my caves is almost priceless. It is the rarest type of diamond in the world. The story of how I came to be in possession of it, as well as its previous history, would make that bracelet look like child's play."

"I would very much like to hear that story," Patty said, getting up. "If that cairn secures an invite, it'll be something to share, for sure."

"Patty is going to be my best friend when those gargoyles come," Nessa said, batting her eyes at the older woman. "Oh, the fun we will have, Patty."

Patty smiled and hooked her arm through Nessa's. As they started walking out, Patty quietly asked Nessa, "Those pieces of jewelry the old gargoyle was talking about…have you seen them? I'm a little concerned that they will be clunky, horrendous things that will give everyone a fright. Somewhat like most of this house's interior…"

They passed through the door after the others. I hung back, waiting for Austin. He picked up the bracelet to get a better look.

"It's definitely well made." He took it from the box and turned it over, looking at the back. "All the gems are secure and the artistry is definitely on point. The gems look pristine, though I can't really tell how many carats they are with a naked eye."

"But…" I said with a grin.

He returned it to the velvet box and closed it. I slipped my hand in his as we headed for the door.

"But…" He glanced back before we turned the corner. "The design is a little chaotic—not entirely refined—and the worth…is lacking."

"Did you see all those gemstones? That's gotta be…hundreds of thousands of dollars, if not over a million. I'm no expert, but I've browsed jewelry I'd never be able to afford before…"

He smiled as we walked slowly down the hall. He clearly didn't want the others to hear our conversation. I wondered if he thought it would insult them.

"It's the pride of the cairn," he said. "It sounds like the leader showed it off as though it was the finest thing they'd ever produced. With their own mine and their own artisans, I'd expect the piece to be jaw-dropping. Extravagant. Elegant. I'd expect them to go way overboard. Think of the pieces that jewelry establishments like Harry Winston or Cartier drape across the necks of celebrities. Or Tiffany's yellow diamond, worth over thirty million."

"Right, except those are multimillion-dollar Dick companies, and this is a gargoyle cairn firmly entrenched in their neck of magical society, a species that Nathanial said likes to stick to its own. They aren't like the mages who filter into the Dick world and acquire the riches to show for it."

Austin was quiet for a moment as we neared the front door. "Some of the shifters have big bankrolls. I wonder if that's because we aren't as entrenched in our own kind as gargoyles seem to be. We don't mess around with Dicks for the most part, but we don't shut them out, either. We're open with the rest of the magical society, too."

"I wonder why gargoyles are like that."

"Slow to change from the olden days, perhaps. This territory might not be their cup of tea because of it. That might work against you."

"Or it might work in our favor if people want a little more excitement in their lives, like Dave."

"Let's hope."

We exited the house to find the others standing around the extravagant carriage that had been delivered as one of the cairn gifts. I slowed to a stop before reaching the group and glanced at Austin.

"There is one thing." I gazed back through the door. "That bracelet *is* pretty. It does have craftsmanship. It's modern. Ivy House has fine things, worth much more than that bracelet, but everything is outdated."

He grimaced, pulling me close. "A bit, yes."

"And some things are a little…gaudy."

"A little, yes."

"It's pretty far from the modern era, and it sounds like the new gargoyles won't look favorably on that. I need to make time for an Ivy House refresh. Maybe even a complete overhaul."

He nodded in agreement. "So does the town. Patty stopped by the bar earlier today and informed me of that. If we want to attract the gargoyles—"

"And we need to."

"We have a lot of work to do."

CHAPTER 4

JESSIE

GIVEN THE CARRIAGE had been parked on the front lawn for days, we'd seen it a good few times and admired the gold accents and the sturdy craftsmanship. This cairn had a few production cairns as well, including one who mined gold. The sentiment was apparently along the lines of "transportation fit for a queen," something very on brand for the gargoyle culture. I just couldn't help wondering what we were supposed to do with it. I didn't plan to buy draft horses to pull me around the town. My old Honda was just fine if I ever needed to go anywhere. That thing would run forever.

"Okay, let's head around back," Patty said, leading the way.

She took us around the side instead of back through the house, and from the way her head swiveled this way and that, I could tell she was assessing the grounds. Those at least looked good. The front of the house, anyway. Edgar had stayed modest with his designs and flower planting. We just couldn't allow anyone out back or near a back window to witness the explosion of flowers and the eccentric hedge maze.

A doll waited in the center of the back lawn, facing the wood. More still held their positions as sentinels farther back and to the sides. They walked or stood guard with their instruments of death, waiting for a gnome to show itself.

I really should've been thankful for them, but I just couldn't see my way to it. The little buggers still creeped me out something awful.

Patty didn't seem to even notice or question the insanity of animated dolls. She marched right on past without a second glance.

"Where's Hollace to kick these things?" I muttered, following the others.

The closest doll must've heard, because it turned and looked at me. An evil grin spread across its babylike face.

"Gross."

Patty reached the flower line. There was a stone path through the swamp of flowers, but she ignored it and trudged on through.

"Mom, look out," Ulric said, jogging for the path. "Don't stomp all over the flowers."

"It'll do the yard good. There are far too many of them," she replied, reaching the other side. "The floral stench is overwhelming."

"The basajaunak eat them."

"Then plant them in the woods where they aren't such an eyesore." She beelined for the trees.

"We're all thinking it, like," Niamh said, trudging along after Patty.

"Don't you start," I told her, taking the path. "Edgar will either freak out or ask to be retired. I don't need the headache."

"I'm sure he will do both," said Mr. Tom, the third to trudge through.

I sighed.

"Here we go. Just in the trees here," Patty said. "Ulric hid them so you'd be surprised."

I peered through the trunks and into the shadows, looking for those horrible gnomes. If they were there, though, they were hiding.

In a small clearing stood a large wooden sculpture much too chic and modern to belong in these woods. About as tall as the basajaun, it curved and twisted into a shape like a funnel. The piece rested on a marble base.

"It's a serious piece of art." Austin ran his hand along the smooth wood, following the contours while walking around it. "They included different kinds of wood to make this. It looks like one solid piece, but it isn't. That takes incredible craftsmanship."

"Which cairn is this again?" Nessa asked.

"The Nikken cairn." Patty pointed at the computer in Nessa's hands. She'd reclaimed it from Sebastian on the way out here. "At the top of the spreadsheet."

"Here, Sabby, put out your hands." Nessa placed the laptop on Sebastian's outstretched hands before opening it up, using him like a table. "Ah, yeah, got it."

"The Nikken cairn has a production cairn that specializes in woodworking." Patty put her hands behind her back. "They have one other—"

"The textile one you mentioned earlier, right?" Nessa pointed at her. "The one where Pierce learned his trade before possibly stealing their secrets and taking off."

"Good memory! Yes, the very one. I met a woman who knew a woman who'd mated into this cairn. She said all of the townships had nice residences, there was a community feel despite the size, and the streets were clean. She went on and on. Of course, she was from a dingy little cairn with no status, so there's that. Also, she liked to gloat, that one. Or so I heard. But the cairn is doing well, so…"

"Yeah, I've always heard good things," Ulric said, looking up at the sculpture. "Kind of a weird thing to send as a connection request, though. I'm not really into sculptures."

"Me either," Jasper said. "It would make for good firewood."

Patty turned to head back the way we'd come.

"Wait, Mom," Ulric said, looking back the other way. "I forgot—there's that other thing back there, remember? It came yesterday. I completely forgot about it."

Patty hesitated in confusion before her expression cleared. "Oh yes, right. One of the cairns with middle status, I believe." She sighed. "Well, we might as well have a look. Just one more after this one, though. We're almost done."

"Good." Nessa paused to wipe her forehead. "I'm actually exhausted from gift opening. I never thought I'd see the day."

"I'm exhausted by how much work we suddenly have in front of us," Sebastian replied.

The rest of them walked farther into the trees, but Austin lingered a bit, his gaze tracing the gentle curves of the sculpture.

"Like that, huh?" I said, hanging back with him.

"Yeah. There's something about it."

Sebastian, who'd clearly overheard, stopped just beyond a tree and turned back.

"It's not just beautiful," Austin said. "I can almost feel the passion and care that went into it. I didn't get the same sense with the carriage or even that bracelet. This, though…"

He minutely shook his head, walking around it. Sebastian's gaze bloomed with curiosity as Nessa walked back to him, looking for the computer.

"It was crafted by a master," Austin went on. "By someone who loves what he or she does. It's definitely a risky gift, because art *is* so subjective, but the type of wood negates that."

I furrowed my brow. "Why is that?"

"Because it is the same wood that is featured so prominently in Ivy House."

"Whoa," Nessa said, stopping dead.

Sebastian handed off the computer to her before drifting closer to us. "Come again?"

Austin glanced back at him before pointing out the two different colors and types of wood that had been seamlessly fitted together within the sculpture.

"The archways and fireplaces, the coffered and beam ceilings—this sculpture would match them. It would complement the rooms where different types of wood are used."

"Are you sure about this?" Sebastian asked, looking hard at the sculpture.

"Yes. I've always noticed the craftsmanship in Ivy House. This reflects the best the house has to offer."

Sebastian stopped on one of Austin's sides, Nessa on the other, both of them looking at him with wide eyes.

"And this doesn't trouble you?" Sebastian asked.

Austin glanced over before returning his gaze to the sculpture. "It impresses me, actually."

"How would they know about the wood used in Ivy House?" I asked, more alarmed by that than the items that had worried the others.

"I've come across a few pictures of Ivy House's interior in my research," Sebastian said. "But I did extensive research. They weren't easy to find."

"We've had gargoyles in that house." Austin tore his eyes away and took a step back, his gaze finding mine. "The ones who didn't make it on your team either flew home or stayed in town. None of them are expressly loyal to you. Not if an influential cairn comes asking questions, that is."

"They all have eyes and ears in town," Sebastian whispered. "I wondered if someone would exploit that obvious advantage."

"They might not have," Austin said. "We have no way of knowing." He paused for a moment. "The cairn could've tracked down some of those that returned home. I can't imagine it would take long for news to travel."

"If we have time, we should try to track that down." Nessa opened the laptop and stepped up to Sebastian so he'd hold it again.

"Our to-do list is already really long," he told her. "Let's hit the important things first and circle back to this."

"We're dealing with gargoyles, at least. They can't possibly be cleverer and more devious than mages. They don't steal, they raid. They present themselves in plain view and offer their opponents the advantage of preparing. I don't think we'll have to work nearly as hard as we're used to."

Austin grabbed my hand and tugged me in the direction of the others. "Just make sure you don't break any of their societal rules," he told them. "Don't insult them or cause Jess to lose their respect."

"In the words of the great puca..." Nessa straightened up and lifted her chin in mock importance. "Do I look like an amateur?"

We found the others gathered around a stone statue of a naked man with a stone leaf covering his private parts.

"Wasted opportunity," I murmured.

"Amen, sister," Nessa replied.

The statue didn't have nearly enough detail in the face, lacked nipples, and had abs that were strangely off-center. It stood on a rough stone base that didn't jibe well with the dull gray stone used for the rest of it. Its height barely topped Austin's, and the body didn't at all measure up.

"Not…great," Jasper said, crossing his arms and circling the statue. "It gets worse the longer you look at it."

"This is a middle-status cairn that is very proud of their production cairn." Patty's face creased in confusion, and she squinted into the trees.

I had a moment of alarm, thinking it might be a gnome. Cluing in to my surroundings, though, I quickly realized she must be reacting to Dave, who'd gotten very close to us, his companions in tow. He was clearly having a little fun with Patty.

"They work stone, obviously," Patty went on. "I'd always heard that…" She frowned, now staring at a small branch that was gently waving despite the lack of wind.

Jasper grinned and looked away to hide his expression.

"What's up, Mom?" Ulric asked into the silence, his expression patient but his eyes glittering with humor.

Patty lightly shook her head and pulled her focus

back to the statue. "Nothing. Where was I…"

"You'd always heard…something," he helped.

"Ah yes. Yes, I'd always heard they were quite good with stone, actually. If they could just get a better group of guardians, their cairn would easily elevate in status. This statue doesn't support those rumors, though."

The branch wiggled again. Patty snapped her head that way. After staring for a moment, her brow furrowed, she wet her finger and held it up, probably checking for a breeze.

When she felt nothing, she swept the ground with her gaze, probably looking for gnomes, and then shrugged.

"Okay," she said. "One more and we're—"

Dave burst out of the trees. His giant arms were held aloft, and his massive jaw exposed large, jagged teeth. He roared, all his hair puffing out to make a nine-foot-high and robust creature look that much bigger.

Patty screamed, her whole body jolting. Dave slowed his advance, his expression softening with humor, which quickly turned to surprise. Her scream turned into a snarl of rage, and she launched forward, hands out like claws. She barreled into his stomach, not at all daunted by his size.

Dave made a sound like *ha-oooah* as he tried to back-pedal. Her weight wasn't much compared to his, but such a solid hit was plenty to knock him off balance. He tripped over his own feet and tumbled to the ground. She rode him down with fists flying. His back had barely touched dirt before she was up again, standing over him, kicking his midsection.

Loud laughter erupted from the trees, and the two other basajaunak showed themselves, bent over and guffawing.

"Mom!" Ulric lurched toward her, laughing. "Mom, stop! It was a joke. Stop kicking him!"

"That was…excellent," Nessa said, watching with a delighted smile. "I will remember that scene for the rest of my days."

Patty gave one more mighty swing of her foot before she stopped, looking down at him.

"Oh. You must be the basajaun," she said, all friendliness now. "I've heard so much about you! It's nice to finally meet you. Here we go." She reached down for him, and he flinched away. The other basajaunak laughed harder. "Oops. You're okay now. You can get up. You just startled me, is all. You'll be okay. Just walk it off."

"What manner of creature are you?" Dave asked, avoiding her continued reach.

"She's a garhette," I said, walking forward. "A female gargoyle that doesn't shift. And who have you brought? I recognize one of you, of course. Welcome, *Her*. Treat these woods as your own. Let me know if you need anything."

The basandere I'd met in Dave's lands stepped forward, still chuckling. "Hello again. Thank you for having me. I am very excited to start this new journey. Your wood is very lovely. More than a wood, though, right? It has a presence within it."

"Oh…" Dave had never mentioned that, but I guessed it had to be true, since it was connected to the house. "Yes, Ivy House is magically connected to these lands. Or did you mean the gnomes?"

"Not the gnomes. Funny little creatures, those. One cleaved my foot, so I stomped on it. But the other, yes, I feel it. The living things are a little confused about it. That is why the wood is not quite settled. I can work them around, though, do not worry. They are eager for harmony."

"She is very good at managing a forest," Dave said. "I cannot feel all that she does. She has a real gift." He turned to the basajaun I didn't know. "*He* was intrigued by your visit to our lands. He expressed an interest to stay on my mountain and check things out."

The new basajaun stepped forward, a hair taller than Dave and just a bit sturdier.

"Greetings," he said, and bowed to me. "I request

admittance into your territory. Forgive me for not seeking it earlier, but Bul—Dave said you were busy and that we could wander through the wood until you were finished with your meeting."

"Perfect timing, yes." I offered him a small bow. "Welcome."

"In exchange for my admittance, I will help Dave protect these lands," he continued, and it occurred to me that I should've initiated the trade. That was how these creatures worked, which could be a bit tedious when you didn't feel like bartering. Thankfully, this basajaun was doing it for me.

"That sounds good," I told him, then repeated, "Welcome."

Stepping around me, he stood in front of Austin. "Alpha," he said, lowering his head. "I wish to make a similar trade. I know that your territory is vast, and also that you have non-magical humans within it. I understand the perils of showing myself to such humans and will be careful."

Austin nodded his acceptance.

Finally the basajaun turned to Niamh. "I want that rematch. I will soon start making the special brew."

Ah. So this was the basajaun who'd wrestled drunk Niamh through a fire. Promising a rematch was as good a way as any to get him here.

"Use my back garden for making it if ye want," she said with a shrug. "It'll keep the human hikers from discovering it on the mountain and drinking it all up, thinking it's moonshine. In exchange, I'll want an equal share in what ye make."

The basajaun's face split into a smile. "Good trade."

"Yes, those hikers can be very curious," Dave said, looking off in the direction of his territory. "They would probably do as she says and end up poisoning themselves. I do not need a bunch of dead humans littered around my camp."

"Great. Let's get to that last connection request, shall we?" I lifted my eyebrows at Patty.

"Good idea!" Patty turned and swished through us all, headed back toward the house.

"You know," I said to Austin as we followed the others, "you can have that sculpture if you want. If you can find a use for it."

"It wouldn't work in my place. It needs to be kept inside, and my ceilings and space can't handle a piece that big. It was made for Ivy House. The size, the wood…"

"So I have to find a place to put it?"

He laughed. "Only if you want to. Isn't that how these things work? You keep what you want and get rid of the rest?"

"Well, since you can't make use of the wood sculpture you like so much, you can have that statue. You're welcome."

He laughed softly. "You're so giving. How did I get this lucky?"

"I know, I know. Don't worry, I'll let you make it up to me."

He hooked an arm around my waist and pulled me in closer. I bumped against him as we walked. "Before I make it up to you, which will take some time because I've missed you these last couple of days"—heat flash-boiled my blood, and I leaned a little harder into him—"maybe we can talk about a direction for Ivy House's refresh."

I sighed, and the heat quickly cooled. "Yeah, we probably should, and thank you for the help. I have terrible taste, and when I asked Mr. Tom for help with the office, because he's always harping on to me about *making it mine*, he came up with the strangest stuff."

"You have great taste—you just don't know how to pull things together. Did your ex decorate your old house?"

"No. My mother-in-law. It was gauche and terrible, but I didn't have much say in anything because my ex always sided with her."

"My grandma used to pick everything out for me,"

he said. "It would annoy the hell out of me until everyone started raving about how good my place looked. I learned what I could from her so she'd leave me alone. Turns out, I have an eye for it. Not as good as her, but good enough." He smiled, his eyes distant. "She's a hard woman with exacting tastes, but I had a lot of fun learning about that stuff. That's probably why it stuck so well. My brother isn't remotely interested in interior design. His mate handles all of that, and she is constantly badgered by Grandma Mimi about her choices. Poor thing. They don't have the same taste."

We reached the flowers, another few patches of which had been trampled down.

Austin took a deep breath. "But I won't have time to handle the nitty-gritty details with Ivy House. It's much too big, and we have way too much to do. So after we work out a direction, Patty can bring in an interior designer."

"Or…" I trailed my fingertips along the hand he was resting on my hip. "You could call in a favor and have your grandmother come help…"

His body tensed, and a brief smattering of longing filtered through our bond before he crushed it into submission.

"I'm sure she's busy."

"Or maybe she needs a vacation and wouldn't mind

seeing her grandson after all this time. I'm sure she'd like to visit."

He shook his head as we passed a doll, and I wished again that Hollace were here to kick it. I didn't dare to myself. I worried it would latch on to my leg and bite me, or something else nightmare-inducing.

I could feel Hollace and the rest near the house. Good. I was sure Dave was eager to show off the magical flowers, but he knew better than to do it without Edgar's consent. We'd all been down that road.

We approached the entrance of the large labyrinth made up of hedges taller than the basajaunak. They were all trimmed to perfection, their tops flat and the sides without a stray leaf.

"Oh." Dave, who'd been following us with the other basajaunak, slowed to a stop. "I will wait out here, Miss Jessie. I do not have fond memories of that maze."

He and my son Jimmy had gone through the maze at Easter, and it hadn't taken Dave long to freak out and crash his way through the walls to escape.

"Sure, no problem. Edgar will be here in a minute anyway."

"Get out of here, you blasted thing." Patty kicked wildly, just missing a gnome that jumped out of the hedge with gardening shears and took off running. "Get out! This isn't your home!" She hiked up her skirts and sprinted after it.

"She's not a fan of gnomes," Ulric said by way of explanation. "Just this way," he continued. The wall of hedge in front of us had been torched down to the burned grass. Another wall beyond had seen the same fate. "Edgar assured me he could repair the damage. I don't think he realized Cyra would be helping me, but that's fine. It'll give him something to do. Above all, I wanted this one to be a surprise, Jessie. I didn't know where else to put it."

We followed the trail of destruction to the right, then back left; the path was surprisingly irregular. A little farther in, we met a wall of green magic that formed a sort of box, attaching to the living hedge and draping across the top.

"They didn't want you to see it from your bedroom window," Sebastian said as I traced it with my eyes. "This spell is weak, but it works great from a distance if a person isn't specifically looking for it. I was assured you'd stopped noticing the minutiae of this yard a long time ago. Edgar was not impressed to learn this. Sorry about that. He might be more mopey than usual about his gardening…abilities."

"In other words, he's going to ask to be retired again," I said.

"Probably, yeah. Sorry." He looked over my shoulder. "Nessa, I need you to take this computer so I can pull the spell down."

"I can do it," I said, applying a grabby sort of spell over his and then ripping it away.

Peeking out from behind the living hedge was a sleek headlight and the gentle curve of a metallic blue bumper. Burned ground crawled up to the wide tires and large black rims.

"They got me a new car?" I asked as everyone parted for me to walk closer. "Oh wow, it's a Porsche."

It was the sleekest Porsche I'd ever seen, actually. A black convertible top spanned over the classic Porsche body. A few little embellishments to the fender and spoiler made it look especially fast. Black leather seats matched the top, and subtle wood trim traced parts of the dash and along the doors.

"A Porsche 911 Turbo, if I'm not mistaken," Austin said, lightly running his hand along the fender as he took the car in. "This baby is quick. And pricy."

"The color nearly matches your eyes," I murmured, standing back with my hands on my hips, surveying it. "How pricy?"

"About two hundred grand, all told," Patty said as she re-entered. "It is ready to be registered in your name."

"Cairn name?" Nessa once again hovered over Sebastian's makeshift computer table. "And nearest drag strip?"

"The Khaavalvor cairn," Patty supplied. "It's a great gift for Jessie. She can't keep driving that…eclectic little deathtrap that was parked in the driveway."

I frowned at her. I most certainly could, especially since I didn't drive that much. Most of the time Austin drove us around, and if I was going somewhere in town, I walked. A fancy car would be wasted on me.

Then again, apparently the gargoyles at the top of the heap were expected to flash their wealth and status. In this case, it would be flashing Ivy House's wealth, since I didn't bring all that much to the table, but the sentiment was the same. Not to mention the crew shared my car, and they might like to drive something without a lightly cracked windshield or gently worn-in seats where the seams were starting to fray and the interior padding was making its way to the exterior.

I shrugged. "It can be the crew's car. Like a company car for Ivy House."

Sebastian cracked a smile. "Perfect, Jessie. That is absolutely perfect."

Patty didn't look so sure, but she didn't voice her objections.

"Great, that's that finished. Finally." Mr. Tom's wings ruffled. "Who would like some more refreshments or a snack—no, I will not bring you a beer, you lush." He turned away from Niamh and strode out of the maze.

Sebastian handed the computer off to Nessa and stepped in close to me. "A word? With you and the alpha."

"Yeah, sure." I hung back with Austin.

Sebastian cleared his throat. "I have many…unsavory talents that I have employed to great effect in my tenure as Elliot Graves. One of those talents is knowing how to manipulate people using various items. Like gifts, for example." He put out a hand. "The gifts I gave you and your team at our meetup in the caves were personal. They were my way of saying thank you for taking me in as a nerdy mage. Those were from *me.* Sebastian. They weren't business. I hope you know that. I wasn't sure if you'd be killing me in the next few days, and I wanted a way to show my appreciation."

"When I thought those gifts were from Elliot Graves, I was very annoyed at how amazing they were," I said with a smile. "You were starting to thaw me even though I hated you. *Him.*"

They'd all been perfect, building me up and rejoicing in who and what I was. The gifts for the crew had been equally amazing—Sebastian had clearly internalized each person and found a sentimental gift that complemented them perfectly.

He nodded. "The talent is great for friends and family, but until recently, I didn't have any of those, save Nessa. She makes out like a bandit. Christmas is going to be amazing this year. I'm already thinking of gifts. Anyway." He closed his eyes and shook his head. "Anyway. The unsavory part of this talent is how I can use certain items to elicit a reaction. You didn't see it, but the other head mages got gifts, too. I didn't bother with their crews. Those gifts were little trinkets that…set them on edge, mostly. Made them wary or unsettled. Exposed a secret they thought they'd kept. Things like that."

Austin adjusted his stance, slipping his hands into his pockets.

Sebastian wilted a little. "Unsavory, I told you. It's—"

"You misinterpret my posture," Austin said. "That's ingenious. Masterful, even. I think your ability will be a great help when Jessie is dealing with cunning and sly opponents who are openly her adversaries…"

Sebastian put up a finger. "And that is exactly what you are about to walk into. Their range of emotions and expectations regarding Jessie are all over the place, as evidenced by the connection requests. Most of them didn't know whether to treat her as a Jane or a gargoyle. The top tier, the *cream*, as Patty said, were just as scattered. One hinted that they'd done their homework—the sculpture. One showed their own status—the bracelet. One just randomly sent you a car—I bet that was about monetary worth. The carriage was the only one that hinted at your status in the community. A leader. A pinnacle of success. But that very gift makes zero sense in the modern world. The cairn that sent it must be vastly out of touch, and whatever they think it's going to be like meeting you is probably going to slap them in the face."

He paused to let all of that sink in. Austin didn't comment. Sebastian had some *very* good points. Points Patty had been circling since all of this had started.

"You are very good at reading people, Austin Steele," Sebastian said. "I am very good at reading *motivations*. Political motivations, motivations based on power, manipulations—I've survived all these years through my ability to read the room. And this room is going to turn hostile very, very quickly. You need to prepare for the worst. For war."

CHAPTER 5

AUSTIN

LATER THAT NIGHT, Austin sat at the little table in Jessie's room, looking out over the darkened grounds. She lay cozy in her bed behind him, the sheets pulled up to her neck and her hair fanned out across the pillow. Her soft snores drifted across the room, the sound tranquil and safe. She was protected.

For now.

He drummed his fingertips against his thigh, watching Edgar in the moonlight as the vampire attempted to stand up the flowers that had been crushed earlier in the day. It looked like he was tying sticks around their bases and staking them in the ground. That vampire was not right in the head.

Austin let his gaze slide away, noticing a shape looming not far behind Edgar. Large and hairy, it peered out of the trees. Austin couldn't tell from this distance, but he guessed it was the basandere watching

Edgar's antics. Or maybe just waiting for him to leave so she could sneak a few more flowers. Both she and the new basajaun had been given a large sampling earlier, and it was as though they'd grown up without sugar and were trying chocolate for the first time. Their sounds of delight could be heard throughout the yard. Dave's joy was easily felt through the Ivy House link, along with his confidence. He thought he'd hooked them, that he'd get them to stay.

Austin hoped he was right. He hoped they'd tell their friends to come too. He needed them.

He let his gaze keep wandering, his mind whirling. He'd thought a lot about what Sebastian had said earlier. A *lot*. The mage had made some very good points.

At this point, they all expected at least a little pushback from the gargoyle leaders. He hadn't thought of the possibility of their getting hostile, though. Thinking on it now, he honestly wasn't sure why it hadn't occurred to him.

Hadn't Austin experienced something similar when he walked into this town and forced order? The hostility he'd faced hadn't diminished until the troublemakers either left or submitted.

Growing up, he'd watched and/or helped Kingsley aid smaller packs that suffered from poor leadership.

They'd had to force order there, too. They'd had to force change, and often that only came by fighting and physically removing the existing leadership.

Change was a tricky bitch. It was best done over time, gradually.

They didn't have time.

Nathanial's approach—to accrue guardians now, and work on winning over the leaders later—sounded good in theory, but it didn't account for the status issue. Austin couldn't imagine the better guardians wanting to work with them if Jess couldn't guarantee them some modicum of status. To gain status, they'd need support from powerful gargoyles.

Jess would need to manipulate, coax, push, shove, and then dance around these leaders, working them around. To do that, she would need the help of Sebastian and Nessa. Niamh. Even Patty. Austin's role would be territory stability.

He'd also need to provide the element of flashy sophistication that his brother managed so well.

He let out a breath slowly and thought about grabbing his phone.

Edgar had stood up all the crushed flowers, and now ventured into the trees in the direction of the statue Jess had received. Maybe he planned to move it. Or pickaxe it until it was destroyed.

Not long after Edgar disappeared, the basandere moved gracefully across the yard and went straight for the flowers. She chose a particularly thick cluster and began delicately plucking one flower at a time. After obtaining a handful, she turned and sprinted into the trees, disappearing quickly.

Edgar came running out a moment later, hands out, looking around the garden wildly. He walked directly to the place the basandere had just been and scratched his head. He clearly couldn't tell what had been stolen. He'd met his match in the subtle flower thief.

"Damn it," Austin said softly, grabbing his phone and standing from the chair.

This call had to be made.

He walked from the room so he didn't wake Jess, making his way down to her private sitting room. Other than her bedroom, it was the most comfortable place in the house.

"Do you need anything, sire?" Mr. Tom, mostly obscured by deep shadow, asked from the end of the corridor.

Austin hadn't even noticed his presence. How was that possible?

"No, I'm fine." He paused. "Why were you standing there?"

"You've been toiling over something, have you not?

While the miss is sleeping soundly? I thought I would remain on hand in case you needed a nightcap or an ear. Maybe a brandy. How about some marijuana? I hear it is all the rage nowadays. I picked some up from the dispensary just in case someone might need it."

All Austin could do was stare for a moment. "I'm good. Thanks."

He went to turn down the hall, then paused. *Damn it.*

"Whiskey. Neat. Something top shelf if you've got it."

"Of course I have it," Mr. Tom replied stiffly. "What do you take me for?"

Austin resumed his course without comment. Really, what was there to say?

In Jess's sitting room, he took the soft recliner covered in a loud floral print. His phone was still in his hand. He rested it on his lap, staring down at it.

"And here we go." Mr. Tom bustled in wearing his full tux with the moth-eaten edges and set the glass beside Austin on a little table. "Will you be needing anything else?"

"Thank you, and no." Austin reached for the glass. "You'll need to get some new attire, Mr. Tom. Tailored. The house crew will need something other than oddly fitting purple muumuus."

"I am one step ahead of you, sire—"

"Don't call me sire."

"Master, then."

"Alpha is fine."

"Yes, sir. I will leave you to your affairs. Call me if you need anything."

"I won't, Mr. Tom, thank you. You can go to bed."

"Of course, sir. I'll just be in the kitchen if you need me."

Austin stared at nothing for a moment while Mr. Tom made his way out of the room and closed the door after him. It had been a while since someone had so flagrantly ignored his directives. Strangely, it didn't bother him. Expecting Mr. Tom to act in any way normal was an exercise in disappointment.

He took a sip, stalled a little longer, and then finally picked up the phone. If he was lucky, he'd get the answering machine. It was late, after all. Maybe she'd changed her usual hours…

"Austin," she said on the third ring, her voice that familiar tough sandpaper rasp. "Do you want information or need help?"

He couldn't help a smile as he leaned back into the chair. She'd always cut right to the chase. Zero room for superfluous words. Even in this situation, when they hadn't spoken in so long.

"Hello, Mimi. Both, if possible."

She didn't comment. He'd started the conversation by calling, and now she expected him to lead it.

He hadn't realized until this moment how much he'd missed her.

"Firstly," he said, "just to get this out there…I'm sorry. For leaving like I did, for not calling…for everything."

"Even as a boy, you've always gone your own way. You found any barrier that existed and wouldn't rest until you'd crashed your way through it. I'm glad you eventually found your destination. The thing about family is, we're always here when you find your way back."

He let out a slow breath and then took another sip of whiskey. "I can't get back quite yet."

"Has your brain gone soft, boy? I didn't mean physically."

He huffed out a laugh and then shook his head. "Point taken. What's going on over there? Kingsley says that mages have been sneaking in to test his defenses. He says the attacks are weak. Is that true? You know him—he won't admit he actually needs help until danger is breathing down his neck."

"The attacks do seem weak, yes. They attack the defenses in seemingly random patterns. That mage has never attacked a pack as strong and well organized as Kingsley's. He might be realizing he's bitten off more than he can chew."

Austin took another sip of his drink. Wouldn't that be a miracle. He wasn't sure, though. That didn't sound like the mage Sebastian had talked about.

On the other hand, the people they'd dealt with in the basajaunak lands hadn't been as threatening as Sebastian thought they would. Maybe the weird mage still wasn't properly assessing how fierce shifters could be.

"I'll speak to our resident mage about this. He hadn't had any word from his network last time I checked, but I'll stay on top of it."

She made a little hum. "You have acquired some useful people, it sounds like. Kingsley raved about some of the creatures you have in your pack."

"Not mine. My mate's. She brought in the power players."

"And you tamed them, yes. Did Kingsley tell you about his talks with other packs?"

"That he was communicating with whoever he could about unifying?" he asked. She didn't comment. "Yes. He's got some interest, but he's not really in a position to do anything. No one wants to jump into the fire with him."

"Even when he was, he wasn't enough to bring everyone together."

"Maybe he wasn't. But I will be. It'll be my focus right after we prove our strength by crushing the mages."

"That's my boy," she said softly, and he couldn't help smiling in pride. She'd always had unwavering belief in his abilities.

"What do you need help with?" she asked.

He took another sip of whiskey, welcoming the fire burning down his throat. "We have what'll probably be a few cairns of gargoyles coming to this territory. Jess needs to create an army of them, and it'll be tough going. Part of their culture is flashy displays of wealth. That's what the most prestigious cairns expect, at least."

"Damned waste of time."

During her reign as alpha, she'd never gone for posturing for the sake of show. She'd never played games. She saw no purpose in it. Neither did he, come to that, but he'd do worse for Jess.

"Our focus in this territory so far has mostly been centered around pack organization and training. We haven't had a lot of time to devote to sprucing the place up, especially the house Jess inherited. You have excellent taste in interior design. I wondered…if Kingsley could spare you…if you'd humor me and help decorate Ivy House. After that, maybe take over some of my projects or identify some establishments on their last legs that I could take over and improve."

"You need a business manager."

He tilted his head from side to side. "First I need an interior decorator. After that…"

Her dry laughter rolled through the line. "You don't want to give up control. I know a woman like that."

She was talking about herself. He released the tension he belatedly realized he'd been holding.

"A couple of things, though." He took a big gulp of whiskey this time, finishing the glass. "Her house is massive. A mansion. It hasn't been updated in… I really couldn't say."

"Anything else?"

He grimaced. "Her crew is…eccentric. The gargoyle butler might get in the way. The groundskeeper can't take criticism well; he often asks to be killed. The neighbor shouldn't be a problem, but she does throw rocks—"

"Austin, I am not concerned about strange people and their antics. What about your mate? It is her house, solely?"

"It's…kind of its own entity. It's magical. Alive, kinda. I'm sure Kingsley mentioned it. But it belongs to her, yes. For now."

"For now?"

"For as long as she lives. When she dies, the house will choose a new heir."

The silence on the other end stretched until his grandma finally said, "When you ultimately choose a destination, you really go for extravagance."

He chuckled softly and leaned his head back against the chair. "It seems so."

"And what about the tastes of your mate? Your brother's mate and I don't see eye to eye about such things. She can't stand when I come around."

Austin bet Mimi hung around often then, just to annoy Earnessa. She found humor in things like that.

Which, now that he thought about it, seemed an awful lot like something Niamh would do. Maybe that was why Niamh never bothered him, no matter how surly she got.

"Jess is very easygoing with stuff like this. She'll be happy not to bother with it. I'll be the one with the critical eye."

Mimi scoffed. "Then I'll be done in no time. The only opinions you have came from me. You say you're in a hurry?"

"Kingsley is in a hurry. We're going by his schedule. Having gargoyle allies will help our efforts immensely. So yes, ultimately this needs to be done yesterday. Can he spare you?"

She scoffed again. "Can he spare me? He'll be happy to get rid of me. I ask far too many questions for his taste, and he's got your mom for counsel."

His sigh of relief was audible. He'd get nervous later.

"How is Mom?" he asked, almost too quietly.

He hadn't spoken to her in all this time, not even after he'd met Kingsley again. She was a patient woman. Too patient, probably, allowing him to find his way. Now, speaking to Mimi, he realized how much he missed her. Missed them all. It had been too long. He should've called. He should've kept in touch, at least after he'd gotten somewhat settled. He'd been a coward. Was still a coward, actually. He couldn't bear to hear her disappointment, or worse, traces of the hurt he'd caused in her tone.

"She's how she always was."

How she always was—still putting the territory ahead of herself, even after stepping down from the alpha role. He'd expect no less, not from any of the Barazzas, and he knew Mimi wouldn't either. He'd been the only one to disappoint in that way. Hopefully now he could return with a little pride after finally stepping up into the role he'd been born and bred for. Trained for.

Mimi left it at that, and so did he. Now wasn't the

time.

"I can arrange travel—"

"No need," she said. "Just send me the address. I'll come as soon as everything is arranged. Don't send me pictures of the house. I'd like to see it for the first time without preconceived notions. Get together a list of vendors in the area. Ones that can handle big orders. Ones that'll jump all over themselves for a good client. Do you have an idea of the budget?"

"Unlimited."

Her tone turned disapproving. "I have no need for monetary theatrics, Austin. Even the richest people have budgets. Make sure your mate has some idea—"

"Mimi, you are not working on a commission. I'm not worried about you going crazy where you don't need to. But she'll need you to go crazy when the situation warrants it. *There is no budget.* The house came with more than enough riches to cover any renovations you might dream up. The wealth randomly stuffed in drawers would probably cover it, and that's only the few drawers in the attic I've seen. Lord knows what else is lying around this place." He paused, and couldn't help the thread of pride weaving through his words. "This house is unlike anything you've ever experienced. There is a lot of history rolled up in these walls. A lot of stories to tell. You'll know what I mean when you get here."

Her silence felt different this time. He suspected she was intrigued.

"Fine," she said. "I'll be there in a couple of days, probably. Get some sleep. You sound exhausted."

The phone went dead. His heart beat rapidly.

Part of him couldn't wait to see her. He'd leaned on her through the years when the others had thought him too dangerous, too volatile, and too like his father. She'd been his shelter, his quiet support when he was trying to get his life on track.

But she was also a hard woman with exacting standards. She'd scrutinize Jess without meaning to. She'd have *opinions* on Austin's house, his bar, his restaurants—opinions she considered as good as facts. Anything she thought was out of place…she'd force back into her perceived order. Her world existed in a series of squares and rectangles, and she was about to enter a circus of circles.

He needed her, though. He trusted her. She was family.

At least they'd have a little practice for the stubbornness of the gargoyles.

CHAPTER 6

NESSA

TWO DAYS AFTER the gift opening, Nessa stood in front of Ivy House, just barely off the property, waiting for Sebastian to arrive so they could tally up the house's goodies. They needed to know what Jessie was working with so that they could come up with a cohesive strategy for the gargoyles.

She had an electric notepad and stylus in hand, ready to jump into action. Jessie had mentioned there was a lot of wealth lying around, but Nessa had no idea what exactly to expect. Were there gold coins sparkling in the bottom of bathtubs like pirate booty? A cauldron filled with gems at the end of a rainbow Mr. Tom had randomly painted across an attic wall? Swords and cleavers and other bloodied weapons decked out in sparkling jewels and mugs crusted in gold? She could envision all of the above.

"Captain," Sebastian said as he walked briskly toward her, right in the middle of the street.

"What took you so long?"

Sebastian shook his head. "I met Patty in town. She told me her life story. Or maybe I told her my life story? I can't be sure. Every time she stopped talking, it seemed like a terrible void that had to be filled. There was a dinner invite in there somewhere, and something about the Porsche. It's all very confusing on this side of it. Anyway, doesn't matter. I've got news, and then I need an update."

Her excitement drained away immediately. She recognized that tone.

"What happened?" she asked. "What's going on?"

He shook his head, stopping beside her on the sidewalk. "I just heard through our network the kind of numbers Momar is pulling in to attack Kingsley. It's more than he's used for anyone else. He clearly knows what sort of power he's up against, and he's not taking chances."

"How many more?"

"Lots more. He's also approaching this attack more cautiously. He's systematically testing Kingsley's defenses and mapping out the terrain. He's getting his game plan in order so that when he finally attacks, it's going to seem like the thunder of God. The shifters won't stand a chance."

"Which is why we are going to their aid."

"Nessa..." This time his tone and the corresponding pause sent a shiver up her spine. "We're not enough. We have two magical workers and Austin's pack. Big whoop. Momar is preparing an army of mages and a ground troop to stand between them and the shifters. Without the basajaunak to pump up our numbers, we're sunk. We're as good as dead."

"Well..." This time it was Nessa who took an audible breath, as her brain churned quickly. "Okay. What can we do?"

He nodded, obviously expecting her to say that. They both knew they couldn't let the shifters get crushed. That would be the death rattle to their cause. Because of that, they couldn't run away or remove themselves from the altercation. They had to get stuck in this time. They'd need to figure this out.

"I've been thinking." He walked forward, onto Ivy House soil.

"Whoa, whoa, whoa." She put out her hand to stop him. "The house can hear you once you're on the grounds."

"I know. This house wants to protect the heir above all things. It doesn't care how that is accomplished, as long as it is. It won't care that this plan goes behind Jessie's back."

"We'd have to go behind Jessie's back?"

"Yes. We'll have to be the bad guy, but it'll be for a good cause. This time, anyway."

Nessa shook her head, looking at the ground a few steps ahead of her. "Unless it does care, takes the plan as an affront, and kills you before you can get off its soil."

"Unless that, but I've talked over things with it before. It hasn't killed me yet."

"That is not exactly confidence inspiring," she muttered, crossing the threshold. "What'd you have in mind?"

"Okay…" He started for the front door. "Nathanial has said multiple times that gargoyles are a battle species, and they would want to be dragged into our trouble if we had it. That they would want to battle."

"Correct. I've heard the same thing."

"And we both know that Jessie always rises to the challenge. She seems sweet and caring and like a pushover until it's time for action, and then she's a beast."

"A very colorful, sparkly sort of beast, yes. I love how confusing she will be to mages."

"Yes." When they reached the porch, the door swung open on its own.

Shivers washed across Nessa's skin, and she hesitated again. "Doors opening on their own make sense when the heir or one of the crew is around. It feels like they are controlling it. But when it's just the house…it's a little creepy. Like the walls have eyes."

He laughed as he walked in without any trepidation. "You know how you always make fun of me for being jumpy around the shifters?" He paused for a reaction he didn't get. "Well, you'll never live this down."

She rolled her eyes, following him. In the foyer, he pointed at the grand archway where the wooden carving had been changed from a sort of valley to a woman in a fancy dress. Two stick figures held the hem of her skirt like they were about to lift it up and peer underneath it.

"She's going to reveal all her secrets," Sebastian translated. "And yes, the house is communicating with us. Ivy House, do you want to show us around and point out all the hidden gems?"

The door to the most-used sitting room slammed shut, making Nessa jump. Then it opened again slowly, the hinges squeaking softly.

"We also know," he said as they entered the room and various paintings in their gaudy and gilded frames wiggled, "that they won't want to be led by her. Or at least we strongly suspect that."

"They are slow to change," she said, squinting at the painting. "Looks like these might be of value, then?" The paintings wobbled a second time.

Sebastian nodded, clearly quite good at communicating with the house. "I'll take a picture and try to look them up." He studied them for a moment. "They could certainly do with nicer frames."

Nessa looked at the oil paintings, trying to find any sort of signature or tag. Not finding anything, she made note of the two pieces on her spreadsheets, leaving the dollar amount blank, as Sebastian took pictures.

"Slow to change, yes," he said. "But as we know, if the right pressure is applied in certain situations, it acts as a catalyst. When it comes to those gargoyles, I am willing to bet the farm that a catalyst should be centered around battle and strife."

"Stands to reason—Sabby, the wooden mural on the fireplace is changing. Ugh!" She grimaced at it. "It's like we're inside of a person…like…in its belly. Will your magic be able to fend it off if it gets in a temper?"

The door to the room swung hard and slammed shut. Several other doors, out in the hall or upstairs, some sounding very deep within the house, slammed shut as well. A thump sounded overhead. Something else slid against the inside of the walls.

She stood frozen with what she knew were hugely rounded eyes.

The mural that had just changed to the stick figures from earlier holding magnifying glasses now changed to one of the stick figures cowering low with ghosts flying all around them.

Sebastian laughed, of all things! It was clear this house delighted him, weirdo that he was.

"The house is playing with you," he said as she unstuck herself from the floor and reached the door first. She turned the handle, but the wood stuck fast.

"Oh my God, we're trapped." She yanked on the door, then beat on it with her fists. "We're trapped! Help! Jessie, can you hear me? Help!"

"Nessa, seriously, what…" Still laughing, Sebastian gently pushed her out of the way and turned the handle himself. The door opened smoothly. "The house isn't a microphone. Jessie can't hear you." He passed into the hall. "Which way, Ivy House?"

The door to the opposite sitting room, which probably had some formal name she didn't know, swung open. Sebastian calmly went that way.

"This house definitely needs an update," she said, noting the three paintings that were moving and then crinkling her nose at the stale air and gaudy furniture. "Can you imagine how absolutely amazing it would be if it was updated? Like…the bones of the place are amazing. And I see what Austin was talking about in terms of the woodwork. Except for those stupid pictures, it's all pretty awesome."

"It just needs a refresh," Sebastian said, peering in the drawers of an old-fashioned desk in the corner. It looked like one that a character in a Jane Austen novel would sit at to write a letter. "Check this out, Nessa."

One drawer held yellowed paper with rough edges. Another held quills and dried-up bottles of ink. Still another held antique fountain pens with old ink staining the velvet-lined drawer.

"Nessa!" Sebastian flared his hands, half knocking her out of the way, as he bent over the next drawer. "Oh my God, Nessa. Oh my God. Is this… Look at this!"

"Well get"—she shoved him over—"out of the way and I will. *Oh!*"

A pocket watch sat on the velvet drawer lining with its chain askew. The gold top plate was shaped like a flower, the twelve petals spaced evenly, the style based on the clock inside, no doubt. It was decorated with embedded pearls and dulled sapphires, and the space between the petals was colored red to show off the pearls and gems.

"I don't dare touch it," Nessa said, moving a little to make more room for Sebastian. "It's obviously antique."

"Yeah, we should use gloves," he said in a hush. "That design…is ringing a bell. I can't…put my finger on it."

"Historical?"

"I bet you anything it is. I'm guessing whoever owned it was royalty, or as good as." He blew out a breath, straightening up. "And it's just been thrown into a drawer in a writing desk and forgotten about for…who knows how long."

He went through the other drawers, but nothing else held a candle to the pocket watch discovery. Then again, they were watch people. All mages were. It was like when women used fans to communicate. Subtle hints or bold statements could be made with the choice of a watch. It was a hidden language—subtle enough, sometimes, to require a cipher.

"Jessie should be a pocket watch person," Nessa said, writing down a wiggling end table and then the shaking lamp on top, not knowing which Ivy House was actually trying to identify.

"An antique pocket watch person," Sebastian said, nodding. "She should have special clasps on her dresses—"

"No! Pockets sewn into every dress so that she might properly carry her antique, notable, hard-to-acquire pocket watch."

"Yes! But only to formal events and functions. During casual times, she should have simple yet exquisite collector's editions from all the top watchmakers. Excellently crafted, one of kind, simply done."

"Perfect."

They walked into the next room, still in a watch daze.

"I wish we didn't have so much to do right now," Sebastian said, "because I would love to start working on her watch collection. Imagine the mages' faces! They'll know she's making a statement, but they'll wonder if there is a cipher because they won't understand the language."

"Oh my God, so perfect. And she'll play clueless to a T—"

"Because she *will* be clueless…"

"—and they'll think there is a secret club that they haven't been invited to but are suddenly desperate to join."

Sebastian laughed and clapped.

All the lights went out, creating a murky pall in the large room with its heavy drapes only slightly cracked. The house felt like it had stilled, somehow. Like it was waiting for them.

"We should get back to it," Sebastian muttered, looking around. "Sorry, Ivy House. We get carried away."

"Spoilsport," Nessa muttered to the house.

"The last heir was a couple of hundred years ago," Sebastian said as he began looking in end table drawers in the next room. "During that time, the house had caretakers but no actual heirs. Which is why it hasn't gotten updates in so long. Now I guess Austin's grand-mama will be heading up the redesign project, huh?"

"Yeah, how have we not talked about that? What do you think she's like?"

He shook his head as they jotted down everything that shook in the room and moved on. "I'm afraid to find out. Scary, probably. I mean…he had to come from somewhere, right?"

"I will *die* if she's this sweet older lady with a bun and a little hunch and she smells like cookies."

"That could almost be Patty, and I think we can both agree she is only sweet until some fearsome creature tries to get the drop on her."

They both laughed.

In the next room, Nessa sighed. "Why does this place need so many sitting rooms?"

"Because they didn't have home theaters back in the day."

"Oh! A home theater. That's a good idea. One of these rooms should be turned into that."

"Yeah, maybe upstairs. Anyway, circling back, these gargoyles need a catalyst. They need to feel what a real battle is like. Nathanial was talking about raids the other day, and they seemed like sanctioned affairs. Pretty safe in the scheme of things. But that's not the kind of creatures gargoyles are. I've read up on them—"

"Just look around. The gargoyles in our house are pumped after battles."

"Right. Except when they're hurt. Anyway, they all want to be guardians, which is apparently the most fearsome of their kind. Those types of creatures don't want to play at fighting—they want to actually fight. To protect. To win."

"Yes, yes, I get it. So you're proposing we stage a battle?"

They wandered through the kitchen. Not a single thing moved. It clearly needed a remodel. Mr. Tom would not be pleased.

Sebastian held up a finger. "It won't be as easy as just staging a battle. Not this time. The battle is just one of the overall components." They stepped into the next room. Nothing moved and the furniture looked a little rickety. "We need to get tensions running high. We need those cairn leaders at a boiling point so that their people are on the edge. They need to be holding in aggression so that when they meet that catalyst, it feels so damn good to let it out and claim victory. That way, they'll look to Jessie in the most favorable light. She'll have led them in their triumph, and they'll love her for it. They'll want her to keep leading them, despite all their hang-ups."

Nessa wasn't even going to ask if he actually thought that would work. If there was one thing Sebastian excelled at, it was the art of subtle manipulation by working the environment around his target. He constructed their whole world and then watched them dance. It was truly a marvel.

He stalled in the next room, looking all around. "I have no idea what this room is. Oh, that looks like a thing for hand-washing clothes. Wow. This is old. This room could be made into something else. *Anything* else, actually."

"Moving on."

"Yup."

They wound a little deeper into the area that had clearly been designed for household staff and large-scale washing and ironing. The first floor done, they used the back stairs to reach the second floor.

All the doors were closed, probably from when Ivy House had slammed them to mess with Nessa, and they continued on until one slowly swung open.

Sebastian made a sound like *ewah* and clasped his phone a little tighter. "This is Jessie's room. I don't know that she would want her private stuff looked through—"

The door wiggled and opened a little wider.

Sebastian sighed, his shoulders slumping, and walked forward. “Fine,” he said softly.

“Maybe don’t look in the drawers in here,” Nessa advised, following him. “We don’t need to know what kinks Jessie and Austin are into.”

“Are you saying that for my benefit or yours?”

“It’s hard to say,” she replied. “How are you going to get the cairns wound up? With their gifts?”

“Naturally. It’s the easiest way. One we’ve had a lot of experience with, and a proven track record. The battle should be hard enough that they fear for their lives, but not so hard that we lose anyone. Jessie has to truly believe they are all in mortal danger. She’ll want to protect them, and to do that, she’ll unite them like she did in the basajaunak lands.”

“She knew all the players in the basajaunak lands. She won’t know the people here. How can we be sure she’ll unite them?”

“We can’t, and that’s just one of the dicey parts.”

“What’s the next dicey part?”

“Ah, how cute—the dolls are all standing in a line, watching Edgar fuss with his flowers.”

Nessa stopped and bent over the little table by the windows, looking into the wood. “Do you see any of those horrible gnomes?”

“I’d rather not.” Sebastian straightened and looked

around before a painting near the closet started to wiggle. He frowned when the painting wiggled again, and then shook his head and addressed the house. "I'm not getting it. I already took a photo. Why are you still wiggling the picture?"

Cracks and pops sounded, like an old house shifting, followed by a deep wooden groan from somewhere in its bowels. Shivers broke out on Nessa's skin again, and she backed up, looking at the door.

"Yes, I know you're annoyed, but that doesn't help me figure out what you're trying to say." Sebastian lifted the edge of the wobbling painting and peered behind it. "Ah."

He removed the painting to find a wall safe without a combination knob. It popped open, obviously controlled by the house. A shiny briefcase waited inside. Sebastian pulled it out and popped the clasps. Stacks of bundled one-hundred-dollar bills filled up all available space.

He picked up a few of the bundles, flipping through them. "All hundreds, so there's probably about two-point-four million in the case, assuming they are bundled as normal. Why is it in a briefcase, though?"

"In case they need to do a shady transaction, and only a Hollywood-grade briefcase will do?"

He shook his head, replacing everything. "This isn't

flashy. It's odd, but not flashy. Ivy House, lead us to the flashy stuff. I want something better than that pocket watch. Something we can wave in the gargoyle leaders' faces to blow their minds."

As they followed the house's prompts out of Jessie's room and down the hall, Sebastian continued.

"The next dicey bit is obvious. Controlling the length of time the gargoyles are here."

"I'm not sure how that's obvious. I doubt they'll be suspicious of us. It'll be easy to rile them up or cool them off, as the case may be, to keep them long enough to get the attack into position."

"Except Jessie is incredibly unpredictable. If they rile her up too much, there will be no cooling her off. Or cooling them off after she's made an example of them. Then there is Austin. Rile him up and he's liable to kill them all. Remember, aggressions need to be high, at least by the most battle-savvy of the guardians. It'll be a pot ready to boil. Hopefully. That's the goal, at any rate."

"And we can't tell Austin because he'll batten down the hatches."

"Exactly. He's not rational where it concerns her, which is cute and great and I love, but he won't want her in any danger at all, even something she should be able to handle."

She blew out a breath.

He trailed off as a door down the hall opened. He walked through. "Mr. Tom's room."

Nessa hurried in after him, incredibly curious. It was spotless, with very little clutter—everything looking like it had a specific location and he was vigilant in ensuring anything he used went back to that location. A nightshirt waited on a hook in the en suite bathroom.

The walls were devoid of pictures, save one—a man in his twenties with a full head of hair, chiseled features, and a stuffy air. That had to be Mr. Tom in his younger days. He used to be a looker, actually. Thick chest, muscular arms, tall. Age hadn't been kind. That was probably why he was so annoyed Jessie hadn't let the house make them all young again.

"Here we go," Sebastian whispered, pulling out various boxes from the closet and resting them on the bed.

He opened each, and Nessa knew Mr. Tom had been correct. These jewelry sets were extravagant. Obviously worth a fortune, given the size and sheer volume of the jewels. Nessa would be greatly surprised if some of these hadn't once adorned the necks of queens. Perhaps some of the jewels had even sat in crowns. They were enormous, cut in a way that screamed *relic*.

Sebastian had his loupe out, checking the quality of

the stones.

One of the sliding closet doors closed slowly and opened again.

"Go check what else is in there," Sebastian said distractedly.

She did as instructed, pushing the door wide and then snapping her hand back when the door pushed back against her. Ivy House did like to play games.

When she made no move to try again, the door slid fully open and something clinked on a little shelf in the corner. She found smaller jewelry boxes. Below that, more. Below that, larger ones.

She pulled them all out.

"We've got more." She laid them on the bed in rows before opening all the lids. "Holy hell, Sebastian, is this for real?"

A huge blue gem winked up at her from one, surrounded by sparkling diamonds. It hung on a thick diamond chain. Each emerald-cut diamond ranged from a carat to two. They winked and sparkled as they looked up at her.

"That looks like a blue diamond," she whispered, stroking a finger across the surface. "It's gotta be twenty carats."

She moved on to the next case—these were all individual pieces rather than sets. A radiant-cut diamond solitaire ring had to clock in at over three carats. Another ring, similar in size, had an emerald with diamonds on the sides. There were finely worked bracelets and other necklaces, earrings, and rings. She'd never seen a collection like this in the flesh. The fact that it had been randomly kept at the bottom of a closet boggled her mind. Mr. Tom had stowed two million in cash in that safe, but he'd stuffed this collection, worth a whole lot more, willy-nilly into a closet.

"I bet these all reek with fascinating history," she said into the hush of the room. "Stories untold. Thievery, battles, ransacked castles…"

"The heirs probably got them as gifts, but who knows how the gift givers got them?" Sebastian shook his head and motioned for her to pack them up. "There isn't one cairn leader who can come even remotely close to matching this. Not *one*. Now, when we get into the mages—"

"No, no." Nessa held up her hand. "We don't need the house getting pissy again. Meeting mages is farther along in our plans, after we hopefully *do not die* in Kingsley's territory."

"Right. True. Sorry."

"What's next? Let's see if this can be topped."

She needn't have asked.

After skipping over the crew's rooms, they found

themselves in a room that was completely empty, save the closet.

"What in the—No." Nessa just shook her head, hands on hips. "No. This is ridiculous. Why did Mr. Tom waste his time putting cash in a briefcase in a wall safe when this is up here? He has royal jewels in a closet, and now this? What—"

She was at a loss for words. Sebastian's mouth hung open.

Stacked in the closet, floor to ceiling in side-by-side stacks, was a crap-load of gold bars.

Gold bars.

This closet, with no lock to speak of, in a random, empty bedroom in the house, was the house's own private Fort Knox.

"I can't even." Nessa threw up her hands. "How do you even flash this around?"

"I'm sure we can figure out a way, but it won't be with gargoyles. My God, Nessa…" Sebastian's mouth opened and closed like a fish's. "Just…my God."

After a great lot of staring, some counting, and much shaking of heads, they continued on to the rest of the house. The office held a few really old-looking books and a financial ledger with a bottom line that didn't seem possible.

"That is an awful lot of zeroes," Nessa said, once

again shaking her head. "An awful lot."

Sebastian started laughing. Nessa joined him, and the two of them leaned against each other as they wrestled with the enormity that was this house.

Much to their disappointment, the third floor wasn't that impressive. Other than a billiards room that was old and in need of refurbishing, most of the space was empty. There was a small ballroom as well, grand but *very* old, and oddly placed on the third floor like it was an afterthought. It looked like it had been shut up long ago and not bothered with since. Some of the chandeliers were worth a pretty penny, and there were more paintings and furniture to write down, but nothing like those closets.

"Which mages are you going to use?" Nessa asked.

"I'm going to have to use some of our people in the reserves. The ones in hiding that we know about. We'll promise them that we'll wipe the slate clean, give them a hefty payment, and, of course, assure their protection."

"Lies, of course."

"Of course. I'm expecting Jessie and Austin to kill them dramatically. They'll be desperate to believe us, though. They'll assume a grisly death if they don't. They'll do it with the hope I want to use them another time."

"How many?"

"Ten."

"*Ten?*" She stopped on the way to the attic stairs, her mouth dropping. "*And* mercenaries?"

"A couple dozen mercenaries."

"Sebastian, that's crazy. That's too many mages! The shifters will be able to eat through the mercenaries, but that many mages against you two?"

"We'll have the gargoyles."

"We *might* have the gargoyles, Sebastian. Might. *If* we can pull this off. If we don't, and that attack team goes dark, we're going to have to fight that company. There won't be a way to stop them."

Going dark meant deploying. It meant the attacking team closed communications to the outside world and operated in secret so that they couldn't be detected by the enemy. It was the way Elliot Graves always operated.

In this instance, it would be better to forgo the practice, but they'd found that if they ever deviated from what people expected of their operations, they lost trust. Losing trust meant the company scattered, and they had to be tracked down and killed and more people found, and it was a whole mess.

"We need a sizable attack, Nessa," he said. "We need the odds stacked against us, and mages are the best way to do that. She's ready for this. If we have those gargoyles—the fliers to help us—we can handle this."

"Right. But we're back to *if*. There has to be another way." She started forward again, heading for the attic stairs. "Jessie turns people loyal like no one's business. If we help her, and set things up that might delight the gargoyles, at least some of them"—he started shaking his head—"will want to join her cairn."

"That's just it, Nessa. She doesn't really *have* a cairn. That, and she has zero status, which apparently means everything to them, like how mages think of magic. I overheard Patty speaking to Nathanial the other day, after the connection request thing. They're worried. They both are. Waving money in the guardians' faces might've won a couple people over if it was just the newness thing, but it's not. It's so much more, including Jessie's lack of history with gargoyles, them operating like a pack instead of a cairn…" He stopped at the base of the stairs. "I feel this, Nessa. In that way I sometimes do, I *feel* this. It's dicey, as I said, and the whole structure of the plan is loose at best, but it will work. If we can see it through, it *will* work. I know it. She'll turn them. She'll be the battle leader she was meant to be, and she'll turn them. You have to trust me. We need those gargoyles if we're going to defeat Momar, and this is a way to get them."

She knew about those feelings, a strange little offshoot of his magic that sometimes led them out of a dead end by some miracle or other. His sister had been a *Seer*, and the family gene pool had clearly touched him somehow.

But things always went wrong. Always. This was clearly why he hadn't mentioned it before now. He hadn't thought up this plan; it had come to him in a flash, in bits and pieces that never seemed to fit together perfectly.

That was where she came in. Her job was to keep their fragile house of cards from collapsing. She'd gotten them out of scrapes a million times, but there'd always been casualties.

"The goal is not to lose anyone, I thought," she said slowly.

"We won't. I know we won't."

She didn't know if she believed him. Sometimes he focused too hard on the big picture and didn't see the Mack truck bearing down on them. That was her job, after all. Damage control.

She paused, studying him. "Are you going to tell them about Momar's numbers, or leave that as a surprise, too?"

"I'll tell Austin some of what I found out. Basically that Momar is checking Kingsley's defenses. That his goal is information gathering. Momar wants to preserve his people for the actual attack. The rest he doesn't need to know yet. It'll agitate him and pull his focus from what is most important right now—getting those gargoyles on board."

"Austin is a very dangerous man, Sebastian. I don't like the idea of sneaking around behind his back. If he finds out we planned an attack on his pack, on Jessie, while simultaneously keeping important information about his brother from him, he'll skin us alive."

"I know. He's not cunning, though. He won't know our plans unless we actually tell him, and we're not idiots."

"He's not cunning, but he's smart. He's going to see how we dance around those gargoyles. He'll see our tactics. What if he somehow puts two and two together and reads into this?"

"How would he do that? He'd have to know more than he does. That part I'm not worried about."

She sighed, leaning against the railing. "I just don't know. This plan isn't just loose—it relies on a lot of factors we have zero control over. It's almost reckless."

"Maybe, but it'll work. That's the bottom line. All we're doing is pushing Jessie a little, like we've done in the past. Besides, if we don't get the gargoyles, we can call off the attack before they go dark. Going dark only lasts three to six days, depending on the team. We should know by then."

She didn't comment, looking away to think.

"We won't be able to keep her from helping Kingsley," Sebastian said softly. "If we told her and Austin the risks, they'd go anyway. They'd do everything they could to help, and they'd likely die trying. Securing those gargoyles will go a long way to saving her life. It's worth trying to make this happen."

He had a point there. So why did she still have a very, very bad feeling about this? Why did she feel like the price for success would be incredibly steep?

CHAPTER 7

NESSA

THE SOUND OF doors creaking and opening echoed down the hall. Other doors popped and then opened—those to the secret tunnels within the house. From all the rooms, the lights flared and then glowed brightly.

"That's a yes," Sebastian said, looking down the hall. "That's Ivy House's yes to the plan."

"I forgot that the house got a vote," Nessa murmured. "Will the house help me try to patch up all the holes in the plan as it gets underway?"

"You know it will, if it can. We'll be able to do this, Nessa. Maybe it'll even be easy, since those gargoyles don't know what they're walking into."

Famous last words.

She'd think this all through later.

"Let's see what's in that attic," she finally said, starting up.

"Why don't you tell me where we are with the gargoyles?"

She did so, quickly telling him about the huge amount of information Niamh had pulled together in such a short time, and their ability to hack into the cairns and get everything, from their guardian information to how much and what their production cairns were producing. They'd done good work in a couple days and now needed to lean into information gathering on any dark secrets the cairn leaders might be hiding.

"Yikes," Nessa said, finally taking a look around the attic and noticing the rows of weaponry hanging on the wall. A grin wrestled with her lips, and then she burst out laughing. "They're named."

Sebastian had a lopsided grin as he investigated. "Who did it, do you think? Mr. Tom or Edgar?"

"Mr. Tom. Edgar doesn't get to make decisions about the inside of the house. Just the outside."

"And vice versa?"

"Yup." She chuckled, tracing one of the names. "Jake the battle-ax. They aren't even interesting names. They're all common. Ron, Ralph, Carl…"

"Here we go." Sebastian picked up a stake from the top of a chest of drawers. "Silver stakes. Are these for killing vampires and shifters?"

She shrugged, counting them up before opening the next drawer. Then she started laughing again.

"Holy crap-cakes, look at this." She held out an enormous loose stone for Sebastian. "Tell me that isn't a ruby." He took it and pulled out his loupe magnifier as she pushed other gems around. "And tell me these aren't other enormous semiprecious gemstones just randomly kept in a drawer in the *attic*."

"It's a ruby, and this is what Jessie was talking about, remember?"

His phone rang. He put the loupe away and handed back the stone before digging it out. "It's Jessie," he said, tapping the screen. "Hi. What's up?"

Nessa attempted to count the gems, but really, what was the point? The enormity of this house's wealth wouldn't register to gargoyles. Not most mages, either. Not most people, full stop.

One thing did occur to her, though.

"There weren't any watches in the jewelry in Jessie's room," she mumbled to herself as Sebastian said, "No problem. We're done anyway."

"I didn't see one pearl." She looked over her notes. "Oh yeah, there was that huge one. But no pearls of regular size. Like everyday size, I mean. She needs a better wardrobe, too." Nessa tapped the stylus against her lips. "She has *a lot* of golden oldies, but she's pretty sparse with modern jewelry and other accessories. Stuff that screams *wealth*, I mean. She has the normal jewelry one might wear around town. She needs more sunglasses, handbags, shoes… We still have our work cut out for us."

"Yes, it's a bit mind-boggling, actually," Sebastian was saying to Jessie. They were clearly talking about the riches randomly stored around the house. "I have what I need, yes. I'll be able to use some of it, for sure. Okay…okay…okay, bye."

He hung up and started for the door. "Someone is coming up the walkway," he said, heading down the stairs. "Jessie wants us to intercept them in case it is Austin's grandma. I think we should take some of those loose stones and have them made into some really swank jewelry. Something modern that'll compete with that gargoyle's bracelet. The old stuff is impressive, and it'll be perfect for impressing some of the mages, but we want to show that we have better modern designers too. That'll get that gargoyle's goat."

"One thought ahead of you, bro," Nessa said. "We need to find a really amazing artisan, though."

"Do you know of any?"

"Not on the level we need. I'll ask around. Austin plays chill with his monetary status, but he's got some gold coins jingling around in his purse, too. He probably has a list for when he wants to pamper Jessie."

"He definitely has a refined side, I'll say that much. I've seen some of his remodels. They are chic. He'll do perfectly with the gargoyles. He won't need any coaching, I bet you anything."

"We'll need to figure out his persona for the mages."

"Scary," Sebastian deadpanned.

"Well…yes…but let's delve a little deeper, shall we?"

They reached the front door in time for it to swing open. Nessa jumped back with her hands up, her electronic notepad flying.

"Steady, Captain," Sebastian said, his words riding a laugh.

A regal older woman was just stepping up onto the porch. She held herself with great poise, her posture perfect and her chin just a smidge elevated, as though she was a very important person who'd come to call. Her gray hair was curled around her head and into a bun, surprisingly artful for such a mundane type of hairstyle. Nondescript black slacks covered her bottom half, ending in black flats you wouldn't look twice at, and a thin line of lace topped her black shirt. It would've been a plain outfit if not for her statement piece: a freaking cool-ass light coat that draped down to her thighs. Nessa couldn't figure out what it was made out of. Kinda seemed like velvet, but it wasn't, though it did look soft. It had a sort of sheen but wasn't exactly shiny. It flowed gracefully along her body, elegant and chic.

This was where Austin had gotten his sense of style. Nessa would bet her life on that.

"Hello," Sebastian said, his shoulders hunching a little. That meant he recognized the alpha shifter in her.

Nessa stifled a snicker.

"And you are?" the woman asked, her blue-eyed gaze like frost-tipped spears.

Sebastian hunched a little more. "I'm Sebastian. Jessie…Ironheart. Alpha Jessie Ironheart, I mean…of the…here. The house. Uhm…"

Before a laugh broke free, Nessa stepped partially in front of Sebastian with her hand out.

"Hi. I'm Natasha, but my friends call me Nessa. Sebastian is the mage training Jessie, and I am his accomplice. With Jessie's approval, we were just making note of all the worth stashed within Ivy House and coming up with a game plan for making her shine for the coming gargoyles and eventually the mages."

The woman looked down at Nessa's hand but made no move to shake it.

"You seem very forthcoming with information, Natasha." She turned her gaze to Sebastian. "Sebastian."

That must've been a hello. Back to Nessa now. "I am Naomi Barazza of the Gossamer Falls pack, grandmother of Austin Steele, alpha of this territory. I've come to help my grandson, and he has asked that I start with outfitting this house. I've received word that they are tied up. I believe I've been permitted to start my analysis of this property. Will you be leading me around?"

"Oh…" Nessa drew out the word and turned to shoot Sebastian a look. "Uhm… I'm not sure we're really qualified for that sort of thing."

Naomi showed zero expression, but her tone worked wonders at relaying her feelings. "You are not qualified to show me around a house that you've just cased?"

"It's just…" Nessa randomly pointed behind her. Okay, yes, this woman could rattle the nerves a little. "It's magical, and it has decided I'm a fun joke. I'll probably just get in the way. It's fine, though. I'm sure it'll show you around itself until Mr. Tom gets back to take over."

"Mr. Tom?" she asked.

"The gargoyle butler. He runs the place. Mostly. Kinda."

"I see."

The disappointment in those two words was evident. Her non-reaction to the idea of a house showing her around was just shy of incredible.

Nessa had a feeling it would be awfully hard to fluster this woman.

"Do you have *any* relevant information for me?" Naomi asked, the words carrying a snap of command.

"I'd rather not," Sebastian muttered, and then hunched some more and stepped out of her line of sight.

Nessa's smile at Sebastian's antics withered under that icy stare. She widened her eyes and stepped back a little.

"Sure, I guess," she said. "I mean…kinda. Ivy House pointed us toward the things that were worth something…"

Naomi stepped forward, and Nessa found herself clearing out of the way.

"The items that are worth something are a great place to start. And you said the house pointed those out?"

"Yes."

"And how did it do that?"

All the doors that had been opened slammed shut. Those that had been shut creaked open. Then they switched. The wooden carving above the entryway changed to Nessa's stick figure pulling at a door, a discarded magnifying glass flying through the air behind her. Paintings wiggled and tables and vases shook.

"That is enough," Naomi barked, loud and sure.

The wooden carving changed to Nessa looking out the door and Sebastian's stick figure cowering behind her.

"The house is magical," Nessa said.

"Yes. I see that." Naomi stared for a moment, and her expression could give stones a run for their money.

"Go, Nessa." Sebastian pushed at Nessa to get walking. "Let's just follow the same path as before until Mr. Tom gets here."

But the second time through was *much* different than the first.

"Hmm," Naomi said in the first room, taking a long moment to look at the very first painting Ivy House had wiggled. Her gaze traveled the edges before she stepped back. "The frame does not do that one justice. It'll need to be changed."

She ran her finger along one of the couches and then stopped for a longer period of time on a painting Ivy House hadn't wiggled.

"The world thinks this painting has been lost," she finally said, taking a step back but still seemingly entranced. "Records were not well kept when it was in its infancy and have since been damaged. It is part of a formerly lost collection that has been distributed to museums around the world. All the paintings in the collection have been found except for this one. And here it sits, on the wall with no protective covering, no security, and no acknowledgment."

Nessa and Sebastian looked at each other in slow motion, his wide eyes probably mirroring hers.

"So you know a little something about art," Nessa said, restarting her notepad that Sebastian had picked up for her.

"I know a lot about art. It is a passion of mine." Naomi continued along the room, stopping periodically. "You know what they say: those who can't *do*...covet those who can."

"Those are some serial killer vibes, right there," Sebastian muttered.

After viewing the art, Naomi glanced at the furniture. "All of this will have to go, of course. The wallpaper will need to be changed. The floor sanded and re-stained. Maybe even replaced. It has not weathered well." She looked up at the coffered ceiling. "That looks like the original wood. It can be polished up, I think. The craftsmanship is...incredible. The fireplace, too. Ah...the mural on that changes as well. Interesting."

Without another word, she walked from the room.

"Okay..." Nessa jogged after her. "Were any of those other paintings worth anything?"

"Yes. All, I'd wager. They are paintings out of time, probably with a good story attached to each. A pity the house doesn't talk."

She paused in the foyer for a moment, her gaze tracing the wood on the stairs, the wallpaper next to it, and the worn rug along the center of the steps.

"The house does talk." Nessa poised her pen over the notepad. "To Jessie."

Naomi spared her a glance before continuing into the next sitting room.

"Those are apparently worth something." Nessa pointed out odd lamps, but Naomi still had her head tilted back, wandering close to the walls and taking in all of the paintings.

"It's like a moment out of time," she said again. "Many of these I have never seen or heard about. That doesn't make them any less enjoyable, of course. A couple, though..."

"The Ivy House heirs were a really big deal back in the day," Sebastian said, giving her a wide berth. "The books say they were invited to dine by kings and queens. Fawned over by powerful magical players. Showered with gifts by prospective suitors..."

"Is the heir no longer a...big...deal?" She drew out

the last word, finally going to the lamps Nessa had mentioned earlier.

"Not yet."

"And you are going to elevate her to that status? That is why you are being meticulous about documenting her worth?"

Nessa went to give Sebastian a *look* again, because wow this lady was intense, but he didn't notice. He'd straightened up, his hands at his sides, his brow creased.

"I am going to do everything in my power to try, yes," he said, his tone defiant. "And yes, that is exactly why I am being meticulous."

"These lamps are themselves a work of art. They'll need a certain kind of style to shine, but it *is* worth showing them off. Everything else can go." Naomi eyed Sebastian before she crossed into the next room, speaking to him over her shoulder. "As a past alpha, I understand why someone might wish to show off a pack's success, using material goods to do so. But such posturing is on the level of cheap parlor tricks. The solidity of a leader is not in the…*bling* around their neck, but in their actions. In their people and the community."

"I beg your pardon, Ms. Barazza, but you have no idea what you're talking about. When I come here and root around in my friend's things, it is because she is my friend. It is because I know *exactly* what I am doing and how best to help her, more than anyone else in this particular situation. Gargoyles expect that kind of posturing, and so do mages. *I* am the one who'll keep her alive in the snake pit, not your grandson, and not her gargoyles. You might think you know better because you led a pack once, but with all due respect, when it comes to what she's about to walk into, both in the near future and in the distant future, you don't know dick."

Nessa grimaced and stood very still. Sabby was, at his heart, a non-confrontational introvert. But when you threatened his family, he was every bit the alpha.

Naomi stopped…and then turned very slowly.

Menace pulsed out from around her and shone in her icy stare. But Sebastian didn't buckle. His spine didn't bend. He met her stare with one of his own, hard and cool and calm, the part of him most people only saw when he was in his Elliot Graves persona.

She nodded, just a curt jerk of her head, before turning for the next room.

Nessa followed like a little lamb, suddenly not sure which was worse—this house or Grandma Naomi. She'd never longed to see Mr. Tom so much in all her life.

CHAPTER 8
AUSTIN

AUSTIN GLANCED DOWN at his phone to check the time. They'd gotten a lot done, but the day had run long.

"This is never going to be done in time," Jess said, standing in the middle of the tasting room downtown. She had her arms crossed over her chest, surveying the makeshift setup they'd agreed on. Niamh sat at a high table a little removed from the rest, drinking tea and eating a scone. "We'd have to rush it, and I don't want that. If they ask, we can bring them in here, share our ideas, and leave it at that."

"You're right." Jess knew exactly what she wanted for the tasting room, and Austin had every intention of making her vision a reality.

"We should go, though." She took a step back, surveying the space with a critical eye. "Your grandma is at the house. We need to get to her."

"No, no." He waved her away, leaning against the wall by the door. "I'll see her later tonight. I know for a fact she'll enjoy interrogating Sebastian and Nessa. We'd just get in the way."

Jess looked away left, then right, her hand on the wine bar. "We need more light. How hard would it be to put in a window?"

"Do ye hear her?" Niamh leaned back with eyebrows at her hairline. "She'd want to be on one of those home makeover shows."

Jessie spread her arms at Niamh. "This isn't a dive bar. We need a little light."

"I'm not sayin' we don't. I'm just sayin' ye're awfully opinionated about this place when ye couldn't give two shakes about Ivy House."

Jess shrugged, looking over the table setup one last time, and then pointed at the far corner. "Maybe a little area for selling wine things there instead of across the room." She stared at it for a bit, looked around one more time, and nodded. "Yes. I think that's it. This feels right."

"Oh it *feels* right, does it?" Niamh looked to where she was pointing as Jess took a chair at Niamh's table and motioned Austin over.

"Yes. There is a nice flow through here now," Jess said. "It'll be perfect. And in answer to your…accusation or whatever it was…" She shrugged again. "My ex-mother-in-law kind of put me off house decorating. But also…Ivy House has its own personality. I am the heir, but it'll never be truly mine. So…I don't know, I just wouldn't know where to start."

Niamh nodded. "That's why I bought my own place. I didn't want to live in the house with that clown Mr. Tom underfoot all the time. Ivy House is a place of work. I need me off time, too."

"Yeah, exactly." Jess nodded again. "That's a great way to put it."

They passed a bit more time, sitting at the table and chatting, looking up colors and items for the interior. When they'd exhausted their efforts for the day, Niamh wandered away and left Austin and Jess standing in the center of the space.

"It's going to be really nice," he told her, pulling her close.

She wrapped her arms around his middle. "I think so. Though the tasting room doesn't have to be perfect. It's the wine people will care about."

"The team is working on it. Honestly, if you're sure about delaying, it's probably for the best. But in the end, I believe we will have a good finished product."

"We'll do a pre-opening at the actual winery to taste, inviting whoever wants to come, and then open a week later or whatever. That'll start it off with a nice buzz."

"That…is an amazing idea." He kissed her forehead. "I love it."

A glimmer passed through her eyes and her eyelids narrowed just slightly. A flurry of emotions filtered through the bond, too fast for him to pick any one out.

"How about we make use of the lack of windows?" she murmured, her breath sweet.

He ran his hands down her back and cupped her butt, grinding her hips against him. "We're kind of short on time. I was hoping you'd have dinner with me? Afterward, I need to check out one of my properties. We also need to meet up with Mimi at some point."

"Hmm." Her kiss was languid but intense, her tongue swirling with his. "I'd love to have dinner with you. We can be really quick."

She trailed her hands down the sides of his body and then pushed back a little so her fingers had room to feel along his belt. She ran her teeth along his lips and pulled at his button before quickly unzipping his pants.

"Super fast. Then we'll run to the car." She slid her palm in and captured his hard length. "We'll have lost no time at all, you'll see. Or if we go a little longer, so that maybe I can use my mouth a little, we'll just go without an appetizer."

She dropped down to her knees, sucking him in. He groaned, his fingers in her hair and his head falling back. There really was no point in resisting. When it came to her, he wasn't a strong-willed man.

She wasn't hurried, using long strokes that drew his eyes down to her. She looked up, repeatedly taking him in, working him with her hand as she did so.

"You're so beautiful," he blurted, and her rhythm stalled a little so she could smile up at him. Even a smart man had trouble with original compliments in this situation. She was lucky he could do more than continue the marathon of grunting.

He curled his fingers around her wrist to stop her. If she kept going, he'd finish before she'd even begun.

Knowing this, she gracefully rose before stripping off her shirt and then her bra. Her shoes then pants went next, leaving nothing but a lacy pink thong. She sauntered to the counter, her hips hypnotizing him, before turning around and leaning back. Her nipples constricted from the chill, pointing right at him. Her curves set him on fire.

Pants around his ankles, he lurched toward her like Frankenstein's monster. His hands ran along her flesh. His mouth sucked the hard peak of her breast. He meant to fall to his knees and worship her, but he was too far gone. Instead, he sucked in a tender spot on her neck that she liked and pushed her thong aside.

"Hmm," she purred as he trailed his fingers through her wetness.

She hooked a silky thigh over his hip. He ran his tip along her heat before thrusting, earning a long feminine mew.

"I'm so happy to be doing this project with you, Austin," she whispered, lifting the other leg so that he held her weight. "Thank you for including me."

His answer was a grunt. He couldn't even be embarrassed about it.

Her smell, the heat of her skin, and the glory of her lips sent him to paradise. He closed his eyes and strove harder, his heart full, his body on fire.

His climax smashed into him, and he drove in deep, emptying inside of her. He pushed in two more times, his body shaking, and she cried out with her release.

A strange feeling curled through him, something primal that he couldn't really distinguish. She clutched him, as though feeling it too.

In a moment, though, it subsided into the glorious euphoria that always came from their joining.

"I love you," she whispered into his ear.

"You're my forever," he replied, holding her.

After they'd freshened up, he escorted her out. "I had Mr. Tom bring the new car over," he said as he gently tugged her toward the Porsche. "The reasoning was twofold. The first was to give Mimi a little more time before Mr. Tom descended on her and slowed everything down. The second…" He grinned, ignoring the people passing by with nods or hellos. "I want to see how fast it goes."

He left her by the passenger door and bent near the back tire, retrieving the key fob from on top.

"Is that okay?" he belatedly asked. "My Jeep's down the street if you'd rather not put miles on it."

She rolled her eyes with a smile. "I don't care about putting miles on it. Honestly, the whole connection request situation with these extravagant gifts seems a little overboard."

The bucket seats hugged his butt just right. The smell of new car and leather greeted his senses, and the metal sport pedals near his feet begged him to stomp on the gas.

"They do, but think of it this way—these big cairns don't extend connection requests often. Or ever, maybe. I'm guessing they get them often enough, though. They're about due to drop a little money."

"A *little* money?" She laughed and shook her head.

At the entrance to the highway, he stomped on the gas. The thing shot off like a comet, throwing him back in his seat. Jess grabbed the door handle but didn't squeal or scream. All too soon the fun was over and he had to let off the gas. He'd reached the speed limit *quickly.*

"I'm not really looking forward to having to dress up just so I can show off when the big cairns come around," Jess said. "I know we'll have to invite them. It just seems like so much hassle."

"It does, but it's part of the job. Babe…" He wasn't sure how this would go, but she needed to hear it. He reached over and took her hand. "You do need a better vehicle. I love my Jeep, and I drive it almost exclusively, but I have my flashy sports car for when I want to take out my girl or impress her snobby friends. You have a new job now. You need to drive the part."

"Yes, yes, I know. Everyone has been bringing that up since I got this car." She looked out the window and quietly said, "What a hassle."

He couldn't help laughing. He loved that she was so down to earth. Most people would've gone gaga over being thrown into a whirlwind of money, but it hadn't changed her even a little. She was in it for the people, not the material goods.

Austin pulled into a parking place in the rear of his new restaurant, the spot reserved for him or Jess. Probably Mimi too, because he knew full well she'd butt into all his businesses and assert her opinions. The restaurant was newly opened, having been purchased by him and closed for renovations.

"If you like this restaurant," he said, "we can host the gargoyles here when it's necessary. It's the nicest I have. Assuming everything was done to the specifications I requested."

"I'm sure it'll be perfect," she said, getting out of the car. It wasn't until they'd approached the restaurant that her face filled with wonder. "Oh Austin, this is gorgeous."

CHAPTER 9

JESSIE

AUSTIN'S PHONE CHIMED. He pulled it from his pocket and glanced at the screen. A moment later, he looked up at me and then resumed eating in the loveliest restaurant I'd ever been in. The décor was modern and tasteful and beautiful, like some sort of swank fairyland with excellent food. It had given me the idea to do something similar for the tasting room, as well as changing my plans from tasting room to wine bar.

I knew that look.

"What's up?" I asked.

"Mimi is leaving Ivy House."

"Wow. So late?" I checked the time. She'd been there for a little over four hours.

"Yes. She's headed back to my place. I have no idea how she's getting there, but she has the address. Apparently she didn't want to stay the night in the house."

His smirk was hilarious. I remembered him essentially feeding Kingsley to the dolls on his brother's visit.

I finished as much of the plate as I could, then sat back and put my hand on my belly.

He glanced at me and then speared the meat on my plate. He knew I didn't take home leftovers. It annoyed Mr. Tom, and Austin always insisted on cooking fresh when we were together.

"You know," I said while he finished, "we should probably set up an additional housing development that is solely Ivy House's. Property has a good shelf life if we can keep the territory going."

Over dinner, he'd proposed a number of things, the most notable being inviting one of the production cairns to live in the territory. We didn't have the resources to send protection to anyone, but if he and I could collaborate on housing, we could protect them here.

"Ours can be for magical people in general, and hers can be exclusively for gargoyles," I continued. "Assuming we can find someone to stay here."

"That is the hope, certainly."

"We'll definitely need a manager for all of this, though. I'm already stressed just talking about it."

"A manager, yeah." Austin shook his head. "People have always said Mimi has a sixth sense." He hit me with a hard stare that made me lean backward. "She is very intense. In her heyday, she was named one of the most intense alphas around. She was also one of the most generous. Her pack thrived, but it wasn't until she took over leadership."

"She fought for placement? Challenged, I mean."

"She mated the alpha. When they'd only been mated for a few years, another pack attacked and took his placement. I understand that there were a few very dark years under that leadership. No other packs would come to their aid. So Mimi orchestrated an uprising within her pack to overthrow the alpha and his enforcers. She didn't do it all at once, though. She knew they didn't have the brute strength, so she resorted to sly maneuvers. The enforcers disappeared one by one. Slowly. Systematically."

"But wouldn't the alpha wonder where they'd gone?"

"Eventually, yes. But her plans were already in motion. Finally she was down to a mere handful, and then every able-bodied shifter worked together to take down their captors. They named her alpha on the spot, and she led that pack until she *chose* to step down. She couldn't withstand challenges, but her people supported her regardless. They wouldn't allow anyone to replace her. And they thrived under her leadership. She took that pack from an unknown to one of the most prosperous in the country. My mom, who learned from her, continued on, and now Kingsley. The money we all have is because Mimi invested every dime she had into that pack, over and over again, and eventually saw incredible returns."

"She sounds amazing."

He regarded me silently again.

"She's tough," he finally said. "You probably won't like her. I ask, though, if you can, that you humor her. Or humor me, maybe. Just try to get along with her as best you can."

"Of course I will!" I frowned intensely at him. "How could you think otherwise? Trust me, I've had experience getting along with troublesome in-laws. It'll be great."

✧ ✧ ✧

AUSTIN

AUSTIN PULLED OPEN the door of the Porsche for Jess, trying to keep his nerves in check. Truthfully, though, he was worried about Jess's reaction to his grandmother.

Jess stepped out and looked up at his house, and her joy at seeing it melted his heart. He needed to get her on the deed. Hell, he needed to get her a key. They hadn't had time to hammer out the details of more thoroughly (and legally) joining their lives together. It was way past due.

"Ready?" he asked, trying to ignore the butterflies in his stomach.

"Honestly, Austin, you're freaking out over nothing." She clearly felt his emotions through the bond. "In-laws know that they aren't always going to get along with spouses. We make the best of it until the holidays, and then we all get drunk and argue. It's basically a Jane tradition."

He couldn't help but smile as he slipped an arm around her and pulled her close. "I feel like you don't know what you're getting yourself into."

"I haven't known what I was getting into since day one in this magical life. Why change things now?"

He laughed, pushing open the door and following the glow to the kitchen. Mimi sat at the table with a clean plate and a glass of water. She held a book against the tabletop, her eyes glued to the page.

Austin turned a little so Jess could see him put his finger to his lips. Mimi didn't like to be disturbed when she was in the middle of a good part. Then he led Jess to the island and had her take a seat.

"Do you want any coffee or more wine?" he asked

quietly. "Or second dessert?"

"A glass of wine would be fine." She checked her phone, reading whatever she found there.

"I have brownies…"

"A glass of wine and a brownie would be fine," she amended.

"I'll have the same." Mimi snapped her book shut and stood from the table.

"Here, I've got that." Austin grabbed her empty plate and glass, removing them to the sink.

Jess stood as well, facing Mimi with a kind smile. "Hello," she said, clasping her hands in front of her body. "I'm Jacinta. People call me Jessie."

"Jessie." Mimi nodded. "I am Naomi. I hear you are the mistress of Ivy House."

"Yes." Jess hesitated before sitting back down. "Would you care to sit at the island? We could also retire to the living room. Which would be more comfortable for us?"

"For you? I have no idea." Mimi took a seat at the far end of the island. "I'm fine here."

"Great." Jess resumed her seat. There was not an ounce of irritation through the bond. So far, so good. "I am the mistress of Ivy House, yes. The steward, really. I've never been in this kind of position before."

"And which position is that?"

"Lady boss, I guess." She laughed, and Austin paused in opening the wine to glance her way. He loved that musical sound. "I'm suddenly in charge of a lot of people's wellbeing. It's new to me."

"You seem to have already accrued steadfast loyalty. I was able to meet a few of your…team."

And now Austin paused, because that was a compliment from Mimi, and he'd never heard her give one so quickly upon meeting someone. That house and the people in it must've made an impression.

"We share mutual respect and loyalty," Jess told her. "We're a team. Together we are greater than the sum of our parts. But you know all about that. Austin told me about how you became pack leader. Alpha, I mean."

"Yes…" Mimi scrutinized Jess, holding the silence for a few long moments.

Jess's gaze slipped away to land on Austin. "Do you need a hand with anything? Should I get the brownies?"

Oops. That was code for *hurry up, I need a distraction.*

"Nope. Here we go." Austin popped the cork and poured the wine before moving to the pantry to grab the brownies.

"Austin obviously mentioned why he called me in?" Mimi asked, pulling a filled glass toward herself.

"Yes. Thank you! You're a lifesaver. It's a huge undertaking."

"It is, yes. Austin mentioned that you don't have a budget. Is that accurate?"

Jess sipped her wine slowly. "That's tricky. Ultimately, I need Ivy House to be modernized and returned to her former glory. I will pay whatever is necessary to achieve that end. That said, I don't want to pay for extravagant things I don't need. Does that make sense?"

"Perfectly. What about the third floor? It's essentially a wasteland. The billiard room will be redone, of course, and I propose moving it to a larger room."

"There's a billiard room?" Austin asked, distributing the brownies to plates. "How did no one mention that?"

"The ballroom needs a complete makeover, as well," she went on.

"There's a *ballroom* in there?" Austin stared.

Mimi met his eyes with a scowl. "If you don't have anything to add, why are you speaking?"

He tightened his lips and looked down at the plates. Humor gushed through his bond with Jess.

"There are empty rooms, most with en suites. Most have good views. I assume they must've been guest rooms at one time, but neither your mage nor your butler could understand the house's response to my question."

Jess cocked her head a little, her eyes losing focus. Ivy House must've been speaking to her.

"They were," she finally said. "The last heir had initiated some remodels before meeting with an untimely death."

"But heirs are immortal, are they not?" Mimi asked, her eyes narrowing slightly.

"Until they are killed, yes," Jess responded.

"Ah." Mimi cleared her throat. "I would propose outfitting those again. The mage suggested a theater and bowling room. That could certainly be arranged. There is plenty of space for it. A theater at the back of the house on the first floor, I think. A bowling lane…somewhere. I'm not sure. An underground floor would be ideal because of the noise, but Ivy House doesn't seem to have one of those. Not one they would show me, anyway. Eventually, I would wonder if an add-on might be prudent? It might open you up for additional tax issues, though. We'd have to look into it."

She paused, her gaze steady on Jess.

"Sounds good so far. If we were to add on, an indoor pool would be amazing." A smile slowly crossed Jess's face, and she glanced at Austin. "If we're going to do it, we might as well do it right the first time, and do it big, right?"

He laughed and moved around to her side. Given

she was at the edge of the island, he was still facing Mimi. "Exactly. I wouldn't mind a pool."

"In the interest of time, I propose that we focus on remodeling and repurposing the areas of the house you will need for your coming visitors," Mimi said, picking a corner off her brownie and popping it into her mouth. When she'd finished, she continued. "The sitting rooms at the front of the house should be done, of course. The kitchen should be fashioned into more of a commercial kitchen, though maybe that should come later. It'll need walls knocked down for more space. We can cater for now. All the guest rooms. Any rooms you inhabit. Am I leaving anything out?"

Jess just stared at her. Mimi nodded, apparently taking that as a no.

"The grounds…" She let the words linger.

Jess grimaced. "Yeah…I don't really have control over that."

Mimi quirked her eyebrow. "You don't have control over your garden?"

"No. I mean, I do, yes. It's just that the gardener is a bit—"

"Senile, yes." Mimi picked off another bit of her brownie. "I met him. I'd thought they killed vampires that old."

"Well, that's just the thing. If I express displeasure

in his work, he asks to be retired. Killed forever. And the basajaunak eat the magical flowers, so that's why there are so many."

"I'd be happy to retire him for you, if that's what it'll take?" Mimi's eyebrows lifted, her demeanor as serious as the grave.

"You wouldn't know it to look at him," Austin said, "but he's actually incredibly useful. Whenever Jess seems out of reach for anyone else, he always finds a way to get to her. He's great at confusing enemies, too. Even if Jess would let you, and she wouldn't, killing him isn't the answer."

"Fine." Mimi pushed away her brownie. Her stubbornness was creeping in. "I can manage him. Finally, there is the subject of art."

Jess finished her brownie and took a sip of wine, waiting. She'd clearly figured out that Mimi wasn't one for idle chitchat. That realization didn't seem to trouble her in any way.

"Art is a soft passion of mine," Mimi began.

"A *soft* passion, huh?" Jess grinned but then put up a hand. "Sorry."

"I've taken pictures—no flash—of all of the pieces in Ivy House. I'll be looking them up. A few, however, I already know by sight. Many people in the art community would, in fact. They know everything but what happened to them. There are no photographs of them, only written records, because they were painted before photography. What might appear on them is speculation. I feel privileged to have gotten to see them with my own eyes. A privilege many would love to have."

"Oh?" Jess leaned her elbow on the countertop.

"I was told the house has a way of communicating with you?" Mimi paused for an answer.

"She does, though at present—in my life, I mean—I don't have time to rehash lengthy stories. My downtime is sparse."

"Understood. The issue is, if you ever planned to allow museums to rent or borrow them, there is the question of how they were acquired. We'd need the history to make sure ownership was not in question. If they were stolen, for example, we might have issues. There is also the subject of use tax, imposed by certain states. I'd hate for you to pay for doing the world a favor. We could have museums cover that fee or find a way to write it off. More importantly, however, you'll want to secure those pieces, and any other pieces of note, should word get out that you have them."

"They are secured," Jess said. "Plenty secured. Move them to the ballroom, cover them up, and they'll be fine. Ivy House is better than any security a museum could hope to offer."

"Yes. The house showed me an example of that earlier today when I raised the issue. Fine. I do think one of the larger third-story rooms can be fashioned into an art hall, if you're willing. Your own museum. That would give the residence some real prestige. Your mage's eyes gleamed when I mentioned it."

"Yeah, that sounds like an amazing idea. And we can procure some suits of armor and those sorts of things. That'd be cool."

Mimi's eyebrows arched. "I'm sure…that could be arranged. Fine, I'll add that to the list for future improvements. We don't have the time to catalog and set everything up now. I'd want a room in the middle of the house so that it—she?—has plenty of time to protect the assets."

"I'm getting excited!" Jess beamed. "These are the finishing touches that are going to make the house sing. And you're right about the paintings. If they have special significance, we shouldn't keep them to ourselves. Ooh, we should start a charity! Maybe turn the ballroom into more of a banquet room for charity fundraisers and things like that? We'd definitely need an industrial kitchen for that."

"Yes…" Mimi drew out the word again. "I think we have the same direction in mind. There is one more room I wanted to bring up. It's a bit perplexing. The library."

Jess's face dropped into a confused frown. Austin prevented himself from saying, "There's a library?" He'd seen full bookcases in the sitting rooms, but he hadn't realized there was an actual room dedicated to it. No one had ever mentioned it.

Then again, no one had mentioned the billiards room, either. He and Kingsley would've made great use of that. He'd had no idea he knew so little about that house. Not that he'd ever wandered around to the rooms that weren't in use. Besides, most of the secrets the house revealed were in the nightmare category—they weren't something a guy would seek out.

"What about it?" Jess asked.

"The house is littered with collector's volumes. I am no expert, but there are many first editions and ancient volumes that must be a prize in and of themselves."

"Oh. Yeah, everything in that library feels ancient. It feels almost like a book crypt, which might be cool if it were anywhere but Ivy House. I'm afraid to touch anything and haven't had a lot of time to read with my schedule, so we generally keep it closed up. It would be great to redo that room."

"I would mention that reading expands the mind, and it's a better pastime than many other things I can think of, but I've learned that the one TV in the common area was installed for your visiting father and you never use it. So I would mention this instead: all work and no play makes Jane a very dull girl."

"Except I'm not a Jane anymore, so…" Jess shrugged, smiling.

"Yes, well, I would encourage you to take more time to relax. Anyway, the library is like stepping back in time. Books are another passion of mine—I have had to find numerous hobbies to keep from interfering in my family's running of the pack—and I have no doubt that the library will prove a similar situation to the art you have around the house. Some of the volumes you could display—in a protective glass box—in the art hall. Some might head to museums—if they can travel. Most should stay as they are, amazingly well preserved. I suggest we get an expert in to catalog all the finds."

"Won't that be similar to the art situation, though?" Jess asked. "Won't we have to know the origins?"

"There are far too many for that. The puca, after a lively bout of arguing with the butler, mentioned that she knows someone who owes her a favor. He'd publish results anonymously, and we could see if any disputes arise. She assured me that he fears for his life in her presence and would follow our instructions to the letter. I am inclined to believe her."

"You can," Austin said, finally able to add to the

conversation in some way. The thought made him chuckle helplessly for some reason. He collected himself within the stern stare of his grandma, one of the few who'd ever sobered him up when he was younger. "You can always take Niamh exactly at her word. The trick with her is to figure out what she's *not* telling you."

"Noted." Mimi sipped her wine. "I advise you to keep that room closed for now."

"Easily done. Will there be an opportunity to make it into a less crypt-like reading room? We can leave the books off-limits if they are fragile, but people can always bring in books from other parts of the house."

"If you do that, you should create an additional room, temperature-controlled, for the oldest and rarest books. Many rare book collectors have this. It wouldn't be hard to set up and, as I said, there is plenty of space. That house is currently like a skeleton. Its best attributes are being wasted."

Jess tugged Austin a little closer so that she could lean into him. He put his arm around her and squeezed her upper arm.

"I think Austin chose the perfect person to bring Ivy House back into her glory, Naomi," Jess said. "Again, thank you. All of your ideas are perfect. If there is anything you need while you're here, please let me know."

"Austin mentioned there was space within Ivy House for me to stay, should I need it?"

Austin didn't hide his surprise. "I thought you came here because the house had chased you out."

Her frown was one shade away from threatening. "Of course not. Don't be ridiculous. I wanted to see your home and speak to you without the house listening. Apparently it hears all."

"Um…" Jess coughed into her hand and pushed out of his hold. She took up her wine glass and gave Naomi a smile he knew to be genuine. "She can hear you whenever I'm around as well. There has to be a way to muffle that link, but I haven't found it yet. Maybe Sebastian can dig it out of one of the books. So on that note, I'll leave you guys to catch up without a sentient house listening in. It was lovely meeting you, Naomi, and I'll ensure a room is set up for you immediately. You'll be welcome there as long as you like. Which seems like a generous thing to say until you spend a little time with the other inhabitants."

She tugged on Austin's arm with her head tilted up. He bent to kiss her, his lips lingering. He simply couldn't help himself.

"I'll be up in a while," he murmured, then grabbed another soft kiss before he let her go.

"Thanks for dinner. It was perfect." She said good-night to his grandma and sauntered out of the room.

The kitchen was silent as he watched her go. Then he topped up his grandma's and his glasses before sitting down.

"Be kind," he said as a warning. "The effects of mating haven't worn off. I'm not rational where she is concerned."

"Bah." She waved that away. "That's not because of the mating. It's because you're head over heels for her. I haven't seen you smile this much since you were a child. I've heard about your territory. You are rising to your true potential, my boy, and it's plain to see that she has been a direct influence on that."

"It's true. Part of my drive is that I want to be in a better position to protect her. But at this point…I also want to provide for her and make a home."

He thought about holding back the next bit, and probably would've if it were anyone else save Kingsley, but he'd always been close with his grandmother. He wanted to rekindle that closeness now, and part of that was being honest.

"I want to impress her."

"Of course you do," she said as though he were an idiot for saying it. "You want her to be proud of you. That's what it is to be a mate. A true mate, not something nature kicked up to try to create the best offspring. And I think you've found your true mate. I hope you enjoy how it feels, because the very few true pairs I've ever heard of say the effects don't really go away. Maybe they dull a little with the mundanities of life, but…it doesn't look like you'll have that for a good long time."

"No. All seems peaceful at the moment, but—"

"Austin, what do you take me for?" She pulled something out of her pocket, turned, and threw it at his face.

He ducked and turned at the right time—the object thudded off his shoulder instead of his cheek.

"Ow!" He peered around his shoulder, wondering if any more would come. When he saw she was back to sipping her wine, he glanced behind him to try to find the projectile. "Was that a rock?"

"Yes. And I have two more where that came from. When I was walking the mages out, I decided to look around the neighborhood a little more. That's when I saw the surly Irishwoman—Niamh—sitting on her porch. She yelled at me to go home and then started throwing rocks. She only introduced herself and offered to answer questions when I caught one of the rocks and threw it back at her. The sting from catching it was worth it when my rock landed."

"Why do you have them in your pocket?" he

barked. "And why are you throwing them inside my house? That could've broken something."

"I have them just in case. She hinted that she'd get me back for the rock that landed. I want to be prepared. And I threw one inside your house because you are speaking like a fool, and you should know better. Hopefully I *do* break something. The furnishings are lovely, but the accessories here… Austin, have I taught you nothing? They look cheap. I am all for saving money, but sparing this much expense on the accessories lessens the whole *look*. You can't have pricy furniture and then throw out some cheap plastic merchandise you got on sale. It's a shock to the system."

He rubbed his face, and then the part of his shoulder that throbbed. It had been a hard throw at close range. "It's not plastic, firstly, and I bought this place with the bar money. I didn't use any of my inheritance on it. I wasn't going to spare any expense on the stuff that's hard to switch out, so I saved where I could. I just haven't gotten around to changing out the accessories. It didn't bother Kingsley."

"Oh, what would Kingsley know? Earnessa handles all of that for him. Badly, I might add, but I don't mention that anymore. I always have a book. When I am forced to spend time in their mutual company, I get a lot of reading in."

"Fine. Please stop throwing rocks in my house."

"Then stop talking like a fool. Peaceful? Not even Kingsley's territory is so wound up, and they are under threat of invasion. Jessie's crew is buzzing with wariness. I also met the phoenix and the thunderbird before I left. It felt as though they might sneeze and accidentally burn the whole house down."

"That's just their way. They're always like that."

"The puca is on edge and the mages seem like they are preparing for war. Not just Kingsley's war, either. They were talking about what seemed like some huge, elaborate mage war on the horizon. Your people are keyed up and suspicious—I saw it as I passed through town—and the vampire thought it necessary to outline all the ways I could die if I mistreated the house or its mistress in any way."

"There is obviously trouble ahead of us, and no, not just Kingsley's, and there was trouble behind us, but *right this moment*, it is peaceful. That's what I—Don't you get a rock! This is normal behavior for all of them. It always has been."

"I haven't even mentioned the basajaunak that came charging out of the bushes when I was looking at the landscaping. The butler was grabbing me a cup of coffee, so I was by myself. They clearly thought I was some kind of threat because they surrounded me aggressively. I didn't dare shift in case they thought that was a challenge. The butler merely waved them away as though it was no big deal."

"Are you okay—Sorry, don't grab the rock. I'm going to kill Niamh," he muttered. "They clearly thought you were trespassing. You know how basajaunak are."

"I've met a couple basajaunak in my day, way up in the north. A different clan of them, obviously, but they are all very similar. I was on their land, but they didn't get this riled up. They approached me calmly."

"Is that because they wanted to trade with you for passage?"

She didn't reply, which was a grudging yes.

"You must see how different that is," he said. "Ivy House has been attacked. Repeatedly. Shifters intent on attacking my pack and Jessie's crew have run through its grounds. Dave, the basajaun on our crew—don't call him that; you aren't permitted to know his name—"

"I am old, but I am not as senile as that vampire. Stop treating me like I don't know how the world works."

"Sorry. He must've smelled that you were a shifter, but I doubt he knew you were my relation. He's been making the new basajaunak feel at home. He's out of the house loop. So he was absolutely ready to defend the territory. To repeat, we've had trouble *in the recent past,* but at the *moment*, things are peaceful."

She shook her head at him. "I don't know who you are trying to fool, me or yourself, but I see the signs. This is a territory under extreme threat."

"Why do you think I had to call you in? I don't have time to play designer when I'm working on our defenses and the things we need to attract an army of gargoyles. Or maybe defend against an army of gargoyles turning hostile."

"Yes, fine, I just hadn't realized it was this dire. Kingsley hadn't mentioned it."

"He always had Jess on hand to distill her crew. You got the wild side of them. It can shake anyone up."

"I'm not shaken! Merely concerned. Anyway, it doesn't matter. I'll move my things in there tomorrow and roll up my sleeves. Now, go enjoy your pretty mate. You did well there, my boy. She has the right ideas about what it means to be a leader. I can see why you smile so much around her. It's a good look for you. Kingsley mentioned you'd relaxed, but he didn't tell me that you'd finally found your peace, even if your idea of peaceful isn't one shared by most people. Don't roll your eyes! They'll get stuck like that."

Warmth filled him, and he wished she was a hugger. "Thanks, Mimi, for coming. For everything."

"The sentimentality isn't such a good look, though."

He huffed out a laugh and got off the barstool.

"Oh, and by the way," she said as he was leaving, "I think that nutty vampire is making some sort of shrine in the backyard with a naked male statue. That creature should be stopped. He's absolutely fruit loops."

CHAPTER 10

JESSIE

TWO DAYS LATER, we all shifted into our human forms after training.

"Crap." Ulric bent down to rest his hands on his knees. "Tell me that was the hardest training yet. It *felt* like the hardest training yet."

"That was the hardest training yet," Jasper said, lying flat onto the ground.

"I feel great!" Cyra beamed at everyone. "It's been a long, *long* time since I worked this hard with a team."

"What about that battle on the basajaunak land?" Hollace asked, slipping on one of the purple house muumuus.

I'd told Mr. Tom in no uncertain terms that he needed to find new team workout attire, and he'd responded by buying rather nice sports sweats. Did anyone on the team use those sports sweats? No. They continued to use the horrible and often ill-fitting purple muumuus.

"Didn't count," Cyra said.

"Why not?" Jasper asked.

"Because we weren't really working as a team. We were just flying all over the place, trying to kill the enemy while simultaneously trying not to die. But now we have some team direction. The next one will be better."

"Unless it's an enemy we haven't experienced before," Jasper said, pushing up to sitting. "That'd probably mess everything up."

"Way to cast a black cloud on a good training, bro," Ulric said, running his fingers through his hair and straightening up. "We're learning how to build off each other. Even if it *is* a new enemy, or an old enemy who throws a wrench in our plans, we'll find it easier to improvise and regroup."

"Hear, hear," Hollace said.

"Ready, alpha?" Nathanial asked me as I zipped up the black jacket of the sports sweats. Only he and I had chosen those instead of the muumuus. Niamh apparently didn't plan on putting on anything at all.

"What are you ready for?" Cyra asked, stepping closer. "Are we interrogating someone?"

"No, we are not interrogating anyone," I told her. "We're about to choose which cairns to invite."

"I'll get her this time!" Edgar's shout came from behind us. He went racing through our area with his high-kneed lope. "Hi, Jessie! Great flying! Pity about the…"

His words trailed away as he disappeared.

"What's he up to?" Ulric asked, watching him go. Ulric's muumuu was bunched around his neck.

"The basandere is stealing his flowers," Mr. Tom said. "He can't seem to catch her in the act. Nor can he find any evidence. He's as blind as a bat. She's doing a wonderful job of trimming things down, though, so I haven't troubled myself to educate him."

"Are you sure we need those gargoyles?" Cyra asked as we all started for the house. "They don't seem to pack much of a wallop. One in town picked a fight with me. I let him have the first three punches, but he was so weak I barely felt it. It was so disappointing that I just burned him on the spot and moved on. He posed absolutely zero threat."

"I thought we agreed you weren't supposed to tattle on yourself about that," Hollace said through his teeth.

"Oh yeah." She curled her lips as I stared at her with wide eyes.

"It's not like no one knew who did it," Ulric said. "Next time, clean up after yourself. Jasper and I had to quickly hide the evidence before one of Alpha Steele's people found the mess."

"Oh, thanks, Ulric! That was nice of you." Cyra pushed into him from behind and squeezed his middle, trapping his hands at his sides. "Teamwork, see?"

"Your hugging still needs work," Hollace replied. "That's more of a tackle."

I spread my arms out. "Hello? I'm an alpha. I shouldn't be hearing this."

"Don't you mean that she shouldn't be burning people on darkened street corners?" Mr. Tom asked.

I pointed at him. "Yes, exactly. Cyra, stop burning people."

"I might've provoked it, but he threw the first punch, so he technically started it," Cyra said. "I was defending myself."

"Provoking it *is* starting it," Jasper told her.

"Oh." She twisted her lips to the side. "Hollace, did you hear that? So technically that shifter—"

"Don't," Hollace said quickly. "And if you do, let's all remember that I have nothing to do with anything."

"Oh yeah. Right." Cyra scratched her head. "I'm terrible with secrets. Anyway, like I was saying, I don't think the gargoyles will be worth all this fuss."

"The gargoyles in town are *nothing* like the guardians that will be coming," Nathanial said in a low tone. "Nothing like us, either. If one of the top four cairns make it, you won't want to offer up the first three shots."

"Oh." Cyra gave a thumbs-up. "I like that challenge. I'll do it just to see what happens."

I thought about veering off course to check on Naomi's claim that Edgar had set up some sort of a shrine, but I didn't want to waste the time. I also didn't really want to find out she was right.

In the hall, we had to stop and wait for a line of shifters carrying old furniture toward the front of the house to be removed. I had to hand it to Naomi—when she got to work, things happened at lightning speed. She'd already showed me her vision for a few of the rooms, with colors and drape options and sample furniture. They'd all looked absolutely amazing. Better than anything I could've imagined.

She hadn't been happy with my immediate sign-off, though. I was apparently supposed to seek out more opinions. She then took the designs to Austin, and the two of them bickered about who knew what. I just stayed out of it.

"Out with the old," Ulric said as the last of the moving people headed down the hall. "Are we just going to have bare rooms for a while? Because I thought I heard her say the stuff she ordered yesterday wouldn't be here for at least a week or more."

"They need to paint or wallpaper or whatever

they're doing," I said, reaching one of the smaller sitting rooms that hadn't been touched yet. "The floors, too, I think. So yeah, they are taking the furniture to storage for now. I think some of it might come back? But the majority will be sold off or donated or who knows."

"A waste," Mr. Tom said with a sniff. "Furniture these days lacks in quality. We'll have to replace it within the year, just you watch. We're throwing money away."

He'd been grumbling about all this since Naomi first showed up, probably annoyed that she was the one making the decisions. We knew better than to engage.

Patty knelt next to the coffee table with various cards spread out in front of her. Nessa and Sebastian stood nearby, looking down at the table. Austin sat in a chair a little removed, watching me enter.

Hollace pointed down at a chair. "It's cool if I sit on this when I'm sweaty, right? They'll all be dumped anyway?"

"Not if I have something to say about it," Mr. Tom blustered.

"You can sit," I told Hollace, crossing the space to run my fingers over Austin's knee in hello before I took my place at the coffee table. "What've we got?"

"Okay—" Patty paused as Naomi poked her head in, sweeping her gaze across the room.

She zeroed in on Austin. “Are you busy? It’ll only take a moment.”

“Oh!” Patty jumped with a huge smile on her face. “I keep seeing you here and there, always in motion, but we haven’t gotten a chance to properly meet. I’m Patty!”

Patty reached Naomi and opened her arms for a hug.

Without warning, Naomi punched Patty’s chin and snapped her head back.

Austin jumped up as Patty paused in confusion for a second…and then she launched at the other woman, fists flying.

“Oh crap! Mom, no!” Ulric ran in as Austin reached them, catching one of Naomi’s fists intended for Patty. Niamh started laughing. Ulric pushed in between the two women as Austin grabbed his grandma by the shoulders and forced her back.

“Let it go,” Austin told his grandma in a low voice. “Control yourself.”

Ulric stood in front of his mom with his hands out. “Mom, stop attacking people!”

“She punched me,” Patty replied. “I hardly think this was my fault.”

“He meant hugging strangers,” Austin offered.

Patty wet her finger and smoothed a piece of hair back into place.

"No, I didn't," Ulric said, "though why did you think to hug her?" He dropped his hands at his sides, exasperated. "Since when are shifters huggy people?"

"A good many of the more mature women in town treat physical touch as a normal form of social interaction. I just assumed it carried through." Patty *harrumph*ed.

"I'm not sure which I find more offensive," Naomi said, "your calling me old, or your trying to hug me. I think the latter. Anyway, if I can get out of this unfortunate net of social interaction, Austin, might I have a quick word?"

"Yeah, sure." Austin glanced back at me with a tortured look before following her out into the hall.

Niamh was still laughing.

"Can we *please* get this over with?" I said, starting to fray. "I have a bunch of spells to learn and items to choose for the winery."

"Just try to get along, okay?" Ulric whispered to Patty. "It'll make things easier."

"Of course. But honestly, Ulric, the woman punched me. What was I supposed to do, stand there and take it?"

"What did you expect? You tried to hug her. There are non-magical women in town, you know. They're probably the ones who go around hugging people. You might've mistaken them for shifters."

"Oh no, I don't think so..." She didn't sound too sure, though, and for her, that was as much as an admission of guilt.

He gave me a tortured look when returning her to the table before mouthing, "Sorry."

"Okay, what have we got?" I tried again, ignoring Nessa's shaking shoulders as she tried to hold in her laughter.

"We've sent out the invitations you approved yesterday," Patty said.

"Those were for the production cairns Austin has an interest in?" Nathanial verified.

"Yes," Patty replied. "We put both of their cairn names on the invite, so they know they've both been invited. They will each take the first of the three dates, of course. They won't want the other cairn to have Jessie's undivided attention. It's a little unorthodox, but it'll get the job done."

"And the first of those dates is in three weeks?" Nathanial took out his phone.

"For the production cairns, correct, three weeks. The larger cairns get a different set of dates. It will leave the alphas one week to discuss business with the production cairns before the big dogs come in—if the high-status cairns choose the first date, as well."

"And how likely is that?" Nessa asked, all humor gone. "How likely is it that the more powerful cairns will turn up on schedule? Or…you know…at that first invite date?"

"Given the caliber of these connection requests, I'm confident they'll come as soon as possible. So." Patty moved some of the cards around as Austin walked back in. "First, the top four. How many of the most prestigious cairns did you want to invite?"

"All of them," Sebastian said immediately, opening up his laptop. "We've found that there is intense rivalry between them. From what Niamh can tell, they've never all been at the same function. Usually they host, and they invite lesser cairns. They never invite each other to events. Lesser cairns usually choose between them when inviting, and at max two might show at the same party, but they don't tend to interact too much. The top four are islands. We are going to pit them against each other."

"Well…" Patty put her fist to her lips and cleared her throat, looking down at the cards. "That is…unexpected. You've learned, I'm sure, that the four have very proficient guardians. Those guardians can be tough to manage. I'd worry about hosting so many people in one territory…"

"Managing them will be no problem," Austin

growled.

Patty lifted her eyebrows. "O-kay. Well, that's four, then. How about any others?"

"I think we should stick to just the top four," Niamh said. "We don't want to be wastin' our time and effort on the lower gargoyles that can't guarantee us status, so we don't. We need one of the top four. Let's focus on that."

"Agreed," Austin replied.

"Yeah, that sounds good with me," Sebastian said as Nathanial nodded.

"Great. That was easy." Patty collected the cards. "This is probably the only thing that will be easy with those four, but we have to start somewhere, don't we? We'll need to limit the number of guardians they can bring. Sebastian, do you have a number ready?"

"Alpha?" Sebastian said, then explained to the rest of us, "I gave him the number and approximate power scale of each cairn's guardians yesterday."

"No more than a dozen each within territory lines at any one time," Austin said. "I am interested to see if they try to sneak in more."

"If they bring more, they'll post them just outside of the territory," Nathanial said. "Some will spread them out, and some will cluster them. They won't breach the territory line with their extras, though. They'll follow the rules because they'll be wary of grievances filed against them by the other cairns, which could reduce their status."

"No families." Nessa glanced up from her computer. "Let's not drag nonessential personnel into our cross hairs."

"Yeah, that's probably for the best," I said, taking a seat next to Austin. "I'd rather not have to entertain them, anyway."

"Who do they file the grievances to, their mammies and aunties?" Niamh asked. "I've never heard of any sort of governing body."

"The cairn leaders, most notably the higher-status crust of leaders," Nathanial said, "act as a sort of overall leading force of gargoyles. Filing a grievance is essentially making known an issue that went against gargoyle standards. The filer of the grievance is backing the claim with their honor and their status—no small thing. It's taken very seriously in the gargoyle community."

"It can be fought," Patty said, "but seldom is. Our rules and way of doing things are very well established at this point, without much change through the years. A person doesn't file a grievance unless it's a grave offense and they are prepared to stake their reputation on backing it. The more status the filer has, the more weight the grievance carries."

"Sounds like a load of bollocks." Niamh went back to the computer. "They could use a proper governing body. Or a kick in the arse."

"Maybe both." Nessa bent to the side and leafed through the stack of pages on the couch cushion next to her. She picked one up and held it in the air. Everyone stared at it until she glanced up, scowled, and shook it. "That means someone needs to take this piece of paper to the person who needs it. In this case, it is Austin. Steele. Alpha, whatever." She shook the paper again. "Look alive, people!"

Ulric jumped forward and snapped up the paper, handing it to Austin.

"That is a summary of the top four's average defense strategy," Nessa said, still leafing through the stack. "That's all the cairns. Here are…" She grabbed up another piece, then another, then two more, and held them up. Jasper grabbed them this time. "There's a more detailed look at each of those four cairns. Also what their respective uniforms look like so your people can identify them if they try to sneak in. Though why they'd attempt sneaking in in uniform, I don't know."

"You'll definitely want to keep your eye on them," Nathanial said. "We're not setting any real rules for this meeting, other than guardian number. If they decide to attack, the alphas will want to know where their people are coming in from."

"Don't worry about them attacking," Niamh said. "If one pops off, the others will rise up against them. That's why they don't all get together. The first one to break is gonna get smashed down. Their precious status might take a hit from that."

"She's guessing," Nessa said, "but in the past she's proven to be a damn good guesser."

"I know people." Niamh crossed an ankle over her knee, then looked around. "Where's me cooler?"

Mr. Tom's wings rustled. "You annoy people, you mean, and I removed it. Only derelicts and parents carry coolers. Which are you?"

"About to shove me foot up yer arse, that's which one I am…"

"Okay, okay." I waved them to silence, ignoring the jab about my parents carrying a cooler. "Are we sure about these dates? A month out doesn't give us much time to prepare. Or do much of anything, honestly. Do we have any new information about Kingsley's situation? Other than Momar testing the defenses and gathering information?"

Nessa quickly glanced at Sebastian, who answered. "Nothing new, but we don't have a lot of time to dawdle. If the gargoyles get weird about the wine bar or something, you can just explain the situation."

"I'd like to get to Kingsley's pack as soon as possible and assess the situation for myself," Austin said. "I'll need to work my people in with his, and that'll take a moment."

"True," I murmured, resting my hand on Austin's thigh. "Okay. That means we have a month. Three weeks, really. I guess we'd better start picking and choosing what to focus on. Time will go by in a flash. Before we know it, we'll be inundated with prickly gargoyles."

"Some worse than others," someone muttered.

CHAPTER 11

NESSA

TWO DAYS AFTER the invitations were sent to the four biggest cairns, Nessa found herself wandering down the cutest little neighborhood, looking for Broken Sue's abode. Somehow Patty had talked him into hosting a dinner party. It was a wonder he hadn't canceled. He apparently didn't even know who'd been invited! It wasn't at all like him, an intensely private man who drank alone and kept his business to himself.

Patty was magical. There were no two ways about it. She manipulated people in a way that left everyone with a smile on their faces. Nessa really needed to learn how, but she suspected the tools needed weren't in her tool chest.

She ran her thumb along her screen, searching the notes on her phone for the info on the Cashmere Cairn leader. That was the guy who'd hacked into their system so he could send Jessie and Austin appropriately sized sweaters. He probably thought he was a cunning little fox.

He had no idea what he was up against.

She glanced up again, frowning at the house signs. "Wasn't it fifteen-thirty?" She glanced behind her, then back in front. "Fifty-three-thirty? Crap."

Still walking, because this neighborhood was too cute not to enjoy, she tapped out of her work notes and into her life notes, looking for Broken Sue's house number. Then the street name, because the numbers here were much too high for what she'd written down to be correct.

"I didn't even get his phone number," she grumbled, swiping to the home screen and tapping the phone image. She'd hit Sebastian's name and put the phone to her ear before the feeling registered.

Tingles whispered across her skin. Goosebumps rose, and her stomach twisted. *Danger.*

She forced herself to continue walking with the same halting, distracted sort of steps.

"Hey, Nessa," Sebastian said when he answered. "I'm running a little late. Just about out the door. Is everyone there?"

"I don't know. I think I wrote down the wrong house number..."

Sebastian paused for a moment, obviously registering her tone. An edge crept into his words. "What's wrong?"

"Well, I can't very well tell you that, can I?" She laughed good-naturedly, using him as a prop. "Hang on, let me look."

Forcing calm, she veered to the side and lowered her phone, getting her hands closer to her knives.

A sick feeling crept through her.

She'd forgotten to strap on her knives.

"Crap," she breathed out, feeling the presence bearing down on her.

What had she been thinking? She *always* brought her knives. At least one, anyway. Always carefully hidden. Always within reach.

This was the fault of her subconscious! She'd been desperately curious about Broken Sue's private habitat, and excited to see it, and excited to see *him*. The profound feeling of safety she always felt in his presence had crept in. And now she was a sitting duck, with shoes not made for running and magic that wouldn't help her if this feeling in any way belonged to something powerful.

Given the prickly sort of panic creeping in, it was definitely something powerful.

A shape loomed large in her peripheral vision. Very large. Robust and tall and striding purposefully toward her.

She glanced up as though distracted, lifting her phone back up to her ear.

A block of a man took up a large portion of the sidewalk up ahead. Long wings flowed down his back and nearly scraped the ground behind him. Dark jeans squeezed powerful legs, and the black jacket he wore must have been crafted out of sails for it to cover his shoulders.

Gargoyle, obviously, and not one of the residents. She would've noticed a guy like this wandering around town.

More importantly, Austin would've noticed.

He walked with purpose, and his poise bespoke a mix of confidence and arrogance. A stern expression covered his handsome face and his eyes almost glowed, like embers plucked from a dying fire. Each movement screamed *strength*. His bearing shouted *powerful, keep away!*

"I might have found myself in a little situation," she said into the phone, not daring to take her eyes off the stranger.

"I'm jogging that way now. What do you need? What can I do? Should I call Jessie or Austin?"

"No time. Let's see how this plays out, shall we?"

She lowered the phone again and stepped back, giving the gargoyle plenty of space. Most women would've probably crossed the road, but she didn't want this creature at her back. From what little they'd learned about gargoyles, the powerful ones were aggressive and unpredictable. Jessie's antics had nothing on them. Nathanial was a spring day compared to the reports she'd seen.

Her smile was disarming. She'd spent a lot of years practicing it.

"Hello," she said pleasantly, holding her position. She didn't want him to think she was intimidated. It might call to the predator in him.

He slowed, his gaze flowing over her. He must be six-eight if he was an inch, and solid muscle. Absolutely freaking enormous.

"Hello," he replied in a whisky-drenched voice, smooth and slow and wicked. "What is a pretty little thing like you doing out here all alone?" He inhaled deeply, smelling the air.

And if that wasn't a little unsettling, she didn't know what was.

"You smell delicious," he said with a release of breath. "What sort of magic do you possess?"

The frown was hard to keep off her face. Had he never met a mage?

"The smell is likely my new perfume, so thank you."

She laughed, making sure it reached her eyes. "Just headed to a party."

His focus on her was acute as he studied her face, dipping his eyes to take in her body. He stepped closer, his size dwarfing her, his intensity lighting sparks of unease while simultaneously driving heat straight through her middle. His eyes seemed to spark, glowing a little brighter. She hoped to hell she was seeing things, because she hadn't heard of a gargoyle with that trait.

"I love parties." His voice dropped a fraction. "I'd love to meet you at a party. Tell me, are you lost—"

His words cut off, and he stiffened. His wings rustled as he half turned, looking over his shoulder.

Another large shape loomed in the growing darkness. He walked toward them with fluid grace, not hiding an unspeakable menace tethered on a very weak chain.

Broken Sue stepped between them. His large arm came out in front of her, covered in a crisp green dress shirt. She'd always thought he was huge, but his height and muscle mass seemed almost average compared to the new guy. He was a few inches shorter and less bulky.

"Who're you?" Broken Sue asked the stranger, his voice rough and deep.

All the tension immediately left Nessa's body. She flattened her palm against Broken Sue's side, the equivalent of holding a knife in a shaky hand. Feeling it, he hooked his arm around her, his hand finding her side, and tucked her a little more behind him.

The stranger bristled, and a blend of danger and violence leaked into the air around them. "Who's asking?"

"The beta of this territory. You'd better declare your intentions, or I will remove you myself."

Nessa peered around Broken Sue to get the stranger's reaction.

His ember-like eyes had a hard gleam in them. His wings stilled completely, and his muscles tensed in preparation for battle. When he leaned forward, warning shivers erupted all over Nessa's body.

"You should take a care how you speak to me," the stranger said slowly. "I am the lead enforcer of Gimerel."

Holy hell.

Gimerel was the cairn that had sent the bracelet, known for their battle strategies and ruthless fighting prowess. The cairn leader was hailed as a battle mastermind, but his second-in-command was considered a battle genius in his own right. He led with an iron fist, maintained excellent aerial organization and flight patterns, and statistically lost the fewest raids out of any cairn. Or so spreadsheets and hearsay would have Nessa believe.

The Gimerel lead enforcer was practically a celebrity in the gargoyle world, with garhettes happy to throw their knickers at him and brag to their friends about one-night stands. Niamh was excited to poke holes in what was sure to be an enormous ego.

She grabbed Broken Sue's arm and attempted to move it out of the way. It didn't budge, so she ducked under it, but he immediately grabbed her to him to keep from going anywhere.

"Wait, let me—you're going to crease the dress, man!"

Broken Sue's arm came away, but he angled his body to keep up a solid barrier between the stranger and her.

Sighing in annoyance, she hooked her arm around his and stepped a little closer.

"Gimerel's invitation only went out two days ago," she told the stranger, looking up at him. Her low heels weren't doing much to close the gap between their faces. "You can't have gotten it so quickly."

"We are always prepared, miss…"

"Nessa." She put out her hand to shake.

His hand was large, scarred, and rough, and his entrancing eyes held hers. "Nessa. Short for?"

"Natasha."

"Beautiful," he said in that whisky voice. "It suits you, that name. I'm Tristan."

"Why are you here early, *Tristan*?" Broken Sue asked, his voice cutting through the handshake. "You shouldn't be here for over a month at the earliest."

"How'd you even know you were invited?" Nessa asked, suddenly nervous their security had been breached. In addition to hacking into the cairn's systems, they'd created—what she'd thought, at least—was an ironclad cybersecurity system.

"To put your mind at ease, beautiful Natasha…" Tristan's eyes twinkled, and Broken Sue tensed. "Certain news travels quickly in the gargoyle community. In a historic situation such as this? It travels at light speed. All the cairns are anxious to meet the only living female gargoyle, regardless of how that came to be. The moment we heard of a possible meeting from a reliable source, I flew out." His gaze shifted to Broken Sue, and a little smile flitted across his lips. "I am in this neighborhood to check out a home for sale. I figured you'd ask. We don't know how long we'll be here. Real estate is competitive here, though. These small homes are selling for a pretty penny."

"Homes cost more when they're in a desirable location, yes," Broken Sue replied, his tone even and face a hard, unreadable mask. "You should leave your lonely mountain more often."

One of the stranger's dark eyebrows arched. "I am within my twenty-four-hour window. Isn't that the time frame I have in which to declare myself to the alpha?"

"In a routine situation, yes," Broken Sue replied. "You are well aware that this is not a routine situation."

"Isn't it?" Tristan spread his arms. "There were no stipulations barring entry before the planned meeting."

"How would you know?" Broken Sue countered. "You're going off hearsay. You haven't gotten your invitation yet."

Tristan stilled. Broken Sue had him there.

"Go to the Paddy Wagon bar downtown," Broken Sue said. "You'll find it easily. Wait there until either of the alphas or their people show up to speak with you. It shouldn't be long."

He pulled his arm from Nessa's and draped it around her, directing her toward the street.

As they walked away, they heard, "Yes, Daddy."

Nessa burst out laughing, turning within Broken Sue's grasp to look back. Tristan stood in the center of the sidewalk, facing them as they walked back the way she'd come. He had a charming smile, and those entrancing eyes tracked her progress.

"I'll see you soon, beautiful Natasha," he said, his voice low and smooth.

Broken Sue pulled his phone from the pocket of his black slacks. She remembered the call of hers that was still live.

"Hello?" she said, lifting the phone to her ear.

"Hey," Sebastian replied. "I'm nearly to Broken Sue's. I stopped running when I heard him show up. Was that really the lead enforcer?"

"First of all…you have a car. Why were you running?"

Silence. Then, "I'm an idiot, I guess. I've gotten so used to only using the car when I go shopping or to another town that I forgot it was an option. Good thing you didn't get gruesomely murdered."

"I know. I would've haunted you. Anyway, the gargoyle was intense," she said as Broken Sue pulled his arm from around her to tap his phone screen. "Not too intense, though. Like, at first I was worried as all hell, I'll admit it. I felt like I definitely needed a knife, which wasn't great, since I don't have one."

"Why don't you have a knife?"

"I forgot it. Don't ask. Anyway, there was no real reason for my wariness, just a *feeling*. I felt like I should be ready to brawl at any moment, you know? Except I didn't have the tools. Regardless, he wasn't actually as stoic as I was expecting. He joked and smiled and taunted Broken Sue a little."

"Yeah, but why is he here?"

"Scouting, I think. Broken Sue sent him to the bar. Go listen in. And try to keep Jessie from meeting him. I think we should leave her a mystery until the official meeting. Otherwise her weird team will crowd her, and it'll set the wrong precedent. Try to keep her gargoyles away, too. I don't think they're going to stack up to this guy."

"Okay."

"Alert Niamh about the whole situation. She'll weasel in to get close to him and do his head in. Maybe she can chase him away. We really aren't prepared for guardians to be nosing around quite yet."

"I'll see what I can do."

After she hung up, she realized Broken Sue had fallen quiet as well.

"Did you tell Austin Steele?" she asked.

"I did. He's at the bar already. He'll handle it."

She sighed, her mind suddenly churning. "We should expect other scouts. Because unless Patty amended the invitations, there was no stipulation that they couldn't come sooner than the suggested dates. Crap. We can't unveil the weird that is Jessie's crew this soon. The stories will get much too big before she can negate their weirdness with her awesomeness."

"I wouldn't worry about it. Alpha Steele didn't seem

impressed that one of their lead battle commanders was wandering around a quiet neighborhood, whatever his reason for being there. He'll push the issue."

"Meaning he'll throw his weight around and make the other guy feel really uncomfortable?"

"Yes." He paused as he pointed across the street. "You missed the house. I saw you walk by, looking at your phone. Why don't you have your knives?"

The last comment was said in a growl.

"Oversight. Don't worry, it won't happen again. I felt completely vulnerable without them. I hate feeling like that. I couldn't even run, though that probably doesn't matter when the enemy can fly."

"If you ever feel threatened…" He stopped walking abruptly and leaned down to catch her eye. "You call me. Day or night."

Butterflies flurried in her stomach from his proximity. "I don't have your number."

He held out his hand, and she filled it with hers.

"No…" He squeezed her hand before shaking it a little to dislodge it. "If you give me your phone, I'll program my number in."

"Oh." Her face heated. "First let me close out of all the soft-core porn…" She handed over the phone.

He tapped at it as he started across the street. "The weird mage isn't coming, then?"

"No. He has to work." She held out her hand for the phone as they hit the next sidewalk, out in front of his house. "Wait a minute. Let me take this in. This is *not* how I envisioned your digs. Who even *are* you?"

CHAPTER 12

NESSA

HIS LAWN WAS a little square of heaven. A lovely oak sat in the far corner of the yard with a tire swing hanging from a reaching branch.

"Do you ride?" She pointed at it with a smile.

"The neighborhood kids are welcome to use it anytime. There used to be more of them before the Dicks and Janes started moving away."

Gray pebbles lined the walkway to the front porch, which had a welcome mat and a little park bench next to a pot growing lively pink flowers. A stationary garden gnome stood under a wide window, hunkering under a bush with his shovel tip touching the ground.

"That better not come alive," she said.

He threaded his hands into his pockets, looking at it. "I admit, I put that there before the gnome issue at Ivy House."

"And you kept it because…?"

"I *want* it to come alive. That'll be the last time it does."

A wave of shivers coated her skin, and she leaned away from him a little, looking up with wide eyes and a grin. "That is literally the hottest thing I've heard in two weeks. Slay dragons? How could you? But kill gnomes? You're my knight in shining armor."

His face remained impassive, very shifter-esque. "In two weeks? Who said what two weeks ago?"

"Some random guy at the bar said, 'I'll go punch myself in the face, then, will I?' He was actually really good-looking, just an incredible dickhead, so it was definitely pretty hot when he said exactly what I was thinking."

He studied her for a moment, his sharp cheekbones looking even more severe in the falling night. With his narrow nose ending in the cutest little uptick, teamed with the crazy in his eyes, he looked almost like a hot Bond villain. But she knew this guy could never be the villain he thought himself to be. He was pure and honest and good, with a wholesome house and a tire swing for the kids. The protector. The provider. The guy who would look down on all that she was and all that she'd done, regardless of the why. Maybe *because* of the why.

She wasn't looking for Mr. Right, though. He didn't

exist, not for her. She was looking for Mr. Right Now, and if he'd just loosen up the cinch of his belt a little, they could both have a lovely time. It wasn't like he was keeping himself abstinent. He took ladies home from the bar now and again, just never her. She had no idea why.

"Your bar for hotness is pretty low, huh?" he asked, his eyes showing the smile that his face didn't.

She laughed. "Excuse me if I happen to care more about things like humor or personality than strictly appearance. But let's see how you rate, given your personality is terrible and your jokes are worse..."

She stepped back in mock seriousness and crossed her arms over her chest, assessing him for the first time since he'd intercepted her. He wore a crisp green dress shirt, made from quality material and ribbed with a darker green to give it a little depth. The first couple of buttons had been left undone, showing his man-cleavage, that indent at the top part of the chest that hinted at the large pecs filling out the shirt. It was pulled a little too tightly over his shoulders, not tailored, and molded to his popping biceps. A shiny black belt secured his black slacks in place, the ends dusting the tops of his dress shoes. His dark hair was parted on the side and combed like a 1950s do, and while she usually wouldn't be into that, on him it made the spit dry up in her mouth. Because that goodie-goodie look offset the sharp lines of his face and the arching brows over those heavy-lidded eyes.

"Hideous," she croaked, then had to clear her throat and will some moisture back into her mouth. "Absolutely terrible. Anti-hot. You're so not hot, you leach all the hotness out of the rest of the world."

His eyes sparkled harder. She wished, just once, he'd show her a smile.

"Shall I do you now?" he asked, a gleam of competitiveness in his eyes.

"Yeah. Wait…" She looked around and then took a seat on the little bench.

"Ready?" he asked, playing along.

"No, wait." She tossed her hair, blow-dried and lightly curled for dinner, over her head so it was all on one side. Then she crossed her legs at the ankle and swung her knees his way, making her dress ride up to mid-thigh. Leaning back, she gave him a seductive pose she'd seen in a million magazines with women a lot better at it and made a kissy face with one eye half squinted. She was sure she looked ridiculous.

"Now?" he asked, his voice suddenly subdued. His intense gaze traced her body.

Her stomach fluttered as his gaze returned to hers, deep and penetrating.

"Now," she responded, a lot too breathy.

"You are absolutely stunning," he started. "I haven't seen a woman as beautiful as you since…" He didn't finish that thought. She swallowed hard and suddenly felt strangely exposed. "But if I have to take your humor and personality into account…boy, are you awful."

She spat out a laugh, slipping in her pose and nearly sliding off the bench entirely.

He grabbed her before she got far, hauling her up, much too close. Much too warm. His cologne smelled like cedar wood and nutmeg and man, a delicious combination that soaked into her senses.

"Should I just go punch myself in the face now, then?" he asked when she righted herself and stepped back, his hands slow to fall from her arms.

"Definitely, yes. Past time."

He nodded and stepped toward the door, but hesitated before opening it. "I feel like I should warn you… Patty invited the vampire. No idea why. He doesn't eat. It's a small party, and out of all the people she had to choose from, she chose the blood drinker. Here we are."

✧ ✧ ✧

Brochan

Brochan watched a look of incredulity flit across

Nessa's face before she threw back her head and started laughing. "Here we are, indeed."

"At least we have Ulric and Jasper. Ulric can be counted on to keep conversation going."

"Ulric can? My dear sir, you have Patty in there. She's a one-woman show. We're in good hands."

God, he loved her smile. So bright and carefree, as if it could chase away all the clouds in a thunderstorm.

"Just one thing, though," she said. "You didn't lock your drawers, right? You know, in case I get bored and want to snoop through your things."

An uncomfortable feeling lodged in his gut. He had family pictures in some of those drawers. Keepsakes from a life lost. He didn't want someone scrutinizing those, or telling him he should move on. Telling him it wasn't good to hold on so tightly. And even though she'd said it jokingly, she was exactly the type to go through drawers. To snoop. To gather information she might need on a rainy day. They were opposites in how they viewed the world, both of them too complicated for their own good. Maybe that meant they weren't exactly compatible—not that either of them were looking for more than a distraction.

"Hey, whoa." She put up her hands, alarm in her expression. "I'm kidding, bud. I am absolutely kidding. I'm going to keep my hands in my lap the whole time, promise. I'll tell Patty to keep a close eye on me."

"Tell the vampire," he replied, feeling slightly ashamed for the thoughts he'd just had. "He doesn't seem to miss much."

"Ah." She held up a finger. "But will he rat out his shadow? I'm not so sure."

"Good point." He pushed the door open and stepped aside. "Ladies first," he said quietly, accidentally catching sight of her popping cleavage and tearing his eyes away quickly. Hopefully she hadn't noticed.

"Well, my goodness. Quite the gentleman," she said, passing in front of him. "That must be your professional training, since we all know you'd shove me out of the way to enter first if this were any normal situation."

"I still might. Watch your six."

"What has Patty made Edgar for dinner this evening?"

He stepped inside after her, and his heart beat a little faster. He turned to close the door; the familiar smells of his home mingled with the unfamiliar fragrances of others in his space. He took a moment just to breathe, this being the first time he'd had people over. The first time he'd entertained since losing his family. The first time—

He swallowed, his face breaking out in a sweat. He'd gone through with this dinner because he'd wanted to challenge himself. When he joined Austin's pack, he'd decided that he should try to make a new life for himself. He'd longed for the easy friendliness Jessie shared with her crew, for a sense of community. Patty had presented the perfect excuse for him to try.

Now, in his space, he realized how little he had to offer any social evening. How bad he was at small talk. How close he was to the memories of a different time and place, a different home—his kids thumping around, his mate and her friends chatting…

"Hey, hey. Whoa, hey." Nessa was there in a moment, her hands on his arms, pushing at his chest. Cool air blanketed him, and his butt touched down on the wood of the bench. She'd gotten him back outside. "What can I do? What do you need? I can call the whole thing off in two seconds. No problem."

He looked away, his throat tight. He wanted to scream or fight. He wanted to tear himself apart and end this eternal night that he was trapped in. He wanted to drink so much he couldn't feel. Couldn't remember.

"Incoming," she said, and her firm butt touched down on his thighs. "Here we are." She scooted in close until her shoulder leaned against his chest. "Here we go. Just pull that around here…" His arm was yanked around her. "And that one around here…" The other followed. "Your arms are really heavy. It's like they're stuffed with lead. Okay, now squeeze." She tugged on his arms. "Squeeze, squeeze. Like a teddy bear. It'll make you feel better, I promise. I used to do this all the time to Sabby after his sister died. Ordinarily you'd think I'd be the one hugging, but he was too big. You're definitely too big. So you hug, and I'll try to keep my guts in my body. It's better than—"

She wheezed when his arms constricted. He hadn't even meant to tighten them.

"It's better than a teddy bear, I think," she continued, her voice breathy. He tried to relent, but he couldn't seem to follow through for some reason. "Teddy bears aren't real. They don't give anything back. But people have energy and heat and compassion. So when you hug me, you give me your energy. And then I merge it with mine and give it back. And then we just kinda stew in each other for a while until you feel better. See? Also, I talk nonsense. Sebastian always liked to hear chatter because it helped take his mind off things. I can be quiet if you want, though. Just tell me what you need."

He needed to have a better grip on himself. He needed to get off this porch before any of the pack saw the state he was in. He needed to be stronger.

He needed to break down.

God, he hated this life.

"I'll go scare the others away," she said, and moved to get up.

"No, it's fine." He buried his face into her hair, breathing her in for a moment. She always had this pillowy-soft scent he'd recognize anywhere. It wasn't the magic that gargoyle had smelled. It was just…her. Sunshine in a bottle, beautiful all year round.

"See?" she asked. "Do you feel that? The buzz?"

It took him a moment to recognize that she'd spoken. And then he *did* feel it, a deep electrical current, running through the very fiber of his being. It crackled in the air around them and vibrated through their touch.

"I can only do that with some people," she said, snuggling a little closer. "Then again, I only actually try with some people. And I don't really make it a habit of randomly sitting on people's laps. I should, just to see who I can energy-connect with."

"Why did you sit on my lap? If you don't make it a habit, I mean."

She shrugged. "I felt like you needed it. I figured that if you didn't feel comfortable, you'd just remove me. You are certainly strong enough. You could probably throw me across the grass if you wanted to."

"I'd never throw you."

She didn't comment, just burrowed in that much

deeper so he could squeeze her tightly and close his eyes. It did help. He liked the buzz. It felt good. Comforting. He knew that was the point.

She didn't come back with a witty quip for him, which was unlike her.

"Do you not believe me?" he asked softly, the buzz settling down deep, the growl in his words hinting at his desire.

"Of course I believe you. But you set me up for a sexual taunt, and it didn't feel like the time."

"A sexual taunt?"

"Yeah. Like—sex would be really boring if you never threw me down on the bed..."

He squeezed his eyes shut, feeling his groin pounding. She wiggled a little, maybe to try to give him more space, to make this less awkward for him. But with all the emotions tumbling through him right then, shame was the last emotion he could've felt.

His fingers were in her hair before he knew what he was doing, trying to find a port in the storm. His other hand went to her knees, turning her, dragging one leg over his hip until she straddled him. Her dress rode high, and he traced her inner thigh with his fingertips, wanting to sink them into her heat. Her breasts heaved against his chest, and hot breath tumbled out of her open, waiting mouth.

"Is this what you want?" she asked, and he knew *she* did. She'd made no secret of her interest.

He also knew it wouldn't be personal. It would just be physical, for both of them. It would ruin any hope of their having a friendship, the thing he needed most.

But he was hard-pressed to stop as his hand found her center and rubbed against her panties, feeling along the edge of the lace before dipping in.

Her soft groan set him on fire. He trailed his fingers through her slickness. Her hips jerked forward like they were out of her control, and he plunged his fingers into the core of her.

He took those lips, thrusting his tongue into her mouth before sucking hers into his, devouring her sweet taste. He worked her hard with his fingers. Too hard, probably, but he couldn't seem to calm down. His desire to take her nearly undid him. He'd dreamed of it more than once. Fantasized. He didn't care that they were on the porch. He didn't care that this would ruin everything between them. That, once this was done, she'd cease to exist for him. That his guilt over being with someone other than his mate would corrode any feeling, even friendship, he had for her.

He knew all of that. But he wanted this anyway. He wanted to drown out the nightmares and shadows that were rising and trying to consume him.

He worked his belt with his other hand, trying to get it free. Trying to get himself free.

Tight fingers squeezed his wrist. A shock of magic flooded him, cold through his center. More magic, pushing pain into little pricks across his body.

He froze, a hard thing to do, wrestling with all of his control. He knew what the signal for *stop* was.

"I want to do this," she said softly, her lips still against his. "I really, *really* do. I've wanted to since I first laid eyes on you. This is not me rejecting you. But you don't seem in control, and besides, we can't do it like this. Whatever you're facing, this isn't the solution. This would be me taking advantage of you, and I will not do that. When you're back to being a surly asshole, let's bump uglies then. Not like this."

He angled his face to catch her lips again, slow this time. Softer. He loved her taste as much as her smell. But she was right. Not about taking advantage of him—if something more had happened here, on his porch, he'd be guilty of that, too—but about the situation. About the mood. Hell, about their location and who might walk by and see. This was crazy.

"I'm sorry," he said, his voice gruff. "I'm sorry, I—"

"I shouldn't have let it get that far," she said, delicately taking the blame.

He shook his head as she turned, fixing her dress

and leaning up against him again as though nothing untoward had happened. She was effectively covering the moment. Smoothly covering it, as though she'd had a lot of practice handling dangerous things.

She thought of him as a dangerous thing.

His heart caved in and he dipped his head, guilt consuming him. "I'm not usually that rough. Or that…uncontrolled."

"Pity," she said lightly, and while it sounded sincere, it was probably just another smoothing technique.

"I'm not the monster you think I am," he said. "I'm really not."

"I don't think you are a monster, Brochan. *You* think you're the monster. I think you're a man with a scarred heart and a really hard past. A man who's trying to find his way. I am a woman who'd very much like to help him do that." She paused for a long beat. "I will tell you this once, and then I will never mention it again unless you want me to." The pause was briefer this time. "You could not have saved your pack. I've looked into it. You could've asked for help from nearby packs, but if you'd done that, they would've died too. The number of mercenaries and the number and level of mages who attacked your remote pack were too many. They knew this."

"We could've run," he countered. "We could've

left."

"They figured you would, actually. I pulled up the mercenary orders. They assumed you'd run and had a plan to pick you off when you did. Instead you stayed and took way too many of them down with you."

He stiffened.

"Sorry," she murmured. "That was in their reports. They concluded that the attack came at too high of a cost for them. The battle leader was killed. Regardless, you couldn't have saved your pack. It's the same fate that has befallen many shifter packs across the country."

"Everyone I loved died, damn it!" he ground out. "I said I would protect them, and they died." His voice broke and he hated himself for it. "I should've died with them."

"But you didn't," she said. Her tone was so soft. So understanding. "You lived. And now you have a duty to your family to continue living. Your mate and kids wouldn't want to see you so unhappy. Healing takes time, I know that, but it's a better journey than this continued purgatory you're forcing yourself into now." She looped her arms around his neck, hugging him tightly. "In the meantime, work with us to ensure mages can't keep doing this. Work with us to stop all of this so you can finally find some peace."

He nodded and took a deep breath, trying to find

some shred of control.

"What do you need from me to find that happiness?" she asked. "What can I do to help you?"

His heart was so heavy. So broken. He wouldn't be able to hide the desperation in his next words if he'd tried.

"I need a friend," he admitted. "I need guidance back into the world of the living. I need your sunshine."

"The good ol' friend zone, huh?" She kissed his cheek and squeezed him. "I am that friend, Brochan."

He held her tightly for a little longer, needing a port in the storm.

"This wasn't how I saw this dinner playing out," he murmured.

"How did you see this dinner playing out?"

He blinked rapidly a few times, his gaze sliding to the side. "You caught me—I'm not really sure. Normally, I guess. Like a normal dinner party."

"She invited Edgar." Nessa cocked her head. "*Edgar.* How normal could it possibly have gone?"

"This is true."

She got off his lap. "The good news is, you won't have any normalcy in this town to compare to your old life. You just won't find it. So if we can get past the front door and to Edgar, I'm pretty sure you'll find plenty of reasons to never host a dinner party again."

He stood, grateful.

"You must be a guardian angel," he whispered.

She shook her head sadly. "No. *I* am the monster you envision yourself to be, Brochan. And the worst part is, I have zero guilt about it. Being morally gray keeps me alive."

CHAPTER 13

AUSTIN

AUSTIN GENTLY PULLED his arm from under Jess and slowly removed himself from the warmth of her body. The production cairns were due in today, and he needed to get his territory prepared.

He paused by the new table sitting in front of the window, glancing out at what he knew would be a big difference in the view.

The hedge maze was gone.

Somehow, Mimi had convinced Edgar to let it go in favor of a more cohesive gardening plan, all without Edgar's threatening to retire himself.

The decision hadn't been without its issues, however. Edgar hadn't wanted to witness its destruction, so he'd slept last night, a rarity for him, and would wake up to find it gone today. How he'd react was anyone's guess.

Austin grabbed a shower and then made his way

downstairs.

"Good morning, sir," Mr. Tom said as Austin walked in. "Fine morning, isn't it? Which kind of coffee would you like? Espresso, Americano, caramel macchiato? Or what about something different today, like a chai tea? I've just learned how to make it. Very easy, really. I have oat milk, regular milk, unsweetened almond milk if you're watching the waistline…"

Mimi had outfitted the kitchen with an espresso machine, and Mr. Tom was in rapture. No one really knew why, but they were happy to drink his creations. He'd been so busy learning its tricks that he'd mostly stopped harassing Mimi about all the changes around Ivy House.

A strange keening started, catching Austin's ear.

He turned toward the sound, which was coming from somewhere at the back of the house, maybe. Or outside?

"Is that…" Austin cocked his head. "Is that a cat howling? Did we get a cat?"

Mr. Tom lifted his eyebrows while listening. "Oh, that's just Edgar. He must've found Naomi's handiwork. Honestly, it's about time. No one ever used that maze. It was time for it to go. Did you decide on the coffee?"

"Black." Austin continued to the island.

"Maybe without the hedge maze to repair…" Mr.

Tom muttered almost incoherently.

As he worked on his creations, he drank his creations. The result was a lot of hurried babbling, wings fluttering, and zooming around.

"He can finally turn all of his attentions to those gnomes," he continued, seemingly talking to himself as he grabbed a mug out of the cabinet. "He seems to have completely forgotten about those gnomes. Out of sight, out of mind isn't a wise tactic where those creatures are concerned. The gnomes just use the time to gather more troops and organize a battle strategy. You wouldn't think animated garden accessories would go to such lengths, but trust me, they do. At least they stay away from the house. I think that's Ivy House's doing more than Patty. I can feel the buzz within the house. Can you feel it? It's excited for the gargoyles to come. And as much as I hate to admit it, I think it's happy for a little spruce-up. I know I pushed back on that grandma of yours, but she does have an eye. She's dressing Ivy House up like a new penny."

Austin crossed to the fridge, but then stopped at the counter. A plethora of plates had been set up, each with a different chopped ingredient on it.

"What's this?"

"Oh." Mr. Tom filled the mug and set it on the counter. "I took the liberty of chopping some ingredients for your breakfast. You've been cooking breakfast more often over here—dare I say you feel more comfortable now that you've had a hand in redecorating?—and I thought you might like a fuse chef."

"Sous chef."

"Yes." Mr. Tom stared at him.

"It's called a *sous* chef."

"Right. That's what I said."

They stared at each other for a moment.

"Right," Austin said, letting it go.

"However, if you're in a rush and don't need my capabilities as a *fuuuuse* chef, I've made you a breakfast burrito. It's sitting in the oven on warm."

Letting it go again, he glanced over the various ingredients. A dozen things he could quickly whip up rolled through his head.

"You don't need to do this, Mr. Tom," he said out of habit. "I'm perfectly capable of making breakfast without any help."

"Of course, sir. I wouldn't presume to say otherwise. Is there anything missing that you'd like me to chop up?"

Austin sighed as his phone rang. He checked the screen. Brochan.

"Just the burrito would be fine, Mr. Tom. It's probably best if I get moving."

"Yes, sir. Coming right up. Are you sure about that caramel macchiato? Or what about an affogato? That has a scoop of ice cream. A little morning treat never hurt anyone."

Austin ignored him as he crossed to the other side of the room. He accepted the call. "Yes?"

"Goman cairn just crossed the territory line. They have a convoy of five large vans."

"Destination?"

"Looks like they are heading for the warehouse."

"Don't mind if I do," Mr. Tom said right before the espresso machine whirred to life.

Austin headed into the smaller-scale formal dining room off the kitchen. It'd been completely refurnished and outfitted, comfortable but decadent, one of many jaw-dropping makeovers. Mimi had really outdone herself. Then again, she'd had one helluva space to work with.

"Our people are in place?" he asked.

"In position now, yes," Brochan replied. "Additionally, we have another guardian scout checking out the territory. This one is for Khaavalor."

"Khaavalor…" Austin took another sip of coffee as he tried to place the name.

"Mr. Porsche," Brochan helped.

"Right, yes. I need to drink this coffee faster."

"Understandable. It's his lead enforcer, but not nearly the caliber of Gimerel's."

"Accommodations?'

"He mentioned that he has a line on a house. This will be the third cairn that's opted for buying property rather than staying in a hotel for free. It's odd behavior unless they plan on staying awhile."

"That or they're showboating. Time will tell."

"Yes, sir. This guardian was every bit as arrogant as the others."

"Easily cowed?"

"Yes. Only Gimerel's seemed impervious to my posturing. He took it as a joke."

"Gimerel's, yes," Austin said slowly before sipping his coffee.

He thought back to that meeting in the bar. Tristan, Gimerel's lead enforcer, was more dangerous than any of the others, not just because he was physically powerful, but because he had a thorough knowledge of his limitations. Austin had noticed the way he silently surveyed the bar and every single threat in it.

He hadn't been arrogant, though. Not to Austin. He'd been businesslike and straightforward, with no humor or mincing of words.

Of course, that might be because he'd found a bigger threat than himself.

"I'm sure it goes without saying, but keep an eye on him," Austin said.

"Yes, alpha. There is something I've gathered from meeting these people."

"What's that?"

"They don't seem to have much respect for shifters in general. They might back off their attitudes with me, but there's an underlying disdain."

"That could just be a product of their position, but well noted. It's something to watch."

"The lead enforcer is waiting for you in the café," Brochan said. "Do you need me to stay until you arrive?"

Austin and Brochan hadn't seen much of each other in the past month. They took opposite shifts, always with a strong team as backup, to ensure the territory was covered with solid leadership at all times. They'd needed it.

Solo gargoyles had been coming in all month, some intensely powerful. Patty had told them that was the norm. Gargoyles looked for guardian placement like Dicks looked for jobs, and the situation Jess had created was essentially a job fair.

The visiting gargoyles had been rowdy, testing the limits. They'd quickly learned the hard way not to do that.

"I'm on my way," Austin told Brochan. "Get some sleep. The fun starts tonight. You have all the info?"

"Yeah. Nessa dropped off the potion last night."

"Remember, you might need to pivot at a moment's notice. Jess often throws a wrench into these types of situations. Just roll with whatever happens."

"All due respect, sir, I don't think I can be shocked at this point."

"I thought that once, too. Now I know better. Get some sleep. See you tonight."

Austin hung up the phone and finished his coffee. "Mr. Tom, can I have a cup to go?"

"Of course, sir. Coming right up!" Mr. Tom hummed to himself as he grabbed a travel mug and filled it up. "And here you go." He put the burrito in a sleeve to keep it warm and handed it off. "Oops, the miss is waking up."

Mr. Tom unceremoniously put the travel mug on the counter, without affixing the lid, and filled a different mug of coffee.

"Do you have your instructions—"

Austin cut off as Mr. Tom hurried from the room.

It was pretty clear who ranked highest in this household.

✧ ✧ ✧

JESSIE

"HERE WE GO, miss. Not a moment late!" Mr. Tom walked in briskly with a cup of coffee and a manic smile. He'd dabbled too frequently in his coffee making again.

"What's that strange keening noise?" I asked, rubbing my eyes. "It sounds like it's coming from outside."

"That's Edgar. He's just missing the maze. He'll get over it. Now, up we go. We have a lot of work to do today. I was listening in on Austin Steele's conversation, and I think one of the production cairns is already here."

I glanced at the clock. Seven thirty. It was early, but Mr. Tom was right. I had to meet with Mimi to figure out a few hiccups—we hadn't finished as many rooms as we'd hoped, so we'd have to decide which could be used for entertaining. Then I needed to finalize my wardrobe and get in some training and a handful of other things before the pageantry officially began with a tour of the production cairn's goods.

"Right. Okay." I took a sip of coffee as Mr. Tom laid a not-so-fresh T-shirt out on the bed. Austin's. "No, Mr. Tom—" I pushed it a little. "He hasn't left the property yet. I'm not going to get caught in one of his shirts that you stole."

"Borrowed, miss. I simply borr—"

"Borrowed without asking, whatever."

With a huff, he gave me my robe.

Edgar sat in the middle of the desecrated hedge maze, bowed over his legs, sobbing in a high-pitched sort of wail. Dolls lingered around the outskirts, their hands clasped in front of them and their heads bent in sympathy.

As I watched, the basandere, whom I'd hardly seen anything of since she and the others got here, walked out of the trees toward Edgar. She stepped over each root and branch that had been left behind from the maze massacre until she reached him, then she sat down next to him and put her hand on his bony shoulder.

My heart squelched, and if Mimi hadn't convinced Edgar to agree to the plan prior to bulldozing the maze, I'd probably have let him start on another.

"Hello, dear. Good morning!" Patty came bustling in. "My, you're up early. Okay, I have the gift baskets ready for the production cairn leaders." She gave me a pout. "So terrible about Venavin's leader. Nessa will never want to let off a little steam with him now, and she no longer has the lovely Brochan to chase. Things completely fizzled with him, did you hear? Friend zone. Ugh! Weren't they so cute together? She's so perky and upbeat, and he's so gloomy and *black cloud*! Opposites attract! Anyway, doesn't matter. Here we go, let's head to the shower."

She fluffed the air beside me, getting me moving. "It seems the Goman cairn's leader didn't bring any guardians. I'd heard that, but it doesn't make sense. How bizarre, right? There must be some sort of mix-up."

"How do you know that? Didn't they just arrive?"

I made it to the bathroom door, pausing so she'd find somewhere else to be.

"In you get. I'll just sit here on this lovely modern bench and fill you in while you suds up." She ushered me in, following me, and grabbed the front of my robe.

"Whoa. Hang on—"

"Don't be bashful. I've seen you naked a million times. Here we go…"

"It's diff—erent." I gave her a stern look before stepping into the shower, pulling closed the shower curtain that I was happy I'd insisted on, and took off the robe. Then I had to cower in the corner so the cold water didn't freeze me before it warmed up.

"He arrived at the warehouse without any guardians, I heard," she said. "I just got a call from that lovely young woman who turns into a wolf. She's on the warehouse protection detail. I asked her to help me keep track of things so that I could make sure you were up to date. So at dinner—*dinner*, mind, not in the warehouse—you'll need to very casually ask why he made that unusual choice. It's a character assessment."

"Got it."

"I've written it down so that you'll remember. Now, I've got it on good authority that Pierce—Mr. Cashmere, the others call him—will be here a few hours before the meeting. He has a lot of swagger. He shows very well."

"Swagger isn't going to impress Austin."

"Swagger is just icing. What's important is that he gets the job done. The Dark Three may have dug up information about how he came by his position, but honestly, there were no grievances filed, so he is absolved of any wrongdoing."

The Dark Three were what we now called Niamh, Sebastian, and Nessa. The dirty pool players, Nessa always said.

I held my head out of the water so I could hear. "They didn't mention that. How'd he get his position?"

"Relax for this week," Patty went on, ignoring my question. I'd need to ask the others. "These are just production cairns without any status. Any gossip they spread can be turned around, don't you worry. I have all my girls on standby. Use this time to get to know how lesser gargoyles work, how they speak, what they do, all that. Get used to them, and then you'll hit the ground running when the high-status cairns come through."

I knew all this, of course. I'd been told a million times.

After all the preparation, turning the house upside down, getting new jewelry made, a new wardrobe—finally it was time to meet the first wave of gargoyles. I was both extremely curious and utterly terrified.

CHAPTER 14
JESSIE

WE ARRIVED AT the warehouse punctually and separated ourselves as we usually did, Austin's line clean and crisp and mine a little meandering but mostly in sync. Two shifters opened the double doors, and Austin and I went first, side by side. The others came behind and then fanned out, as we'd planned.

The two production cairns waited in the middle of the spacious warehouse on either side of the large space. Each had plenty of room and had used it fantastically differently.

On the left stood what I had gathered to be the Goman cairn, their rugs spread out in front of them with the sometimes odd designs and an array of colors. Textiles were draped on tables behind that or hung on rolling garment racks. The various gargoyles associated with the cairn stood among their products, their faces impassive and their stances patient. The whole setup seemed organized and thought out, everything placed *just so*.

In contrast, the Venavin cairn setup was a mess of textiles. Items were heaped onto the tables or throw blankets seemingly tossed onto the ground. I couldn't see any rhyme or reason to the setup, and it certainly didn't seem like they cared.

In a moment, I saw why.

One of the gargoyles clustered in the back took us in and started snickering. He elbowed the guy next to him, and that guy barked out a laugh before shaking his head in disdain. Grins sprang up on the faces of the others, and who I recognized as their leader from pictures I'd seen crossed his arms over his chest with a smirk. He didn't plan to call them down. Worse, it seemed he agreed with their sentiments. They stood amid a mess of their product, a terrible display of their worth, and they had the audacity to laugh at *me*.

Both anger and support radiated through the bond, my people urging me to keep a stiff spine. Tightly coiled rage worked through me from Austin as Patty *tsk*ed and started murmuring furiously to herself.

I didn't need support or to be reminded to keep a stiff spine. I needed to cool the rush of fire fueled by my gargoyle to dominate those jerks and wipe those insufferable smiles off their faces.

This was how it was going to go, was it? They thought they could laugh at my crew and I wouldn't retaliate? Just what kind of outfit did they think Austin and I ran here?

I pushed out a hard slap of magic. Let them see who they were messing with.

It rolled over that cairn like a wave, wiping the smiles clean off their faces. Wings fluttered, eyes widened, Edgar randomly put up a fist.

"Put yer hand down, ya gobshite," Niamh murmured to him.

"Hello," I said with a firm voice. "Welcome. My name is Jessie Ironheart."

I took a step forward, and Austin did so at the same time, in perfect sync. The cairn on the right, the ones who'd mocked me, all took a step back. Except for the leader. Pierce. A.k.a. Mr. Cashmere.

He stood his ground, a cocky sort of playboy grin curling his lips. This one wasn't mocking like the others—it was an obvious attempt at charming, boosting his handsomeness. It wouldn't do him any good.

"I am the alpha of this territory," I continued, "along with my mate Austin Steele. This is a multi-species magical territory, as you can plainly see. We have different rules than you are used to. I'd advise you to learn those rules as quickly as possible, because we are unforgiving if you break them. You will address me as Alpha, Ironheart, or a combination of both. My mate will be addressed as Alpha, or Alpha Steele. Do you understand?"

None of the gargoyles acknowledged me, and so I sent a blast of magic at both cairns this time, eliciting various forms of acceptance. That would do.

"You are all of course aware," I went on, "that I have not been a gargoyle long. I became a gargoyle the day I got magic, which was about a year ago. I'm still learning the ropes, and I make a lot of mistakes. I imagine you'll see those mistakes as a sign of weakness. If you snicker at them, though, make sure to do so from a distance, because my mistakes kill people. Alpha Steele is not new to his magic, and he doesn't make mistakes. If he means to kill you, he'll do so viciously. This is the only warning you are going to get. Now…"

I smiled at Venavin's cowed postures. They were lucky all I'd done was hit them with a little magic and address them with words. If it had been a shifter situation, Austin would've leveled them all.

"Let's see what you've got." I looked at Austin. "Who would you like to start with?"

His gaze beat into Pierce.

Maybe he still planned to level them all.

He started forward.

The man of the hour met us with a flawless smile oozing charm and charisma. He had a face that would make photographers weep and a toned body he clearly worked hard on. His hair was styled long, just past his ears, and a lock of hair had a habit of falling across his right eye, accentuating his brilliant smile.

"It's legendary to meet you, Jessie Ironheart," he said, offering a shallow bow. "Gargoyles in general have been so curious about you. It's been an age since there was a female gargoyle. Most of us had started to think they were a myth." The wattage of his smile increased as he leaned forward. "I'm Pierce. I make the softest, most luxurious fabrics you've ever had the pleasure of feeling. You must've liked your sweater. I excel in creating the perfect fit."

"Why are these not uniform?" Naomi asked in a stern voice, standing at the side of his setup and holding a blanket to catch the light. I hadn't noticed her following us over.

"Well…" Pierce jerked his head to get the hair out of his eye, and his perfectly manicured eyebrows lowered. "That is an artisan piece. They are handmade and rarely uniform."

Naomi looked over her half-moon reading glasses at him. Without a word, she dropped the blanket to the ground and moved on. It didn't take a genius to know that she hadn't liked his answer.

Without skipping a beat, Pierce turned back to us. "Our specialty is in our knits." He gestured for me to follow him. "Please. Let me show you."

"Not me." I hooked a thumb Austin's way. "He's the one in the market."

Pierce swung his gaze slowly, and his face visibly fell. Charming women was in his wheelhouse, it seemed—no surprise with that face. He didn't seem so confident about the big alpha staring him down.

"Of course," he finally said, leading Austin to the table.

"His appearance lives up to the hype," Patty whispered as she stepped up beside me. "His personality, however…" She grabbed my arm. "Oh look, Goman cairn has more of those infuriating rugs. Naomi made that other one work so well. Let's see if there are any others that will drive me crazy."

We crossed the space to the organized setup.

"Hi," I said to the leader—Anthott, his name was.

He stared at me silently, his hands stiff at his sides.

"Do you need to flip a switch to activate him or something?" Hollace asked, wandering closer.

"Oh, Hollace, look at this one!" Cyra tramped across the rugs to get to the one she liked.

"Don't step on those," Jasper said softly through his

teeth, trying to grab her.

"Why?" she asked, out of his reach. "They're rugs. What do you do with them if not walk on them?"

"Solid logic," Hollace drawled.

"It really is hard to argue with her at times," Patty told Anthott, patting his forearm. He flinched slightly. "Well? Don't keep Miss Ironheart waiting—what do you have for her?"

Sebastian and Nessa drifted in behind me. Edgar skulked around to the side, and the rest of my crew wandered closer to hear.

"Yes, Ironheart," the gargoyle said crisply. "I stand ready to answer any questions."

I grimaced at him. "Uhm…" I shook my head, looking at the rugs spread out behind him, then the perfectly folded or delicately draped items on the tables. "Well, why don't you tell me a bit about your operation?"

"Artistically, stylistically, or mechanically?" he asked.

"This feels like a test," Sebastian said. "At least it's multiple choice."

"Artistically," Nessa stage-whispered. "Do artistically."

I gestured Anthott on to say that that was fine.

"Yes, of course." He turned ninety degrees. "There has often been a divide between purpose and art. If something is made for a working purpose, it is not generally crafted to be a piece of art. I blur those lines. I have simple rugs, as you see." He lifted his hand to indicate a plain beige rug. "It can go with almost anything. It blends in to allow other things in the room to pop. It's functional and durable and very boring. Or is it?"

"I'm going with no," Nessa said, poking Sebastian. "What's your guess?"

"There's a face in it," Hollace said.

Anthott craned his neck to see who'd spoken. "Interesting," he murmured, looking again at the rug. "Any other guesses?"

I narrowed my eyes at it, realizing it wasn't an all-beige rug but actually a series of dots in various shades similar to beige. When closely observed, the dots seemed to move, like they were forming patterns or pictures. It reminded me of Ivy House's wood murals, which did actually move.

"I see a monster face," Sebastian said. He squeezed his eyes shut and shook his head. "This is stressing me out. I don't like inkblot tests."

"How about this one?" Anthott led us around to a rug with a geometric pattern.

The more I looked, the more the shapes popped out, one by one, until it almost looked 3D.

"Weird," I said. "I mean…cool, definitely. I haven't seen anything like that before."

"Better," Sebastian said. "I like this one, actually. Except for the colors."

"Yes, so the rugs can be plain at first glance but take on a life of their own once studied," Anthott said, walking us around to another. "The inkblot beige, the geometric purple. And now we get to the type of rug I sent you. This is a harder rug to create. It is a statement piece all its own. In the right hands, it creates interest and depth. It elevates a room. In the wrong hands—"

"It's hideous," Edgar said, nodding slowly. He'd drifted toward one of the cairn's gargoyles, nearly shoulder to shoulder. The gargoyle didn't seem to notice.

"Exactly, yes," Anthott agreed, seemingly not offended. "It would've been better to send you something simple, probably, but I find that there is an emotional charge with rugs like this. I've found that people either like them or hate them."

"What if she'd hated it?" Hollace asked.

"It wouldn't have mattered. It was the emotional reaction I wanted. *Any* emotional reaction. It's that emotional connection that would make me memorable. I made sure to put it in a well-made and more traditional trunk, and to include some luxury apparel in a bland color. It would make the rug stand out."

"Huh." Hollace peered over my shoulder. "Smart."

"All of these rugs are made to be used. They are made for foot traffic. But the materials are good quality, too, soft enough to make love on."

Nessa's eyebrows climbed high, and her mouth popped open with a smile. "Tell me you're a gargoyle without telling me you're a gargoyle…"

"We've found Ulric and Jasper's people," Hollace said, laughing.

Anthott paused in obvious confusion.

"Never mind." Nessa waved him away. "What else ya got? I see trunks over there. Are they sturdy enough to lock Edgar in them?"

"I'm not sure I'll like that game," Edgar said, backing up now.

"Come on, Edgar, you'll never know until you try."

CHAPTER 15

JESSIE

"VENAVIN HAD THE better material in the textiles," Austin said as our limo driver brought us to the restaurant we'd used for other high-profile visitors. Austin had listened to the alphas' spiels, given a detailed look at all the products on display, and asked intelligent and insightful business questions that had blindsided Pierce and not at all thrown Anthott.

When he finished, he'd thanked the two gargoyles for displaying their goods and said we'd see them for dinner in an hour.

Our team was heading there early. We had to set up. It was time for a little sneaky reconnaissance.

I leaned against Austin's arm and threaded my fingers through his. "Not put together well, though," I reminded him. "Your grandma was not at all impressed with the inconsistencies."

"True. The issues were obvious. But it raises the

question, how could his people have come up with such amazing craftsmanship in one aspect, and not in others?"

"There's some sort of scandal surrounding him. Maybe she should ask the Dark Three about it. They've been cagey, which means they're definitely planning something."

"What'd you think of him?"

"Who, Pierce?" I leaned away to get a read on Austin's face. It was blank and his emotions didn't give away anything besides that simmering rage I'd felt before, turned down low. "He's very handsome." Austin gazed down at me. "Very charming." Still he stared. Nothing new came through the bond. "Lovely smile."

"Small wings, narrow shoulders, lacking muscle tone for extended flight. He's not great in the air and worse on the ground. Yes, I know all his physical attributes. What about him personally?"

"*Oh*, him *personally*." I laughed and leaned back into him. "Not jealous, huh? Not even a tiny little bit?"

"It's impossible to be jealous of such a fop."

"A fop, wow. I don't think I've ever heard that word spoken aloud. Apparently you don't think much of him."

Austin's breath fell around me on a sigh, and he glanced out the window. "Apparently he doesn't think that much of you. I'm not telling you how to do your job, Jess, but if that had been a shifter, I would've kicked him around the warehouse. He's not taking you seriously."

"I think we should prepare for none of them to take me seriously, Austin. But it wouldn't have done me any good to kick him around the warehouse. He's not someone I need to impress. He's someone who should be trying to impress me."

"Except he isn't. First he allowed his people to laugh at you, and then he humored you in an attempt to charm you. If he's here for business, it's not yours."

That pulled me up short. "Then whose would it be?"

"I don't know, but if the mages don't figure it out, I'm going to shake it out of him. I have no tolerance for his behavior."

I smoothed my free hand across his forearm. "As I said, he's not someone I need to impress. I can ignore him for now. It's the big dogs I need to worry about. This is just a practice round."

He shook his head, and his anger spiked. "All these cairns seem isolated at best and closed in at worst. The Goman cairn has their operation on top of a mountain, no one for a truckload of miles. The larger cairns might not be quite that remote, but they are still removed from the rest of the world. Will they even be helpful if we were to form an alliance with them?"

"Don't we need them?"

"We can do without if we have to. We'll just have to leave fewer shifters here to guard the territory while we're gone. The territory should be safe, though."

"Just…let's wait and see, okay? There *are* good gargoyles out there—we have them on our crew. We're making a lot of assumptions. If we flaunt our bling and show off our strength, we should be able to moonlight guardians looking for placement. We've already had an influx of them into the territory, right? We have the money to pay them. You have experience. We have the building blocks. We can reel in the rest."

He was quiet for a beat. "Fine. But I cannot guarantee I won't make an example out of one of the leaders if they allow their people to laugh at you. Or belittle you. It was a real struggle to keep myself calm earlier. It is a struggle I won't win for very long."

"Okay, then. What about the rug-making robot? Did you see anything you liked? You didn't comment much, just asked questions."

"His textiles weren't as fine as Venavin, but the workmanship was first rate. The woodworking was amazing, equal to the sculpture you got from Nikken. The rugs were… I can't decide if I want to say ingenious or wacky."

"Your grandma raved, which is not something she does often."

"I think that's why I want to say ingenious. I saw what she did with the one in Ivy House. It absolutely adds the depth he was talking about. It might be a hard sell, though. I doubt I could make them work."

I snuggled a little closer as we glided down the highway. "Think you'll make a move?"

He let go a soft sigh. "I really want to be done with the whole species, honestly. I haven't much enjoyed the guardians I've met, save one. They've been a handful. Then there's that douche in the warehouse… In addition to the strength of the pack, I've gotten reports that the basa—Dave is entertaining more basajaunak on his mountain. Some are coming and going, but many are lingering. Or going and then coming back."

"I didn't realize you'd been watching Dave."

"I had someone ask him about a territory breach, and they reported a gathering. Curiosity got the better of me, and I started a rotation to watch—from outside of his territory, of course. I'm not crazy."

"Niamh hasn't mentioned anything. I've felt her head to the mountain a good few times in the last few weeks. I assumed she was going for the moonshine and good times."

"She probably is. And it's probably benefiting our

cause. We just have to make sure they don't get carried away."

I'd wondered why Dave hadn't been coming by the house for his flowers, or to check in. He used to do that all the time. I'd just assumed he was busy with his friend.

"So with more basajaunak and with a strong pack," I surmised, "you're less worried about making connections where the gargoyles might not want them?"

He squeezed my knee. "The basandere in the redwoods saw strength in your crew, as odd as they are. She saw strength in *you*. They never once disrespected us, and when they came close, they compromised and backed off. They welcomed us and treated us as family, and they had a very good reason for not making an alliance. I saw no fault in them. I'd welcome a connection with them, anytime. Which is why I'm so encouraged that Dave is fostering their interest. The gargoyles are nothing like them so far."

"Again, we have some gargoyles who are."

"Three out of all the many you've called in. I've met the best they have to offer, and I wanted to throttle each of them, save one."

"Save one," I repeated, since it was the second time he'd mentioned it. "Who's the one?"

"The Gimerel lead enforcer. He's someone I could

lead without all the hassle the others have given us."

"You have to remember, though, the shifters didn't treat me very nicely at first. One of yours tried to challenge me with the intent of making a fool out of me. I think the mages will be worse. With the basajaunak, we had an *in*. Dave is the son of that clan's leader. It's not like we were starting from scratch. Just..." I watched the landscape outside start to slow as the limo took the off-ramp. "Just give them a chance, okay? Let's see how I handle the big dogs. I plan on letting my gargoyle call the shots. I'll put it in her hands. If I can't make wine out of crushed grapes, then so be it."

"A wine metaphor, huh? Thinking about your new tasting room?"

I laughed. "Yes, actually. I can't wait to open it. I've gotten a crapload of questions about it. I just wish I had time!"

We pulled up to the restaurant and stopped, and the limo waited to drop us off before moving off to the side to park.

"I'll think about Anthott's production cairn," Austin said. "I'll get more information. He and his people were professional. I can't fault them for Venavin's reaction."

"Whatever you think. But for what it's worth, I don't think it would hurt to have some artisans in the territory."

"No it wouldn't, especially since Ivy House would foot the bill for keeping them here."

"Oh I see," I said as my door opened. The driver stood beside it, waiting for me. Austin got out his side. "You're just trying to save yourself a buck. It's free, so why not, huh?"

His eyes twinkled but he didn't allow himself a smile. "I've always loved a deal."

I laughed as the limos behind us emptied, our people walking our way. The first wave of limos went to park and the rest pulled up, the doors opening without anyone waiting for the drivers.

"Okay, guys," I said as Sebastian and Nessa stopped beside me. "No more Mrs. Nice Gargoyle. It's time to play dirty. Tell me what I need to know for this dinner. You've been holding out on me about Mr. Cashmere."

"Niamh!" Nessa screeched, turning to look behind. "Niamh! She wants to play hardball. Get up here!"

"Who needs a bullhorn when they have you?" Broken Sue murmured at Nessa as he passed by.

"Be nice or I'll play dirty tricks on you," she quipped.

"Your humor is already a dirty trick."

At the front door, Niamh reached for it first. When it didn't budge, she said, "What clown didn't unlock the door?"

"That would be me." Austin shot her a look as he threaded through us with the keys.

Her back straightened within his stare, and she swore under her breath. "I hate when he does that," she muttered.

"The chef and line cooks use the back entrance." Austin opened the door and peered inside. "They're prepping. We've got a little less than an hour. Make it count."

We followed, and I saw that not much had changed since our last visit. It was posh and well constructed, but I'd remembered it coming off as more of a fine-dining experience. Then again, it was hard to hold a candle to Austin's newest restaurant.

The space was still largely open, with the tables spaced evenly, nowhere to really hide. Unless you had potions to make you invisible, of course. Which we did.

"This place is great," Nessa said as she started dragging one table toward another. Sebastian quickly stepped forward to help.

"So what'd you think of that cairn leader, Nessa?" Niamh asked, surveying the tables they were moving around. "Handsome fella."

"Yeah. Very." Nessa adjusted another table and stepped to the wall. "This is my spot. And from the way Austin reacted to him, he'll probably die very soon."

Niamh laughed. "Ah, sure, he'll be run out of town before Austin Steele can get at him, right twat like that."

"If everything is too calm, and the guy is too light and easygoing, I always get this extreme paranoia that I'm going to get stabbed in the back. Anyone else feel that way?" Nessa asked, still sizing up the room.

Niamh kept laughing. Everyone else just looked at Nessa.

"What?" she asked. "It's better if the most dangerous man in the room is the guy I'm with, because then I know he's either got my back or he's going to kill me. No guessing."

"The job has done a number on ye." Niamh shook her head, still chuckling. "Not like I can talk, mind. I once stabbed a fellow puca because he smiled at me. I thought he might've poisoned me or something. Turned out he'd just had gas. Sometimes ye just can't shake *the fear*."

Sebastian's expression fell as he gazed at Nessa. "I did this to you. I've made your life unlivable. Yours and Jessie's. Every connection I make, I—"

"Don't get sentimental on us now, Sabby." Nessa rolled her eyes with a smile, then bounded over to Sebastian and wrapped him in a big hug. "*I* chose my path. If anything, I forced you to end up like this. It had to be done, and I did it. I don't regret it."

"Well of course ye don't," Niamh said. "I heard about that bollocks mage who broke into yer lab. He knew what he was about, and he should've known he was goin'ta die. Fair play to ya. The Anal Repository will pay for what they did to Sebastian, we'll see to that."

She was talking about the man Nessa had killed in self-defense. Sebastian had claimed responsibility, knowing a weak mage like Nessa would be killed for the offense but he would be allowed to live, and he'd been tortured for days by the Mages' Guild.

Neither Nessa nor Sebastian seemed to hear what Niamh was saying, though, and a shiver arrested me. Something about the way she was hugging him, and the way he curled into her, spoke of a long and deep history. This was some sort of shared trauma carving away at them. The odd thing was that I didn't think it was because of the mage Nessa had killed. When they'd told me that story before, they'd delivered it almost as a joke. This was something darker, or maybe something earlier.

I wished I could help in some way, but I didn't want to pry. I doubted I'd get a straight answer out of them anyway, not from the way they were hugging each other and ignoring the room.

Niamh must've realized it too, because she turned in that unaffected way of hers. "Right, Jessie, let's get down to business. We need to talk about that *gobshite* that mocked us in the warehouse. He's some piece of work, he is. We're going to make him sizzle. Here's how…"

CHAPTER 16

JESSIE

I STOOD AT the wall five feet from the main table where we'd all eventually have dinner. Austin's pack stood outside in their orderly formation, making a show of the protection detail. My people were interspersed with them.

Sebastian and Nessa stood in their positions, chosen earlier, and Niamh sat at a table in the back with a flask. She'd been given strict orders to maintain her grip on that flask at all times. The potion we'd taken would mask our sight and sound, even our smell, from onlookers, within a small aura around us. The same potion would allow us to see one another, an elusive quality Sebastian had been trying to add to his potions for years, and he'd only succeeded with our combined power.

We'd be covered, our clothes would be covered, and elements that touched us would be hazy at the edges.

For Niamh to render that flask invisible, she would have to keep her hands covering most of it at all times.

Someone mentioned that it would've been easier just to tell her she couldn't bring it. That guy clearly didn't know Niamh very well.

Austin stood to one side of the entrance to the dining area, his back to the wall and his hands clasped in front of him. Broken Sue stood opposite him. Both of them had also taken the potion.

We wanted to test the instincts of the gargoyles. A shifter would be able to feel them lurking there, even if they couldn't see, hear, or smell them. We wondered if these gargoyles had the same abilities.

"Ready?" Austin asked, his words as hazy as his appearance, but easily understandable.

Nessa put out a thumbs-up. Sebastian nodded. Niamh took a sip of her flask. Thanks to the potion, I could see them all.

"Bring them in," I whispered.

Austin brought up his phone and sent off a text. A moment later, the sound of rubber soles on hardwood came our way.

"Right this way," a host said, carrying menus and stopping at the two tables we'd pulled together. The tables had all been adorned in white tablecloths with flickering candle centerpieces. The lights on the walls had been somewhat dimmed with softly glowing sconces.

Pierce sauntered in first, looking around as he did so. He took a seat with a flourish as Anthott followed behind, not bothering to glance around the room or look beyond the leather billfold he carried.

"Miss Ironheart and Alpha Steele will be in shortly," the host said, handing out the menus. "They have been momentarily delayed. Can I get you something to drink while you wait?"

"Grab me some bread, will ya?" Pierce said, not looking up at the man. He pushed his menu to the side, disturbing his place setting. "And a wine list."

"The wine list is just"—the host leaned forward and tapped the third menu he'd set on the table—"here, sir."

Pierce picked it up without preamble.

"Soda water for me, please," Anthott said, placing his menu atop the empty decorative plate in front of him. He set his billfold to the other side of his napkin and silverware, and then straightened everything in front of him.

After his host left, Pierce put up his finger with a sly smile. "Wait…" He pulled a device out of his blazer. Clunky and black, it was clearly a sort of technology, and he placed it on the table next to his plate. "This should scramble their security cameras' audio. And your phone. Hope you aren't waiting for an important call."

Anthott pulled his phone out of his pocket and checked it before putting it away again. He didn't seem troubled. Austin did the same, as did Broken Sue. Both looked incredibly annoyed.

"That's why they are late, obviously." Pierce leaned back in his chair and put his hand over the chair top next to him. "They want us to talk amongst ourselves, revealing our secrets."

"I don't have any," Anthott said.

Pierce frowned at him before shaking his head with a condescending smile. "Well, it's clear why no cairns have picked you up. How long you been looking?"

"I've sent samples to a few of the larger cairns every six months for the past two years. My cairn is only five years old."

Pierce laughed. "Maybe stop aiming for the stars, bro. A few of the larger cairns? With your setup, you need to aim low and settle quick."

"Smaller cairns won't have the starting capital for the kind of production I envision. We'd have to pick and choose what to produce, when it would be optimal for profit to produce sets. People like to buy sets. If given a choice, the average person would rather buy a bedroom set, for example, at a higher price than buy one piece and bargain-hunt for things that would match. They simply don't have the ability, time, or desire to piece together a room by themselves. You sell more, and in turn make more, with sets."

Broken Sue glanced at Austin with a lifted brow. Pierce's eyebrows were also lifted, but in a different way. He blew out a breath and leaned forward, hitting the edge of his plate and making it wobble.

"Wow, bro," he said. "With conversational skills like that, you'll get a big cairn, no problem." He laughed, leaning back again. "No offense, but you don't have the right stuff to lure in a big cairn. I watched my old cairn pitch new products to Nikken's buyers. The big cairns look for a certain charm. They want someone who talks a good game. I'm great at that sort of thing. I was rising in the ranks faster than anyone in history."

"Why did you leave, then?"

"Why?" Pierce flared a hand. "I want a bigger piece of the pie, that's why. I was making peanuts while securing big orders. It was crap. A lot of the other guys felt the same. I figured screw it, you know? I can do it myself. No one to tell me I was aiming too high or thinking too big. You get that part at least, right? Now I just gotta secure a big cairn, and I'm golden."

"I might be wrong, but I don't know that laughing at the benefactor of a cairn is the best approach."

"Who, the chick?" Pierce's face screwed up. "*Please.* The alpha shifter clearly has some power, but his territory has almost no fliers. Not to mention shifters are social pack animals. They aren't built for protection. How would they protect against a raid? And then there's her…" He flung his hand. "She has three gargoyles on her team—"

"I counted four."

"The old one doesn't count. Three gargoyles, and only *one* could remotely be considered for a guardian position. Not even a high-status one at that. They've got more gargoyles in the shifter pack, but none of them are worth a glance. Then she's got a bunch of odd…whatever creatures they are. I couldn't identify *any* of their smells. Besides, since when has a female gargoyle led anything? That's all myth and legend. And even if it isn't, *she* certainly can't. She has some magic, whoopee. But does she even shift? She has no wings."

"I believe the female gargoyle's wings—"

"Whatever. I'm not here for this…pack. I'm here because in a week I'll be in the same town as the four biggest cairns in the world."

"Except you already burned a bridge with one of them. Or did I hear that wrong?"

Pierce's demeanor changed in an instant. "What do you know about it, *Anthott*? Did you even bring any guardians?"

"I'm not sure what that has to do with—"

"I'd think long and hard about any allegations you want to make against me. Without any guardians, you won't be able to protect yourself. And if you open your mouth, you'll definitely need to protect yourself."

Anthott lifted his hands immediately, fear edging into his voice. "I just heard rumors, is all. I don't have any allegations. I don't know anything concrete—"

"The rumors aren't true, or wouldn't they have filed a grievance against me?"

"Production cairns with high-status alliances almost never file public grievances. They worry about causing a big stir that will reflect negatively on their operation. If that happened, it's all too likely the affiliate cairn would call them down or sever their connection to maintain status. No production cairn would risk it. Which I'm sure you knew—"

Pierce stood, and his chair tumbled back behind him. He reached forward and grabbed Anthott by the shirt, yanking him forward.

I stepped forward quickly, reaching for a vial of potion to counteract the last. My magic pumped into the room even as Austin started moving, crossing the space. He grabbed Pierce by the neck and threw him back. Pierce's legs hit tables and knocked over chairs before he struck the back wall with a loud *thud.*

"Help!" he hollered as he fell, hitting the ground with a grunt. "Help! I'm being attacked by…by magic."

Austin drank down his potion as boots thudded against the floor in the reception area. We'd allowed four of Pierce's guardians to play sentinel outside the room. They ran in now.

Broken Sue was ready, though, newly visible after taking the antidote. He stepped in the way, and the first guardian slammed into him and bounced back. The next was right behind, though, trying to push through. Two more followed, all four barreling into Broken Sue.

He handled the onslaught without so much as stepping backward. Although his blank expression didn't waver, I could feel his enjoyment through the bond. He grabbed the first gargoyle, much smaller than him in every way, and used him as a plow, ramming into the others and forcing them all back. He marched them out of the space, then—judging by sound—into the reception area then out of the building entirely.

"What the hell?" Pierce panted, Austin standing over him. "What the hell?"

"You don't need cameras to listen undetected," I told him. "Magic will suffice."

"Sit our friend down, Austin Steele," Niamh said after drinking her potion. "I think we should have a little chat."

"What the..." Pierce's eyes were huge as Austin reached for him. "No, please! No! Please!"

"Isn't it delightful," Nessa said, twisting off the cap to her vial, "that they all beg in the same way when Austin Steele grabs them?"

"I was just thinking that." Sebastian tucked his now-empty vial into his pocket and wavered into public visibility.

Austin roughly sat Pierce down in his chair. Anthott sat frozen in front of him, shock and fear etched onto his face.

"Let's get rid of these, shall we?" Nessa grabbed the candles and plates, gesturing for Sebastian to take away the menus, silverware, and tablecloth. "We don't want to get blood on anything."

"What are you going to do to me?" Pierce asked, cowering in his seat. "Who put you up to this? W-was it Aadath's d-doing?"

"Anthott..." I put my hand on his shoulder, and he flinched. "You can leave for a while, if you'd like. Or maybe sit at another table and drink your soda water?"

"How about a snack?" Nessa stopped at his other side and pulled at his arm. "Up we go. Let's have a snack, shall we? Here, you can sit right over here and watch the show. You'll be safe, don't worry. *You* didn't laugh at a female gargoyle and her incredibly powerful crew…"

Sebastian patted my shoulder. "You get started. I'm gonna grab that guy something to munch on. He looks a little shaken."

Niamh swiped the scrambler off the table and switched it off before pocketing it. She apparently liked that little gadget and didn't plan on giving it back.

I took the seat opposite Pierce as Austin continued to stand by his side like a mobster's hitman. A moment later, Broken Sue reentered and stood in the middle of the entryway, an enormous bouncer.

"Aadath." Niamh sat down beside me. "He's the lad in charge of Gabauve, right? The production cairn ye pulled a runner from?"

"You know how he is," Pierce said, his face a mask of scared rage. A little drool leaked down the side of his mouth. "He doesn't have any vision. He knows it, his people know it, and *I* know it. Why do you think so many people agreed to go with me?"

"Because ye promised them a huge cut, I imagine," Niamh said before taking a sip from her flask. She made a face. "Like fire, that stuff. Goes down rough. Anyway, what was the cut you promised, twenty percent? Thirty?"

"None of your business! I left that cairn fair and

square. I followed the rules! I gave my notice in writing, I stuck to my job until it was time to leave, and then I left peacefully. You've got nothing on me!"

"But…" Nessa sat down beside him and leaned to the side away from him, her elbow propped on the table, her chin in her hand. "Are you sure, though?"

"Where are we?" Sebastian asked as he reentered with a plate of what looked like bacon-wrapped shrimp.

"We were just getting to Koru," Nessa said, gazing pleasantly at Pierce.

All the blood drained from his face. He opened and closed his mouth several times, but nothing came out.

"Yes, exactly," Nessa said, nodding. "You didn't think anyone knew about Koru, did you? A married woman—"

"Mated," Sebastian amended.

"Mated to the head weaver. Bored, though, poor thing. Tired of hearing about her husband's—"

"Mate's."

"—mate's day, and how he recalibrated his machines… But when a handsome, charming gargoyle half her age showed a little interest, suddenly she was eager to share all she knew. She even started asking her husband more about certain aspects of his job, like what his secret was for making a product no one else had ever been able to duplicate. Until you…"

"I didn't do anything wrong," Pierce shouted, his voice quavering. "It's not my fault she shared information with me! I just listened, that's all. She's the one who talked."

"Hard to listen with her thighs clamped around yer head," Niamh drawled. "Then again, it's a right easy way to get her to come back for more of yer tedious company. Ye must be at least decent at it."

"So?" Pierce said. "Having sex with a garhette in a closed mating isn't against cairn rules. That had nothing to do with my job. Her being unfaithful is between her and her mate."

"Hmm." I tapped my chin in mock thought. "I could've sworn bribery and blackmail were against cairn rules, though, no? Did I get that wrong?"

"I didn't—" He swallowed hard and choked on his spit. "I didn't bribe—I didn't do those things!"

"You didn't bribe her with fancy jewelry and then sex acts to get her to ask her mate for detailed information?" I quirked an eyebrow. "You didn't blackmail her into stealing his private documents out of the safe by telling her you'd reveal the affair?"

"You can't prove that," Pierce said. "Those were gifts."

"How about blackmailing the head weaver?" I asked. "Didn't you threaten him with termination if he reported the incident?"

"I just said I'd tell on his mate, that's all! I didn't say he couldn't report me. It's not blackmail. He's got nothing on me!"

I sighed, leaning back. "That's true. This is all hearsay. There was no actual money exchanging hands for it to be considered a bribe—if we count the jewelry as a gift—and there is no evidence of direct blackmail."

"That's why they couldn't file a grievance." He crossed his arms, looking smug. "I didn't do anything wrong. It wasn't my fault."

Nessa put up her hands, her mouth open in a pantomime of incredulity. She swiveled to Sebastian and then Niamh. "We literally just went through a whole list of why he's a scumbag, but because he didn't get caught, he thinks that means he did nothing *wrong*? That's wild."

"Ye know what I think?" Niamh took another sip from her flask. "I think cider tastes better than this, that's what I think. I also think his old cairn didn't file a grievance because they couldn't be bothered. He might have the know-how to make the stuff, but he is absolute *shite* at everything else. Who would take him on? He can't even set up a display, like. Pure useless, this lad."

"True." Nessa pulled her lips to the side and nodded. "Why risk the loss of your benefactor—"

"Affiliate," Sebastian corrected her.

"—affiliate cairn when you could just cut him loose and hope he crashes and burns?"

"The only problem would be if he failed but then used that face and his charm to get another job," Sebastian told Nessa, pacing. "That would be annoying. He could take that information to anyone."

"Like us?" she replied.

"Maybe not us, no. Nikken is probably really annoyed about their secrets being stolen. We wouldn't risk striking up animosity with them so early in the game. But…someone else, maybe…"

"Who in their right mind would *touch* him with that kind of track record?" Niamh asked, playing up her disgust. "Not a hope. The second people know what he's really about, he won't get a job anywhere."

"Well, what if he finds someone to smooth out his operation?" I asked. All of this for show, carefully rehearsed at the last minute. We wanted it on record.

"But what sort of affiliation could he get?" Niamh asked. "None. He's done. Sure, he's basically admitted that all the rumors are true."

"Who cares about rumors?" Pierce sat back, stubborn to the last. "That's just bored garhettes chattering. It doesn't mean anything. No one listens to it."

"They *were* just rumors." Nessa's smile stretched

wide. "It was surprisingly hard to connect the dots. No one had quite pieced it together until our pal Niamh here had our associate ask the right questions to the right people. This is the first time the story has been told in its entirety, and you've confirmed every aspect."

He stared at Nessa with a slack face. "What do you want? Do you want the information? I can give it to you. I—"

"No, no." I held up my hand, standing. "We already have it. You scanned all the documents and uploaded them to the cloud. Turns out, our hackers are better than your security team. We've gone ahead and downloaded all that…and then corrupted the files for you. You're welcome. I hope you have a good memory."

"No!" Pierce shot up to standing.

Austin clamped a hand onto his shoulder and slammed him back down into his seat.

"No! You can't do that," Pierce wailed. "I need those files. We don't have the process perfected yet."

"You'll have to ask Nikken for them," I said, tipping my head to study him. "They'll be going into their care package for when they arrive, along with a record of this meeting. Edited, of course. It's always nice to start a new friendship with the other party owing you a favor. As for your employment, we'll make sure everyone knows what you did, don't you worry. No one will want to touch you. And why would they? You no longer know anything. Enjoy your new Dick life. It's not so bad. I should know, after all."

Austin reached down and grabbed him. Broken Sue strutted to his other side, and they literally carried him out. Pierce kicked and screamed the whole way, turning back to beg forgiveness and ask for leniency.

I stared at nothing for a moment in the aftermath.

"That was, like, incredibly easy." I frowned at the others. "You ruin lives as easily as that? Just—here's some info, good luck creating your own witness protection setup!"

"Easy? Do ye *hear* her?" Niamh groused. "Do ye know how long it took me to get to the bottom of all that? And then I had to get that chatterbox Patty to plant the right seeds. She had to go to some people two or three times. It was absolute bollocks. Easy? *Pffft.*"

"We don't ruin lives, Jessie," Sebastian said seriously. "We expose people's bad deeds. They ruin themselves—they just sometimes need a bullhorn to complete the work."

I sat down again, tired. "Fine. Well, that's him out of our hair, and also payback for being a dick. Let's eat. I'm starving."

From the side, Anthott slowly raised his hand. "If you've found something on me, can I just confess? I don't think I have the nerve for your teamwork interrogation process."

Laughter burst out of me, unbidden. "It's fine, Anthott. Sorry about that. He had it coming."

Nessa helped him up again and brought him back over. Sebastian re-dressed the table.

"You mentioned blood…" Anthott checked the table before the tablecloth glided over it.

"Sometimes words create a scarier picture than physical violence." Nessa patted him and moved away. "Why didn't you bring any guardians, by the way?"

Anthott straightened the settings in front of him. "I don't have any."

She furrowed her brow. "Your database lists them, though. It says that you have some, I mean."

He craned his neck to look up at her in surprise. "That is a breach of privacy."

"Yup."

"Did you look in on all the cairns, or just the production cairns?"

"All the cairns. We have more information than you would believe, my friend. We know some secrets the big dogs will wish we didn't. Think of this as Dick politics—when you run for office, you open up your closets and show off your skeletons. You're pretty clean, though, except for the guardian discrepancy."

He went back to facing front. "I'm not sure what to think."

"You have time to figure it out. About those guardians..."

"I chose my current location because it had housed a small production cairn that couldn't attract an affiliation. The premises had been abandoned after the cairn dissolved. Or so I'd heard. It turned out a few of the old-timer guardians still existed there, so I put them on the books at first to allow them to retain their home. One by one, they left or gave up the job. Instead of bringing in others, I chose to spend the money on craftsmen instead. I never got around to updating the logs because I don't need them. We're running at a loss right now, trying to come up with our designs and business plan and sending expensive samples to affiliates."

"You're not worried about raids?" I asked.

He huffed out a laugh. "If you saw the mountain where we live, you'd understand why I laugh. It provides its own defenses, and when it fails, the elements gladly pick up the slack. It's not a nice place to live, which is why we have very few garhettes. They won't tolerate it. When we get enough money together, we can look for more permanent lodging."

Nessa gave me a pointed look, patted him on the

shoulder, and stepped away. It was like he was hand-tailored for our setup. The question was, would Austin bite? Was this guy good enough?

As the dining room was set to rights, Anthott picked at his nail and mumbled, "I would've liked to look over those documents. Just for curiosity's sake. I always like to improve on my craft when I can."

"Would ye *schtop*?" Niamh shook her head at him. "We have the notes, like. Ye didn't think we'd go through all that trouble and give away the only copy?" She rolled her eyes. "If ye work for Jessie and Austin Steele, ye'll get'ta pore over the information to your heart's content."

"Then why give Nikken a copy?" he asked.

Niamh winked at him. "Knowin' a secret is no fun unless other people *know* you know that secret. Let the games begin."

CHAPTER 17

SEBASTIAN

"GIVE ME GOOD news, Captain," Sebastian said as he took a much needed and very long walk through the fields around O'Briens.

His nerves were shot. Shot, mangled, and then left for dead. He knew he was doing the right thing by calling in an attack, and he felt certain this was the best way to propel the situation forward, but the guilt was starting to eat a hole through his gut.

He'd thrown attacks at her before, yes, but he'd had his sister's visions as his guide. Plus, he hadn't known her then. He hadn't gotten so close to her. This time he was going at it alone, and he was scared something would go wrong.

Because the truth of it was, ten mages *were* a lot. If the gargoyles didn't join their cause, quite possibly ten was too many. He was taking a risk, and Jessie and her people would be in the balance. If they lost even one of their pack, he knew the alphas would feel the loss. He didn't want to be responsible for that, not to mention he feared what Austin Steele would do to him if he found out.

"I've got good news and bad news," Nessa said.

"Good news first."

"Though it wasn't easy to wrangle, all mages are on board. Mercenaries have been secured, as well."

"Okay. Bad news?"

"They are located all over the place, and getting them grouped together and then brought here is incredibly messy with the limited time frame."

"You can't group them closer to here and just have them drive a larger distance in?"

"That would increase the time they'd be in dark mode, because I wouldn't want them too close. I'd worry a shifter who is traveling might see them or Austin has friends we didn't know about, or some other contingent I didn't have time to assess. It's too risky. We need them in the area as briefly as possible before they are en route to attack."

"True. Good point. I should've known you'd thought of that."

"Because of all that, though, I'm concerned about timing and nervous it won't be easy to call them off. It's like herding cats. It would be easy to get delayed, as well. I'm also concerned about the paper trail I'm leaving. I don't have the time to be as clean as I'd like."

Sebastian let out a breath, stopping and staring at a field with ambling cows. Nessa was incredible at her job. He would never be able to maintain Elliot Graves without her. For her to sound this stressed meant things weren't going smoothly. If he hadn't felt the rightness of the outcome in his very bones, he would call the whole thing off right now.

"The timing issue is definitely not ideal," he said. "The paper trail shouldn't be an issue, though. It'll just show that Elliot Graves's people were sent in to attack Jessie. We don't care if people know that."

"Unless that Irishwoman goes sniffing around."

"She's too busy with the gargoyles. We're good. We just need to pay attention to that timing issue. We need to be able to stop the attack if needed."

"I know. I'm on it."

"Ideally, how long do we need to keep the big cairn leaders here?"

"You mean how long do we have before Austin Steele pulls all their heads off?" He could hear the humor in her voice. "At present, we'll need them to stay for *at least* a week and a half to hit the projected date, and longer still if we hit delays. That wouldn't be too hard if we weren't amping up their aggression with those gifts, and if we didn't already see an example of how she might be treated. Keeping Jessie and Austin in check might be the hardest part of this situation."

He paused for a moment, assessing. "We might need to pull back a little with the gift boxes. Maybe not amp up their tension so much out of the gate. Gimerel especially. That cairn seems to be the mightiest in terms of social influence, mostly thanks to their lead enforcer. Maybe if we avoid offending the Gimerel leader, the others will mind their manners a bit longer. It'll be easy to throw a wrench in their moods if things go too smoothly."

"Probably a good idea. If any of them treat her like Pierce did, this situation will go pear-shaped in a hurry. It's a lot more precarious than I like to plan. We have a lot less control than I'm comfortable with."

"I hear you loud and clear, Captain. We're on track so far. We just need to keep Jessie and Austin from exploding."

"Easier said than done."

Wasn't that the truth.

CHAPTER 18

JESSIE

A DAY BEFORE the cairn leaders were due for dinner, I was doing everything in my power not to let nerves overcome me. I sat in the TV room with a sandwich, butterflies swarming in my stomach and my gaze continually straying to my phone.

The leaders would be arriving today. Their guardians had scouted the area and secured lodgings, and they would be settling in for the foreseeable future, dependent on me and my crew to keep them entertained while we got to know each other.

They'd also get their gift boxes.

I swallowed nervously as Naomi walked around the room, surveying everything.

I still wasn't sure about those gift boxes. The actual gifts were lovely, of course, but some of them sent very pointed messages. These people were hiding secrets. Dark secrets, some of them. Gross and terrible.

The Dark Three had all agreed this was necessary. Even Austin had given their plan the go-ahead. The cairns needed to know I was a power player right off the bat. This would show them that I wasn't afraid to dig for dirt, my crew was capable of finding it, and also that I could keep secrets. I was showing them I could play the game better than any of them. Or so I'd been assured.

"Jessie?" Naomi stood with her eyebrows raised. I vaguely recalled hearing a question about the blanket she'd just artfully draped across the new couch like we were preparing for a magazine shoot.

"That looks great, but when my dad comes, it won't work," I told her as I finished my sandwich.

She put her hands on her hips. "Why not?"

"Sorry, let me rephrase." I held up a hand. "It'll work as a blanket for warmth but not as a fart blanket."

She stared at me silently for a long moment. I'd come to realize that could mean a handful of things, most notably that she was irritated, full-out angry, or didn't understand.

I figured it was the last one. My dad's fart blanket mystified the brightest of people.

"He sits on a blanket to keep from getting too hot and sticking to the leather," I explained as someone I didn't know stepped onto the walkway leading up to Ivy House. "He has a flatulence problem, kind of like the basajaunak after too many magical flowers. The blanket collects—"

"Say no more." Naomi raised her hand. "Please, say no more." She shook her head, grumbling under her breath. "Fine, I'll get a trashy butt blanket for when he comes. We can store it in the linen closet. I'll ensure it matches the couch so it's not so offensive."

"It would have to be a soundproof blanket for it not to be offensive, but yes, that'll work."

I crumpled the napkin as I stepped out into the hall, feeling Mr. Tom coming down the stairs to see who was nearly at the door.

Oh God, what if it was one of their guardians saying the gift boxes had been too much and they were pulling out? Or a guardian wanting…something else. I'd seen some large gargoyles downtown lately, guardians potentially interested in a job, but I hadn't met anyone affiliated with the top four cairns. I had no idea what to expect.

The doorbell rang, an eerie series of gongs that had Naomi stepping out of the room behind me.

"What in the world is that?" she asked, looking around at the walls. "That can't be the doorbell. Can it? Is that the doorbell and no one thought to tell me?"

I frowned at her as Mr. Tom glanced back. "Didn't you ring the bell when you first came?"

"No. I never got the chance." She started forward. "Well, that'll have to go. You can't have a beautiful interior, like this is shaping up to be, with a gong bell! Disgraceful."

"It still matches the exterior." I shrugged. "It'll give it a little authenticity until we paint."

"What is all this commotion?" Patty asked from the top of the stairs, Nessa's electronic notepad in hand. Her reading glasses were perched on the end of her nose. "It sounds like we're preparing for a raid."

Without another word, Naomi removed herself to the back of the house and her makeshift office. She was still a little offended that Patty had tried to hug her.

Mr. Tom opened the door, straightening his back and lifting his chin.

"You rang?" he said, and I was pretty sure he didn't realize he was mimicking Lurch from the Addams Family.

"I want a word with the female," a gruff voice said, the arrogance of the speaker evident in his tone.

"*The female?*" Ivy House said, clearly annoyed and borderline angry.

"May I ask who is calling and what this is in reference to?" Mr. Tom asked, his wings fluttering.

"I've got it, Mr. Tom," I said, putting my hand on his arm.

"Well now, Jessie…" Patty started down the stairs.

"Of course, miss." Mr. Tom stepped out of the way.

A man in his late sixties stood at the top of the steps, his gray hair parted down the middle and his big frame a relic of the power and strength he'd once possessed. Wrinkles now heavily lined his face and drooped at the corners of his hard brown eyes. He wore a navy blazer buttoned over a white dress shirt without a tie, and navy slacks that ended at brown suede shoes.

I recognized his face from the studying I'd done. Withor, leader of the Nikken cairn, a little older than the picture I'd been given.

Behind him, parked by the curb, waited an empty sporty Mercedes. No guardians stood beside it or seemed to have accompanied him here. I didn't feel anyone in the air above Ivy House and couldn't see anyone in the blue sky over the street. He appeared to be alone.

I was almost positive I knew what this was regarding.

"Can I help you?" I asked evenly, stepping just outside the door.

He surveyed me for a moment, his gaze taking in my face, hair, and then my jeans and plain T-shirt.

"You're the female gargoyle, correct?" he asked as Patty joined Mr. Tom behind me.

"Yes. And you're the leader of Nikken." I stepped forward and put out my hand. "Jessie Ironheart."

He looked at my hand but made no move to shake it. I'd been told he was a hand shaker or occasionally a fist bumper. Apparently not with me.

"Ironheart is the name given to you by the shifters," he said, his wings fluttering in obvious disapproval. "It has no relevance here."

It took everything I had not to allow my eyebrows to drift up to my hairline.

"*Who in the hell does he think he is talking to?*" Ivy House said, and I could feel her deep well of power start to rise. "*You are his queen. He should be bowing to you, not condescending about your choice of name. The Ivy House heirs were ruling his kind long before his cairn was even established. Teach him a lesson!*"

I took a deep breath, trying for calm. Even still, a blast of magic rocked the front porch, my annoyance teaming with Ivy House's anger.

He tensed, and his eyes slowly narrowed.

"I am going to excuse that lapse in judgment," I told him. "I will warn you, however, that you'd be wise not to tell me what does and does not have relevance while standing on my property and within my territory." I paused for a moment and pretended not to notice the sky darkening around Ivy House. She was not so eager to excuse his lapse in judgment. "Checking the calendar might also be wise, since you are a day early for the welcome dinner. What is it you want, Withor?"

"You may call me master or lord. My given name is reserved for equals, of which I cannot imagine you will ever be."

The house rumbled, as though from a small earthquake. I'd probably need to get this guy out of here before Ivy House took matters into her own hands. As it was, I was still trying desperately to keep my eyebrows out of my hairline.

Act with decorum, I told myself. *Act with decorum!*

"What can I do for you, *bub*?"

I couldn't help myself.

Anger heated his eyes, and his expression turned to granite. His wings fluttered, though, indicating he was not as self-controlled as a shifter would be.

"I got your package," he said curtly. "Enlightening."

I shivered. He'd gotten the information about Pierce, but also a little surprise hinting that we knew an enormous secret he was keeping from the world.

"Was it?" I arched an eyebrow. "I expected you to have a better grasp on what goes on in your territory, home, and with your affiliates."

Now his eyebrows lowered and one of his fists clenched. "How did you acquire that information?"

"By doing my due diligence. You know something about that, don't you? I noticed the two woods used in the sculpture you sent me. They nearly matched the inner construction of my house. Very clever."

He held out a paper bag. When I didn't reach out to take it, he shook it at me, stepping forward to push it into my chest.

Without moving, I threw up a magical blockade. His knuckles hit off the spell, and sparks flew. He let out a yelp, jerking his arm back to cradle it against his chest. Apparently he was not fond of electrical charges. Baby.

I tsked at him, so incredibly in control of this situation that I surprised myself.

"No touching," I said. "If you have something to show me, you may take it out of the bag and hold it up."

Shaking with fury, he threw the bag onto the ground. I could hear the baby rattle inside.

"Is this blackmail?" he demanded. "Because you won't be hurting me if you bring this information to light. You'd be hurting my family."

"*I* wouldn't be hurting anyone," I replied, my resolve hardening. "The honorable thing to do would be to tell your family, not to mention your cairn. I can't imagine any of them would like to hear about your mistress. Sure, you're not the only cheater, but messing around while your mate is sick? Telling your mistress she'll take your mate's place once she dies? Of course, we both know you'd never let that happen. She's got almost no status and not a lot of world experience."

I paused for a moment, allowing the beat of silence to stretch. The worst was yet to come, and we both knew it.

"You wanted to get an heir from her, and you did. If your mate had succumbed to that nasty bout of pneumonia, you could have run with your plan and told everyone your mistress was a surrogate. That you and your mate had made the arrangements together. But she *didn't* die. And now you're not sure what to do, because your mate would never have agreed to the arrangement. Especially since you gave that surrogate a child the old-fashioned way."

"What do you know about any of this?" He pushed closer to me, anger lining every inch of his face. His eyes raked the air in front of me; he knew I was protected. Knew he couldn't do whatever he was envisioning.

"I know you're screwed," I said, ripping the magic away and closing the distance. I poked the center of his chest, and he took a step away from my heated rage. "You got the timing all wrong, and now you have a baby you can't use. You have a mistress *you are still banging* who'll talk if you turn your back on her. Your cairn's status hangs in the balance, because these are certainly not the actions of a *stable* leader. You're not a very good one, either, anymore. Your worsening management is dropping the cairn's overall profitability. In other words, you've slacked off, Withor, and instead of replacing yourself, you kept pushing forward. Now you've got a real clusterfuck on your hands."

I kicked the paper bag, making it fly off the porch. The rattle broke free and smashed against the concrete, breaking in half.

He studied me for a long time. I held his gaze, daring him to get aggressive. Daring him to try to push me or punch me or fling me as I could tell he wanted to. Unlike the shifters I was accustomed to, he broadcast every thought that flashed through his head.

He must've known I was ready to fight, though. He must've suspected I would blast him across the yard. He held his position, not even bending forward over me.

"What do you want?" he finally said. "What is it going to take for your silence on this matter? You need guardians, is that it? You're trying to establish a cairn with a bunch of shifters, so you must need guardians."

When I didn't speak, he tried again.

"You want more direction on that textile information, then." His eyes pinged back and forth between mine. "You obviously have the notes my production cairn let slip, but you don't have the people to make sense of them. Fine. I can put you in contact with that cairn."

I had no idea where it came from, but I felt a smile bud. And then stretch. I knew the sentiment didn't reach my eyes.

I let the words come slowly.

"You think my silence can be bought?" I shook my head. "I'll tell you what. You keep those guardians. Send them to your production cairns and batten down your hatches, because I am going to show up with my shifters and take or destroy everything you own. They'll beg me to take their affiliation when I'm done just so they can have their equipment back. You think plenty of warning is enough to defend against me in a raid? Think again. I'll crack your whole world wide open and show you how your name fits your personality, *Withor*. Now get off my property before I lose my temper and make you call me ma'am."

He didn't budge for a moment, staring me down. Slowly, though, as if it greatly pained him, he took a step back. Then he turned, fists tight, and took the two steps down to the walkway.

"Who will you tell?" he asked stoically, not looking back.

"You will send the woman and the child to me," I told him. "I'll ensure they are looked after. I don't want her to have a fatal *accident*, since I know how those *accidents* tend to happen under your leadership. I won't allow the child to become an orphan. If you do that, I won't let this information slip. However, leave here knowing that I have a lot of proof that would call your leadership into question. If you're thinking of setting up a smear campaign against me, you'd better think again. You're outgunned in every way. I'm more than happy to prove it, but I doubt you'd want me to. Do we understand each other?"

Once again, he didn't speak for a long moment. His body stayed tense. Finally, though, he cracked his neck and started forward.

"Understood." He climbed into his Mercedes before screeching away.

I let out a shaky breath, adrenaline coursing through me. The door opened behind me. Patty and Mr. Tom were still standing there. They'd clearly been listening through the door.

"So…that didn't go very well," I said softly, turning toward them.

"For him, no it did not," Mr. Tom said stiffly. "Calling him master—as if you would ever!" His wings fluttered. "No, miss, that would be preposterous. How *dare* he!"

"You hear some stories," Patty said, "and you think

to yourself, *That can't be true. No one is that evil and ruthless. Not to mention that dense!*" She shook her head and tsked. "He didn't even bother denying it. I can't believe it."

"Maybe that gift basket thing was a mistake," I murmured, heading into the kitchen. I needed some chocolate.

"You heard how he addressed you," Patty said, following me closely. "I hate to say it, but he wasn't ever going to be your biggest fan." She shook her head when we reached the island. "I have no idea why. He didn't know anything about you. He still doesn't."

"He knows I'm in league with shifters," I said, breaking off a square of Godiva from a bar on the counter. "And he hinted that I should have guardians to form a cairn, which I technically don't if Nathanial and Ulric and the others don't count. I don't have the set up to impress him."

"Hmm." Patty broke off a square as well. "Unfortunately, that is probably true. But! He's always been a curmudgeonly sort of leader. I think I must've mentioned that before, haven't I? I'm sure I have. And he had the worst secret out of all of them. Being exposed would make anyone grumpy. We still have hope with the others. They'll be in better moods, I'm sure. There are still three more. You only need one to like you! Just one!"

I sat down at the island as I felt Austin heading my way. He'd been downtown, probably in the bar, so it wouldn't take him long.

"All things considered, I think you handled that beautifully," Patty said, taking out her phone and laying it on the island. "Just like a female gargoyle should've." She set her hands on the island. "I just cannot believe his leadership is sprinkled with so many dirty deeds. I mean the"—she did bunny ears with her fingers—"'accidental deaths' used to happen more back in the day, but that practice has gone out of favor. Hard to put faith in a leader who kills off anyone who disagrees. It's not the epitome of stable, I'll say that much."

Mr. Tom put some lemonade in front of me. "A little sugar will help with the come-down of adrenaline."

Patty tsked and shook her head. Then threw up her hands. "Well, I have to tell someone *something*! I can't just not say anything about all of this. He's too good at keeping secrets. The community has a right to know."

I knew she was just blustering. We couldn't say anything, not until he made a move against me. For now, it was enough that I could help his mistress and her baby.

After a deep breath, I sipped a little lemonade. "This really was a terrible start to the big meeting. What if they all go like that?"

"They won't. Definitely not." Patty leaned over and put her hand on my forearm as Austin walked toward the door. "It'll work out, you'll see."

Austin's heavy footsteps echoed over the freshly polished wood floor. He turned the corner into the kitchen with an air of ruthless power. His gaze traveled my face as he closed the distance between us, and then he put his hand on my shoulder to lean me back so he could glance down my body.

"I heard one of the leaders left this house incensed." He smoothed his hand down my back. "I felt your anger through the bond. Did he touch you?" he growled.

"No, it's fine. I'm fine."

"He tried," said Mr. Tom, the tattletale. The last thing I needed was Austin keyed up about my safety. That sort of thing would turn a very rational alpha into an utter nightmare.

"It was Withor from Nikken. He just went to give me back the rattle," I quickly replied. "Speaking of which, Mr. Tom, go throw that horrible thing away. It hurts my heart to even think about it. Poor child. How disgusting is that leader?"

"Dis-*gust*ing." Patty turned her nose up. "I am absolutely appalled. How has he been allowed to maintain his post? What are we, in the Dark Ages?" She slammed her fist onto the counter. "This is an outrage, and I can't tell anyone! What am I going to do? I can tell Ulric. I can at least tell him. And Nathanial. Nathanial won't like this one bit. He looks up to all those leaders, but he won't look up to this one anymore. I can at least do that much. *Someone* has to know."

She stomped from the room.

"He thought I was trying to blackmail him, and he offered me guardians," I told Austin as he moved around me and lowered into the seat to my right.

"Like he'd offer them to a production cairn?" Austin asked.

I hadn't thought about it that way. "Yeah, I guess so. It didn't sound like he was planning to hand them over, free and clear. Then again, I didn't ask for more information. I just threatened to raid all his production cairns and destroy his business."

"Hmm." Austin lifted his eyebrows at me. "That's one way to go about it, I suppose. It would save us from buying some of the equipment we need."

"As well we should," Mr. Tom said, placing a glass of water in front of Austin. "I would offer you lemonade, sir, but you really do eat too much sugar. We need to cut back on that. Water will be fine for you."

Austin looked at Mr. Tom like he'd grown a third eye before shaking his head and leaning back.

"You did the right thing, Jess," he told me. "A leader

who's made that many questionable decisions is on a path to implode. I've seen it in the shifter world. The Dick world, too. If you ask me, his age is starting to grate on him. Without children to carry on his line, he's looking in the face of mortality. He'd have enough money to comfortably sustain himself after he steps down, but I'm betting he doesn't want to relinquish power."

"What does that have to do with his lack of an heir, though? Wouldn't he be in a similar situation if he had one?

"When an alpha's child succeeds him or her, there is an element of pride. The alpha isn't stepping down so much as passing on the torch. The business stays in the family, as it were. I assume the sentiment is the same for Withor. He's worried about losing his grip on the cairn and he's starting to get desperate to secure his interests. Maybe it's past time for him to step down, and he is doing anything he can to stay in the game. That would certainly explain some of his rash actions."

"So…" I tucked a strand of hair behind my ear. "That's not good, though. He has a big cairn. That's a lot of people depending on his leadership."

"It's a great thing, babe." He put his hand on my leg. "I've heard Nathanial mention that cairns that undergo a change in leadership are given plenty of time to find their way. No one kicks them when they're down. They all kinda regulate each other, it sounds like. It'll give someone else the chance to keep the cairn in high status, and maybe that someone will look a little more favorably on you."

Silver lining.

"In the meantime..." Austin picked up my half-finished lemonade and took a sip.

"Cheating on your diet is only cheating yourself," Mr. Tom intoned.

"He's a grown man, Mr. Tom," I said. "He doesn't need you to restrict sugar from his diet."

Mr. Tom sniffed. "Tell that to his evening mood swings."

Austin finished the lemonade and set the empty glass down in front of him. "In the meantime," he said again as he stared pointedly at Mr. Tom, "some of his guardians might look elsewhere for placement. Granted, most of them will probably hang on to see what happens, but we're presenting them with a different option—with a situation where they'd see a lot of action and excellent leadership. We might entice a few this way. Maybe Patty should be allowed to gossip."

I frowned at him as Naomi walked into the kitchen with a few cloth place mats in hand.

"What happened to you not wanting to bother with

the gargoyles?" I asked him as she stopped and stared at me. That meant she wanted something.

"That was before I realized the rank-and-file guardians are actually pretty easy to manage. They aren't like the lead enforcers or stray gargoyles we've had in town. In fact, they are taking an active interest in how I've structured our defenses. I get the feeling their operations aren't as organized."

"I mean…they are a battle species," I replied. "It's right up their alley to be interested in your fighting approach."

"I think you mean *we* are a battle species, miss," Mr. Tom said. "Now, you'd better acknowledge Naomi or she will stare holes right through you."

"I am capable of waiting for my turn to speak, Mr. Tom, or didn't you notice my silence?" Naomi told him. "And of course the guardians settle down quickly. They are watching one of the best alphas in the world. They can't get this sort of battle training with those stuffy old gargoyles. Present company not excluded. Anyway, Austin, Jessie, what do you think about this for the table settings tomorrow?"

CHAPTER 19

JESSIE

A JET OF magic seared through the sky, right for me. Sebastian had joined our training today, and he wasn't pulling any punches.

Nathanial grabbed me around the middle and tilted wildly, tearing me from a forward trajectory and careening us both haphazardly toward the ground. I let him, closing my eyes to finish the spell I was working on, and then opened them again to find the direction of the ground. He leveled out, nice and low, and I let the spell fly.

Sebastian didn't have the ability to counter. Not with how close I'd released the spell and its complexity and strength. He dove out of the way, leaving him vulnerable.

"Ta-ake him!" Nathanial yelled out.

Cyra dropped forward immediately, opening her mouth for a fire attack. Sebastian rolled, knowing he wouldn't get any time to flail. Not with my team. He shot a spell at her, prompting her to dodge away. Ulric and Jasper dove with her, sweeping apart when he spread his hands and then targeting him as soon as his spell shot between them.

They should've known better.

It ballooned out and then condensed, knocking them together and tying up their wings. They started to fall, slowly at first and then like stones, straight for the ground.

Nathanial threw me in their direction. I snapped my wings quickly to stop from tumbling and then hit the gargoyles with a counter-spell. Mr. Tom flew in to grab them and give my spell time to work. Hollace soared overhead, raining down lightning.

Sebastian threw up a protection spell, but it took a hit and fizzled immediately. I could hear him swear from below.

I helped him, keeping Hollace from accidentally giving Sebastian more than he could handle, while also throwing a spell Nessa's way to keep her hidden in the bushes.

Ulric and Jasper snapped out their wings, freed, and Mr. Tom dived down toward Sebastian. Niamh followed right behind. When Sebastian shot off a spell at Mr. Tom, sending him careening, she was right there, smashing down onto the dirt. Her hooves hit beside his body and then she was up again, showing off all the ways she could kill him—hooves, stabby horn, whatever.

Breathing hard, Sebastian just lay there for a moment with his eyes closed.

"Get me in the air," he finally said, climbing to his feet. "Get me up in the air, and let's see if I can get at Jessie that way."

Ulric dove down to grab Sebastian. Meanwhile, Jasper had gotten hold of Nessa, pulling her out of the bushes.

"Whoa, whoa, I didn't sign up for aerial combat," she hollered as they rose into the sky.

"Come on, Captain," Sebastian called to her. "It has to be better than being trampled to death by a nightmare alicorn."

"I wasn't the one in that predicament. I was hiding safely in the bushes. Crap! Please don't drop me, Jasper."

"*Do you know that gargoyle who has wandered onto the property to watch you train?*" Ivy House asked me.

I didn't get a chance to look, as Ulric flew Sebastian quickly toward me.

"*Who? I've been a little busy,*" I thought as Sebastian fired off three spells that I was hard-pressed to handle.

"Don't counter those," Sebastian yelled at me as Nessa fired off a spell at Niamh, who was bearing down on them. It was now a little confusing as to who was on whose team. "Deflect them."

I spared a moment to clue into Ivy House property, feeling the person standing below us, immobile, on the back lawn. Dave also blipped onto my radar, traveling with a bunch of others, all making good time through the wood and toward the house.

"*Why didn't you stop him or let me know sooner?*" I asked as Ulric thundered toward me and Sebastian fired off more spells.

"Mo-*uve*," I garbled out to Nathanial, pitching my body to get the point across.

He understood immediately, but instead of quickly tilting right to get out of the way of those spells, he threw me left and he went right. The spells sailed uselessly between us as he doubled back around to get behind the mages.

I darted farther in the direction I was heading before twisting in the air. The wind went out of my wings, and I started to fall, but I fired a few spells off as I did so.

"Get out of the way!" Sebastian yelled as Ulric dipped down. A portion of one of my spells raked across Ulric's backside. He threw Sebastian into the air.

"Motherfu—"

Sebastian rushed to work the spell to catch himself as Nathanial attacked Ulric, throwing him farther away. Nathanial dipped down to them and grabbed Sebastian to keep the mage from eventually going splat.

"Is he attacking or saving?" Nessa hollered, firing off a spell regardless. "Am I hurting or helping?"

I caught altitude and zipped a spell at her, forcing Jasper to steer off course to get out of the way.

Nathanial let her return spell hit him, and it sliced a gash into his tough gargoyle hide. With Sebastian in his grips, he shot up into the sky.

Jasper, who had Nessa, was on the chase immediately, trying to catch the stronger and faster Nathanial. The mages were reduced to screaming, and I figured that was about it for the day.

"*Hello?*" Ivy House said.

"*What?*" I asked her, seeing the basajaunak moving fast though the trees. Dave was in the lead, heading straight for the trespasser. He had eight or nine others with him, two of whom I recognized as the ones who'd initially shown up with him.

"*I* said..." she started, and from her surly tone, she clearly thought I'd been ignoring her rather than in the middle of an intensive training session. "*I can feel his power. He's got a lot of it. I'd be a fool to turn away a gargoyle of his magnitude. If something happens to the bear, this would be the perfect replacement. Actually, maybe the bear would agree to bringing this gargoyle into your relationship. That way we wouldn't have to choose, and you'd get to have twice as much fun…"*

I ignored her, stalling a little as Dave and the basajaunak broke the tree line, bearing down on the stranger.

The stranger saw the basajaunak and took a large step back, lifting his hands immediately. I could hear their combined growling from here, see their hair all bristled and their arms puffing out to the sides. That oughta make the strangers' bowels a little watery.

As the basajaunak circled the stranger, I sent up a plume of magic that would shower the trees in color. That meant the end of our practice session. Lowering to the ground, I shifted and then snatched up my house sweats. Those on, I tied up my hair as I threaded through the flowers.

"I'm here to see the mistress of the house," the stranger said, his voice cool and calm but tight. He wasn't completely hiding his nervousness.

"That's me." I reached the first basandere and put my hand on her arm.

She stepped out of the way, smiling down at me. "Hello, Jessie, good to see you again. Beautiful wood."

"Thanks," I said, not exactly sure who she was. "You're welcome to visit anytime."

"Thank you." She beamed at me. "When on your grounds, I'll protect it as my own."

"Oh, great. Yeah, thanks," I said, realizing I'd just made a deal and chastising myself to be more careful in the future. Thankfully, it was a good one.

The gargoyle's black wings dropped down nearly to his heels—no small feat, given his incredible height of six foot eight or nine. His large shoulders and broad chest suggested he'd earned his strength in flight or fighting. He wore a black blazer and black slacks with a black dress shirt and tie to go with it. His wavy hair lightly curled around his ears. He wasn't Pierce's caliber in the looks department—not many were—but he was no slouch, with a strong chin and high cheekbones.

It was his eyes that made him stand out. They looked almost like glowing embers. His face seemed vaguely familiar, but I couldn't place him from the pictures I'd studied.

"Hello," I said, wiping the sweat off my face. "Can I help you?"

He surveyed me for a long moment as the mages continued to yell above us.

"Shall I shake the words out of him?" Dave asked, and two of the basajaunak must've thought that was a great idea because they stepped forward to help.

The gargoyle raised his hands a little higher. "As a security measure, I had hoped to scout the location for tonight's dinner. I knocked on the door, but no one answered."

"When no one answered, you decided you might as well go on a little trespassing expedition?" I braced my hands on my hips as I caught my breath.

"I heard shouting and decided to trespass enough to check it out, yes." He shook his head at me, his stare so intense it could rival Naomi's. "Your gargoyle form is…unlike anything I have ever seen. Stories don't do the female gargoyle justice."

"Yeah. What I lack in the wings department, I make up for in the sparkly glamour area. What access did you need? The house? The yard?"

A smile flitted across his features. "Your magic is powerful."

"Yes, I got it from the house."

"I heard. Forgive me; I'm struggling to process everything. Do you practice like this all the time? It looked like you were in a life-or-death situation."

"We practice in a way that'll hopefully help us in battle. Have you battled much…?"

"Tristan."

Ah. He was the lead enforcer for Gimerel.

"Have you battled much, Tristan? Where the enemy had more resources than you and their sole purpose was to kill you?"

"They did not intend to kill you last time, miss," Dave said. "They planned to kill *us*. You, they planned to kidnap and torture."

I blinked up at Tristan slowly. "Yes, Dave, thanks for refreshing my memory."

A little line formed between Tristan's eyebrows. His eyes seemed to burn, the glowing intensifying. I stood strangely transfixed, practically *feeling* the humor and fascination emanating from him.

"You expect more battles?" Tristan asked.

"Yes. Always." My fatigue got the better of me. "Now, if you'll excuse me, I need to start preparing for dinner. Mr. Tom will be down shortly—I think he's hanging on to make sure the mages don't die—and then he can show you whatever you'd like."

He still had his hands raised in the sky as I walked around him and toward the house. At any other time I might have laughed, but today I just couldn't find the humor. Sebastian had been a problem in this training, and he was only one mage. We'd taken far too long in bringing him down. Momar would be bringing in many more mages to act against Kingsley. We had to do better.

"Miss Jessie, I would like to speak with you," Dave said, his one stride matching two of mine.

I slowed and stopped again, squinting into the sun. "Sure, what's up?"

The yelling above stopped, the gargoyles apparently having decided the mages had had enough.

Dave smiled down at me, his heavy mustache splitting to reveal his large teeth. "I wondered if you would allow your wood to play host to more of the basajaunak? I have offered my mountain, but now that the gargoyles are here, I would like to stay closer. That means they would like to stay closer, as well."

"Sure, Dave, that's fine. You'll just need to work out with Edgar which flowers can be eaten when."

"Yes, Miss Jessie, I figured as much. *Her* will be in charge here, since she has been given the task of waking up the woods. The visiting basajaunak will respect her and the environment—I hope you know that."

"Yeah, it's totally fine. No problem—"

"And in repayment of your hospitality, they will help protect you and the wood." He lowered his volume a little. "I think they are eager to do it. We were already en route here when I felt the stranger's presence on Ivy House soil. Given you were all busy, I thought the situation needed my attention. They were quick to volunteer their help."

I smiled, patting his forearm. "That's really awesome, Dave. Thank you for hosting them until now. It means a lot."

"My pleasure, Miss Jessie." His smile broadened. "Shall I invite them to trail the gargoyle while he is outside? I do not like his curiosity."

"Sure, if you think they would want to and it wouldn't put me out too much in trade."

"No." He winked. "They will enjoy themselves, I think. The gargoyle behind you was trying not to show his wariness, and it was not working!" Dave started to laugh. "Did you see his face?" He laughed harder.

"Right. Okay." I stepped away a little. "Is that all, or…"

"Yes." He lowered his voice to a whisper. "I knew they would come. I knew they would."

I patted his arm again and this time offered a squeeze. "Okay. I need to head in."

"What are you doing here?" I heard, and turned to find Nessa stalking up to the gargoyle. Her hair was windblown, standing every which way, and her chest heaved with breathlessness.

A smile slowly spread across his face. "Beautiful Natasha. I didn't realize you'd be here. Were you up there singing your praises to the sky?"

Sebastian stopped beside her, his eyebrows lifting.

He shook his head and then shot a glowering look back at Nathanial. "I'm not sure what they were trying to prove, but they probably proved it."

Jasper spread his arms, his muumuu gathered in one of his hands. "Just proving my mage was better."

Nessa lifted her hand, and Jasper air high-fived it. Tristan laughed—a deep, joyful sound.

Nathanial also had his purple muumuu clenched in his fist, but his stare was on Tristan.

"Is this taken care of, miss?" he asked me.

"He wants to be shown around for security reasons. Mr. Tom can handle it unless you want to. I have to get ready."

Tristan met Nathanial's stare, his humor not failing.

"Mr. Tom is capable," Nathanial said before escorting me toward the house, pulling on his muumuu as we walked. "I was thinking about that bracelet, miss."

Gimerel was the cairn that had sent the bracelet for the connection request.

"What about it?" I asked as we entered through the back door.

"I don't think it was a gift. Given the way Pierce and Withor both treated you…and the fact that the Gimerel lead enforcer has been snooping around—I wonder if their plan all along was to get it into the house and then raid and take it back. They have a lot more guardians outside of territory lines than the other cairns. If they were to take back that bracelet, it would cement their claims of greatness."

"Firstly," I said as we climbed up the stairs, which Naomi had stripped of carpet before having the wood sanded and polished like the gleaming floors, "their guardians aren't supposed to come into the territory."

"Those rules don't apply in raids."

"They do in this territory, and we'll make them suffer for breaking them. Regardless, what would it say if they weren't able to take it back?"

He stopped as we reached my room. His grin spoke volumes.

"Wear it tonight," he said softly, confidence leaking into his voice. "I know they were going to have you wear a better-made, more expensive bracelet, but wear that one. Show it off...and then lay it down in one of the sitting rooms in plain view. They'll all know that for the challenge it is. *Come and get it.*"

CHAPTER 20

JESSIE

LATER THAT NIGHT, I had to cut out the house link to all my people so they weren't constantly inundated with my nerves. They ran through me like a living thing, shaking my limbs and quickening my breath.

I stared at myself in the mirror, checking over the silky cream dress with the plunging neckline and a slit up my right thigh. Sapphires surrounded in diamonds dripped down my chest in a fairly simple but incredibly expensive design that matched the cut of the dress. More swung from my earlobes. The multicolored Gimerel bracelet adorned my wrist.

I'd already had a run-in with one of the cairns, and now I was about to issue a challenge to another. I was really betting on aces. And this time we'd have that huge lead enforcer to answer to. If he was as good as he was big, he'd be a real problem in the air. A problem *I* would struggle to deal with, what with my small wings and slow maneuvers.

Thank God I had magic, or that whole thing would probably be over before it had begun.

"Right, okay," I whispered to myself, checking my hair and makeup. "Head in the game."

A car rolled up the driveway. It was too early for the dinner guests, so I was guessing my new wheels had arrived. Mr. Tom had chosen the perfect ride—he'd said so himself. He wouldn't tell me what it was, though. Or maybe he had, but he'd had too much caffeine for me to make sense of whatever he was babbling about. All I did know was that it was supposed to make the Porsche somehow seem inconsequential.

It would do nothing but sit in the driveway and look pretty tonight. I was the host. The leaders, along with two enforcers each, were coming to me.

Breathing out a nervous breath, trying to dislodge the butterflies filling my middle, I left the mirror and headed downstairs. Austin waited right at the bottom, turning toward me as I descended.

The breath left me in a gust of air, and I slowed and reached out to clutch the banister. He wore a crisp and tailored tuxedo, the jacket flat black with a wide and shiny lapel. A black bow tie matched the black buttons down the front of the cream dress shirt beneath. Draped around his neck was a black-and-cream-checkered silk scarf, giving the ensemble a little flair. A sparkling watch, a gift from Sebastian, encircled his wrist, and his hair was styled in that spiky, messy style I loved. The best thing, though, was the five o'clock shadow gracing his gorgeous face, making him look a little more rugged than those clothes might suggest. He looked fit and strong and powerful, but posh and sophisticated and incredibly handsome. Perfect.

He waited for me with a soft sparkle in his eyes, one hand at his side and one bent behind his back. I finished descending the stairs to meet him.

"My God, Jess, you look beautiful." He leaned in to kiss me softly on the cheek, probably so as to not disturb my lipstick.

"You do handsome look." I grimaced. "Those aren't the right words."

His smile took my breath away. His hand came around from behind him to present a fragrant bouquet of blue, yellow, and fire and ice roses. The blue and yellow were a running theme with us, matching the color of the wildflowers I'd chosen on our perfect date. Austin being Austin, he'd planted flowers of the same color outside of his home as a romantic gesture.

"Yellow roses mean friendship," he said, holding them between us. "It's how we built our bond, and I am so thankful for the rock-solid foundation it gave us. We are unshakable. You can always depend on me, and I know you will always be there for me." He paused to take my hand. "The blue symbolizes attaining the impossible, and that's what I've done with you. I have a love I never thought I'd find. A life I never thought I'd live. A woman I never in my wildest dreams thought I could deserve. In you, my hopes and dreams have become a reality."

My eyes teared up as I listened.

"The fire and ice roses have two meanings. The red is for passionate and undying love. A mating bond is supposed to cool after a time, but my love for you burns stronger now than ever. I don't think it'll ever cool. It certainly won't ever die. I will love you until the end of time, and I will fight for you until I take my last breath. The white means childlike purity and innocence, and that's how you entered the magical world. I've cherished staying by your side as you change and grow and reach for the stars. It's prompted me to be a better man. You've made me great, Jacinta. Without you, I never could've gotten this far. I thank you and I love you."

He handed them forward, and I took them with shaking hands. A tear tracked down my face.

"I love you," I whispered, moving forward to hug him. "That was beautiful."

"Not done yet," he said softly as Mr. Tom whisked

through.

"I'll just find a vase for these," he said, taking the flowers. "Let those tears fall, miss. Don't go wiping at them and ruining your makeup. I'll be back after the next heartfelt and very well-done speech to clean you up, don't you worry."

Austin waited for him to go before shaking his head a little and smiling. "I'm pretty sure that was high praise from Mr. Tom, and it's worrying me that I'm okay with it."

"He's growing on you."

"Sadly, yes." His eyes were liquid cobalt. "I got you a little something."

He dug into the inner pocket of his jacket and came back with a little blue ring box with *Tiffany's* written across the top.

I waited with bated breath as he creaked it open, displaying a gorgeous sapphire and diamond ring that looked like it was made of vines, each side curling toward the other as they lay flat on the finger.

"I wanted it to look unique but still match your ensemble for tonight," he said, taking it out and slipping it onto my right ring finger. "I thought this looked fitting for the mistress of Ivy House."

Smiling through more tears, I held out my hand to survey the ring. "I love it. It's perfect."

His scent fell around me as he kissed my forehead, and then the tip of my nose, and then my lips. I fell into that kiss, wrapping my arms around his shoulders and swiping my tongue through his mouth. He groaned softly, sliding his hands down my body and pulling me in closer.

"I've never met someone so incredibly romantic," I murmured against his lips. "I love you so much. I'm so glad I found you."

He cradled my face gently, his thumbs out to wipe away my tears. "I don't want to mess up your makeup," he whispered, not letting his thumbs touch down.

"A little late for that, sir," Mr. Tom said, bustling up. "Miss, let's get you fixed up. Oh no…" He tsked at Austin. "You're all lipstick. Come on, I have something for that. Up you go; let's get to the bathroom."

"I can handle it myself," Austin said, trying to gently extract himself from my embrace as Mr. Tom descended on us. He wasn't quick enough, though, and before he knew it, he was up in my bathroom with Mr. Tom fussing over us both. He watched me with a put-upon expression the whole time but endured it, and I knew he was doing it solely for my benefit. I also knew I'd never loved him more.

We arrived downstairs again in time for Sebastian to walk through the door. He wore a black tux without a bow tie, and his white dress shirt sported gold buttons. He'd popped his shirt collar and styled his hair in a "bed head" sort of look, and it stuck up all over the place. His watch gleamed with a great many diamonds, and his shoes had a mirror shine. He looked like a trust-fund bad boy.

A little smile crossed his face as he looked me over. "Gorgeous, Jessie," he said. "Absolutely gorgeous. They'll get a shock when you let loose the hardass."

"I am aiming for decorum, thank you very much," I told him, and really hoped I could stick the landing.

"Okay, quickly now." Mr. Tom shooed us toward the door. "We're running behind schedule. Miss, you need to check over your vehicle. Sebastian thinks Mr. Porsche, as Nessa calls him, will inquire about it. It's best you know what he's talking about."

The guys all stepped to the sides to allow me to exit first, a show of gentlemanly respect that nearly had me tearing up again. Austin followed at my back, naturally protecting my six, until we got near the driveway. Then he fell away. "Fuck off."

"What?" I asked, turning in confusion.

He'd stopped, now slightly leaning forward with his mouth hanging open, staring at the car in the driveway.

"How?" he said, having momentarily forgotten me. "How in the hell did you get a hold of one of those, Mr.

Tom?"

Sebastian stopped beside me with a smug grin. "Sorry to interrupt such a romantic moment, Jessie, but I'm not gonna lie—I'm enjoying his reaction."

A gorgeous car waited in the driveway, the paint a sort of copper yellow with brown overtones, unlike any color I'd ever seen on a car. The opulent design spoke of high fashion and the convertible top screamed *fun in summer!* Walking a little closer, I saw the hood badge.

"Oh wow, is that a Bentley?" I widened my eyes, looking through the window at the interior.

Sebastian opened the door for me so that I could sit in the plush leather interior.

"It is a Bentley Bacalar, to be precise," Sebastian said as Austin circled the car with his phone out, snapping photos. "Turbocharged six-liter engine, six-fifty horsepower, and six-sixty-four pound-feet of torque."

"The miss doesn't care about any of that," Mr. Tom said. "Miss, it has a handmade interior and an ultra-luxury feel and drive." He put his hands behind his back and nodded. "I know how you like to be pampered. I thought this brand of car was a perfect fit for you. It's not as pretentious as a Rolls-Royce. I mentioned that to Sebastian, and he thought of this model."

"Weren't there only a handful of these produced?" Austin asked, his hands now on his hips as he looked in at me.

"Twelve total units were produced," Sebastian replied. "This model makes the limited production runs of other cars look plentiful. It's truly a collector's edition."

"They were all bought, though, right? How did you get one?" Austin asked, taking a picture of me inside and then turning around to get a selfie with me in the background. "Who in their right mind agreed to part with it?"

Sebastian spread out his arms. "I must confess, it wasn't the owner's idea."

I stepped out and leveled Sebastian with a *look*. "Tell me you didn't kill someone or threaten their life to get this car."

He put his hand to his heart. "I didn't, I swear. I knew you wouldn't accept it if I had. In fact, when I showed up on his doorstep, the only mage in the magical world to have tracked him down, I promised I *wouldn't* kill him. At least until he crossed me again, which I have no doubt will happen so I wasn't too put out by my promise."

I narrowed my eyes, and Sebastian put up his hands.

"He's a mage too, Jessie," he said. "He's screwed over most everyone in the magical world. I let him off easy. In order to save his own miserable life, all he had to do was sell the car. Honestly, the guy's scum. He used blackmail to get the car in the first place. It's not like he deserved the thing. We'll make much better use of it, especially when we take it to a mage function and show it off. They'll know you found the mage that they never could." He took out his phone. "Speaking of which, I need to make sure the trail we uncovered is re-hidden. Otherwise our leverage will be ruined."

Austin caught my mystified look. "It's how things are done in his world, Jess," he said softly. "I'd ignore the details."

"You're just saying that because you want to hold this car over Kingsley's head."

"In large part, yes."

His boyish smile melted my heart, and I shook my head. "We can't very well drive a collector's edition all over the place."

"Of course not, miss." Mr. Tom indicated I should go back in the house. "With Austin Steele's guidance, we have procured a temperature-controlled warehouse to store the pricy automobiles you both own. A little overkill, if you ask me, but I know you like to make him happy. This vehicle is for special occasions only. I took the liberty of parking that hideous connection gift you received in the warehouse, as well. Soon we'll purchase some about-town vehicles for the crew. Oh, and we have procured a mating gift for your mate, to be presented to him when you aren't so outrageously busy. I must warn you, though, the weird mage did not play by the rules for that one."

Sebastian spread his arms. "Okay, but seriously, the mage had it coming. He was poking around in Nessa's affairs, and once he gained access to some private files, he started sending her lewd messages and pictures. She paid him a visit, and I helped myself to some of his effects. We reap what we sow."

"What is it?" Austin asked.

Sebastian smiled. "You're going to love it. More importantly, your brother is going to be so jealous."

Austin shook his head, still looking at the car as headlights appeared down the street. "I don't want to make that kind of gift procuring a habit."

"I hear you loud and clear, alpha," Sebastian said, crossing his arms in front of him. "But these people really do deserve it and more. Much more. You'll see when you dip your toes in the mage world. Anyway, we should probably get into positions. Time is running out. Nice watch, by the way."

"It was given to me by a guy who is excellent at gift giving," Austin replied, walking back toward the front of the house. I assumed it was his people arriving to make a show for the arriving gargoyles. "I can't wait for

Christmas."

Sebastian laughed as the cars stopped, the most relaxed he'd ever been in Austin's presence.

"Miss, I really think we should sojourn to the house," Mr. Tom pressed. "You should be relaxing in comfort while the rest of us handle the details."

I ignored him as Broken Sue stepped out of a black Lincoln Town Car. He said something in a clipped tone, too low to hear, before walking around the hood of the car to open the passenger door. Nessa's bare legs swung over the side as Broken Sue reached a hand in. She took it and gracefully allowed him to help her out.

"Wow," I said, taking her in. I barely recognized her.

An off-the-shoulder, asymmetrical chiffon evening dress hugged her tightly at the bodice, decorated in sparkling silver sequins. It loosened up around the legs, higher in the front and then flowing down to the ground in the back, light and airy. Her hair had been piled on top of her head in an intricate design, decorated with what looked like diamonds woven in to appear like fairy dust. She'd aimed for dramatic makeup, completely the opposite look to my simple dusting, with a thick smoky eye under dark brows, accentuated with dark lipstick. She looked like the devil to my angel, and I knew that was by design.

"Yes, she's a knockout when she makes the effort," Sebastian whispered.

"No." Broken Sue put his hand on Nessa's shoulder to stop her from bending over. She turned back in confusion, and he gently but firmly escorted her to the sidewalk a few steps away. "I'll get it."

He returned to the car to retrieve her notepad. When he handed it off to her, she smiled up at him, batting her eyelashes dramatically. "My knight."

Ignoring the comment, he passed by her to stop in front of Austin. He wore a similar tuxedo that molded to his large frame, but with white buttons instead of black and no scarf.

As always, Austin's people lined up quickly and in an orderly fashion. Kace, the pack member next in the hierarchy behind Broken Sue, headed up one column and Broken Sue headed up the other, both standing tall and broad amid hard-faced shifters. Austin would wait with me inside.

A pulse of magic brought my people to the front of the house.

"And we're just supposed to leave you alone with these gargoyles?" Cyra asked me before I'd gotten to slip inside. Mr. Tom was practically dancing from foot to foot to get me moving.

"I'll have more people than they will, remember?" I

told her. "Austin will be with me, for one. I'll have Broken Sue and Kace standing by the front door and Sebastian and Nessa loitering around with an invisibility potion—"

"If they don't sense us," Sebastian said.

"Niamh will be very close, at home, and a bunch of basajaunak will be blending into the trees around the house, not to mention Mr. Tom is acting as butler and Naomi is leading the catering crew. I think I have half the team on hand. I'll be more than fine."

"We'll stay close in case they bring extra people," Nathanial said. "We'll shift in Niamh's backyard to be ready."

"Or have her make us some sandwiches inside and shift when we're needed," Ulric muttered.

"I volunteered to accompany your mom downtown to find gossip with all their people at the bar," Jasper said. "Request denied."

"I'll be lurking around," Edgar said, at the end in a suit that somehow looked good despite his current hunch. "I'm very close should you need me."

"It'll be grand," Niamh said. "Now, Jessie, ye best be gettin' on. There's headlights down the way. At least pretend ye're the high status they should expect."

With that, I finally trekked back inside with Austin next to me and Mr. Tom on my heels. We'd chosen the front sitting room for our reception, one of the done-up areas of the house. The wallpaper had been taken down and the walls painted a deep gray-green. A large trio of chandeliers dripped down in the center of the space, and a set of hardwood bookcases in the back featured various volumes that were old enough to be impressive yet fine to be handled. The oil canvases had been replaced with modern stylized photography or various other non-picture art. It had a general old-school masculine sort of feel while still being cozy and comfortable. It seemed the perfect fit for the leader gargoyles.

Butterflies swarmed my belly and a text silently lit up my phone.

Nessa: *Here comes a limo.*

Mr. Tom walked in with a stiff back and a silver tray, polished up to a high shine but *very* old school.

"We couldn't have bought some more modern trays?" I asked as he handed me a glass of wine and Austin something brown in a sipping glass. Probably scotch.

"This tray is perfect," Mr. Tom said. "She doesn't need to remake the wheel."

"She hasn't gotten to the kitchen yet," Austin said as Mr. Tom left the room again.

Another text came in.

Nessa: *Solgid cairn, givers of cool but useless carriage.*

Nessa: *leader name Eram.*

I showed the screen to Austin. He nodded, sitting back with his ankle crossed over his knee and his arm resting on the back of my chair. He sipped his drink casually and gave off the aura of someone who didn't have a care in the world. Given the utter calm I felt through the bond, that might've been true.

I was not so calm; my nerves rattled through me as I waited for a bunch of people I either didn't know or had already had altercations with.

"What's going on with Anthott?" I asked, needing a little small talk. Not to mention it was probably good to know. I'd mostly let Austin handle that so far.

"He is easy to talk business with if you accept that he talks like a robot and has very little understanding of humor. I like the direction he's thinking and agree with his ideas for size and scale. I think he'd be a good asset."

"So you're going to go further with it?"

"He's getting cold feet. He's nervous about working with shifters and wary about your interactions with gargoyles thus far. He's worried about status. He's not thinking about the pack, solely your unformed cairn. So we'll see. I have his notes and his ideas. Worst case, I find someone else to put them into motion."

I lifted my eyebrows at him. "First of all, how dare

you! I have a formed cairn. It only has a few people, and they're all weird, but I have them. Secondly, look at you, using the Dark Three's tactics."

"It's business. You work with what you have. I doubt anyone else will have the resources to give him what we can, though. He cares about his work more than status. He'll come around."

Nessa: *Leader has sneer painted on. Barely looked at shifters. Sized up Nathanial, then puffed up chest.*

Nessa: *headed your way.*

I felt them coming up the walk. Mr. Tom waited at the front door.

"Did your people sneer at the gargoyles in town before all of this?" I asked Austin.

"Likely. They definitely aren't fond of some of the guardians. But I think the leaders and more powerful guardians tend to sneer at anything that isn't their own reflection. That's the vibe I've gotten, anyway."

"They are at the top of the food chain."

"They *were* at the top of the food chain. Then they wandered into my world."

The shivers that raced across my flesh were decadent. I leaned into him. He put his arm around me and touched down on my shoulder, rubbing with his thumb.

"Here we go," he whispered.

Mr. Tom opened the door, his back stiff. "Right this

way, if you please."

He walked in and half turned. In his wake entered a six-foot-tall man—short compared to the guardians strolling in behind him—who looked to be in his mid-fifties. Gray lined his temples and streaked through his short, dark hair, which was parted at the side and moussed down flat. His tux didn't fit to perfection, buckling a little around the shoulders where it had to accommodate his wings. His shoes were heavily polished, though, and his guardians looked mean and important. They filed off to the sides, their gazes finding Austin and then sticking to me as they took up their posts by the wall.

Mr. Tom cleared his throat. "I present Eram from the Solgid cairn."

Austin uncrossed his legs and stood, setting down his drink before turning back to me and offering his hand. Only once I took it did I also stand, setting down my glass and clasping my hands in front of me.

"Mr. Eram, welcome," I said, offering a slight bow. We knew from our research that he didn't like handshakes or to be touched at all. Gargoyles didn't use last names, instead using their cairn as their second name. "I am Jessie Ironheart of Ivy House. This is Austin Steele, original alpha of the Dusky Ridge pack."

He'd come up with that name a while ago. Dusky

Ridge was where he'd been when he decided to come to this town—it was the first step in the journey that had led him here. Original alpha simply meant that he had started the pack.

"Jessie—may I call you Jessie?" Eram asked, his tone a little rough, like he'd been a smoker in his youth. When I nodded, he continued, "And Alpha, correct? That is how shifters do things?"

No scowl yet. He was apparently on his best behavior.

"Yes, though Austin is fine in private company."

I wondered if Eram knew Austin was making a gesture, changing how shifters did things to accommodate the gargoyles.

"May I get you and your guardians something to drink?" Mr. Tom asked.

Eram looked Mr. Tom over, from his lined face to his slightly tattered wings. "You've been out of the game for a long time. Were you ever part of a cairn?"

"I was, of course," Mr. Tom responded, still looking straight ahead. He didn't volunteer which one. Never had, in fact, even though Ulric and Jasper had asked multiple times since joining us. "The magic of Ivy House has physically restored the vitality of my youth, even if you can't tell visually. With that and my experience, I am a force all my own."

It was not easy to keep my face expressionless.

"I see." Eram sat down, still looking at Mr. Tom. "And this is what you're happy doing? Playing maid to a Jane?"

There went his best behavior.

A surge of anger blistered through my bond with Austin, and though he didn't move, and though his expression didn't change, suddenly the guardians tensed and looked hard at him. Eram's gaze swung his way, as well, concern flashing in his eyes. They'd all felt the blast of raw, primal power from an alpha shifter.

"Excuse me," Eram said smoothly if a bit too quickly. "I didn't mean any offense. I am genuinely curious why he would squander his returned…vitality in this way. Especially with his experience."

"We are all very aware what offense you did and did not mean," Mr. Tom said loftily. "Some of us are also very aware of how ignorant you sound. Rest assured, I would rather be looking after the heir of Ivy House on her rise to greatness than holding up a wall for a washed-up cairn leader who doesn't recognize the very extreme danger he is in after insulting an alpha shifter's mate. Care for a drink?"

Anger bloomed on Eram's face, and he shifted his focus to me. I could feel the next cairn leader coming for the door. The phone lit up at my side—likely Nessa filling me in on who was arriving.

"This is how you allow your staff to address—"

My blast of stinging magic shut Eram down.

"We as a whole have no interest in your dramatics," I said. "Would you like a drink, yes or no?"

Mr. Tom received the order but stopped at the door to admit the next cairn leader. In walked my dear friend Withor, his eyes wary and his guardians clearly stressed.

"Hello," I said after he was introduced and his guardians backed away, still hovering close. "Nice to see you again. Mr. Tom is just headed out to get a drink for Eram. Would you like something?"

He placed his drink order as Austin stood, helping me up in that way we'd practiced. It gave the impression he was the lead enforcer, a cue for the gargoyles that he would protect me violently if necessary.

"Since we already met yesterday, this is Austin, original alpha of the Dusky Ridge pack."

Austin didn't reach his hand forward for a handshake, having heard my story yesterday. Instead his power pumped out in waves, filling the room to bursting as he stared Withor down.

"What do you mean you met yesterday?" Eram said, pushing up to standing. "I didn't hear anything about a meeting! What were you discussing?"

Mr. Tom walked to the door again, followed by one

of the catering people carrying the tray of ordered drinks.

"He turned up unexpectedly," I said, gesturing for them to sit down. "Alone. We shared some words on my front porch and then parted ways."

"My business here didn't concern you," Withor said, his eyes not having left mine. He took his drink and found a seat.

Another man entered the room, a brick of a human with jet-black hair thinning on top, a layer of fat covering what must've once been a powerful body, and an aged but handsome face sporting a few laugh lines. His height topped Austin's, but he was shorter than the guardian that walked in after him, whose face I knew from earlier.

The others quieted down. The other guardians, I noticed, were peering over Nelson, Gimerel's leader, to Tristan.

"Hello," I said, still standing. "You must be Nelson. I had the pleasure of meeting your lead enforcer earlier."

"What?" Eram hadn't sat or grabbed his drink. "First Withor and now Nelson's lead enforcer? What's the meaning of this? Why didn't I have access to her before today?"

"Sir, may I offer you a drink?" Mr. Tom said from

his position near Nelson.

"You may, thank you. How about a bourbon, neat?" Nelson walked in like he owned the room and stopped near me. "I am Nelson of Gimerel, yes. And you are wearing my bracelet."

CHAPTER 21

JESSIE

"I AM, YES," I said, stretching out my hand for him to shake.

He took it, his eyes dipping to the bracelet, and then moved my hand this way and that to catch the light. He couldn't keep his gaze there, though, instead finding the necklace draped delicately around my neck and the ring Austin had given me earlier. It was clear that his jewelry wasn't the nicest I possessed, nor the costliest.

I refrained from issuing the challenge now. It was too early in the evening, and not all of the leaders were present. If the bracelet didn't come up again, Austin had a few things he could say to restart the conversation.

"Austin Steele, the famous alpha." Nelson took Austin's hand. Their arms flexed and hands tightened until their fingers turned white. A pissing contest. It was Nelson who let go first, swinging his gaze to the others. "Eram, Withor—I haven't seen you in…how many years?"

"Not enough," Withor murmured.

At least I wasn't the only one getting animosity. That was actually a little comforting.

"So." Nelson sat down and flung his arm over the top of the couch. "What were we all carrying on about when I showed up? Something about previous access to the female?"

Mr. Tom came back in with the man's drink as I felt more strangers enter the property. That had to be the last cairn.

Eram revoiced his concerns.

"Did you not send your lead enforcers to check out the premises?" Nelson asked before taking his drink with a thank you. "I'm shocked. You sent them to check out the…territory ahead of time, I heard. To secure housing. Quite a market, alpha. You have a lot of shifters falling all over themselves to move in here."

"Shifters at present, yes," Austin responded, getting comfortable again, but wariness rung through our bond. "Eventually we're hoping for more magical people in general. Gargoyles have already found their way—"

"Those gargoyles don't mean anything," Withor said.

"Everyone in this territory means something," I replied. "They can be a viable part of the territory without joining our defenses."

"Very true," Nelson said, nodding at me. "Everyone in this room should know that. What do you plan to do about housing?"

"As soon as we have some breathing room," Austin replied, "we'll be expanding the territory to accommodate the growing pack and building more housing within the established territory. I am from a large, prosperous, multigenerational pack. I'm well versed in how to establish and run a territory. Our people are our top priority and will be looked after."

"Even in the event of a…skirmish?" Nelson's eyes glittered.

Austin's didn't. "Especially in the event of a skirmish. We are always ready for an attack."

The last cairn leader, the youngest of them all, finally reached the door with windswept blond hair, wide brown eyes, and a large smile. He clocked in at around Austin's height but thinner, in his mid-forties, with a perfectly tailored navy suit, no tux. His brown leather shoes were trendy and cool and his wings fluttered as he walked into the room.

"Gentlemen," he said to the room at large before bowing to me. "I have to hand it to you, Miss Ivy House, you have raised the bar. A Bacalar? This has to be a joke of some sort, right? How…" He put his hands on his hips and leaned forward somewhat comically. "How? That's it. That's the only question I have. How in the world did you come by that automobile? You weren't even magical when they were all sold. I looked into you. I don't feel bad about admitting that because you very *thoroughly* looked into me. When you were a Jane, you didn't have the means or connections to grab a car like that. How'd you manage it?"

He leaned back and tilted his head to study me, dropping his hands.

"Who do you know?" he said slowly. Speaking faster then, like his brain couldn't keep up with his mouth, he added, "Who do you know and do they have any others that they might want to sell to a schlub like me?"

"Gerard, Gerard," Nelson said, rolling his eyes. "Take a breath. Give the woman a chance to warm up to you."

He put his hands together in a prayer style and bowed to me. "You win this round, Miss Ivy House. I'm a big enough gargoyle to admit it. But"—he waggled his finger—"I'll rise to the occasion. You just wait."

The guardians behind him seemed so much more serious than their leader. They took their places at the wall, staring straight ahead.

"Where are we?" Gerard fell into a love seat, making

our grouping into a sort of an oval. "What'd I miss?"

"Well…" Nelson held up a hand and studied his nails. "Withor visited the female yesterday and Eram is pissed about it. Tristan visited this morning and Eram is also pissed about that. She's wearing my connection gift request, displaying Eram's in the front yard for some reason, and there isn't any sign of yours or Withor's. Then you came in hollering and here we are."

"She's not displaying my gift because she has a Bentley Bacalar out there," Gerard said before answering Mr. Tom on what he wanted to drink. "I'm not mad about that in the slightest. She has outstanding taste in cars. I'm just happy it got me here. As for that carriage, she probably only kept it around so she could strip it of gold and use the rest for firewood."

"She would've already stripped it down if that was all she wanted with it," Eram said, his brow lowered.

"Tristan didn't see any horses," Nelson said. "I can't imagine she's going to get much use out of it if she doesn't have any horses."

"And just why was Tristan skulking around, anyway?" Eram glanced back at him. "What about Withor?"

"Tristan was *looking* around to prepare for tonight. I wanted to make sure there were no surprises. It's the same reason why I'd like to cordially request that your gargoyle butler show him around now, Jessie, if you wouldn't mind. I'd rather not get a nasty surprise in the middle of dinner."

Gerard pointed at the fireplace. "I think my eyes are playing tricks. That wooden carving just moved. I swear it did."

"Lay off the edibles," Eram told him as I connected gazes with Tristan standing stoically in the corner.

"Have at it. All of you. You don't need my butler to guide you. Check out the house as you see fit, but do not touch anything. I'll know if you do, and you will be punished." I waited for all the leaders to give me their attention. "How would you like to handle those punishments? By yourself, or shall I do it?"

"You think you have the power to punish my guardians?" Nelson's smile was delighted.

Tristan's gaze zipped that way and his body minutely tensed. I might not have noticed if I weren't used to shifters giving almost nothing away. He must not have told his leader what I was capable of, because I was pretty sure he knew from watching the training that I could definitely inflict pain, and so could my crew.

Withor opened his mouth to respond, but Nelson made a sweeping gesture with his hand.

"Have at it," he said, "though you might be surprised to learn that guardians at this level have strict discipline."

Humor and annoyance leaked through the bond from Austin. He didn't have as much faith in our visitors as Nelson did.

Withor's face clouded over and then he shut his mouth, slouching down into a sulk. He also knew what I could do, but if he said anything now, the others would think his people weren't disciplined.

Tristan looked around before nodding. After one last long look at me, he left the room. The others followed on his heels, dispersing quickly once out of the room.

"*I need to focus on these leaders,*" I told Ivy House, "*so let me know if the guardians touch anything. Try not to show your magic to the Gimerel guardians. I don't want them to know what they'd be up against if they attempt a raid.*"

"*Gotcha.*"

Her vibe was that of a trickster rubbing their hands together in anticipation. I did not envy those guardians.

"Now, where were we?" I asked the room at large.

"I think we were all wondering," Nelson began before finishing his drink, "what dirt you had on Withor that he had to turn up a day early to talk about it."

Withor's head snapped Nelson's way.

A smile spread across Gerard's face. "I've been hearing a lot of rumors about you, Withor. What was so incriminating that you had to break the rules and seek her out a day early?"

"She's got nothing on me," Withor said, much too angry for that to be true. "But are we really going to let her get away with this? She clearly violated your privacy, too, Gerard. You said as much." He'd leaned forward as he spoke, his face red and spittle flying out of his mouth. "She violated our trust! I say we denounce her right here, right now. She's not a real gargoyle. She got the magic from a house, of all things. She isn't technically one of us."

I finished my wine just as Mr. Tom walked in with another glass. This one had the potion in it that would allow me to see and hear Nessa and Sebastian once they took their invisibility potions. Austin refrained from the potion, wanting to use his senses for the mages so he could stack his abilities against the gargoyles'.

"Would anyone else like a refresh?" Mr. Tom asked.

"I would, my boy, thanks." Gerard lifted his drink. "I'm flying home. You can't get in trouble for drunk flying." He paused, but when no one else ordered a refresh, he continued, "We've always maintained that to shift into a gargoyle, you must be a gargoyle. If you cannot, your abilities are latent. I've known guys that couldn't shift, though it's rare. They are technically garhettes, though they usually just leave the life behind and become Dicks. However she got the ability, she shifts, therefore she is one of us."

"Let's call a spade a spade—Withor is just pissed that she's got dirt on him." Nelson's eyes glittered. "The question is, how powerful is this dirt and what can she do with it?"

"I won't be blackmailing him, if that's what you mean," I said. "I will be watching him, however. I'll be ready to help his people should they need it, in any way they require."

Gerard's brow lifted and he leaned back. "Whoa. This just got serious. What are you hiding, Withor?"

"It's just that thing with the production cairn," Withor spat before downing his drink. "She's just trying to make it seem worse than it is."

"It must've been pretty bad if she threw that production cairn leader out on his duff," Eram said suspiciously.

"Well, what about you?" Withor demanded of Gerard and then Nelson. "What does she have on you?"

Nelson smiled and spread his fingers. "I got some rather nice little gifts nodding toward hobbies hardly anyone knows about. I'll spare you the suspense—it's just rock collecting and bird watching. I don't fly with the guardians as much anymore. I don't have to, you see, with a lead enforcer of Tristan's caliber. I started collecting rocks and bird-watching to pass the time. She very nicely informed me that they weren't embarrassing hobbies at all and I shouldn't try to keep them hush-hush." He rubbed his chin. "Nice touch, that. Very effective."

I bent my head in thanks. Sebastian for the win.

Speaking of, he and Nessa slowly entered the room, invisible to everyone but me. No one seemed to be the wiser, except for Austin, whose emotions quickly registered recognition.

Gerard scratched his head. "Yeah, I got gifts. There was one little secret she found out about. I have *no idea* how. I won't spare you the suspense. Keep guessing if you want—I'll never tell."

He was mostly joking, and that was good, because the idea hadn't been to shame him for his foot fetish. We'd just given a nod to his "secret" so he'd know we were capable of digging deep.

Eyes turned to Eram, who scowled back at the others. We'd delivered him proof of embezzlement. He was only skimming a little off the top, but it would still reduce his status if people knew, not to mention have people question his leadership.

Patty was bursting with the need to tell people.

The message we'd been trying to convey, in addition

to our power of discernment, was that these cairn leaders weren't perfect and had better not judge me for not being perfect either.

I now doubted they'd understood.

"When's dinner?" Eram barked. These guys had to be terrible poker players. "This meeting is getting tedious. I remember now why I hate being in your company."

"That's hurtful," Gerard said, grabbing his new drink from Mr. Tom. "It's not untrue, but it's hurtful." He winked at Mr. Tom. "Thanks, bro."

"Dinner is ready to be served," Mr. Tom informed us. "Shall we wait for the gargoyles now snooping through the second floor, or will we allow them to continue looking through all of our worldly possessions while you dine?"

"Let's give it another few minutes," Nelson said, swirling the contents of his glass. "This is a big house. I don't want anything popping out at me that Tristan hasn't inspected."

"You're sure giving him a lot of power over your operations," Withor accused. "Word is, there's starting to be some confusion over who is actually leading your cairn, you or him."

"Now, now, Withor." Nelson gave him a sly smile. "Jealousy doesn't become you."

Eram narrowed his eyes at Nelson and then shifted his attention to me. "Why *are* you wearing that bracelet? It sticks out like a bruised thumb compared with the rest of your *much nicer* ensemble."

Austin glanced at me, and expectation rose through the bond. This was the perfect setup. It was time to issue the challenge, especially since Nelson's people were probably making a list of other things they hoped to steal.

"*If they attempt a raid on me, they'll get a nasty surprise*," Ivy House thought as the dolls woke up. Tristan was currently standing in the empty room with the random closet full of gold, and one of Eram's people had made it to the third floor and was walking into the art room. The dolls were preparing, just in case.

"This bracelet?" I lifted it to show everyone, wiggling it in the light. "I figured it was a joke, and I was the butt of said joke. Otherwise why would Nelson just *give* it to me when he'd challenged everyone else to come and take it? He has to be laughing at my expense, right? Making fun of my small team and lack of enormous guardians?"

Sebastian, standing behind Eram right now with only a few feet to spare, slowly put a thumb up.

"Jessie!" Nelson placed a hand to his heart. "How could you think so little of me? I'm just a bird watcher."

I laughed for his benefit. "This is true. Well…" I put down my wine so I could use that hand to unclasp the bracelet. It fell off into my palm, and the suddenness wiped the smile off Nelson's face and captured his focus. "I'm sure I can figure out how to protect an itty-bitty little bracelet like this."

I held it up for Mr. Tom, who was waiting near the door.

"Mr. Tom, would you do me the favor of setting this out on the table behind me? I'd put it on the coffee table, but I don't want one of us to spill our drinks on it."

Nelson watched me shrewdly, all the charm and humor stripped away to reveal sparkling intellect and raw ruthlessness. He nodded at me, just slightly, and my gargoyle thrummed within me. Challenge accepted.

CHAPTER 22

NESSA

"THIS IS REALLY boring, Sabby," Nessa whispered to Sebastian.

This potion was a serious game changer. Sebastian was a genius for concocting it, and Jessie a godsend for helping him bring it to life. They could move around without smell, sight, or sound, *and* they could hear and see each other? If there was the equivalent of a Nobel for mages, he'd get it, hands down.

They stood dangerously close to Mr. Charming, the leader of Gimerel. Friendly, funny, and easygoing, he was a delight to be around.

Nessa had never trusted people like him. Pull back the covers, and there were bear traps in bed.

Mr. Charming reached back to scratch his head, making Sebastian take a step away so as not to be accidentally touched. Wind probably rustled Mr. Charming's arm hair. She and Sabby stilled, waiting to see if Nelson would notice. Jessie coughed into her hand, glancing over.

Nothing.

Austin or Brochan would've spun around, grabbed them by their invisible necks, and clunked their heads together. Most decent shifters would. Nessa had forgotten how easy it was to spy on non-shifters.

"They have to go to dinner soon," Sebastian whispered back. "Let's just give it a few more minutes."

She pointed at Mr. Porsche, the other somewhat funny cairn leader. "Let's go see if he can sense us. Maybe he's got hidden talents."

As they slowly made their way over to them, the leaders finally stopped bickering for long enough to ask Jessie a meaningful question.

"Be honest," Mr. Porsche said, leaning forward. "Did you really like that carriage?"

Jessie grinned and leaned a little into Austin, an action that always made him curl his arm around her and pull her closer.

"Truth?" she said, the wine putting a little flush into her cheeks.

"Yes," Mr. Porsche drew out. "Tell us. Tell us!"

"It is very pretty," she said, and everyone hung on her every word whether they realized it or not, "and the details in it are very cool…"

"Go on." Mr. Porsche rolled his finger in an air circle.

"But what the hell am I going to do with it?"

"I knew it!" Mr. Porsche fist-pumped the air and pushed back, laughing.

His back hit the cushions and his head came dangerously close to hitting Nessa in the stomach. She jumped back, swinging her arms. A wafting of wind feathered his hair.

Nessa and Sebastian froze again. Jessie cleared her throat, frowning over at the wooden carvings on the fireplace. The image had changed to a man with wild hair sitting on a couch with a stick figure in a ghost costume standing behind him.

Ivy House was ratting Nessa out!

She poked Sebastian and pointed at the image.

"Yeah, so I just left it for now." Jessie shrugged. "I'm sure something can be done with it. A focal point in a garden or something. It's cool, don't get me wrong, but…yeah."

"What about his?" Mr. Porsche pointed at Withor, a name so bad he required no disparaging nickname.

"You don't see it, do you?" Withor asked grumpily.

"I actually really enjoyed that piece," Austin said. "I thought it was very well done."

"Oh yeah?" Mr. Porsche, who just could not sit still,

threw his arm over the back of the couch. Sebastian narrowly dodged it. "What does it look like?"

Austin described it as Nessa pointed at the doorway. "Let's go spy on the guardians and see if they notice."

"I'm actually going to put it in an art hall we'll be setting up," Jessie said, glancing their way with tight eyes. It meant she was worried about them.

They'd be fine, though. If they needed backup, Ivy House would intervene. Probably.

"I'd say that I would invite you to see it when it's done, but I'm not sure I could tolerate the company," Jessie said in a flat tone as Nessa and Sebastian exited. Most of the room erupted in laughter.

"She was being dead serious," Sebastian whispered. Technically they could talk at full volume, but whispering just felt safer.

"That's what makes it so funny. Wait, we don't even know which area of the house we're going to."

"I'll just go check on the place settings," they heard Mr. Tom announce in the sitting room. "I *assume* dinner will begin shortly..."

His annoyance was unmistakable, and Nessa couldn't help but chuckle. Only Mr. Tom would passive-aggressively chastise the biggest leaders in the gargoyle world, his employer included.

"But seriously, Jessie Ironheart, tell me..." Mr. Porsche let the words hover for a moment. He was the only one that didn't sound patronizing or condescending. "What sort of cairn are you actually looking at establishing?"

Mr. Tom turned the corner with his chin held high and an unmistakable air of importance. If Nessa hadn't known better, she'd have assumed he was the most influential person at this gathering.

"Wait, I want to hear this," Sebastian said, pausing. "You go on." He motioned her forward before heading back into the sitting room.

Nessa didn't want to hear. They were probably about to poke holes in Jessie and Austin's setup.

Those two would never have a bona fide cairn. Not like these gargoyles. They'd never have a bona fide pack, either, because they were inviting all manner of creatures to join them. The idea of fitting in with a mage organization was just laughable. They were the redheaded stepchildren of the magical world, the misfits on the outskirts of "normal," and they'd be the best there was because of it. These guys wouldn't understand until the truth of it hit them in the faces.

She saw now why Sebastian's plan was a necessity. Handling an attack would be the proof. It would be the evidence of this territory's greatness that slapped them in the face.

If only she'd had more time to prepare. As it was, trying to get it organized was like cupping water in her hands and trying not to let any leak out.

Mr. Tom put out his hand to silently shepherd Nessa in front of him. When they were down the hall a ways, he softly whispered the few rooms she would probably want to head to.

"Take the hidden tunnels," he added, stopping by the wall and touching a spot that looked like all the other spots around it. A door popped open, no lines or cracks hinting at it the moment before. "The house will guide you."

She knew that well enough, though she didn't really want to be trapped in the bowels of this place without Sebastian.

The shove ended her hesitation, and Mr. Tom shutting the door behind her dunked her into complete darkness.

"Oh hell," she said, spinning around and feeling for the door. "I can't do this. This isn't the sort of courage I possess…"

A light clicked on behind her, an eerie pale blue.

"Is that better? I'm not sure." Shaking and not afraid to admit it, she turned slowly and stared at what looked like a stone mouth.

Down the way, another light illuminated the narrow

passageway.

Sebastian had described these passageways to her. He'd worked in the deep parts of the house for a while now. She'd never ventured into them, though. Honestly, she'd never been invited. Apparently this was her chance, like it or not.

"Definitely not," she murmured, following the tunnel slowly. When she got to the next glowing orb, not even really a light and without any sort of wiring she could discern, another lit up farther down the way. Then another, until she was following the house's lead up a set of creaky, narrow stairs with walls on either side.

"Did I ever mention that I have a slight phobia of confined spaces?" she whispered. "Maybe a *wee* bit of blind terror at being trapped in said confined spaces?"

The house groaned, and the unmistakable feeling of humor danced with Nessa's senses. She'd been blasted with raw fear before, while wandering the house. She'd assumed that had been initiated by her. But it would seem the house could orchestrate emotions as part of its defenses. Sebastian had said as much, but she'd never really experienced it for herself.

"That's a little terrifying," she murmured.

It made sense, though. How else would it get people out or stop them dead if there wasn't a door to shut or a doll minion to send?

At the top of the stairs, she lightly touched the smooth wall and stopped, waiting for more direction. When a light flickered on, she followed it, winding through the walls of the house and up one more flight to the third floor. There she walked until the lights stopped illuminating her path.

A little bench sat in an alcove to her right, and on the left was a peephole. Not seeing a door associated with the peephole, she pushed forward and leaned in to look.

The large room beyond was dimly lit with bare, hanging bulbs. Old-fashioned furniture lined the walls around a giant, archaic pool table that would look really cool if it was properly restored. At the far side of the wall, looking at the rack of pool sticks, stood an enormous frame Nessa felt sure she'd remember in her grave. She could still feel the danger emanating from his presence, the strength and power. The strange glowing eyes, like embers drifting through the air.

Tristan leaned in a little, looking more closely at something, and then reached forward as if he couldn't help himself. Most of his back was in the way, but she could just see his fingers nearly close around a pool stick before he froze and then slowly, deliberately, pulled himself away. He was sufficiently scared of being punished by Jessie, that was clear. Seeing the training earlier must've made an impression on him. She doubted he was the type to be rendered speechless often.

He turned, and the light fell over his handsome face. My, but he was a handsome bugger. She'd certainly seen worse. He knew it, too. His swagger spoke volumes. He'd need a flashy watch. A serious statement piece. He'd pull it off, too. He'd have the mages glancing once, twice, and then looking at him warily, knowing the flashier the watch, the more confident the villain.

He let his gaze roam the pool table, close but careful not to touch. He worked around it, studying every inch, even bending to look at the underside at one point. When he neared the wall she was peering through, he slowed briefly…before continuing on, making a full circle. He hadn't been as thorough on that last stretch, though, and when he turned to face her again, she saw why.

His eyes scanned the back of the pool table and then moved up to the wall. His gaze swept the furniture that must be situated in front of it and then moved back to the wall. Up to the ceiling, then back to the wall again, until it landed right on her…and held.

She froze. Sudden movement would catch the eye.

Wait, what was she thinking? She was invisible and

hiding behind a wall! He couldn't see her. He could definitely feel her presence, though. Even through a wall, he'd known he was being watched. Fascinating.

He left the room. The tunnel went dark except for the light above her head.

"Is that you asking what I want to do?" she said out loud, thinking of the other guardians she needed to check out. She'd gotten her answer with this one. She should move on.

"Lead me to him," she found herself saying. "In the walls, lead me to him. I'm…curious."

The house did so immediately, taking her around a back way and depositing her next to the adjacent room. Once again she looked through the peephole. There was a larger bench behind this one. Her mark had just wandered away from an old-style light switch, the plate around it ornate and gaudy as hell. That would've been hideous even back in the day, she was certain. Thank God Jessie had called in help. At least now Ivy House would be able to do what it was meant for—showing off.

He looked around the empty space; there was not even an interesting piece of furniture to catch his eye. He paused, shook his head minutely, and then turned.

This time there was no doubt. His eyes found her location immediately. There they stayed, narrowing as his brow pinched in thought. In a moment, a knowing smile stretched his perfectly sculpted lips. He laughed softly, as if to himself, before nodding, also to himself, and turning for the door.

She stepped back again. Why did it feel as though she'd just been found out? Like actually found out—not just that he was being spied on, but that *she* was doing the spying. Not even shifters had that kind of perception. No one did.

Eyes narrowed like his had been, she hurried to follow, with Ivy House leading the way. This was an act; it had to be. Part of his swagger. He knew how to react in such a way that *anyone* would think he'd marked them personally.

The next room would become the art room, and she decided she was done hiding in the walls.

"Let me out into the hall," she whispered firmly.

The house didn't balk, and the lights guided her around a corner and to a dead end. She paused, waiting, and Ivy House waited with her.

"Can you help?" she whispered. "I don't have enough light to find a latch."

Wind blew through the tunnel, the effect sounding like *shhh*.

Too distracted to be freaked out, she waited until the latch popped. Moving slowly, she snuck out and then turned back, not entirely shutting the door. If she had to make a run for it—for whatever reason—she wanted to get back into the relative safety of the tunnels. She'd endure Ivy House's taunting via murals about her cowardice later.

Light from around the corner cut through the dark hall. She stopped just out of sight, listening for sounds. A door creaked, and then the floor. He'd entered the room.

Heart pounding when usually the sneaking game calmed her into an almost meditative state, she peered around the corner. A boot and the tip of a wing were all she saw, slipping behind the doorframe into the room.

Moving swiftly with silent footfalls, something that would be the case even without the potion, she reached the door and flattened to the wall. Another board creaked within the room, way off to the side. The rooms up here were all large—this one in particular. She clearly had some wiggle room.

Slinking closer, she saw him hovering near the wall, looking at a picture that hung just below his eye level.

Naomi—Nessa hadn't earned the rare privilege to call her Mimi—had rehung most of the house's most valuable paintings in here. There was no rhyme or reason behind the positioning of the paintings, since they'd all be moved. The goal had simply been to put the pieces that would be in the museum in the space earmarked for it. After much contemplation, she'd decided against wrapping them in plastic or encasing them in glass, worried she'd somehow upset whatever phenomenon had kept their aging at bay.

She hadn't yet realized that the phenomenon was Ivy House. The house protected what belonged to it, especially the things that had value. If Nessa had been on that list, she probably wouldn't feel as nervous as she did at this particular moment.

Holding her breath, she slipped into the room, staying near the wall.

He can't see me, she thought, her heart still thumping. *He can't see me. He can't see me.*

He moved to the next painting, leaning closer. His hands didn't move from his sides. There were zero intentions to touch. Then the next, as if he were in rapture.

She mirrored his movements until she was within ten feet, far enough away that a turn and grab would have his hand sailing close but not touching. The twist would leave him momentarily off balance, giving her enough time to dodge the grab and stick a knife in him or turn and run like hell back to the safety of the tunnels.

His wings didn't flutter. His hands didn't move. He

continued on to the next painting; this one was stuck to the wall above another. Unhurried, he studied them both. She watched from a distance. Why wasn't he reacting? He'd found her behind that wall. Both times!

Or was this a ruse by Ivy House? Had the house somehow given away Nessa's presence and this big sucker was going along with the joke? Had to be, because there was absolutely no sign he sensed her behind him. No tension in his shoulders. None of the smooth gliding shifters did when they prepared for attack. No random sniffing or jerks of his head to the side.

Still curious, she drifted a tiny bit closer as she relieved her bosom of the hidden knife stashed there. She was in his striking distance now, and she wasn't the type of girl to take chances unarmed.

The next couple paintings consumed his attention. He barely moved, leaning close to look, bending to study the pieces up close. She had a sudden desire to see his expression. To see what he found so utterly fascinating.

Making a wide sweep, she moved in toward his side. She still couldn't get a good look at his face, though. Six feet away, edging closer, her heart hammering so loud it was pounding in her ears. This was her instincts telling her to back off. She was too close to a very dangerous thing. A naturally unpredictable thing.

He stepped up to the last painting on this wall and finally did give a reaction. One she wasn't expecting.

A soft gasp escaped him, and he leaned closer suddenly. Those beautiful eyes widened, zipping around as he sopped up the details. He stayed for a long moment, his body tense, his focus transfixed—just as transfixed by the painting as she was by him. Both of them were watching something that shouldn't be half so interesting. It was clear he really loved art, that he felt a passion for it that this room had exploited. She couldn't remember feeling so passionate about anything.

His arm jutted out suddenly and his fingers wrapped around her neck before she could blink. Air was cut off, but her reactions were strong. The knife hand darted out of its own accord, blade aiming for his ribs.

As though an experienced dancer, he stepped diagonally and twisted, reaching under his outstretched arm and catching her wrist before she could do any damage. His grip tightened in such a way that agony shot through her.

The knife fell from suddenly lifeless fingers.

"Good girl," he said softly in that whisky voice. She was at his mercy.

CHAPTER 23

NESSA

HE LIFTED HER off the ground with zero effort and, taking another step, moved them nearer to the center of the room, where there was more space.

The lights started to flicker. The air grew heavy and the door to the room widened. The ground vibrated just slightly, and little feet thumped from an undisclosed location.

His arched eyebrows pinched together slightly. His gaze traveled the air around them before making its way back to her eyes, as though he could see her.

"Are you a spirit, I wonder?" He looked behind them at the ground. "The knife is real enough. Crisp edges." Back at her now. Her air was still cut off, her wrist painfully in his grasp. "But you are hazy, like a beautiful angel of death come to snatch me up and carry me straight to hell."

Could he see her? That had to be impossible! There

was no magic as strong as Jessie and Sebastian's combined power. No two mages in the world could match them or produce such an intricate potion. Nessa should know—she and Sebastian had looked high and low. They'd exhausted their search.

As Tristan's eyes moved over her, though, there could be no doubt.

Spots appeared in her vision. Still she held perfectly still, her brain churning furiously. She wasn't sure how to get out of this. With an arm trapped, she couldn't do any magic capable of breaking his hold. Without air, she couldn't use words, and she wasn't strong enough to think any spells into existence.

And so she surrendered to the moment. To his control. To this situation. Fate would take her where it would. If that was to the grave, then it was probably past time. She'd been evading it for so long. She'd always known it would catch up with her eventually.

He swore under his breath.

The fingers on her wrist relaxed, and then her feet bumped down as he switched his other hold from her throat to the back of her neck. He pulled her closer so he could look down into her face.

She used the release to react, smashing him with her strongest spell.

It didn't stick, though. It was like it hit him…and

then split down the middle and fell away. He didn't flinch. The only sign that he'd felt anything at all was a tiny tightening of the eyes.

"What are you?" she managed through a bruised throat.

"A better question is, what are *you*? I felt you spying. I haven't known one of your kind to wield a knife. What sort of sorcery is she practicing here?"

"Wh-what?" Nessa said, so close to that handsome face, to his hard-as-stone expression. He was ruthless—she could see it in his glowing eyes, which were brighter when he was incensed. He didn't have a streak of crazy like Broken Sue—he had a streak of wickedness. Both men were violent, but on opposite ends of the spectrum: the protector and the villain.

The villain was a lot more dangerous, because he didn't give two shits about rules. And now she was in his clutches.

"I'm just a mage," she rasped.

Dolls burst into the room and ran for Tristan, their little faces screwed up in anger and their weapons out. He snapped his head up, and for a moment he froze. His gaze tightened.

"I don't remember dying, but those are certainly agents of hell," he murmured, pulling her up and dashing around a grouping of chairs piled atop a table.

He sprinted for the side, for an open door to the interior tunnels Ivy House must've popped opened after he'd grabbed Nessa.

"No," she cried, but it was too late. He dashed in and yanked it closed behind him, taking a look around.

"So this is how you were spying," he said, noticing the bench opposite the peephole. Apparently they all had seats. "Do you live in these walls, haunting the inhabitants? Magic as powerful as this would require a good few of you, I'd guess, hmm? Very clever, the image you took." He threw her over his shoulder and started walking. "She is certainly alluring. Her beauty would lead men down to hell easily, stumbling after her, hoping for one more smile. Desperate for more of her laughter. My word, but she's gorgeous. Gorgeous and damaged—a lethal combination. A combination that would see through a creature like *you*. Nice try, though. I almost don't want to destroy you." He paused. "Almost."

He turned left, like he knew where he was going. A *snick* echoed down the corridor, a door popping open. The lights shut off, plunging them into pitch black. Her face brushed against something silky, and she realized it was his wing. She pulled her face away again as he kept walking like he could see just as well as before.

"I'm really not sure what's happening," she finally

said. There was no use in fighting. In the short term, it wasn't going to get her anywhere but injured. She'd just have to wait and see if there was an opening down the road. Or who knew—maybe one of the house inhabitants would come for her, presuming Ivy House didn't hide her location in another one of its horrible jokes.

"I find that hard to believe," he replied.

"Clearly. By the by, can you shift me to a more comfortable position?"

Without missing a beat, he hefted her up and pulled her back over his shoulder, cradling her against his chest. His arms were like bands of steel, locking her in.

She went ahead and leaned her head against his hard shoulder. Might as well get comfy until the ride was over.

"How'd you feel me through that wall?" she asked. "That's not normal."

"The magic. I could feel the old magic with her essence mixed in. I am able to do that." He said the last like it would be some sort of surprise, with a little humor mixed in. "I thought it was her until I saw *this thing*"—he shook her a little—"crawl up behind me."

"I didn't crawl," she grumbled as her brain tried to process what he was saying.

It couldn't. She had no line of reference for what he was talking about. It was best to start with the basics.

"Feel who, Jessie? Could you feel Sebastian, too?"

He didn't answer for a moment. "Is this a trick?"

"Hell, man, I don't know. You're in charge here, not me. I was just trying to see if you fellers could sense invisible people. The better shifters can, though none of them can sense someone through a wall like that…I don't think. Actually, we've never tested it. Certainly none of them can see through this potion or see this well in the dark. Jessie can't. Is this something guardians are known for?"

He slowed, then stopped, his breath dusting her face. He was clearly looking down at her.

"What expression are you making?" she asked. "It'll maybe help me know what's going on. Because I have to say, I'm completely in the dark on this one." She chuckled to herself. "Get it?"

He didn't respond.

"'Cause it's dark?" Still nothing. "I've been hanging around Edgar too long," she grumbled.

"Natasha."

"Yeah?"

"Natasha's essence."

It was her turn to pause. "I'm trying pretty hard not to be grossed out, so I have to ask, can you feel other people's essences, too?"

"What—"

He put her down jarringly, and she stumbled. She put out her hands blindly, not sure what she might run into or maybe what staircase she might unwittingly tumble down. His fingers curled around her upper arm to stabilize her, and then he yanked his hand away as though burned.

"Natasha?" he asked in a wispy voice, still whisky smooth, behind her now.

The blackness of the tunnel disoriented her, unsettled her. The thought of being trapped in there squeezed her chest with the beginnings of panic, made worse by his dangerous proximity and obviously off-kilter mental state.

"Oh God," she said, squeezing her eyes shut. But that didn't do anything. There was no difference between open eyes and closed eyes, and she didn't know how to get out. She didn't know which way to turn or how to get away from him.

"Natasha."

"Stop saying my name!" she yelled, breathing hard, panic squeezing her. "Sabby, I need you," she whispered, tears threatening as she was yanked back in time. Tied in a sack. Stuffed in a closet. Left. "Oh God."

She felt with her hands, finding a wall. Feeling along it. Touching forward with her foot to make sure there were no stairs. Tristan's hand touched down on her shoulder, and the panic turned into fear-induced aggression.

Exploding at him, she hit him with her fist, blasted him with magic, then hit him with her other fist, trying to find a face. Kneeing upward to find some balls. Only hitting hard parts.

"Stop, angel. Stop." His arms wrapped around her, and he pulled her in tightly, cocooning her with his body. It almost sounded like he'd breathed her in. "Stop. Please. I'm sorry. I've… You're not… I think I screwed up."

Shaking, breathing hard, she struggled again and couldn't help the tears, all the emotions filling her and then spilling over. She sobbed into him because he was there. She sobbed into him because sometimes she just couldn't help it.

"*Shh, shh*," he cooed softly, his embrace stilling her. "It's okay. I'm going to take you for some air, okay? I'm not going to hurt you."

He didn't sound too sure, like he still feared this might be a trick. Like she was not Natasha the person, and instead whatever he'd been going on about earlier. The thing he'd been walking somewhere to destroy.

Instead of asking, "Why is Ivy House not helping me?" or "What happened to the murder dolls?" or even "Where the hell is everyone who should be coming to my rescue?" she opted to just distract herself with mostly meaningless chitchat he would actually know the answers to.

"How do you know your way around?"

He picked her up again and started walking quickly. "I toured the house, remember? You watched me for part of it."

"But how do you know your way through the tunnels? In the pitch black?"

"I…don't understand the question if my answer didn't suffice." He spoke slower, like her brain had shut off and needed a bit of time to get going again. "I know the layout of the rooms because I walked through them. I have a good sense of direction."

"But…the tunnels are a maze through the house, not exactly following logic. Sometimes Jessie says she just feels her way through, and she knows this house much better than you."

"I don't know what to tell you. There's a little landing on the third floor that I assume is a perch for gargoyles. This house seems to be made for us."

Oh goodie. He could just pitch her off if she got annoying. That would be a handy way to settle this little debacle. Or maybe just fly her somewhere, rip her apart, fly on back, and claim he'd just gone for a joyride. Ivy House probably wouldn't even call him a liar.

"I still have no idea what's happening," she muttered to herself. "There's mocking someone with murals and randomly slamming doors, and then there's just totally ignoring a woman in peril. Is this karma?"

"I don't know what you're talking about."

"Oh yeah?" she snapped. "How does it feel?"

"Where do you come from? Let's start there."

"Rhode Island. Where do you come from?"

"Why were you watching me?"

She leaned her head on his shoulder again as he turned one corner and then another. There was no way a sense of direction would get him through this.

"I will answer that, but first, did you find a map of the secret tunnels or something? Or is Ivy House helping you somehow? I can't help but think this is all a little fantastical. I was led to believe this sort of thing was not possible."

"Again, I don't know what you're talking about."

"If I survive this, I'm going to kick you somewhere that hurts. What was the question—oh yeah, I was watching you because… Well, it's complicated. Short story is that I drank a very powerful potion that masks my sound, sight, and smell."

"A magical potion?"

"I didn't know there was any other kind. Yes, a magical potion. That potion has been tested all around town. On gargoyles, on shifters, on Jessie and Sebastian—it works. However, the decent shifters can all still feel presences. Their primal or magical ability relies on a sixth sense, if you will, and while they can't see, smell, or hear a person, they can feel them. With me so far?"

"I'm not a toddler."

"I know. You're an arrogant dipshit lacking a firm grip on reality. Our gargoyles can typically sense a person who's taken the potion, but they've had a lot of practice. They're looking for it. We wondered if leaders and guardians would be able to sense us through the potion."

"Why test it on me? Why not the leaders?"

She detected a strange defensiveness behind his question. That was interesting. Just what was he hiding? Not that she'd ever know at this rate. She was about to get a one-way ticket to Splatsville.

"We *did* test it on the leaders. They didn't have a clue. I got bored listening to them talk, so the other mage and I were headed upstairs to test the guardians. Except the leaders asked Jessie a question, and he stayed behind. Mr. Tom practically shoved me in the secret tunnel, and the house led me to you. You were supposed to be my first subject of a few. Boy did that go pear-shaped."

"You mentioned that you've never tested shifters

through a wall. You watched me for some time."

"I happened upon you in the billiard room. Before I could find a way in, you left for that empty room. Didn't stay long there, so I followed you to the art room."

"Where you snuck up with a knife in your hand…"

"You *let* me sneak up with a knife in my hand."

He stopped, turned, climbed two steps, and then used one arm to cradle her and the other to reach forward. He must've found a latch or something, because fresh, sweet air rushed toward her, bringing with it moonlight and stars.

"Light," she said softly, smiling as he stepped out onto the little ledge he'd somehow seen from the grounds even though it would take some looking to locate it. It was basically a little flat spot amid the sloping and rising of the roof, right on the edge by the gutter. "You're casing the joint."

"Come again?"

"I'm going to refrain from making a dirty joke just now and repeat myself. You're checking the place out to identify entrance points for a raid."

He set her down and stepped back, finally giving her space. She couldn't help but notice that his smell clung to her—a woodsy scent with hints of amber, all wrapped up in a mouthwatering cologne, and annoyingly intoxicating.

"I'm not at liberty to divulge the plans of the cairn at this time," he said elegantly and with a wicked little grin.

"That was a very long yes. Nathanial figured as much. That's why he had Jessie openly challenge Mr. Gimerel."

He nodded, as though he'd expected as much.

"In the art room, I walked outside of your striking range without pulling my knife."

"You weren't outside of my striking range, but go on. Why did you angle around me and venture closer?"

"Wow. So you knew I was there the whole time. I literally could not tell, and I was watching."

He crossed his arms over his chest, leaning against the wall of the house. "I felt you through a *wall.* Why would you think I couldn't feel you in a room where you were much, *much* closer?"

She held out her hands. "I don't know—I thought maybe Ivy House tattled on me or something." A crease formed between his brows. "Anyway, it didn't really matter. Sure, maybe you'd felt me, but you weren't supposed to be able to see or hear me. I figured you wouldn't have an exact location to strike, so I could run out before you got me. Theoretically."

"Solid plan." That returning grin said he was mocking her. "So why did you walk closer and take out a knife?" The grin dwindled. "Were you planning to rip out my heart?"

She braced her hands on her hips and just stared at him. "Are you dumb or something?"

The bland look turned into one of surprise. A smile budded. "Come—What was that?"

"I could still turn that into a dirty joke. Rip out your heart? Look at the size of you! With such a small knife and my muscle strength—or lack thereof—I wouldn't even be able to get to your heart. Look at your pecs—they're enormous. I'd have to, like, sit on your chest and use all my body weight. If you were defending yourself, I wouldn't even get a chance to land a single strike. And if I did land it? Well, Mr. Wizard, then I'd probably get brained before you lost consciousness. You'd pull out the knife, likely heal before bleeding out, and if you hadn't already killed me, you'd do it then. There are a lot of ways to die in this world, and attempting to stab you in the heart is very likely one of the faster ones. Now, I *would* attempt to stab you in the kidney if I absolutely had to. Neck is better, but you're tall. Eye is great, but it's a small target, and I'd likely miss because you are very fast. Inhumanly fast. Best-case scenario, though, I'd just run away. That's assuming you're limping or something and can't chase me at full speed.

I'm sure you're faster." She paused for a moment. "You know what, after I've thought it all through, it would probably just be easier to lie down and die. At least I'd get to stare at a pretty face before the end, huh?"

He looked both bemused and entertained. "Fine. Why did you walk closer and take out a knife?"

"Isn't it obvious?"

"Obviously it is not."

"Because I was entering striking distance, and just in case you sprang, I wanted defense."

He leaned forward just slightly, making a show of staring at her. "Why-did-you-enter-striking-distance?"

She was trying to evade answering that one. Given she was on a ledge three stories up and apparently no one was coming for her, she decided the truth was probably her best bet. It might even stroke his ego enough that he'd free her.

"Because you were so fascinated by the art, and it intrigued me. I wanted to see your face."

His eyes sparked, their glow enhancing. "And when you snuck closer still?"

"We're at snuck now, huh? You're not accusing me of crawling anymore? That's good, at least." She made a show of adjusting her hair and then her boobs before turning sideways and leaning against the siding that badly needed a new paint job. "You were so in rapture that I wanted an even closer look. Was that for show?"

He shook his head slowly, smug amusement in his expression. "I love art, paintings especially, but photography is nice, too. The alpha was right—that sculpture Nikken gave the female is excellent. It'll find a good home in that room."

"She hates being called 'the female.'"

"I wondered. It's pretty clear no one knows what to do with her. She's a female but brand new, with no family ties or status. She's operating out of a thriving township run by her mate and clearly has some serious funds at her disposal, along with a small but powerful list of guardians, most of them not gargoyles. She's an anomaly, but she's the only living female gargoyle. Calling her 'the female' denotes the 'otherness' of her whole situation."

"She can tell. That's why she hates it. Word of advice?"

"Since you've been making bang-up choices so far this evening, sure, whaddya got?"

She gave that (admittedly funny) dig a blank-stared beat of silence before replying, making him chuckle. "Put your faith in the 'otherness' of her situation. Put it in the 'otherness' of her people. She collects eccentrics no one else wants and makes us shine. She isn't just powerful in her magic; she's powerful in her ability to unify outcasts. She builds them up—as does her mate—and she makes them stronger than they ever could've believed. Get on her side, or she and her people will run over you and flip you the finger as they do."

He was silent for a moment. "That speech started so promising and ended so colorfully. Tell me, are you in public speaking?"

"Fine, whatever. Don't take it seriously. See what happens."

He did get serious then. "I assure you, Natasha, I am. I do not go into my job blindly."

"No. You go into your job raving about essences and old magic and hoopla that makes me question your grip on reality."

He blew out a breath and looked away, and if he was trying to hide his sudden wariness, he wasn't doing a very good job.

"You spoke of a potion. You said it masks sight and sound. Smell." He looked back at her. "Not from me, it seems. I can sense presences, yes. The best guardians can. But I can see you, as well. I don't know why."

She studied him closely through the eyes of someone who had done a lot of interrogations of all kinds. Someone who had been interrogated herself, or found herself at the end of a knife blade, needing to read the other person so she'd know what to say to survive. He'd fooled her in that art room, but he would not fool her again. And right now, reading him, noticing his small cues, she could tell he was lying. He knew why, or at least had some guess.

She let him keep his secrets, though. For now. She'd ferret them out on her own. They hadn't looked into the guardians much. That was an error she planned to rectify immediately. If she lived past this encounter, obviously.

"Your appearance is different, though," he continued. "Hazy almost, like a…dreamscape."

"Do your dreams usually feature angels of death?"

His smile gave her deliciously dangerous butterflies. The worst kind. "Only when your face, or body, graces my night."

"Super sorry I asked. What about all that stuff about haunting inhabitants and old magic and leading men down into the Beyond?"

His eyes flashed—visibly flashed, like a light—before his face settled down into a carefully controlled expression. "The quality of your appearance right now, your glowing beauty—you look like an ethereal agent of hell. Like a sprite from the Forgotten Wood, or a wandering haunt. They assume the face of…someone you know. Someone familiar. They use it to get close to you. To seduce you. And then they…" He shrugged like all of this was no big deal. "They cut out your heart, feast on your organs, and steal your soul to use for their own devices."

"Yeah, totally." She nodded as though she'd ever heard of a supernatural eating organs and feasting on souls. "And you thought I was one of those things? Wandering the halls. Sneaking into rooms. You thought Jessie would be chill with that?"

"She has an army of demons—"

"Calm down with the hell and demons. Those are dolls. They're alive in this house and in a little disrepair from fighting the murderous gnomes—Okay, yeah, I hear myself talking. It's not so far-fetched to think something might be haunting the halls. Except you know that I'm a mage. When you saw me all hazy, why would your first thought be *she's a sprite, I must kill her!* Would you not take a second and assume there's magic at work?"

He laughed, although she didn't see what was so funny. "I have no idea what mages can do," he said. "I've had no experience with them. No gargoyle I know has, until now. Until this trip, I mean."

"But you *have* had experience with demon haunts posing as beautiful women."

"Not quite so beautiful, but yes. And worse things. There are areas of the world rife with old magic and dank creatures. I traveled there for a while before I entered a cairn and worked my way up the ladder. In some cases, I traveled too far off the beaten track. Sometimes you see things that change you. Things you can't unsee ever."

"And sometimes they trigger you," she said softly.

He nodded, his eyes rooted to hers. "Like the dark," he whispered. "Like the deep night. Like feeling trapped."

"How did you…" Her head felt light as unwanted memories suddenly crowded her. A knife. Blood. So much blood. She hadn't realized a man's body held that much blood. Spilled on the floor. Splattered across the wall—

"Natasha!"

She lost her balance, falling before she realized it, too late to grab anything. Her foot skidded across the roof tile; her heel clanged off the gutter. Air greeted her. Empty air. For a moment, she felt utterly weightless, and then she was all too conscious of her weight as gravity used it to pull her down.

Hopefully Jessie will look after Sebastian, she thought as she closed her eyes. She didn't want to see the ground rushing toward her.

The air felt cool against her skin. Like it had been washed clean. Her thoughts turned to happy things. To people she would miss, to people she hoped would miss her.

Crack!

She flinched at the sound, snapping her eyes open in time to see enormous gargoyle arms closing around her. A huge, clawed hand grabbed the back of her head just as her movement changed from a downward fall to an upward pull, and the sensation made her body feel like a stretching rubber band. His great wings, blotting out the sky, beat at the wind, and they shot upward so fast that she couldn't even get breath to scream. Higher they flew before leveling out, the wind washing around them, chilly but for the furnace of gargoyle pressed against her.

"Holy…" She clutched at his neck with her arms and swung up her legs to hook them around him, trying to cling on, not trusting his hold.

"Wa-it." His speech in this form was clearer than any gargoyle she'd yet heard, his voice drum deep but retaining the smoothness of his human voice.

High above the ground, with moonlight cascading around them, he pulled up slowly and hovered in midair, the flight not at all scary like she'd experienced earlier that day in practice. Not at all jarring in any portion except for the part when he pulled out of an insanely deep dive.

"Hee-re." He scooped one hand under her butt, helping her get her legs around his waist. The other hand held her back so she could clutch his neck. No part of it was sexual. He made no jokes or innuendos, instead helping her get secure.

"Read-ee to goo backkk?" he asked.

"Yes," she whispered, shaking against him.

"Oh-kay. Doon't worr-ee. I woon't let you faalll."

His wings once again beat at the sky with incredible power and force. He didn't dive at a dizzying speed, though, as she knew he could've. As the guys had done earlier. His descent was gradual, his hold tight. He landed on a wide, flat area of the rooftop, perfect for large gargoyles. Perfect for a raid, whenever it came.

"Ha-ng oohnn," he said after he'd put her down and she'd unceremoniously dropped to her knees. It wasn't like her to be so dramatic in front of someone, but she'd already made something of a show of herself, so what was one more thing?

He stood back, and his form reduced down to the man. A shimmer of moonlight played across cut muscle and wide shoulders. He bent to her, his hand hovering over her back.

"Are you okay?" he asked softly.

"Did you ruin your clothes, or do you get undressed insanely fast?" She wiped her nose with the back of her hand. "Because I'm pretty sure I ruined my makeup."

He didn't respond to that, instead sitting down by her side with his legs crossed. "I apologize for back there. For all of this. I shouldn't have brought up…" He let the words linger, and she prevented herself from thinking much more about it. "I shouldn't have stolen you from that room and taken you out here. I should've just ignored you, full stop. A creature like I'd thought you were wouldn't have been able to kill me. Maybe in my youth, but no longer. I know this from experience. It's why I carried you like I did. That…and you smell so damn good. I should've known straight away you weren't one of those creatures by smell alone. I just wasn't sure if this house…" He shook his head, frustrated. "The magic in this house—on this land—feels so similar to some dark times in my life. It's messing with my head. You got caught in the crossfire. I apologize."

"What's this? A genuine apology?" She unstuck a strand of hair from her sweaty and tear-stained cheek. "What happened to your charm and swagger and arrogance?"

"The same thing that happened to your sunshine. It's waiting for me to strap it on when I need to, like armor. When we're done here, I will, just like you."

"Why do you bother? You don't need it. Your confidence is so solid it would save a town from an earthquake."

"And you do need it?"

She widened her eyes and leaned back, collecting herself.

"Ah." He leaned back as well. "Back to reality so soon. No problem. I don't want to pry. Last time I did that, you took a swan dive off the roof." He paused with a killer smile. "Too soon?"

She laughed, spraying him with spittle. "Sorry." She wiped her face. "Crap, I probably look like a mess."

"A hot mess. The best kind."

After a deep breath, she tried to smooth back her hair. "I should probably get back. Though I'm not sure why I need to bother. Obviously no one gives a crap that I've been kidnapped by one of the guardians and pitched off the roof."

"*Pitched* off the roof? That's the story we're going to tell?"

"Yes. I don't like being blamed for stupid things."

His smile dwindled. "It wasn't stupid. Life is messy. Sometimes it catches up to us."

"You have no idea," she murmured.

"More than you could ever dream of." He stood, straight and strong and tall. She envied him that confidence she'd just spoken of. "And they do give a crap. A group of basajaunak ran forward from the trees when you fell. So did a vampire who was apparently going to try to catch you. I don't think that would've gone well, especially since he obviously couldn't see you and was waiting in the wrong spot. Three gargoyles and the puca circled me when I was flying you back and are now circling closer, probably waiting for me to step aside so they can be sure another altercation won't send you flying off the house again. A warning has been pounding into me since you fell, promising death—I'm assuming that's the female—and a strange pulse keeps issuing from the house. I'd say they were giving you some space after realizing I didn't plan to harm you—those demons you insist are dolls were following us down the hall—but they're done being friendly. I'm now hoping you'll save me, because the female promised punishment if I touched anything, and pitching you off the house might make that punishment death."

Nessa jerked her head up, looking through the sky. She could just make out Ulric's brighter gargoyle, barely discernible against the black. Then a glimmer of gold from Niamh's hooves. A smile stretched across her face.

"So it *was* Ivy House that blocked off the help." Her heart swelled. "I'll obviously need to burn the house to the ground, but at least the crew came for me, even if it was too late."

"It wasn't too late." His smoldering eyes caught her

attention. "When you're with me, they'll never need to show up at all."

"There's that overconfidence you do so well. Too bad it's hollow. You have no idea what battles wait on the horizon."

CHAPTER 24

JESSIE

"WHAT WERE YOU *thinking?*" I demanded as I hurried down the hall.

"What can I do, miss?" Mr. Tom followed me quickly. "The guardian has left the premises, it seems. Nessa is with Ulric and the others."

"Find the other guardians and tell them it's time for dinner. Get everyone to the dining room—Austin will keep them entertained with his *hilarious* stories about shifter life, the buttheads. Buy me time. I don't know how much I'll need."

"Yes, miss." He peeled away.

"What's going on?" Sebastian jogged to catch up. His expression was screwed up in worry. "What's happened?"

"*I was monitoring the situation,*" the house responded after giving me a chance to fill Sebastian in. "*The guardian came to his senses and they went for a nice chat. How was I supposed to know she couldn't be trusted on rooftops?*"

"This is my fault," I mumbled, turning a corner and finding the first hidden passageway entrance I came to. I could feel her upstairs, in Ulric's room. After letting myself in, I put on a burst of speed, jogging as fast as I could in heels. "I shouldn't have entrusted people's whereabouts to the house. I should've been monitoring them a little better."

"You can't do everything, Jessie," Sebastian said, his voice tight. "I should've been with her. He wouldn't have been able to take her if I'd been with her. Why'd she get so close? That's not like her. Not with a dangerous creature."

"*I agree. You guys are at fault,*" Ivy House intoned.

"*It is not our fault!*" I thought-hollered back. "*It's* your *fault! I was just taking the blame for trusting you.*"

"*Well, you should be taking the blame for telling me not to reveal my abilities to the guardian. I was only doing what you said. I showed the absolute bare minimum of my powers that was needed to make sure she was okay. I even directed the guardian to the safest exit for her to get some air. He thinks his ability to navigate the halls was his doing. Thank goodness he is easily distracted by pretty women, hmm? Bonus for us.*"

"*I swear to—*" I couldn't even form the thought. I

was so mad I couldn't think straight. How could a situation go so wrong? This whole night was one car crash to the next, and now this—one of our own had been in mortal danger.

The leaders had been hammering me on my odd cairn setup with Austin. On the fact that I only handled a few people and he essentially managed our territory. They brought up the fact that money had just been handed to me, I hadn't had to earn it. When I pointed out that they'd taken over for family and that money had also been passed down to them, they moved on to their many years of experience and harped on how I had virtually none. I didn't have proper guardians or many gargoyles at all. My success in battle? Probably hearsay or luck.

They'd told me that I could hope for beginner status at best. My claim to fame of being a female gargoyle? Good enough to get invited to the best parties, not good enough to be handed status, especially since I had no history of status. No family. No connections. Everyone had to start from the bottom and rise, whether by blood or sweat, and I was no different.

Fat lot of good it had done us to invite them. And now I had their stupid guardians wandering through my dipshit of a house, a raid coming that I did not need, and poor Nessa left unprotected for so long she could've died.

"Damn it," I said under my breath, taking the stairs to the second floor. My magic pounded; I couldn't help it. I couldn't even direct it. My mind was fuzzy from wine, and my mood was sour. I was pissed—so pissed—and disheartened.

The door swung open as I got to it. I still slammed it with magic, blasting off hinges and ripping it from the frame. It tumbled into the hall, banging against a wall, half propped up. I kicked it as hard as I could. My toe erupted in pain, but I didn't care, feeling gratification that the door fell to the ground and lay flat. Once I reached it, I stomped over it as hard as I could.

Ulric's door swung open when I got close. He waited beside it, his expression tight.

"We got there as soon as we could," he said, getting out of the way so I could enter. "We felt her on the ledge and moved to get into position, but the house gave us an all-clear."

"I know. I felt it. That's what dragged my focus away from those morons in the sitting room," I groused. "How is she?"

The light in his bathroom was on but the door closed, with Nessa and Niamh behind it.

"She's okay. A little shaky but in high spirits. Nathanial and Jasper are circling the house, waiting for the guardian to come back. Cyra and Hollace stayed back initially because their forms are so easy to see at night. We didn't want to spook the guardian and have him accidentally or on purpose drop her. But now they are keeping pace with him, making sure he comes back here to face you. He had to go get another change of clothes. He ripped all his things when he shifted to go after her."

"What happened?" I asked, guilt tearing at me.

Ulric lifted his hands helplessly as Sebastian knocked softly at the bathroom door. "She says it was a misunderstanding of sorts. She was trying to test the guardian's reactions to a presence, and he responded violently, as they do. The dolls rushed in, and that freaked him out—as they do—so he whisked her into the hidden passageways. I guess Ivy House had left a secret door open in case she needed it. Well, he took it, and they got to talking and calmed things down. So they went outside for a breather, then she lost her footing and pitched over the side."

"*She omitted details from that story,*" Ivy House informed me, "*but what he said is accurate. The guardian came to his senses in the tunnel, got her some air—*"

"*Yes, I know,*" I snapped. "*You've mentioned that part. What you* didn't *mention was the part where you should've informed me of the altercation in the first place so I could've monitored it personally. I can't feel Nessa's emotions; I don't have anything to trigger me when something goes wrong with her. That was* your *job.*"

"*As I said, if I'd known she couldn't be trusted on roof le—*"

"*Oh, shut up.*"

I took a deep breath to collect myself as Sebastian slipped into the bathroom.

"He saved her, then?" I asked, not able to catch a glimpse of Nessa. My stomach churned with the horror of what could've happened. With what almost did. "He dove down and rescued her?"

"Yes. She mentioned that Edgar had planned to catch her, and the basajaunak were waiting at the bottom, but she was invisible. They might have felt her general location in the air, but—"

"Yes, I know. Edgar thought he'd try to catch me once. I know how that goes. And…" I stamped my foot to keep from crying in guilt-ridden misery.

"The guardian must've shifted at an accelerated pace to get to her," Ulric said. "He didn't waste time to undress, so that helped, but still, it's only three stories. Jesus, Jessie, he's a monster. I'd figured he was probably the type of gargoyle whose human form grew to the size of his gargoyle form. No. His gargoyle form must be pushing nine feet. Basajaunak size. You'd think that would make him slow to bank and less agile, but somehow no. He's…"

Ulric ran his fingers through his hair.

"He's a monster," he repeated. "He's going to give us a lot of trouble when they raid. Nessa said she's sure they will."

"First, the house has defenses against fliers, and *I* will be handling those defenses. I can strip the fliers from the sky if we can't handle them. Second, Cyra is agile and can shoot fire from a distance. Hollace is enormous and powerful and can zap moving things with lightning. Niamh could probably figure out how to ram him mid-flight with her horn. We don't only have gargoyles here. And we have magic. Sebastian can cover the rooftop. I can cover the sky. The basajaunak won't let anything get through on the ground. They could all be monsters and we'd handle it. I promise."

"There's one more thing—"

"Jessie," Sebastian said, exiting the bathroom.

"How is she?" I asked again.

"Niamh is helping her with her hair and makeup. She's fine. She always bounces back really quickly. But there's an issue."

He led me through the magical issue. Namely that this guy could see through a potion *no one* else had been able to. He could also feel magic and a person's essence through a wall. He was not an average gargoyle. Whatever genes he had mixed up with the gargoyle half, it had enhanced certain abilities. Abilities we hadn't previously come across.

"What does this mean?" I asked, stepping to the side with Sebastian.

His eyes had a far-off look. "It means I have some research to do. As does she. He mentioned some things that didn't make sense to her. She doesn't want to repeat them until she has more information. The last thing we need is to jump to conclusions when it comes to magic." His gaze found mine. "But I would like to do some testing, and now you have an excuse. He touched something. Her. Doesn't matter why. I want you to blast him with a spell you know well. See how much of it affects him, and increase your power until it is at punishable limits. I'll need to test my magic on him, too, but I shouldn't do it tonight."

"You can wait for their raid."

"Exactly, yes. That's a great time to see what he can endure. Apparently the spell she hit him with, at her full power, barely got a reaction. A tightening of the eyes, is all. Maybe that's just a tolerance for pain."

"Hopefully it's just a tolerance for pain," I said.

He nodded with tight lips. "I don't like this wrinkle, Jessie. I don't like the unknown when it comes to magic. Especially not when it comes to things rendering magic ineffective."

"Well, as I was just telling Ulric, we have a lot of different types of creatures in our arsenal. If our magic doesn't work on him, Cyra can burn him alive."

His smile was grim. "I know that. I was thinking more about mages finding a weakness in you."

Shivers coated my body, and he patted my shoulder.

"Don't worry," he said. "If there are any, we'll find a way to circumvent them. I have no doubt."

Always the magical optimist.

In a moment, Nessa exited the bathroom, her makeup looking great, her hair pristine, and bruises on her throat.

"He did this to you?" I asked, rushing forward and checking her over. Anger and guilt burned through me.

"I was sneaking up on him with a knife. He caught me. It'll go away, it's fine." My lower lip started to quiver, and she tilted her head at me and smiled. "Give me a break, Jessie. I've had much worse in battle. A recent battle, I might add. With you. But I appreciate your feeling bad. I'd thought no one had noticed my…absence."

I could feel Cyra and Hollace heading closer now, and I could only assume the guardian was with them. There was no alarm or giddiness from them, so he clearly wasn't attacking.

"That's my fault," I said, and dared Ivy House to agree. "I told the house that I didn't want her to show what she could do. They'll be raiding, and I wanted her defenses to come as a surprise. She apparently assumed you were fine. So *we* thought you were fine. Then you fell off the roof—" Emotion bubbled up, making my lip tremble more. I didn't want to think about how close she had come. *Couldn't* think about it. "I don't want to lose you, Nessa. Please be careful. You have to make up for us just generally sucking."

"Another misunderstanding. This night has been filled with them." She hugged me tightly and then shot me a serious look. "Did she help him with direction, because that dude knew exactly where he was going. If she didn't, we have a real problem on our—"

"She did, yes." I felt him enter my airspace. Felt my magic pulse, calling him to me. "I have to get back down to those idiots, but first…" I turned for the door.

"Okay, but don't kill him, Jessie," Nessa said, quickly following me. "And not just because he saved me in the end. And not because he's an enigma that I'm dying to solve. Definitely not because he's super hot and it would be a waste. But because I honestly started it, and it's probably not right for him to die because he was trying to defend himself in a stranger's house."

I reached the stairs for the third floor and went up,

debating taking off my dress. Maybe we should handle this gargoyle to gargoyle. Then again, I'd have to take off the jewelry, too, and stow everything somewhere it wouldn't get dirty. That would be a real hassle.

I could feel him waiting for me on the largest flat area on the roof, only gently sloped to allow rain runoff. I pulled open the door and climbed the few steps to it, finding him in his human form with a duffel bag in his hand. It presumably carried his clothes, because they weren't on his body.

"You broke a rule," I told him, and my magic throbbed.

Wind whipped around us. Nathanial and Jasper flew close, watching while in flight. Niamh and Ulric climbed onto the roof with me, spreading out in case they were needed, giving me space. Nessa and Sebastian waited in the doorway behind me. They'd better stay there too. I wasn't letting Nessa set foot anywhere near this platform.

"I did. I apologize for that. Does the master know?"

I didn't think about that part of things. Tristan's crime was touching one of my people…who wasn't supposed to be here in the first place. I'd get heat for her being around, and for doling out a punishment for a crime resulting from my deception.

Screw it.

"No, and I don't intend to tell him. I do still intend to punish you. You can explain as you need to."

"Understood." He held up his bag. "This is my second favorite suit. My first one has already been destroyed. I'd prefer not to lose two suits in one night. Can we keep this in one piece and blood-free, please?"

I frowned at his blasé attitude. He was not at all worried about the punishment. It made me angrier.

"Toss it away. Or put it down; I don't care. How do you want to take this, like that or in your gargoyle form?"

He tossed his bag to Ulric and lifted his hands, looking down at himself. "I guess that depends on how painful you want this to be for me."

"His gargoyle form," Sebastian called up. "Try it on his gargoyle form."

Tristan looked beyond me and pointed. "You can see them too?"

"Not without a potion that allows me to. Which I took earlier."

He nodded and glanced behind him where the flat area ended and a steep roof led to a gutter and then nothing beyond it.

"Do you plan to knock me unconscious and blast me off this roof? Because I don't think I'll survive that fall."

I pointed to Nathanial not far away, then Jasper. "They'll catch you if need be. I won't kill you." I grimaced. "Almost definitely I won't kill you. I'm pretty sure I've got a good hold on my anger."

"Reassuring," he mumbled.

"Any last words?" Nessa called.

A wicked grin pulled at his lips. "Yeah. Stop getting me into trouble."

"Shift," I told him.

His shift was indeed fast, nearly as fast as mine, and I was a much smaller creature. *Much* smaller. The gargoyle rose before me, up and up until he was Dave's size. His thick hide sparkled in the moonlight, tougher looking than the likes of Nathanial or Jasper's. Certainly tougher than mine. His wings ruffled and pushed out slightly, getting some air. Maybe he was preparing to be blasted off the roof.

His eyes hadn't changed color but now glowed brightly, hazel-orange.

"How has no one ever questioned your eyes?" I asked, mesmerized for a moment.

"No one quesh-ons great-nesss."

I gave him a flat stare. "Sure, bub. Whatever you say."

Magic rocketed from my fingers, a doozy of a spell but one that wouldn't kill him, even at full power. It would hurt like hell, though.

It smashed into him center mass but then flowed around him as though hitting an oil slick. It was like he repelled the magic, as though he had a natural deflection spell around his body.

No problem. Sebastian usually had magical defenses. It was really just a matter of altering the approach.

A quick tweak to the spell, then I hit him again. This time only part of the spell flowed around him. The rest struck. Hard.

He jolted back, scrabbling for purchase, and then lowered his head as he took it silently.

I upped my power more, and then more, nearly at max now, hammering him. His claws scraped against the roof tiles. He doubled over, taking the onslaught, clearly trying not to utter a sound.

Something about that really annoyed me. It wasn't logical. I was actually thankful to the guy for saving Nessa and felt he'd endured his punishment admirably. Austin wouldn't have uttered a sound, either.

It was my gargoyle who wasn't pleased. She wanted him to submit. She wanted this mammoth of a gargoyle with hidden talents to succumb to her force, and to do it stubbornly, as befitted his kind. *Our* kind.

Choosing a crushing spell now, one that would force him to kneel before me, I stepped forward and shot it out. Words went into this one. Body movements. It hit him with stinging intensity, nearly full power.

A low growl started within his chest, deep and loud.

"Sabby, apply a soundproof bubble," Nessa yelled.

She was just in time.

Tristan's wings snapped out, and their size was staggering. He straightened up slowly, spread out his large arms, and then leaned forward and roared at me so loudly it was nearly deafening.

Challenge accepted.

He stared me down, taking the pain. Taking the power. He stepped forward, his effort plain. Once, and then again, closing the distance.

"You want to play ball, big guy?" I asked, my excitement rising. "I'll play. Bet your leader never did this."

Another spell, hard and fast and brutal but short-lived. I wanted to let him build up a little confidence. I wanted him to get in over his head. Magic wasn't just physical. The best mages added a mental component to help break their target down.

He stepped forward again, and I stared back at him, daring him to rush me. I'd rip up this dress, no problem. I'd scatter these jewels without hesitation. Austin would understand. What was happening here was more important than stupid displays of wealth. More important than looking good or staying clean. More important than those close-minded leaders and their ideas of what their species should be. I felt that truth deep in my gut. I felt it with an assurance that couldn't be explained.

"Come and get it," I muttered, and he did charge then. With a roar, he came at me with blinding speed.

Good thing I'd spent my entire magical life training with a stronger, faster alpha.

I dodged and countered with a spell, slicing across his tough hide. A line of red opened up, dripping crimson. Not deep enough, though. His natural magic was playing defense.

He turned, his wings whipping around. Nessa had taught me how to fight dirty, so I grabbed one of the thin bones running through the middle of a wing in two hands and snapped it before yanking, tearing it. A strange liquid dribbled out, like blood but bright orange. I shook my head, wondering if it was a trick of my eyes.

His grunt was pained.

Felt that, did you?

A spell at his feet had him hopping in surprise. Gargoyles never expected you to go low. Then I went for the eyes, making him duck while I hurried to his other wing. I snapped another little bone, ripping for all I was worth.

He swung around and grabbed at me, his claws nicking my shoulder. Good thing he was so big—he was practically tripping over himself in this small space. He was used to the wide-open skies, where even a massive brute like him had plenty of room to maneuver.

Another bone, more of that strange liquid. Did he bleed bright orange out of his wings, or was he something other than a gargoyle? Maybe a hybrid monster posing as a gargoyle?

Feet aching, I quickly slipped around to his back. My small size was an advantage here. Without hesitation, I kicked upward as hard as I could, smashing my foot between his thighs. I'd seen what he was working with. He was as big as Austin. This would hurt like the bejeezus, not enough to bring him crashing down, but plenty to piss him off.

He snarled, trying to snap his wings out. The pain of the movement stopped him short, and I grabbed one of the dislocated areas and ripped again, pulling his wing apart in that area. The orange dripped now, pouring onto the ground. His grunt was anguished. He was scared, maybe. There were limits to a gargoyle's healing ability. Too much damage to a wing would be forever. He probably feared I wouldn't play doctor when this was through.

I preyed on that fear. Made him desperate. Wild.

His spin was blindingly fast. His wing thwapped me in the face. He reached forward for my throat, and I had the inkling that he would squeeze and fling, taking this fight to the place he was most comfortable—the air.

Usually I'd battle him anywhere he wanted. This was a challenge I was enjoying. A fun romp. A game between gargoyles. But right now I had a dinner party to get to, so I had to end things quick.

I decided to hit him with a spell I'd only studied on a conceptual level. It was designed to confuse the mind while slashing at the body, inside and out. It didn't hit all at once, though. It started slow and grew, little by little, giving the enemy false confidence.

Then you slammed home the tearjerker and made them wail.

In theory.

I'd never had anyone to try it on. It was at the top of my power scale and old magic, like this gargoyle seemed to naturally defend himself against. We'd see if he could temper its effects a little. If not, I would stop before I hit him with the final strike.

He reached for me as the first wave of the spell hit and jerked, his hand going too far right, missing me. His large gargoyle brow creased and he shook his head, grunting.

Each grunt of his was like a small victory.

I fed it more power, more and more, increasing the pain. The confusion. He staggered now, trying to find a sense of balance.

I ran at him, clawing at his wings. His eyes. Slashing at him with smaller spells that could operate while this one was winding up.

His roar was tortured now. Frustrated. Angry beyond all belief.

He stomped. Swung wildly. Thrashed.

A claw nicked me again. Another scraped down my arm, plunging deep. The pain shocked into me. I staggered but quickly got to work healing it up and stopping the blood flow.

Breathing hard, he endured the first portion of the spell, probably thinking it would be over soon. According to the book I'd studied, most creatures didn't even make it this far.

I slammed him with the final piece, pouring all my power into it. A crap-ton of energy. I needed to make him submit. Fueled by instinct, I knew dropping him would be important in the long run. I knew winning this, and winning it hard, would garner me respect with this fierce and powerful gargoyle-monster.

His wail reverberated across the roof. He wobbled and then fell, crashing down onto his face.

"Make sure he stays here," I yelled, getting onto my knees and grabbing a big arm to keep him put. There went my clean dress. "Don't let him slide!"

Sebastian and Nessa ran forward, but the gargoyles were already there, situating him more securely.

"Straighten out his wings so I can heal them," I demanded, getting up to help.

One of my heels broke, and I wobbled, falling down across his back.

"Sorry," I muttered as Nathanial checked for a pulse. "Don't bother with that. I can feel his chest rising and falling. He's still alive. The effects of the spell will ease in a moment. Stretch out his wings. I need to get him patched up."

Just after we'd gotten them straightened out, though, he shifted, reducing down into a man. He lay on his stomach, arms spread out to the sides.

"Dang it, we just had it." I motioned for everyone to do it again, pressing my hand to the top of his back. "If you value your wings, don't move. We need to make sure they're properly aligned before I heal them or we'll have to re-break them and try again. I doubt that's the sort of day you were hoping for tomorrow."

"You can heal," he said, his voice raspy. It didn't sound like a question, but I treated it like one anyway.

"I would never have done that to your wings if I

couldn't fix them."

"It's forbidden to tamper with wings unless you plan on killing your opponent."

"I have spent a lot of this evening hearing about my shortcomings in the gargoyle world. Add that to the list of grievances, and also the list of 'I don't really care.' No, Nathanial, out a bit." I gestured for him.

"I thought you'd kill me. It felt like you were killing me."

"Liked that one, did you? I haven't been able to try it on anyone yet. Thanks for being my guinea pig. Why do you have a natural resistance to magic?"

"Luck."

"Pain makes it harder to sound convincing when you lie."

"It seems so, yes. You're a lot more pleasant after winning a challenge. Kind of like the deathwatch angel, but without having to try at it."

"Deathwatch angel?" I repeated, cutting out his pain as I fixed up his wings.

"He means me." Nessa raised her hand. "Though last time it was angel of hell, I think. Same difference. It's the only kind of angel I could claim to be. But I resent that comment! I don't have to try at it. I'm always this pleasant, dang it."

He laughed, which turned into a coughing fit, and

his large back heaved. “Naturally pleasant people don’t sneak up on their friends with knives.”

“This is true,” she said. “But what does that have to do with me? I don’t recall sneaking up on any friends today.”

“Enemies, then.”

“Miss—” Mr. Tom appeared in the doorway. “What…? Well, you’ll have to put on another dress. You can’t go down looking like that. What should I say, that you had a problem with your bowels and had a little backsplash? That would explain the delay and the change.”

“Oh my God, Mr. Tom, if you tell them that I will kill you!” I said.

Tristan started laughing. Loudly.

“Don’t you dare tell your leader he said that, either,” I told him sternly. “They’ve been hard enough to deal with. I feel like some sort of…foundling. They barely let me get a word in edgewise, and when I do speak, they argue with whatever I say. I’d assume it was because of my sex, but Austin hasn’t fared any better, even when answering a direct question.” I patted Tristan. “You can get up now. I have to get going.”

Tristan did a push-up before sitting back onto his knees. His chest was scraped and dirty and his hair wild. “They’re ganging up on you because you’re a threat.

You have all the right ingredients to be a power player but one thing…"

"Gargoyle guardians, I know."

He shook his head, getting up and offering me a hand. I took it and allowed him to pull me up after him.

"Battle prowess. Prove you are mightier than them, and they will have no choice but to submit. They might not do it right away, but they will eventually have to accept the new entity in their sandbox. Scare them, and watch them change their minds."

CHAPTER 25

JESSIE

"ANY HINT ON when that raid is coming?" Sebastian asked after the evening training. It was two days after the worst dinner party in history.

I took a deep breath. "I don't know when the raid is set to happen, but it doesn't matter. Whatever Tristan says, the big dogs are going to try to keep my status low to maintain their placement. There are four high-level cairns. They don't want another power player, especially one they don't understand. The best we can hope for is to attract solo guardians to join us."

We started walking toward the house and the back lawn where the others had already headed.

"Have you had any interest from solo guardians? I know quite a few have entered the territory."

"They're watching and asking questions, but so far no one has approached me. Patty thinks they're waiting to see my status." I ran my fingers through my tangled hair. "Everything is about status with these people! It's frustrating."

"You headed to the Paddy Wagon?" Nessa was asking Ulric as we reached the grass.

"Ugh." Ulric held his muumuu, not bothering to put it on. "I don't know. I'm beat. I don't have the energy to fight my way home tonight."

"What does that mean?" I asked as I picked my way through the greatly diminished flowers.

Ulric glanced back at me, and I could tell he hadn't meant for me to overhear.

"Nothing. I'm just tired," he said.

"I'm going," I told Nessa. "I want to sit in when you and Sebastian talk to Niamh about Tristan. Something isn't right with that gargoyle, and I want to know what Gimerel is hiding."

"You're going to finally show your face in town, huh?" Jasper said with a grin.

"I haven't been hiding," I said, a little too defensively.

I had totally been hiding. I'd created mayhem at the dinner party the other night, resulting in its shutting down early.

"It wasn't her fault," Nessa said. "She was so keyed up about my being pitched off the roof—"

"That's the story you're still going with, huh?" Ulric

laughed.

"She was so keyed up about my being *pitched* off the roof," she began again, giving him a flat stare, "she just reacted. Add wine to that reaction, and, well…it got a bit extreme. It could've happened to anybody. Then things…snowballed. Just kind of unfortunate, really."

Understatement.

As expected, Tristan was an anomaly when it came to his ability to see through the potion. He'd gotten cleaned up and donned his second favorite suit before heading back down to his leader, able to watch Nessa and Sebastian meandering through the others, sometimes getting much too close for my comfort level. None of the other guardians could see them, though. Only three others seemed to feel their presence, and that was only if they were pretty close, within grabbing distance. One of them had tried, reaching for Nessa. That had apparently triggered Tristan, who casually pushed his hand forward to intervene.

I hadn't seen the first guardian's reach. I'd only heard about it in the aftermath. I had seen Tristan's movement, though, and reacted. Badly.

In a move that I would now blame on an excessive amount of wine, I tried to blast him. Except I missed—because of wine—and hit the guy on his other side with such force that he flew through the window. He landed on a flowerbed below the window, screaming. The people inside started yelling. Everyone jumped up, trying to figure out what was going on.

The basajaunak outside didn't need to figure anything out at all. They just assumed all the commotion meant the mages were attacking.

They sprinted out of the trees, hackles raised. Dave got ahold of the flowerbed-crushing gargoyle, held him up by the ankles in his favorite hold, and growled threateningly through the window. The other basajaunak gathered around, following suit.

The yelling inside turned to drunken screaming. The gargoyles apparently hadn't believed I actually had a basajaun on my team, let alone two handfuls of them (their numbers kept growing).

Edgar tried to calm things down until he realized his flowers were getting trampled. Then he decided the best course of action would be to swarm-of-insect his way through the window, reform next to Gerard, who hadn't been expecting it, and close-talk about the fragility of flowers.

Gerard freaked out and grabbed Edgar, probably hoping to fling him away. But Edgar held on, wily as he was, and skittered up his arm in an impressive display of gymnastics, dropped down on the other side, and bit him on the neck. Gerard fell, and the guardians lurched forward.

Cue more hysteria.

It had taken Austin and the shifters ten minutes to separate everyone and calm things down. That was when the accusations had started flying about my excessively large crew. Needless to say, it didn't help my status any.

"Pretty unfortunate, yeah," I muttered, reaching the back door. "Anyway, I'll head out tonight. By rule, raids happen in broad daylight, so we're good this evening." I turned back to point at Jasper. "If you're going, take a shower. Body spray does not count as a shower. Use actual water."

"*Thank* you," Ulric said. "He makes an impossible wingman."

"I feel attacked," Jasper groused.

ULRIC AND JASPER waited downstairs. I felt Nathanial on the roof. He'd be rolling in gargoyle form tonight, keeping watch like a sentinel.

"Nessa and Sebastian are going to meet us there," Ulric said, wearing a subdued blue dress shirt and black slacks.

"Where's your usual outrageously bright outfits?"

He looked down at his shirt, and Jasper looked away; both of their emotions went a bit turbulent. His nose crinkled a little.

"Just didn't feel like it," he said. "I felt like being lazy."

Something about his tone—and Jasper's pointedly averted gaze—didn't ring true.

Before I could press, he said, "Cyra and Hollace will probably meet us, too, depending on whether they have an update."

"An update about what?" I said as Naomi briskly walked down the hall, spying us.

"I think it's Nelson tonight."

I shook my head as Mr. Tom descended the stairs with a jewelry box. "I'm not following. What about Nelson?"

Naomi stopped beside us, no notepad or papers in hand, waiting patiently to speak to me.

Ulric frowned, glancing at Naomi before going on. "Niamh tasked Hollace and Cyra with checking out the cairn leaders—what they're doing, who they're engaging with."

"What? Why wasn't I told about this?" I demanded, a shock of fear going through me. If the leaders found out, I'd be in even hotter water. It had become clear to me that they didn't go about things the way mages did. They didn't spy on each other or cunningly try to kill each other. If they had a problem with another cairn, they were open about it. Sure, the sneaky approach had paid off in the beginning, but we'd need to pick and choose when to play dirty politics. It was starting to get out of hand.

"Niamh set it up," Ulric said. "Their target was Gerard last night. Nothing to report there. He was hungover from the dinner, so he mostly just lay around watching TV all night."

"You have to make sure your top people are all involved," Naomi said diplomatically. "If they aren't, they feel left out and restless. Leave it long enough, and when they finally do get to do their jobs, they go overboard and botch it. It's best to keep them occupied with even small, meaningless jobs. It seems Niamh knows this."

That made sense, though Niamh still should've told me. She hadn't even told me about the basajaunak meetups. She needed to be reined in a bit.

I nodded to Naomi, and her crisp return nod back said the matter was closed and she would move on.

"Where are you going?" she asked.

"Oh. Uh…" I hadn't expected such an easy question to answer. "The Paddy Wagon. Austin's bar."

Her gaze slid down my front. "You're going like that?"

"That is precisely what I said." Mr. Tom moved in closer. "How about we dress it up with this?"

He held one of the new pieces of jewelry, which was beautiful but laughable in its extravagance, considering what I was wearing and where I was going.

"No, I—"

"Have you lost what few marbles survived the ages?" Naomi demanded of him. "If you can't help the situation, leave the situation alone. Jessie, please wait a moment. I'll go throw something more appropriate on. I'd like to go with you."

Ulric, Jasper, and I all watched in shock as she walked off.

Mr. Tom gave an aggrieved sniff. "Let's just see what *she* deems is appropriate for that bar. The woman always dresses as though she's going to some sort of fancy recital or dinner party."

In a blink she returned in white cotton pants and a white scoop-neck T-shirt, with a long-sleeved denim tunic over it. She looked sophisticated but casual.

"Yeah, she wins," Ulric said.

"Mr. Tom, you should dress Jessie in that kind of style." Jasper pointed. "That's a little nicer than your standard jeans and T-shirt, but not *too* nice, you know?"

Mr. Tom issued a "humph" before striding away.

"Nice job of rubbing salt in the wound, mate," Ulric told Jasper.

NIAMH SAT IN her usual seat at the bar, and I was surprised to see a basajaun sitting beside her. Not Dave, but one of the others. A large yellow hard hat perched on his head, a burdened safety vest with the yellow reflective strips was wrapped around his middle, and a kilt adorned his lower half. He hunched over the bar with a bottle of Johnnie Walker Red and a pint glass to pour it in.

"That's what we're doing now?" I muttered.

The silky feel of wings brushed my hand as I tried to make my way toward her. The place was busier than usual, and it was impossible to wind my way through without touching anyone. The gargoyle I'd accidentally touched turned, looking down at me. I didn't recognize his face, but that didn't mean much. I hadn't been out much since they'd all arrived.

I pushed around a shifter, who glanced over and then promptly made room. The two gargoyles behind him didn't budge.

A spindly hand closed around my arm.

"No, Jessie," Naomi said, stopping me. "This is not how an alpha moves through a room. Demand your space. Only then will they respect you."

I knew she was right, but it was such a hassle. Couldn't people just be respectful of others? Why did the magical world constantly require a person to throw their weight around?

Annoyed, I sent out a pulse of magic. *I'm here. Move.*

Shifters shuffled out of the way quickly. They knew my magic and remembered the early days when I had zero control. The gargoyles looked around in confusion. Their wings ruffled. Their stubbornness showed.

Another pulse of magic, localized, adding some sting. *Move!*

The two closest stared hard at me, their feet planted and their jaws clenched. Others turned and twisted, trying to figure out what was going on.

I returned the stare of the two men as my magic started to thump within me and my gargoyle rose.

"Clear out of the way," I told them.

Their eyes narrowed. The one on the right said, "Go around," but his body positioning and the spark in his eyes said, *Make me.*

Fine.

I unleashed magic and slammed them, knocking them back before crushing them to their knees. A spell stronger than this had prompted Tristan to challenge me. These guys, though, bent like reeds in the wind before falling. Their knees and then their hands hit the floor as they groaned under the pressure of my magic.

My logic said, *That's overkill*, but fire curled

through my middle and smug pride straightened my shoulders.

The noise in the bar died down dramatically. Wide eyes turned my way and the path in front of me cleared as gargoyles shuffled quickly out of the way.

"Perfect," Naomi said softly.

Making it to Niamh, I found the seat next to her newly vacated and my nemesis, Sasquatch, pushing through the crowd to get away.

I pulled out the stool he'd just vacated, knowing he wouldn't be back. When I used magic, he took off. He was too used to being on the other end of it.

"Here, Naomi, do you want to—"

"Sit down, for God's sake." Naomi gave me a light shove.

Grimacing, I did as she instructed, feeling Austin coming around the corner at the other end of the bar. He'd probably been in the office.

"Here, Naomi, I got it." Jasper grabbed a high chair from somewhere then pushed through the crowd to set it down between but a little behind Niamh and me. We turned to make a triangle. "What are you doing?" he then asked Ulric, who was lingering behind. "I took a shower. I'm ready for wingman duty."

"Nah, man, not tonight. I'll hang here. You're solo."

"All right. Let me know if you get caught up." Jasper

disappeared into the crowd.

"Get caught up in what?" I asked as Broken Sue, taller than most and parting the crowd like water, entered the bar. Menace dripped off him, and his eyes were hard.

"Mush, doggy," I heard Nessa say from somewhere behind him. "Mush, mush."

He stopped next to me, and Nessa popped out on the other side with a big smile. "He makes getting through a busy room super easy, doesn't he?"

She put up her hand for a high five. He stared down at her, unblinking, before moving away.

"No problem, I got it!" she called after him, and slapped her own high five. "*Aces.* What's up, guys? Tell me you didn't start without me."

Sebastian came through the crowd next, given space by the shifters but not the gargoyles.

"It's like they're *trying* to be dicks," I said, watching the scene.

"They want ye to earn their respect," Niamh said before finishing up her glass of cider. "They make a big show of it. It's a huge pain in the arse, if ye ask me. It's a bar. Calm the feck down, lads."

"Hi, Jessie." The basajaun put up his hand. "Nice to see you again. Sorry about the other night. It looked like it had gotten rowdy."

"Yeah, no problem. I initially caused the whole thing, so…" I shrugged.

"Hey, sorry I'm late," Sebastian said, holding his computer. "What'd I miss?"

"We need a bigger circle." Nessa looked around.

Austin walked down the other side of the bar, and his gaze found me and stuck. A beige long-sleeve shirt showed off his broad shoulders and defined pecs. His stubble had been shaved away, and he was rocking that messy hair look that really suited him.

"Hey, baby," he said, grabbing a bottle of wine. "Did you have a good training?"

"Yeah, thanks." I leaned forward and lowered my voice. "How many of the gargoyles in here are with the leaders?"

He scanned the crowd as Nessa rearranged people around me. "Probably about half. They never cause any obvious trouble. I felt your magic a moment ago. I assume they didn't clear out of the way?"

"Yeah. Naomi told me to push through."

He nodded, noticing his grandma. "Welcome, Mimi. It took you a while to get down here. What can I get you?"

She clasped her hands in her lap. "I assume my input is currently of little importance?"

"You assume correctly."

"I'll have a glass of whatever Jessie is having."

He nodded, pulling out another glass.

"And you're fine with…" I hooked a thumb across Niamh to the basajaun, who was being made to scoot down. I recognized him from the first batch of newcomers, the one who'd come to drink with Niamh. Clearly he was still at it.

Austin watched him for a moment. "Yeah. We don't get many Dicks and Janes here anymore. I said I'd allow it until it became a problem. Turns out, the bar fights dropped to almost zero with a basajaun around. His mere presence seems to convince people to mind their manners."

You couldn't argue with that.

He served us drinks and said he'd meet me on the other side of the bar in just a bit.

"Okay, first order of business." Nessa studied her electronic notebook. "Niamh, we got questions."

"Joy," Niamh said drolly.

"As you know, that monster of a gargoyle has a natural resistance to magic. He made many mentions of *old* magic. Of feeling essences. Does that ring a bell?"

"Why should it?" she asked. "I'm not the mage in this outfit."

"Start from the beginning," Sebastian advised.

"Right, right, sorry." Nessa flicked her finger across

the screen and then reminded us of Tristan's ability to feel her through the wall.

"The other gargoyles we tested were nowhere near as effective," Sebastian said. "Not even the shifters have senses that keen. We tried Broken Sue, who has great instincts. He could sense me from across the room, and he knew someone was prowling around his property when we snuck through the other night, but he couldn't pinpoint us. He looked through all his windows, but it was a general feeling, not a localized feeling. So this gargoyle has a sort of perception that isn't normal for gargoyles or for shifters."

"He said it was *yer* essence?" Niamh asked Nessa, her interest already piqued. That was a good thing. She tried harder when that happened.

Nessa explained that he'd thought another entity had taken on her likeness.

"What'd he think you were?" Niamh asked.

Nessa cleared her throat and glanced at Sebastian. "Cone of silence, *s'il vous plaît*."

Sebastian draped a spell over us that would prevent people from hearing our conversation. Except maybe Tristan, but it'd be pretty obvious if he was in the bar.

"So that's where it gets interesting," Nessa said, scanning her notes. "He thought I might've been living in the walls, haunting the inhabitants. He said magic as old as *this*, meaning Ivy House, would have a good few of *you*." She tapped her notebook and looked up at Niamh. "He was talking to me like I was this creature. He went on about how clever it was to assume my face so it could lead people down to the underworld—"

"Didn't he call it something else?" Sebastian cut in.

"Oh yeah. The *Beyond*. He thought this creature would want to lead them down to the Beyond."

"The Beyond," Niamh said wistfully, and it was clear she knew that place. "But he didn't mention what he thought the creature was?"

"Well, later he said I looked like a sprite in the Forgotten Wood or a—"

Niamh sucked a breath through her teeth. The basajaun beside her looked over sharply, puffing up.

"He said that name?" Niamh asked. "The Forgotten Wood?"

"Yeah," Nessa said. "He also mentioned a wandering haunt…" She stared at Niamh with acute focus. When that didn't elicit another response, she continued. "He seemed very knowledgeable about those creatures, like he'd had a personal run-in." She explained what he'd said about it.

Niamh stared at the bar in front of her, obviously thinking. "Now how would a gargoyle his age know anything about all of that?" she said softly, as though to herself. "Is there anything else strange about this lad? The eyes, I know."

"The two kinds of blood, if that's what came out of his wings," I said.

"Ah yeah. I remember seeing that and wondering if it was a trick of me eyes." Niamh nodded. "Anything else? What's his history like? Where'd he come from?"

Nessa and Sebastian both shook their heads.

Nessa said, "That cairn has pretty good records on their people, but there's nothing on him. He was a walk-up, meaning he entered the cairn and asked for a trial to be a guardian."

"None of the other cairns have his name, either," Sebastian added.

"Here, Ulric…" Niamh reached out of the spell, grabbed Ulric by the sleeve, and dragged him in. She repeated what they'd just said about the lack of records.

"Is it any wonder?" Ulric asked. "He's massive, he's fast, he's incredibly strong and powerful—no one is going to question a guardian like that. They'd do anything to keep him happy. Forget the bracelet; he's that cairn's greatest asset. If he doesn't want to give his life history, they're not gonna push."

"Right so." Niamh rattled the ice in her empty glass. "Sebastian, be a good lad and take down this spell. I need me a drink to mull this over, and if I shout now, no one will hear me."

"We'll hear you," the basajaun said, "and wish we didn't."

"Exactly." Niamh rattled her ice cubes again.

Sebastian did as requested.

"Any thoughts?" Nessa asked.

Niamh didn't answer until she'd gotten her cider, taken a sip, and then sat back and crossed her arms over her chest. "Silence spell, Weird Mage."

"Yup. Got it." Sebastian did the spell.

"First," she said, "ye won't hear about the Forgotten Wood in any polite society. Old magic is right, from the beginning of the world. From before time existed. Twisted magic, now. Twisted creatures."

"You've been?" I asked.

"Oh aye, I've been. A cousin dwelled there for a time, long ago. I've done deals with creatures there. Hunted there. That was all in my youth, mind, when I was as dense as they come."

"And wandering haunts? Sprites?" Nessa asked, clearly riveted. "You know about those?"

Niamh nodded very slowly, her eyes far away. "Interesting he thought those types of creatures might dwell within Ivy House. He must not know much about magic if he thought that."

"And why is that?" Sebastian asked.

"If they tried to lead him to the Beyond rather than taking his soul, that says he has blood magic. That'd explain the eyes and his ability to see in pitch black. It would explain the different blood. But he doesn't know modern magic. He's knowledgeable about the area but not knowledgeable about the magic, it seems like. Hmm…"

"What's blood magic?" Nessa asked.

"Old magic," Niamh said. "Ancient magic. It exists in some creatures and dwells in the Beyond. In the Forgotten Wood and a few other places in the world where I'd warn ye never to go. Ye're not able for it. Or, well…" She looked again at the mages, lingering on Nessa. "Some of ye are, maybe."

"We weren't asking to go," Nessa said quickly. "We're just trying to figure out what the deal is with that big gargoyle."

"I'd go," Sebastian said quietly. "I want to learn more about this old magic."

"That's a dangerous game ye're playin'," Niamh told Sebastian. "If ye're not careful, ye'd lose yourself right handy chasing those shadows. Ye'd become something else entirely, something that I wouldn't let back into this world."

"So it's a different world?" Nessa asked.

"Might as well be."

"How could he bleed both orange and red?" Sebastian asked. "Because he did both."

Niamh was staring at Sebastian now, but her eyes didn't seem to be seeing him. "Mixed breed. Blood magic will always be different colored, but if ye aren't full-blooded, ye'll have normal blood too. There is no medical sense to it. That's how magic is. Ye have it or ye don't, and if ye do, it'll show. I've only ever seen green blood in the creatures I've encountered, but that doesn't mean much. There are many types of creatures in the dark places."

"This is blowing my mind," Nessa whispered.

"That's his deterrent to magic, though." Niamh nodded. "My memories from that time are all covered in cobwebs, but I would bet me arse that blood magic is immune to magic such as yours. Mage magic, we'll call it. He's half—or part, maybe—so he isn't totally immune, but he has a natural resistance."

Sebastian gave a pointed look at Nessa.

"And you're saying he's from that place?" I took a sip of my wine. "That wood?"

Niamh shrugged while she gulped her cider. "Can't know for sure. He's from *somewhere*, and it doesn't seem to be a cairn. He's got blood magic, I'd bet me life on it. Other than that, I don't know."

"Why would he hide it?"

"If he *is* from there, I wouldn't blame him keeping it quiet. Most of the creatures with blood magic are taboo. They're twisted. They're hunted and exterminated if they cross the boundary. As well they should be. They don't belong in our world. I'd be interested in knowing why he assumed he belonged in theirs…" She sucked her teeth, her gaze still far away.

"So this is all his doing and not Gimerel hiding something?" I asked.

"I'd guess as much," Niamh said. "Unless he told that cairn leader and the leader decided he'd better keep it under his hat."

"Doubtful." Sebastian looked at his computer screen. "He keeps good records. There was a note asking about origin on Tristan's original intake files, but it was never resolved. This seems like an example of Nelson deciding not to question his good fortune."

"Stop lookin' into this," Niamh said. "Give that gargoyle a wide berth for now. He's survived the dark lands, he's successfully hidden his origins, and he's not afraid to destroy vile creatures from twisted magic—he's beyond what ye're used to handling. I'll look into this. I'll do a little prodding and see how he reacts. I know what to look fer."

Nessa pushed out her bottom lip. "That's a buzzkill. I wanted to play puzzle master for this one."

"Ye'd play, and then ye'd get thrown off the roof fer *real* next time." Niamh took another gulp. "He's not goin' to jeopardize his life for a pretty girl. If he's hiding something foul that resides inside him, he won't be welcome anywhere. That's not something he'll happily expose."

"He can't be that dangerous, though, if I bested his challenge," I said with a little beam of pride.

"There is a face-to-face challenge, and then there are the shadow games of the Beyond," she said, her voice haunted. "Ye might win the first. Ye'd hope not to survive the second."

I released a breath. "So the only way to drag Gimerel down is to take Tristan down?"

Silence met my words. I assumed that was a yes.

The question was, did I want to destroy a life just to get even with Nelson for trying to sandbag me? Could I?

CHAPTER 26

JESSIE

THE NEXT MORNING I lay in bed, staring up at the ceiling. My coffee had gone cold on the nightstand beside me, and Mr. Tom was downstairs whipping up a "comforting and reassuring" breakfast to get me out of this early-morning slump.

I wasn't in a slump. I was wading through a bog of guilt and uncertainty.

I didn't like what I'd become. I didn't like what my team had become. Getting information the cunning way and presenting it to the cairns had been ugly but smart. Those four basically ran the gargoyle world and seemed to decide who got status and who didn't. Despite my power, money, and territory size (thank you, Austin), I'd be fast-tracked as a social pariah if they had their say.

I definitely wanted to play hardball with them. I wanted to squeeze them until they popped.

But digging into the private lives of their people had

pushed me out of my comfort zone.

Cyra and Hollace had returned to the bar last night with news that although Nelson had been boring to watch, Tristan had been full of activity. He'd kept moving locations or even just rooms within the house that Gimerel had bought, constantly making them chase him. He seemed to know they were spying. He probably knew they belonged to me.

Once informed of our suspicions, they'd wanted a green light to spy on him further. A green light the Dark Three had almost given.

The thing was, Tristan was an employee. He was just trying to do a job. If he was hiding something, it must be for a good reason. A reason Nelson didn't seem to care about. And why should he? From what I'd seen, Tristan was a model guardian, commanding those under him with finesse and keeping order within the township. He was Austin, for all intents and purposes, and he'd done a bang-up job. How could I consent to my team seeking out and revealing his secret, when it might rip his world out from under him?

I couldn't. That was the bottom line. I couldn't continue to do business this way.

Making a decision, I sat up and reached for my phone.

"Hell-o lovely," Nessa answered, bright and cheery.

"Are you ever grumpy?" I rubbed my eye with my free hand.

"Uh-oh, clearly you are."

"Yeah, I didn't sleep well last night. Hey, listen, I'm pulling the plug on this Tristan situation, and I wanted to tell you first. I know you two have history, what with his pitching you off the roof"—she spat out a laugh—"but I don't feel comfortable with the way things are going. Let the guy be. It's not his fault his leader dragged him here and forced him into our presence. He shouldn't be punished for it."

"What if he's dangerous?"

"He's no more dangerous than we are, and if he does know these beyond, or below, or whatever shadow games, he isn't playing them here. We're the ones who are being dicks right now, and I don't want to be that outfit. Maybe we'll need it in the mage world, but we don't need to act like this with him. We're going to leave him be."

She was quiet for a moment, and then I heard her sigh. "I get what you're saying. It's just hard for me to shift out of my other life and come here and be a lot more wholesome."

"Tell me about it. It's hard for me to shift out of my other life and be a lot more violent. But I think we should meet in the middle to have the best results, don't you?"

"Yes, I do. You're right."

"And if you do find out his secret, because I'm not so naïve as to think you guys will stop poking at him—I don't think Niamh can help herself—keep it to yourselves. Don't even tell me. Wherever he came from, he has made a life for himself. He has a future. You shouldn't jeopardize that because of the strange orange blood he possibly inherited from a taboo sort of creature."

She sucked in a little breath. "That's not… I'm not…" After a pause, she started again. "I wasn't trying to find out because of any animosity between us. I have nothing against the guy. He was right to grab me how he did—I would've done worse—and he saved a stranger's life at the expense of his favorite suit. In the scheme of things, he didn't act badly. I'm just…curious, I guess. Something about him niggles at me, and I have no idea why. Like he has these…mysterious depths. I can't decide if he's dangerous in that *come hither* sort of way like Broken Sue, or dangerous in that *if you come hither, I will kill you* way. I guess I'd just kinda like to know where I stand."

"Maybe just stand a little farther away."

She laughed into the phone. "Noted, senator. I shall tread lightly and tell no one about my travels."

"Wise." I hesitated a moment, tapping my fingers against my knee. "There's one other thing. Ulric was acting very strangely last night. The way he dressed, how subdued he was… He said something about not wanting to fight his way home, and on the way back, he stuck closely to us. He didn't find a girl like usual. When I asked him about it, he shrugged it off."

"He definitely seemed out of sorts."

"I was wondering… I know I just told you not to spy on people and pry into their lives, but…"

"You'd like to know what's going on."

"Yeah. I'd just like to know if he needs help but is afraid to ask for it."

"Gotcha. No problem. That's easily within my wheelhouse."

"Don't tell his mom."

She laughed again. "Heard."

"Okay. Pass all that on to Sebastian. I gotta call Niamh now."

"Good luck."

I'd need it.

After a deep breath, I figured maybe a shower and some fresh coffee should come first. That finished, I thought I'd better get around to breakfast. My meal consumed, I thought maybe I should go check on Edgar and the weird statue Naomi had mentioned. Or possibly check in on the basajaunak who were hopefully on the complete opposite side of the wood, something that would take all day to do…

"Good late morning, Jessie," Naomi said as I stood in the hallway, staring off into space. "Need a shove toward your destination?"

"No, no. I'm good…"

"Fantastic. While you're standing there doing nothing, you might want to check that skyline."

She strode quickly and efficiently toward her office at the back of the house.

"The skyline…" In confusion, I climbed the stairs to the second floor and looked out the nearest window. There, in the distance, a couple of approaching specks were evenly spread. I could just barely make out wings. "Oh…"

My heart sped up, and I turned, racing for the next window. Another couple of distant figures coming this way. At the back of the house, way out there, another two.

They were coming. The raid! The raid was happening!

"We've got the raid coming," I yelled to no one, racing down the hall and toward the third-floor stairs. "The raid is coming! Make sure that bracelet is where I put it the other night. Mr. Tom likes to move things when he cleans."

"How dare you!" I heard from the other end of the hall. "I know my business, thank you very much."

On the third floor, I ran toward the doorway that would lead to a level area of the roof. Out there, I did a full circle, seeing them coming at the house from all angles.

"Okay, then."

I sent out a pulse. A massive one. My magic boomed out over my property and then shot out wider, farther. It reached town and kept on going, moving to the next town and beyond.

Come to me. Fight!

It wasn't a command so much as an invitation.

Danger! Battle! Glory!

I let the pulses keep going, targeting everyone in the territory, shifters included.

My phone rang.

Austin.

"What've we got?" he asked, and I could tell he was on the move.

"The raid. Check the skyline."

His whistle was soft. "They're certainly giving you plenty of time. What do you need?"

"If Ivy House cooperates, not much, honestly. But it wouldn't hurt for me to down a few and let them see how the shifters can fight."

"And if she doesn't cooperate?"

"*I will,*" she said sullenly, and I repeated the message.

Gargoyles from town rose into the sky. In a moment, though, every single one of them dropped down again. They'd clearly seen Gimerel coming and decided not to get involved. They didn't want to go up against Tristan.

That was fine, as long as they saw me beat him.

I called Sebastian as I jogged down and through the second floor.

"It's on?" Hollace asked, coming out of his room. He had on slacks but no shirt, having paused in either putting on or taking off his clothes.

"That's what the big guardian was so busy about, then," Cyra said, popping out of her room with a big smile. "I called it, didn't I, Hollace? I said it would be today."

After Sebastian answered, I rapidly told him what was happening.

"We saw the gargoyles. We're already on our way."

"What're our orders?" Hollace asked, his hands now at his zipper.

"Fliers, get on the roof and get ready," I replied. "We won't take to the air until they're over the property. The shifters will be here soon. They'll take the ground. Obviously. Most of our defense will be Ivy House. They seem to think I want to hide where my magic came from—probably so I can pretend to fit in. Nope. If they're stupid enough to attack Ivy House, they can get the full brunt of her defenses. I'm not trying to hide anything."

I could feel the basajaunak running away from the house, spreading out within the wood.

"Crap," I said, calling Austin.

"What's up?" he answered.

"Get someone out to Dave and make sure he understands that we are *not* killing these gargoyles. We can hurt them, but we're aiming for zero mortal injuries, even if they say something nasty."

"He seemed to be clear on the rules the other night, but I'll deliver the message."

"I know he was, but you know him…and the others."

"Understood."

Edgar was skulking around his cottage, in no sort of hurry. He'd probably end up saving the day again. You just never knew with that vampire.

Nathanial jogged out of his room down the way, buck naked and no muumuu in sight. He was heading to the roof with the rest of his fliers, though had clearly hung back a bit to speak to me. He wouldn't be in his skin long anyway.

"Are you still going to take Tristan on?" he asked.

"Absolutely, hopefully in front of an audience."

"I'm no match for him in the air," he said, his usually calm and confident tone wavering a little. "I'm not going to be much help to you."

I paused. "I don't want help. I want everyone to see my weaknesses clearly. I can't fly very fast or maneuver very well. I'm tiny in comparison. I'm purple and sparkly, for God's sake. Everyone will see that he has me utterly outgunned in all the ways they think matter. And I will blast him out of the sky. I will not fail in this. I cannot." Fire raged through me. "If that leader turns up, though, allow him into the house. I want Ivy House to make him sweat."

"*With pleasure*," Ivy House said.

Nathanial took a long moment, his gaze fierce and proud. He didn't comment, as was his nature, but his nod said it all.

He knew he was on the winning team. We would all make sure of it, together, relying on each other.

When I got downstairs, Naomi sat at her desk.

"I assume you're not going to fight…" I let the comment linger so as not to offend her. Shifters were prickly about old age and fighting prowess.

"No," she answered.

"Then you'd best stay out of the way. The TV room is probably best, or even just here, at your desk. They shouldn't bother with you if you don't bother with them. Stay out of the hidden tunnels, though. Those are for the enemy."

A little grin pulled at her lips. She nodded, her eyes sparkling so much that I couldn't believe her smile didn't widen. Then again, she was a former alpha, through and through. Without a word, she turned back to her desk and her work.

This woman was made of iron. No wonder her pack had risen from the ashes and thrived.

Speaking of phoenixes…

"No killing!" I reminded Cyra as I jogged toward the rendezvous point. "And no cutting off faces and wearing them as masks, or whatever else you might get up to."

"I have not tried that one." Cyra smiled excitedly at Hollace.

He rolled his eyes. "That was a movie, and he was a sociopath. You're doing a terrible job at pretending to be human."

She let that sink in as she jogged after me. "He was still technically human, right? I'm just doing a bad job of pretending to be a good human. It's a start."

Once we got onto the roof, I looked out at the skyline. Wow, Gimerel was coming *slow*. Were they giving us time to have breakfast before the raid or what?

"Right." I looked toward the town again, checking to see whether any other fliers had decided to join our team. A few more gargoyles had flown into the sky, but everyone was hovering low, ready to watch the show. "Right."

Niamh walked out onto the roof in her muumuu. "What'da… Are they bringing the whole lot into the territory? I thought there were rules against that, no?"

"Not in a raid, apparently," I told her. Then I just blurted what I needed to tell her. "Hey, Niamh, about that other thing from last night. The spying? Don't do that. Don't find out what he is. Just let it go."

"Had a wee bit o' guilt about that, did ya?" Niamh chuckled. "I wondered when all this would catch up to ya. I'll keep ye out of it, how's that? But I half want to know if my cousin is still kicking them woods. He disappeared years ago. Might be related."

"I think you're keeping me out of too much. Like sneaking away to the basajaunak. I don't want all these secrets."

"That wasn't a secret. Ye knew all about that."

"Well…right…but that's only because Austin told me."

"Ye don't think we knew Austin Steele was keeping tabs on us? We knew. But I had to make it seem like I was hiding the truth from yis so that the basajaunak would think they were only permitted on Dave's land. That if they wanted in on the fun and games, they'd need to trade fer it. Once those buggers trade for something, it means something to them. I was just helping Dave usher them to that point. And now look, ye got a small gaggle of them down there, waiting to brain the first thing that falls in their laps. More points if they have'ta do a little work to get at it."

"Dang it, I *knew* they'd try to turn this into a blood sport," I muttered. "Okay, fine, you knew what you were doing. But still, let's all just…stay open with each other, okay? Let's make sure we're on the same page."

Everyone murmured their assent as car tires screeched along the road. A moment later, Sebastian and Nessa were running for the house. She didn't follow him in, though, instead looping around the house, probably for Edgar. The two of them made a surprisingly excellent team.

"This'll all calm down soon," Niamh said as Sebastian worked his way through the house. "If this raid goes well, it'll be grand. If not…well, we're no worse off, really."

The sound of engines heading toward us pulled my

focus. Cars parked at the front of the house. Shifters. Just after, more shifters in animal form entered the wood, coming from all directions. Austin came last, on two legs first and then shifting to four. He paused on the backyard grass to look up at me before disappearing into the trees. A swell of warmth I knew was love came through the bond. I returned the sentiment.

Still those gargoyles flew, slowly closing the distance. Ever so slowly. Like they were nearly suspended in midair.

"This is getting a bit ridiculous," I said at last, half thinking of sitting down to wait.

"We can tell," Hollace said in amusement. "Your pulses of magic went from the equivalent of a battle drum…to a foot tapping. Everyone can feel your annoyance at the wait."

"Oh—"

"No, no!" Hollace put up a finger. "Don't change it. I think it sets the right mood. The battle-hardened will always find games like these tedious. And now all the visiting gargoyles know."

"I'm here!" Sebastian ran out onto the roof wearing a sweat suit. "I'm here." He looked at the sky and sagged, breathing hard. Nessa found Edgar below. "Why does it seem like they are still so far away?"

"What's the story with him?" Ulric asked, indicating

Sebastian. "Is he going airborne?"

"No." I watched the sky, seeing one inkblot that was larger than the rest. Tristan. "We need all our fliers to combat their guardians. Besides, they are coming to us. All he has to do is stand here and prevent them from reaching the house."

"Seems easy enough," Sebastian said sarcastically.

Patty walked through the front door, her steps unhurried. I frowned, turning that way, monitoring her progress through the house, up the stairs, and finally to the door leading to the flat part of the roof on which we stood.

"Jessie, hello! Lovely day, isn't it?" She looked up, stepping out with me.

"Careful, Mom," Ulric warned from his perch. "It's not as flat as it looks. It slants a little."

"Oh, bah!" She waved him away. "Kids, always thinking us parents are feeble. Now, Jessie." She took a spot beside me, looking out at the horizon. "I love what you're doing with your magic. Very funny. I walked through downtown on my way here, and people were snickering and laughing. Great sign. However…"

I prepared for the explanation on why this course of action wasn't fitting with the gargoyle way of doing things.

"The raiding camp can't feel it," she finally said, her

tone delicate. "It's a shame to make a joke at their expense that they can't feel, you know?"

She took my hand, apparently trying to ease the blow of her comments. She must've thought my ego was fragile.

"Maybe it would be better if you sent the hurry-up vibe *to* them?" She gave me an inquisitive look. "And when you fight their lead enforcer—You *are* going to fight their lead enforcer, right? I heard about your rooftop brawl. If only we could've spread that around! What a marvelous story that would've been. In an evening gown, no less. *In your human form!* The garhettes would've raved. But that's okay. We can maybe leak the news after this is all over."

She took a breath, and the silence felt weird after her bombardment of words. I realized she was waiting for me to answer a question, then had to think back to remember what that question had been.

"I am going to fight him, yes," I finally said.

"Right. Well." She squeezed my hand. "When you fight him, can you try to do it over the woods a little? Not too far. Just beyond Edgar's flower line. That'll give us the best shot. I'll just hide up here on the roof, out of the way, to get it on camera."

"No, you can't—"

"Don't you worry at all," she said forcefully. "I have

been through a great many raids. I know how to stay out of the way. And there are no garhettes besides me, so they won't try to take anyone."

"Wait, what?" I said.

She squeezed my hand again. "It's a raid tradition. If an attacking guardian sees a garhette that strikes his fancy, he whisks her back to their camp for the night. She tries to fight him off, of course. What would be the fun in going quietly? Mind you, once she's at the camp, she can choose to walk away, or go back to his cairn with him to see about a life together. It's very romantic. Unless you're one of the prettier garhettes, then I hear it just gets tedious and you have to hide to avoid it. Why, I once knew a girl who'd traveled to five different cairns via raids until she finally found a guardian she wanted to settle down with. It really worked out in her best interest—"

"Mom," Ulric said, "maybe get to the point?"

Niamh started to laugh. "That would've been a riot in my youth."

"If anyone were dumb enough to grab you," Mr. Tom told her as he finally walked onto the roof, coming to stand by me, "they quickly would've wished they hadn't."

"Well, anyway," Patty said, "that won't be a problem here. This isn't a normal raid." She squeezed my hand again. "They are getting a bit closer now. Possibly now would be a good time to—"

"Yes, yes, fine." I sent another peal of magic.

Like before, it blasted out to the town and beyond, but this time it also targeted the enemy. *Hurry up and meet your fate.*

Then I focused on Tristan, the largest shape I'd seen, putting all my power behind it, pounding him with a challenge. *Come and get me. I'm waiting.*

His burst of speed was apparent. Message received.

The rest sped up as well. My crew discarded their clothes if they were wearing them. Even Cyra calmed down, starting to focus.

We as fliers were grossly outnumbered. Hilariously so.

Par for the course.

"Here we go," I said, seeing his shape clearly now, knowing his focus wasn't on this house. It wasn't on this raid.

It was on me.

He wanted payback.

CHAPTER 27

JESSIE

I SHIFTED IN a hurry. I could direct my people through magic and our links. I could direct them from the air, even in the middle of fighting. I'd done it before.

I had to find the darkness first. I had to completely surrender to my gargoyle.

This time there was no hesitation.

I pushed off the roof. A pump of magic told the others not to follow. Not yet. Let the crowds see me meet that monster. Let them see the tiny pink and purple speck fly out to meet that metallic blue and teal beast.

The air felt good around me. I flapped my wings and rose higher, accentuating my gargoyle's shortcomings in flight. In contrast, one pump of Tristan's wings drove him forward at an incredible speed, cutting the distance between us in half as he zoomed right for me.

My stomach wiggled, but only for a moment. Fire

raged in its wake, and then I jutted forward to meet him, feeling paltry at best until I let loose a surge of magic that trumpeted my challenge.

His answering roar was mighty, wriggling through my blood and slicing into my bones. Instead of causing fear, though, it invigorated me.

He straightened, and his claws came forward to ram and rip at me. I threw up a shield and jetted sideways. He slammed into the magic full force, which knocked his head and flattened his body. The spell weakened a little—his natural defenses coming to his aid—but not enough. He began to fall.

The others zoomed behind him, and I sent out another peal for my crew. As one they roared or neighed, issuing their challenges, and the fliers rose into the air. Thunder rolled across the sky, followed by streaks of lightning from Hollace. Fire curled away from Cyra. The gargoyles took off in all directions, needing to cover various angles, and Niamh wasted no time in shooting directly for the first gargoyle she saw who needed a hole in his side.

That was when Ivy House shuddered into action, feeling her time for glory. The door to the doll room opened, and they spread out, finding their placement within the house for the poor sods who would make it that far. Darkness filtered into the blue sky, and shadows reached across the grounds and into the wood. Fog drifted through the trees and upward, making a murky soup.

A spear rose through it and out of the trees, striking a gargoyle. Startled, he flapped wildly, but the weapon had punctured a wing. He was lowered, fighting it, until he disappeared into the trees. I knew he wouldn't come back out until this was all over.

Another spear sailed up, and then another.

Apparently the basajaunak had talents no one had told me about. That was handy and terrifying at the same time.

"*You've been very naughty, little gargoyles,*" Ivy House said in a strange sort of whisper. "*Mommy gargoyle is not impressed.*"

I shivered, both because that was off-putting and because I was suddenly nervous for our adversaries.

Tristan caught himself from the fall and backed off the magic, so incredibly agile despite his size. He rose slowly—for him—his gaze on me. He circled away from Ivy House as a blast of darts filled the air around us. They wouldn't hit my people, and I threw up a shield so they wouldn't hit Tristan either. I didn't want Ivy House's help. I wanted this battle to stay between just him and me.

He saw what I was doing, watched the darts fall to

the ground, then circled me a little longer, sussing me out. Maybe calculating his next move.

I waited. There'd be no point in my attempting to be the aggressor in the air. We both knew it.

He shot forward so fast that I couldn't help but flap wildly and skitter backward. He caught me quickly, scratching down my stomach and across my shoulder to the top of my left wing. Hot agony raced through me, but he hadn't decommissioned that wing. Tried but failed.

Healing myself already, I answered by ripping my claws into him, still in his hold, and shooting spells directly against his skin. Burned flesh perfumed the air. A series of grunts worked up through his throat. A small keening sounded before he tossed me away, unable to take that much pain.

I was after him then, missing Nathanial at my back, struggling to catch him but throwing a slab of magic on his other side to stop his backward progress. I ripped into him, shot him with magic, raked my claws against him. His hide was tougher than other gargoyles', though, and I didn't make much of an impact.

His big arm came around, smacking me. I flew ass-over-tea-kettle, not sure when to open my wings lest I get it wrong and tweak one. In the end, I just threw up a wall to slam against, stopping my fall so I could get my bearings. He was after me in a moment, nearly there—the kill shot.

Fear doused me. I reacted hard, maybe too hard. The burst of magic was so intense, it made my eyes water.

His roar turned into a howl as my spell ripped into his middle. A huge, horrible gash opened up in his stomach, and blood poured out, not all of it red.

His wings fluttered and he hunched over, clutching at himself. He dropped in altitude, hugging the wound. I couldn't tell if it was because of the pain, because of that strange orange blood, or a combination of both.

I could end this right here. I could drop him to the ground and claim victory. But he was losing so much blood. What if he didn't heal in time and bled out? Or what if he continued to bleed that strange blood and someone identified his otherness? I'd just spent all morning deciding I wouldn't reveal him, and here I might've done it accidentally!

Making a quick decision, I crashed into him, smushing my front against his and wrapping my wings around him. Immediately my healing magic got to work; it was quicker with contact.

"Wh-yy?" he asked, and I wasn't sure what he meant. Why heal him? Why help him? Did he think I lacked any sort of morals?

More darts flew as we sank in the air. He scratched at me, but the scrapes were superficial, as his claws barely pierced my flesh. I felt confusion and concern through the bond from Austin. I sent back assurance and confidence, scratching Tristan with my feet to pretend we were wrestling.

He ripped me to the side, his wings snapping. He didn't break my hold, though. He knew I was healing him.

Shifters paced below, wanting to be part of the fight, seeing their opportunity as Tristan and I continued to sink through the air. Hot blood still seeped against me, and I knew he would've bled out. I'd slashed him way too deep.

"Fl-iie," I said. I wasn't nearly as good at talking in this form. "Uup. Hoor-ee."

His wings worked, and we shot up quickly. I could feel his wince as he did so.

"Wh-yy?" he asked again, apparently assuming I had any kind of mastery with my mouth.

Fatigue started to pull at me with too much of my energy going into him. It only needed to go a bit longer, though. Just a little bit longer, and he'd be out of danger.

I pulled my wings away and flapped them wildly, continuing to scratch at him. He grabbed hold of me, squeezing me close, and then tumbled us through the air. Spit flew out of the side of my mouth from the velocity at which we were suddenly moving. I was pretty sure I was the one screaming, now clutching him for dear life. The ground jiggled in my vision, really far away. Then he dove, and I was definitely the one screaming.

His chuckle was dark and wicked as he spun us. My stomach shoved into my back and then out through my mouth as we spiraled toward the ground.

"Am I go-od?" he asked as I squeezed my eyes shut for a moment. I'd never flown this fast and recklessly in all my life.

I unclenched my jaw with effort. "Goo-ud." Close enough.

Nearer the ground now, he shoved me away from him, scratching long gashes across my arms as he did so.

So he thought we'd battle for a bit longer, did he?

This time I would control myself more and end this once and for all (without killing him).

My roar of challenge was dwarfed by his, but it was no less effective.

And then we were at it again—Tristan charging through the air at a speed that was still too fast despite his injury, and me back-pedaling because it was incredibly jarring. I hit him with magic, blunt spells stuffed with a crapload of power. They were much too simplistic to ever use on mages, but even with his natural protection, they rocked his world. He was knocked sideways, then back. His grunts came faster, louder. He visibly flagged, not able to get to me, not able to keep up. I kept shooting them off. More and more, harder and harder, starting to flag now but not easing up. My practice had all led up to this.

With one last effort, which he clearly poured everything into, he darted forward to grab me. His claws sliced down my side. Blood immediately welled up and then started flowing down.

I shoved him back with magic…and then waved goodbye.

The spell I used to snap his wings to his sides shocked the hell out of him. His eyes widened, showing the whites all around. Then he dropped like a stone.

He turned and twisted in the air as he fell, roaring in defiance. When he was ten feet off the ground, I slipped a net spell under him, one that Sebastian had perfected, catching him at a dead stop, then released him to the waiting shifters below.

My roar of victory was all for show. My appeal to Nathanial was urgent. Tristan got to take a break. I had to protect the rest of the house. No way would I be doing it with solely my wings.

He was with me in a moment, lifting me up and away.

Gargoyles swarmed the house, far more fliers than we had at our disposal. Sebastian flung spells like a madman, hitting them hard and turning them back. He could only maim, though, not kill. Without anyone to take them to the ground, they flapped around for a while until they were good enough to return to battle. I'd say this for gargoyles—their stubbornness was a definite advantage in battle.

Hollace swooped down with lightning shooting from him. It caught multiple gargoyles at a time, stopping them and making them shake in the air. It didn't last long enough for them to fall, though. They shook it off much faster than a mage would, than a shifter, even, as their tough hides provided them with some defense.

Cyra darted and dodged all around, fast and agile. She threw nonlethal fire, blasting everyone she came across. Our gargoyles darted in after her, ripping into the stationary gargoyles and throwing them to the shifters waiting on the ground. Spears cut through the air, and one gargoyle flew as fast as he could from a whinnying Niamh. He wouldn't win that fight.

Still they crowded closer, with Hollace and Cyra not

wanting to use their magic over the house. Our gargoyles showed prowess, but they weren't plentiful enough to do any real damage.

"We could use some wind elemental magic to shove them away," Sebastian yelled as Nathanial flew me closer.

I leaned forward so Nathanial would release me, and then sent out a pulse of power. Gargoyles flapped, not liking the tingle that spell sent through their wings. With them stalling, I did as Sebastian had suggested and summoned my power for an intense blast.

A great plume of fire rolled away from me in all directions, hotter and denser than the blasts Cyra had been using and much too vicious for a friendly battle with a nonthreatening cairn.

Oops.

Gargoyles howled. Those trying to catch their breath from Hollace or Cyra dropped from the sky, balls of flame headed for the grass below. Those who'd avoided my blast pushed back quickly, trying to get away in case I did it again.

"That'll work, too," Sebastian said.

Trying again, because I might as well practice, I pulled more energy. My breath became heavy with the effort. Closing my eyes, I thought hard about the spell. I envisioned it in my mind and took care to notice every little detail. Only when I'd done that did I make another attempt.

Snapping my eyes open, I saw a gargoyle dive down for me. Nathanial darted in front, catching the gargoyle and wrestling him out of the way. They spiraled through the air, ripping and tearing at each other, until they hit the roof and bounced off.

Figuring he could handle it, knowing they wouldn't actually kill each other, I let loose the spell.

Instead of fire this time, a great gust of wind blew, out and down. It was plenty strong to take anyone who was less than one hundred percent down to the basajaunak and shifters below.

Unfortunately, it was also strong enough to whisk Sebastian away and throw him off the roof.

My swear came out garbled. I launched from the roof after him, throwing hard spells at anyone who would take my plight as an opening for them to get to the house. Sebastian sailed then started to fall as gravity did its job. A magical net caught him, keeping him stationary in the sky. He looked back my way, his face utterly composed.

When on the job, the guy had courage of iron.

Mr. Tom battled my wind and swooped through the sky to grab him. I put up a magical shield for him, blocking the effects of the elemental spell. Then I did the same for the others, giving them free rein to grab the struggling gargoyles and throw them downward.

That was when I saw him—an older gargoyle, a little stringy and with gray hair, struggled behind two guardians toward the house. They flew low, probably level with the second story, looking like they were trying to sneak in.

Nelson.

My team saw him about when I did, and all of them looked to me for direction. I pointed at the guardians trying to block the wind from him so that he could make his way. Cyra and Ulric dipped through the sky immediately, attacking his helpers. I put a protective spell over Nelson, but if he knew it, he gave no sign. He just kept striving for the house, clearly wanting to be the one to get the bracelet and take the glory.

You should've stuck to bird watching, I thought.

I opened all the windows in front of him and popped out the screens. The dolls waited within the hidden passageways, spread out all over, intending to mess with the minds of whoever came through.

Nelson didn't take the bait, though. He had a particular destination in mind.

He angled up to the third floor, to the little landing that Nessa had pitched off the night of the dinner.

Somehow, he didn't notice me flying just a bit behind him and to the side, watching him labor to that little landing and perch on the edge. Another of his gargoyles managed to evade Niamh for long enough to attempt to join his leader and get into the house.

I waved my hand. A blistering spell knocked him easily away, tossing him end over end through the sky and down. A basandere leapt up with surprising grace and snatched him out of the air. He wouldn't be returning to the battle.

Nelson shifted to his human form and hurried down the couple of steps to the door that was standing wide open. He didn't stop to wonder whether this was a trap. Apparently he thought we'd just welcome him in without even closing the entrances to the house.

I slammed the door behind him, locking him in.

He should've gone in through the windows. At least then he would've had a chance to avoid the hidden passageways.

"*You're mine,*" Ivy House said, absolutely giddy with excitement.

It was the first time I'd actually felt sorry for any of the gargoyle leaders.

That done, I rose into the sky, seeing only a few enemy gargoyles left airborne. My team were closing in on all sides, corralling them toward one another. Ulric and Cyra flitted and swooped, herding them like sheep and, in so doing, showing off their incredible agility in the air. Ulric might've been smaller than most guardians, but he made great use of it, showing he was just as mighty. Jasper attacked a gargoyle that was trying to escape, wrenching his wing, spinning him around, and then throwing him to the ground.

Dave grabbed that one, and his roar of triumph jiggled my stomach a little. God, I hoped he minded his manners. He wasn't the easiest one to talk out of violence.

The five remaining gargoyles put up their hands, surrounded now.

One said something that sounded a little like "Yield!"

Suddenly I didn't feel so bad about my garbled speaking ability.

They lowered slowly, followed by my crew, until they touched down on the grass and into a precise ring of shifters.

This time my roar wasn't just for show. My team had done it! We'd persevered against insane odds, again, and shown what we were made of.

My second roar was joined by my team, including shifters and the basajaunak. I pulled back the magic that darkened the lands, got rid of the fog, and then sent wave after wave of victory to those waiting in the town or hovering in the air, watching the show. I knew the other large cairns were seeing this, their leaders carefully watching. But most importantly, the solo guardians who'd come to check us out were also watching, seeing our strength. They'd felt the call, and now they felt the pride and joy of triumph, whether they'd been in the fight or not.

The first of probably many screams drifted out from somewhere in the house.

Doll sighting. Nelson was just getting started.

CHAPTER 28

NESSA

"IS JESSIE COMING?" Nessa asked Jasper as they waited on the sidewalk in front of Ivy House.

The others were getting cleaned up after another hard training. Three days had gone by since the raid, and Jessie was not at all slowing down. That was a good thing. A very good thing. Nessa just wished she and Sebastian could tell her why it was so important.

Guilt burned in her gut, and she cleared her throat, turning away for a moment. God how she hated this. These people were becoming her family, and a family was something you protected at all costs. It felt like Sebastian and Nessa were doing the opposite by keeping important information from them, not to mention bringing in a bunch of magical users to attack them.

She had to trust Sebastian, though. This had to be done like this, in secrecy. In deceit. It would be far from the only time if their future plans came to fruition.

Still.

At least Nessa could do *something* to help the team. She was going to the bar with the guys to see if she couldn't figure out what was troubling Ulric. After a few preliminary questions and a little digging, she had an idea of what to expect.

"Don't think so," Jasper replied, his hair still wet and his shirt clinging to his muscular chest. He never really put much time and effort into getting dressed, but it didn't seem to matter with the ladies. "She got a notice earlier that the visiting cairns want to have a farewell dinner. They aren't going to hang around much longer, I guess."

"Wait, what?" She turned toward him, her gut tightening. "So soon? When did they say that?"

"She got the note this morning, I guess. Austin Steele is going to clear out his nicest restaurant for it."

Her mind whirled. Their whole plan was predicated on the gargoyles being here for the attack. That was the whole point of the attack, to show those bastards some proof of her awesomeness! The raid hadn't cut it. The house had had a big part in that. It was a watered-down version of the real thing. They needed to show Jessie was a badass without a magical house for backup. More importantly, those gargoyles needed to fight *with* her, not against her.

"When did they say they were leaving?" Nessa asked, trying to tone her reaction down. He couldn't know she was worked up because then, when the truth came out, he'd realize she'd known something. Austin Steele would skin them alive if he found out.

"A few days, I think. The Gimerel leader is feeling the sting of that lost raid." Jasper smiled with pride. "We *spanked* them."

"But…" She tucked a stray strand of hair behind her ear. "Didn't they buy houses here? It sounded like they planned on staying for a while."

He laughed as he shook his head. "Missed that in your digging, huh? Cairn leaders always talk a big game. I guess they didn't buy anything. They're short-term renting. Sounds like they offered the owners an arm and a leg to stay there for a while. First Gimerel did, and then the others caught on and did the same. The houses will still sell, and in the meantime the owners get a nice little paid vacation."

She barely stopped from swearing under her breath. Yes, she had missed that in her digging, mostly because she'd been focused on a dozen other things, and their living situation hadn't been a top priority.

This whole situation was slanting left—her fragile house of cards about to tumble down.

Ulric came out of the house, back to wearing his

bright shirts and crazy pants, with blue and pink spiky hair.

"I can see Gimerel licking his wounds and taking off, but the others?" she asked. "Why would they leave so soon? Mr. Porsche was planning on checking out Austin's fast car. He seemed in no rush to take off. The raid had nothing to do with him."

A smile spread across Ulric's face. "Nelson thought he'd show up with his enormous lead enforcer, make a mockery of Jessie with his raid, and then hang around a while with his bracelet to gloat—"

"The bracelet that's been sitting on a table in the sitting room like a paperweight." Jasper started laughing. "No velvet pillow, no glass case—just taken off, dropped onto a table, and walked away from."

"Yeah. Insult to injury, right?" Ulric started chuckling too. "Then the leader…" His chuckling turned into laughter. "The leader spent the after-party running through the walls, screaming." He bent over, guffawing now.

"That dude's ego has got to be crushed." Jasper shook his head, still laughing. "I'd get the hell out of here too."

"Especially after my mom posted a video of it." Ulric wiped his eyes. "She tried to play innocent. Like she didn't know he was running around screaming in the background while Cyra and Hollace had a casual chat."

There had been two ends to the raid. The first was when Tristan and the rest of the guardians had risen into the sky, roared their defeat, and attempted to get their leader back so they could skulk off.

But Jessie hadn't wanted him rescued so early.

In a move that had apparently shocked the raiding guardians, she'd shepherded them into the house and provided food and refreshments. There'd been no gloating. No smug exhibition of the bracelet. No indication of any kind that they'd just been through a vicious battle. Just a fun little party at the leader's expense as Ivy House tormented him within her walls.

At one point, Jessie had sought Tristan out. "I know what that bracelet means to your cairn. You know where it is. The raid is still technically on, so you're welcome to it if you want it."

"No…miss," Tristan had replied. "The raid ended when my guardians yielded. If *anything* is taken from this house, no matter by whom, I will ensure it is returned to you."

"She embarrassed one of them, fine," Nessa said, thinking over the situation with rising panic. "What about the others? You'd think someone would turn up to offer her congratulations."

"And piss off Gimerel?" Ulric gave her an exaggerated look, basically saying she was being absurd. "She's an unknown. A powerful unknown, but still an unknown. They won't want him thinking they're showing any kind of allegiance to her. They'll all give her space for now and then hopefully try to establish a friendship or some sort of shaky truce on the down-low. She just needs time, I think."

"You know…" Jasper said, staring out at the horizon. A sunburst of color washed across the sky, celebrating the closing of another day.

"Yes," Ulric responded. "For I know everything."

Jasper ignored him. "I used to dream about being a guardian for Gimerel. For any of the biggest cairns, actually. I envisioned myself in Tristan's place, leading successful raids and defending the township."

"We all did." Ulric glanced at the house as Hollace stepped out, always so freaking put together and hot. "We heard stories about their heroics and how much they made and how everyone loved them and looked up to them…"

"How much they made." Jasper scoffed, and it turned into a laugh. "Did you look at that spreadsheet Nessa and the weird mage did? About all the salaries?"

"Yeah. The big cairns don't pay out much more than the small cairns."

"Don't forget the perks, though," Nessa told them,

seeing Niamh step out of her house across the street and bend to check the rocks next to her chair. At one point they'd been stolen or something, and now Niamh always seemed to check them. Though who would steal a bunch of rocks was anyone's guess.

"The perks are what, free food in a cafeteria?" Jasper gave her a *look*. "Do you know how bad that food is? You'd have mac and cheese sitting there for three days."

"Free coffee," she said absently, thinking through all her plans, trying to find a way to speed up that attack. Or maybe slow the gargoyles from exiting. There just wasn't enough time!

"In the let-down room?" Jasper replied as Niamh's head slowly swiveled around.

Nessa knew that look.

Without raising suspicion, she sashayed a little toward the grass, clasping her hands behind her back as though she were looking around the grounds.

"What *is* a let-down room, anyway?" she asked as Niamh picked out a couple winners. "Like a breakroom?"

"Yeah, basically," Ulric said, turning a little to keep her in his sights, giving Niamh his back. Nessa really shouldn't set them up like this. She really shouldn't… "Every cairn has this, like…rec center, kinda. It has pool and air hockey and stuff like that. There's a large room in there solely for the guardians where they can hang out and relax."

"And in that very auspicious room that really only has cards and a couple of sagging couches is free coffee," Jasper said loftily. "The bitterest dredge you'll ever taste. What about our—*Ow!*"

Jasper ducked and put up his arms as another rock came flying. It smacked off Ulric's head, knocking him sideways.

"Damn that woman—*Look out!*" Jasper ran backward. "We're under fire!"

Only when they were out of throwing distance did Niamh put the rest of her rocks down and start on her way to the bar.

"She's not even going to wait for us?" Jasper asked, staring after her. "Rude."

"What about our what?" Hollace asked, still on the porch. He'd clearly seen the writing on the wall and decided to wait it out. Now he descended the steps.

"Our salaries," Jasper replied. "We make *way* more than they do and have…like…a crazy amount of perks. It's insane. We've landed a way better position. We see a lot more action, too. That raid was lame. What was even the point, you know?"

"It was good for training." Hollace wiped a bit of lint off his black button-up shirt. "Who are we waiting on?" He looked back at the door.

"Sebastian," Nessa told him. "He's just chatting with Jessie about a few things. No Cyra?"

"No, she's going to go spy on that lead enforcer. Don't tell Jessie."

"She's gonna get in trouble," Nessa said in a sing-song voice.

"I know, but she really enjoys sneaking after him. He's got this sixth sense about it. She can't seem to ever keep him in her sights for long. She treats it like a game, and even though he's not actually playing, he keeps winning. It's funny."

"He's dangerous," Nessa said seriously. "I don't think spying on him is the best idea."

"Dude, she comes back from the dead." Jasper frowned at Nessa. "What else can he do to her besides kill her—serve her Niamh's dry sandwiches?"

Ulric spat out a laugh.

Sebastian stepped out of the house, his gaze downcast and distant. He was thinking about something, and Nessa had a feeling he'd heard the news as well. This did not bode well for them.

"Hey! There's the man of the hour," Ulric said, stepping forward to pat him on the back.

"Don't bother." Nessa waved him away. "He's thinking. Just ignore him until he comes out of it."

"O-kay." Ulric tilted his head. "Wait, is that your way of politely telling me that he doesn't like me?"

"Ulric, my love…" She patted him. "I wouldn't hold back in telling you that someone doesn't like you—you have my word. In fact, maybe at the bar I'll try to find a bunch of people who don't like you so I can tell you about them one by one."

"You'd definitely find someone tonight," Jasper murmured. "He already knows they don't like him, though."

Ulric rolled his eyes. "I keep thinking those idiots are going to get tired of coming after me, but they always find new people who like to bully a smaller guy."

"The smaller guy who kicks their asses." Jasper elbowed him.

Shivers coated Nessa's body. Their talk was confirming her suspicions. "What's this now?"

"It's nothing." Ulric waved it away.

"This pair of idiot shifters decided they didn't like Ulric when he first got here," Jasper explained. "Didn't you go home with one of their girlfriends or something?"

"She wasn't even a girlfriend—she was just a girl these clowns were trying to pick up."

"Anyway," Jasper continued, "they've been making his life hell ever since."

"Not hell," Ulric replied. "It's not that bad. They're not that great at fighting. But then they bring in more people to outnumber me, and it's a pain in the ass. Everyone else they've targeted has decided to drink elsewhere, so until they find someone new, I get all their attention."

"What joy is yours." Jasper smirked at him.

They got to the corner of the street and crossed over. "Have you mentioned this to Austin?" Ness asked.

Both guys paused to stare at her.

"Are you serious?" Jasper asked. "How's the guy supposed to hold his head up if he has to have someone else fight his battles? That's sure to bring a bunch of other clowns looking for an easy fight."

"And you can't just accidentally-on-purpose kill one of them while defending yourself?" Nessa pushed.

Ulric shook his head. "I've landed a dream job. It might take a second, but eventually other gargoyles will envy us. I don't want to put that in jeopardy by going too hard with a couple idiots. It's fine. They'll get tired of losing eventually."

That night, actually. They'd get tired of losing that night—Nessa would make sure of it. After she identified the troublemakers, she'd make them an offer she hoped they'd refuse, because if they did, she'd get to leave their carcasses in the woods.

"Hey, Ivy Hozers, wait for me!"

Everyone turned at the sound of the male voice. One of the basajaunak emerged from the trees on the other side of the road—the one who drank with Niamh. He had on his hard hat, reflective vest, and too-short kilt. His long legs helped him close the distance in no time, a big smile on his hairy face.

"Hey!" he said again when he got closer. "Are we all going to the same fun-time watering hole?"

"Hozers?" Jasper said as Ulric repeated, "Fun-time watering hole?"

"For a little libation, yes," Nessa said, starting to walk again.

"Good training today." The basajaun slowed down his long stride to keep pace. "You guys are really working as a team. Buln'dan—I mean, Dave is going to see if we can't participate in some way. Harder to help from the ground, but we want to be of more use. That battle the other day was a great time! Too bad we had to pull back. I could've killed a few of them with the spears alone if they'd let me. I am actually an excellent shot. One of the best. *Her* is a little better, but she can't throw as far."

Nessa had thought Dave was violent, but he was nothing compared to a couple of the new ones. They'd been so wound up that Austin needed to step in to protect the gargoyles, lest the basajaunak go overboard. Given there wasn't much for Nessa to do during the battle but laugh at Edgar making all the downed gargoyles uncomfortable, she'd had a lot of time to watch their antics.

"You guys should probably train with the shifters," Sebastian said, glancing up. "I should, too. The non-fliers of Jessie's crew need to train with other non-fliers, I think."

"Welcome back," Ulric told Sebastian.

"What?" Sebastian asked as they reached the bar.

The guy Jessie didn't like stood outside, sucking on the end of a cigarette. He glanced at the newcomers, shaking his head a little when he caught sight of the basajaun. He didn't say anything, though, apparently reserving his wittiness for when Jessie was there and could throw it back at him. Or else not wanting to engage when the basajaun was on hand.

The bar was busier than usual, which was saying something, because these days it was always busy. Nearly half the people had wings flowing down their back, many of them big guys and more than a few from the visiting cairns.

"Wow," Ulric said softly, grabbing Nessa's arm for some reason.

"Hello, boys and girls." Patty appeared out of what

seemed like thin air, her blond hair perfectly curled and a big smile on her made-up face. "Ulric, you're looking well. Come here, come here. Niamh mentioned you'd be by, so I've opened up an area for our heroes!"

"Our heroes?" Ulric asked as Patty tugged them along.

"Of course!" Patty looked behind her to make sure she was being followed. "Oh the basajaun, great! Dear, I have your seat all ready for you. I went ahead and swapped out the chair you had last night for a sturdier one. We wouldn't want you to break it."

"Thanks, Mama Patty," the basajaun said, and Ulric turned back with a confused expression.

The crowd opened up for them, even the gargoyles getting out of the way.

"Everyone is talking," Patty told them quietly. "The question of what a female gargoyle can do has been answered." She beamed. "People are *beside* themselves. So fierce, so protective, so magical! The footage I got"—she lowered her voice a little more—"and *edited* is circling the gargoyle community. People are wowed. We're getting a lot of interest on our cairn's social media page."

"We have a cairn now?" Ulric asked.

"We have a social media page?" Nessa asked as Patty stopped them behind Niamh, where three empty seats waited amid a bunch of people standing.

"The cairn is Austin's pack name with 'cairn' tacked on the end, and yes. Well, it's a website, actually, but there are links to all the relevant social media sites. I've started various accounts—with Miss Jessie's approval, of course. We're getting messages left and right! Now..." She pulled Ulric and Nessa a little closer and leaned in. "The word on the street is that Nelson is livid. *Livid!* He's citing a lot of different grievances, asking for financial compensation."

"How much is his ego worth?" Nessa asked as Ulric rolled his eyes.

"He won't get a dime of it, obviously." Patty patted Nessa's forearm. "Just to be sure, I leaked the tape of him running through the house screaming. That'll shut him up. I posted various clips of the battle on our website. There's a lot of footage of Jessie, of course, but I also put up clips of the rest of the team. Hollace...phew! He's getting a lot of interaction."

"What's that?" Hollace asked, stepping forward.

Patty smiled at him, but he was too far away for her frenzied whispers, so she went back to huddling with Nessa and Ulric.

"I've been hearing that the other big cairns don't really know what to do. They are trying to stay as neutral as they can. I think that's why they all want to get out of here. They want to see which way the wind blows." She squinted one of her eyes, and Nessa figured that was probably her version of a wink. "This'll work out in our favor, just you wait. At that dinner in a couple days, we'll be smooth and gracious and neutral ourselves. We'll say nothing of our demolishing Gimerel and will not rise to the bait Nelson tries to throw at us. That'll give credence to her generosity with the party after the raid…"

She nodded and squinted again.

"Now, Ulric…" She yanked on his arm a little. "A lot of guardians are asking for details about the setup of the house crew." She backed up and gave him a poignant look. "Now is the time to help the house. Be cool about it. Don't showboat. Don't let on that you know your salary is bigger than theirs. But talk up your position. Talk up how great the area is and how smoothly things run here. Talk about all the skirmishes with the mages and that big battle you have on the horizon. Mention all the women here. Get them talking amongst themselves so we can reel in some of these kookie-loo guardians, okay?"

"Lookie-loo, Mom—"

"Okay now." She glanced behind them, pulling away. "Do Jessie proud. You know what to do."

And away she went, immediately smiling and

laughing and saying hi to someone as if they were her long-lost friend.

"That woman is a tornado," Nessa told Ulric, dizzied but envious. "I love it."

"She can get to be a little much." He shook his head, spying a woman on the other side of the bar. "If you'll excuse me…"

Hollace had nestled in next to Niamh with the basajaun on her other side. Jasper had disappeared into the crowd, and once again Nessa and Sebastian were standing outside of things, close but not a part of them.

"We've got a problem," Sebastian said softly, moving his hands to wrap them into a cone of privacy.

She was about to say that she knew when he finished.

"They've gone dark."

A flurry of adrenaline flooded Nessa, and she jerked her phone up to look at it. "*What?* Why wasn't I directly messaged that? There has to be some mistake."

He shook his head, looking over the bar worriedly. "One of the mercenaries got his wires crossed, I guess. He sent an email."

"An email?" She checked into their database but didn't find it. "I don't—"

He showed her his phone with the email brought up.

"But that's…" She grabbed the phone from his hand. "That's the general business email. I only check that every few days. It's not even freaking encrypted! What the hell is he doing? This is not at all the protocol that was *very clearly* outlined for all of them." She read through the message quickly; the email was poorly crafted and the grammar atrocious.

She swore. He'd assembled all but one of the mages and three of the mercenaries. Given the timeline, he didn't think they should wait any longer. They'd deployed that morning. There would be no way to reach them now.

"Who put that idiot in charge?" She handed the phone back. "Not you…"

She let the comment linger just enough to hint at a question.

"No. Not me. But you haven't been able to take a very hands-on approach to this situation because of what's going on here. We both know that when no one is directly leading, there's always someone who tries to step up and assume control. They get off on being in charge. Given we had to assemble all this with heavy distractions and zero time, with a less-than-stellar team we dredged up at the last minute, something was bound to go wrong."

"Bound to go wrong?" She gave him an incredulous

look and laughed sardonically. "Did Jessie tell you the gargoyles are leaving?" She pointed at his phone. "That attack is going to take anywhere from three to six days to get here. Given the state of that email and the bonehead's inability to follow instructions, I'd guess more toward six. The gargoyles will be gone by that time, our status will be in the toilet, so the solo guardians will probably scatter, and we'll get hit with a big attack without the forces to return fire. I've screwed us, Sabastian. I've screwed Jessie. I should've made more time for this instead of showing an interest in that handsome gargoyle-monster. I should've been more hands-on. *Damn it.*"

"It's not your fault, Nessa," he said, moving closer. "I asked the impossible of you."

"You always ask the impossible of me. I should be able to deliver better than this." She turned away from him, angry at herself. Angry at that mercenary. Angry that she'd let everyone down so thoroughly.

A couple people glanced her way, and she could read the curiosity in their eyes. They couldn't hear her, but they could still see her exaggerated movements. She needed to get a grip. She'd screwed up before. This wasn't the first time.

Speaking of time, they still had some. The gargoyles hadn't left yet. There had to be a way to make this work.

She calmed herself down, stilling her movements.

"What do we do?" Sebastian asked, seeing that she was done with the blame-game phase of her disappointment. They were a well-oiled machine.

"We figure this out," she said, chewing on her lip, watching Paul the bartender shake the drink mixer over his shoulder. "There has to be a way to figure this out."

She just, at present, had no idea how.

CHAPTER 29

NESSA

"LET ME THINK about it," she told Sebastian, taking a deep breath. "We have a little time."

Sebastian nodded, his head down, thinking. "I'm going to get a drink and try to sit next to Niamh. She always picks on me when I'm in this mood. It takes my mind off things."

"That's why she picks on you."

"I know."

Nessa watched as he skulked off toward a space at the end of the bar, pulling down the spell as he did so.

She didn't move for a while, clearing her mind and staring at nothing. Now was not the time to panic. It wasn't the time for rash decisions or grasping at straws. She had to push away that she knew and loved these people and this town and focus solely on cold, hard logic. That had always been the way forward, the method with which decisions stopped being hard or cringeworthy, and she started doing whatever was necessary to complete the task.

"Are you okay?"

Nessa startled at that rough but familiar voice. Brochan stood next to her smelling of pine and sweat, his shirt rumpled and his pants stained. He'd probably just gotten off work, monitoring the perimeter and his people. The same people she was three to six days away from putting in danger.

"Yeah, thanks," she said, quickly strapping on a sunshiny disposition. Her armor, as Tristan had said. How had he known? "How about you? How are the troops?"

He glanced down at her empty hands. "Do you need a drink?"

"Why? Are you going to buy me one?" She smiled at him devilishly, knowing that if he did, it might be seen by the other shifters as his desiring a claim on her. He'd always been careful not to cross that line. He especially wouldn't now that they were in a friend zone.

He didn't respond, not taking the bait.

"No, thanks," she relented. "I'm sure Sebastian is ordering me one."

He pressed his lips against his glass, and she watched the brown liquid slide into his waiting, open mouth.

The thought of his kiss came back to her, rough and hot and delicious. His taste. The feel of him underneath her palms.

"Here." Sebastian stopped in front of her and handed her a tequila in a sipping glass. "Let me know when we need to leave."

In other words, let him know when she'd found Ulric's tormentors and could get them alone. She half couldn't wait. She needed a little violence right now.

"Will do," she replied.

"You were left out of the action the other day," Brochan said, one hand tucked into his pocket and the other holding his drink. He looked out at the sea of people, probably not seeing anyone at the same time as seeing everyone.

Austin appeared behind the bar, stoic and stern. His hard gaze touched down on each gargoyle for a moment before moving on. Those who met his eyes hunched, already well versed in the art of submitting. They'd either seen or heard about how he stood up to raging basajaunak without flinching. Ready to go toe to toe. That was no small thing.

Nessa shrugged, continuing to watch the bar.

"Yeah," she said. "And I was totally fine with that. I don't need more ways to die."

"You don't need *any* ways to die."

She smiled up at him. "My knight." Then she laughed at his frown. "You were left out of it, too, for the most part."

"I was playing babysitter to the downed guardians," he growled.

She laughed softly. "Sebastian said they withstood some serious shots of magic. It would be good to have a few of them on our side."

He was quiet for a moment. "When they first got here, I disagreed with that. But now…" He nodded, surveying the crowd.

"We just have to reel them in."

"Not sure what they're waiting for."

Voices dropped to murmurs, and then most people stopped speaking altogether. Bodies shuffled out of the way quickly, bumping into one another to make room.

Tristan stepped in, easily topping the crowd, his expression and mannerisms easy. You'd think he was ready for war, though, with how people hurried to get out of his way.

Brochan tensed next to her, his eyes and bearing now hyperalert. He took a slow sip of his drink as he watched the big gargoyle step up to the bar.

"Alpha." Tristan bent his head in hello, almost a shallow bow. He was acknowledging the leader of this territory and doing so respectfully. That would go a long way to settle any dissenting gargoyles, if there were any left. Nessa only wished his leader were here to see it.

"What'll ya have?" Austin asked, setting down a beer he'd just grabbed and knocking on the bar for whoever had ordered it.

"Hennessy, neat." Tristan stared straight ahead for a moment, not looking at anything in particular as Austin nodded and turned to get it.

When the drink was handed over, Tristan said, "I wondered if Alpha Ironheart will be stopping in?"

"No, not tonight," Austin responded. "She's at Ivy House, if you care to stop in."

Tristan gave him a little grin. "It's been declared a no-fly zone, I'm afraid. I shouldn't even be here. If you would let her know…" He paused for Austin to incline his head. "If you need anything for the goodbye dinner, as they're calling it, let me know. I'm an efficient go-between."

"Goodbye dinner?" Austin's tone carried humor even though he wouldn't allow his face to show it.

Tristan allowed himself to show plenty. "Good riddance dinner, then. I doubt any of the leaders, Miss Ironheart included, will be in a hurry for a gathering like this one again. It was a miracle they all got along as well as they did."

"It probably helped that they had a new kid to team

up against."

Tristan lowered his head slowly, a half nod. "It did. For a time. She seemed incredibly hard to pin down, however. My master wasn't the only one to be a little frustrated she wouldn't be cowed. He'd thought the raid would do it."

"He should've paid more attention to the power in her crew."

"Agreed." Tristan moved to turn away, and then hesitated. He glanced around him, obviously wanting some privacy. He probably couldn't be seen walking off with Austin, though, not if he wasn't supposed to be here in the first place.

"Sebastian," Austin barked, obviously recognizing the problem.

Sebastian, sitting next to Niamh, flinched and then hunched. He got up like a kicked puppy, trudging over to the two men, giving Tristan a wide berth.

"Pretty impressive that you have that mage deferring to you," Tristan said conversationally, watching Sebastian approach. "His skill in battle is incredible. His trust even more so. He was blown off the roof with no wings and didn't seem troubled by it at all."

"Jessie would never allow any harm to come to me," Sebastian muttered when he got up close, and Nessa felt the pang of guilt with those words. "And only an idiot would be cavalier with Alpha Steele."

"Agreed," Tristan said, chuckling a little. He seemed completely relaxed in the alpha's presence, something not even Broken Sue could achieve.

Austin leaned forward and asked a question, too low for Nessa to hear. In a moment, Sebastian worked his hands, probably putting them in a magical cone of silence.

Tristan watched Sebastian for a moment, then lifted his eyebrows at Austin, who said something that couldn't be heard outside of that spell. Tristan's mouth moved next, although he had the sense to look in a different direction as he spoke. He glanced back only once, to make sure Austin was getting what was being said. Once finished, he sipped his drink and moved away, leaving the magic and crossing to a guardian in the back corner.

Nessa was burning with curiosity when Sebastian got back. His look said *wait*, though. He didn't open his mouth.

"WHAT'D HE SAY?" Nessa asked him a couple of hours later, no longer able to contain herself.

Tristan had long since left the bar, never having spared her a glance. Broken Sue had also left, after waiting for the big gargoyle-monster to make his exit first.

Now, it was their turn to leave. She and Sebastian walked just outside of the bar, having easily spotted the idiots who'd been staring at Ulric all night, gathering their courage and their allies. The would-be attackers had skulked out a few moments earlier, and Niamh had tipped them off that the weasels were getting into position. They'd then drink out of flasks and smoke their cigarettes, waiting for Ulric to pass them on his way home.

Sebastian glanced around, slowing when he caught sight of the basajaun exiting the bar.

"He's not coming with us, is he?" Sebastian asked.

"No, I don't think so—"

"Hello, mages," the basajaun said jovially. His hard hat gleamed in the moonlight and the wind caught his kilt and flared it a little too high for Nessa's comfort level. "I wondered if I might join you in wreaking havoc on the shifters terrorizing your crew?"

"Oh..." Nessa let the word ride an exhale. "Uh... That was actually supposed to be a secret. This is against pack rules."

"Yes, Niamh mentioned that. We have to be extra stealthy. Do not worry—I am very good at blending in."

She and Sebastian took in his outfit.

"Yeah, I can see that," Nessa said. "It's just...we

might get in trouble. And Jessie needs you. So you shouldn't get involved."

"Ulric has always been kind to everyone," the basajaun growled. "And the shifter rules are not protecting *him*, so they should not protect his attackers. The alpha is failing in his duty. It is up to us to set matters right."

It certainly was a mystery as to why the sentinels wandering around hadn't blown the whistle on this before now. Nessa suspected some of the shifters still nurtured a dislike of gargoyles, and they were turning a blind eye. Something that would provide Nessa and Sebastian with cover now.

"It's fine," Sebastian said, starting to walk again. "Just don't get caught."

"I definitely will not." The basajaun kept pace. "I'll lose them in the trees if I am seen."

Sebastian glanced back at him. It wouldn't be hard to figure out who he was if he had to run, but she didn't see any point in saying so.

"Anyway," Sebastian said as they walked, knowing where to go courtesy of Niamh. She'd known about all of this for months but had never said anything and never helped, respecting Ulric's request for her to stay out of it. He was concerned that the bullying would just get worse if anyone tried to intervene, something that had happened often enough in his youth.

He clearly hadn't had the sort of support Nessa and Sebastian could provide then. These bastards would know better than to show their faces in public again.

"Tristan told Austin that Khaavalor—"

"Mr. Porsche?" she asked.

"Yeah. Mr. Porsche liked what he saw from Jessie. Tristan said that if we move slowly and play our cards right, we could very likely establish a cairn friendship with him. That would greatly help our status in the long run, even if we don't have much status to start."

"Wow. So he was helping us? What's in it for him?"

"I don't know. Austin asked the same thing after Tristan walked away. Tristan also said that he respects a leader that isn't afraid to get his hands dirty, and suggested the cairn leaders would benefit from seeing what an alpha shifter can really do. He implied there might be some way to get the point across at the goodbye dinner."

"Damn it," Nessa said, curling her hand into a fist. "We *have* a way; we just need to…" She imperceptibly glanced behind her, stopping from saying anything incriminating with the basajaun listening in. "Do you think it's a trap? Is he trying to set us up for failure?"

"I don't know. He'd definitely be defying his leader if he *was* helping us."

"Sometimes our leaders mean well, but they are out of touch," the basajaun said as they stalled in the shadows of a street corner.

"But the question still remains—what's in it for him?"

"One thing is for sure," Sebastian said, checking his phone. "He's very good at evading Cyra. Right before he showed up at the bar, she sent a text to Hollace saying she'd lost sight of him." He chuckled.

"Right, okay." Nessa looked around. "I don't see any shifter patrols. What's the plan?"

"First we find them," Sebastian murmured, working magic. It was probably a simple disguise spell, making the air around them fuzzy. Any mage would know what it was, but people who didn't know magic tended to assume their vision was faulty. It was pretty funny, actually. Very useful, as well.

"I can smell cigarettes," the basajaun said. "They are very pungent. Just…" He pointed up the way. "There is an alley not far. I would guess they are there?"

"Great," Nessa whispered. "We need to get into position to sneak up behind them. I'll take one of the instigators and Sebastian will take the other. Basajaun—"

"Call me Phil, but do not tell anyone you call me Phil. The basajaunak will not understand. But if I am going to look more human, I should have a human name."

She hesitated, sliding him a glance. "Why not. Phil, you take the three who hopped on board. Do not kill them." She speared him with a *look*. "What did I just say?"

"Maim only," he supplied.

"*Maim*, yes. Not mangle. You can pick them all up and head toward the woods for all I care, but whatever you do, don't let anyone see you. Got it? Stealth mission."

"Yes. I have it." He paused as they set a new course. "One question, however. What if I do accidentally kill them?"

She sighed and went over the rules one more time.

Soon even she could smell the cigarette smoke from the end of the alley, deep from within the shadows. The butt at the end of one glowed as someone took a drag.

"Gotcha, you bastards," Sebastian whispered.

He and Nessa immediately drifted into the shadows, and the magic and the darkness made it nearly impossible for them to be seen. Phil disappeared behind the wall of a building, and a moment later he was on the roof, staying low and somehow as silent as the grave.

Closing the distance now, Nessa eased her knife out of the leg holster, thinking of how vicious she wanted to go.

Raucous laughter drifted toward them from the group. A metallic glimmer caught her eye, moonlight reflecting on a flask.

"Shouldn't be long now, boys," someone said, and someone else peered around the corner.

"I'm gonna smash that creep," another intoned, shifting his weight from side to side.

She steadied her breath and focused on her movement and footwork. Easy did it. Soft feet. Smooth walking. Shadows slid over her body. She kept her knife low, ensuring it caught no light or attention.

The basajaun made it to the end before she did, crouching low so people in the street hopefully couldn't see him. He peered over the edge of the roof, watching for her signal.

It had been such a bad idea to invite him. *Such* a bad idea. Hopefully he didn't freak out and raise the dead with his snarls. He was capable of it.

Ten feet away now, Sebastian keeping pace with her. Five, hearing them talking nonsense but letting it flow around her, not sinking in. Her breath was steady. Her hand ready.

She looked up at the basajaun, then nodded.

Her foot scuffed the ground as she darted forward. She grabbed the hair of her mark and wrenched his head back. With a smooth motion, she dragged her knife across his throat, knowing exactly how hard to press to keep it nonlethal. With a shifter, it was a tiny bit harder than a mage, since they could heal so quickly.

Sebastian sprinted across the alley and grabbed the other ringleader—he was not good with weapons, but he quickly took him to the ground with magic. His hand muted the shifter's surprised shouts as the basajaun jumped from the roof and landed amongst his three marks. He backhanded one, slapped another, and conked the third on the head with his fist.

They all stood dead still, their eyes rounded, their bodies in freeze mode. The basajaun scooped them all up like they were sticks and just about sprinted across the street.

"Wait," Nessa said, having to put her body weight on her mark to keep him from writhing all over the place. She pushed both hands down on his mouth. "You have to tell them never to bother any members of Ivy House again," she told the basajaun. "That's the really important part. We all stick together, so if they mess—"

He raced across the street and disappeared. People probably wouldn't think it was anything more than a trick of their eyes.

"Hopefully he got it," Nessa said, dragging her mark a little bit into the light so he could see her face. He gasped, grabbing at his throat, bleeding all over. "If you make a sound"—she put the tip of her knife at his eye—"I'll make sure you never see again. Do you understand me?"

His mouth gaped, and fear was in his eyes.

"Or would you prefer this tactic?" She moved so that she could slide the knife down his stomach, leaving a trail of blood, before stopping at his crotch. "How about I take these? You don't *really* need them, do you?"

His whimper said it all.

She got into his face again. "If you touch that gargoyle with the pink and blue hair, or any of the Ivy House crew, ever again, I'll come back to see you, and next time it'll be in the comfort of your own home. If you tell them who did this to you?" She pressed the tip of her blade against his crotch a little harder, waiting for the whimper again. "I'll do worse than that. Do you understand?"

He didn't say anything, was still clutching at his throat.

She pushed the knife in a little harder. "*Do you understand?*"

"Y-yes," he rasped, very dramatically. That was probably good. It would stick in his brain a little better.

She pushed at his chest to help herself stand, staring down at him for a moment to get the point across. It was an important part of the process, the intimidation situation. Sebastian was just finishing his own speech, using magic to dispense pain and fear until he stood in much the same way.

"Good?" she asked him.

"Yeah. Let's get out of here before someone comes along."

They walked back the way they'd come, turned at the back of a business, scaled one fence, then another, and checked both ways. No one there. Once everything had calmed down, she would say something to Austin about the lack of patrol in this area. It was a lovely, sleepy little town, perfect for a rogue mage to wander through unnoticed.

"I'm going to head to Ivy House," Sebastian murmured when they'd reached the main drag. "I need to make a bunch of potions and talk things through. Maybe Ivy House can throw a spell book or an idea at me or something. Are you okay to get home?"

She gave him a flat stare.

"I know, dumb question. Text me when you get there. Run if someone tries to question you. You don't want to get caught breaking rules in a place like this. These people don't take bribes."

She squeezed his arm. "It's going to be okay. We're going to figure this out. Just worry about you and Jessie.

I'll worry about me."

"Okay. Love you. Call me when you get home."

"Love you—I'll do that or text. We'll see which directive I remember."

"Smartass."

They parted ways, going in opposite directions. She crossed to the side with the trees, then decided she'd better make sure the basajaun wasn't doing something crazy.

Jogging, thanking herself for wearing the right shoes, she threaded through the trees, listening. All was silent. How far would he have carried them?

She moved a little farther, then kinda side to side. Nothing.

A hand grabbed her throat and reeled her in. Her back hit a hard body.

She didn't bother screaming, just slashed, slashed, slashed with her knife until the arm fell away and she could step free, ready to run or fight, depending on the situation.

"Nessa, my goodness, that was very well done." Phil grinned at her in the moonlight, blood now freely running through various patches of his hair.

"Oh! Oh my—I'm so sorry, are you okay?" She stepped forward and reached out with her other hand. "Sorry, but you grabbed my throat and—Are you going to attack me now?"

"Of course not, no." He put out his hand to direct her to the right. "You almost stepped on our friends."

She glanced at her feet, seeing a couple of legs sticking out of the bushes.

"Dang it, you didn't kill them, did you?" She bent to check, but he grabbed her arm.

"No, but I scared two of them so badly that I think they fainted. The third tried to attack me, so I broke his legs. Not too badly, do not worry. He will walk again eventually."

She wilted. "Okay," she said weakly. "Well, if you're go—"

"I grabbed your throat because I know human women do not understand when you accidentally grab their breasts. Your waist is much too low, and I feared I might make a mistake."

"Right. Okay, if you're—"

"Grabbing your face seemed a little unorthodox, but gently grabbing the neck seemed like a good option. Very fast reactions with that knife! I am impressed. You are worthy of Ivy House."

She waited this time to see if he was done talking. When he just smiled at her, she thanked him.

"Thank *you* for letting me tag along. What should I do with our friends?"

"Leave them. You were never here. If anyone mentions any of this, you don't know anything about it."

"I got you. Okay. I will see you soon." He gave a salute, and then off he ran, almost immediately disappearing into the trees.

She watched her footing and got out of there, too. Back on the sidewalk, heart *finally* slowing down, she jogged around a corner, then another, getting close to home. She cleaned her knife as she walked, making sure no one was out and about to see her. That done, she sheathed it and reached for her phone.

This time she didn't have a weapon when a large hand wrapped around her throat. Her body swung with dizzying quickness, and then her back slammed up against a tree trunk and a huge body leaned in.

She recognized the smell immediately—a woody amber scent with a hint of mountain rain. Tristan.

"At least this time there isn't a roof for you to pitch me off," she said, her voice raspy and her hands at her sides.

"You're not going to reach for the knife, little deathwatch angel?"

"No. There's no point. I tried with a basajaun just now, and he commended me on my fast hands. I figure I'll just submit and see what happens this time. Eventually maybe you'll get around to killing me."

"This would be the time." He leaned closer; his breath smelled of chocolate and cognac.

"You don't have any of that chocolate on hand, perchance?" she asked hopefully. "Maybe as a last meal sort of situation?"

"What did you tell your people?"

She assumed he meant about himself. She couldn't imagine his caring about anything else.

"Everything you told me. As much as I could remember, anyway."

"And have they figured out the riddle?" He shook her a little, his voice deep and smooth and full of dark promises. "Don't lie to me. You don't want to know what I'll do to you to get answers."

"I'm sure I can think of a million things you could do, many of which I've done myself. I have a flair for creativity."

It felt so strange saying that out loud. So real. Only Sebastian really knew that side of her. The woman she'd had to become to keep them alive. To keep them safe.

But she felt that this was a man who wouldn't be shocked. Maybe couldn't be. Not if he had been to the places Niamh had described.

"No, they haven't figured out the riddle," she finally said. "Niamh is perplexed that she hasn't gotten anything on you at all, actually. I'm relying on her. What are you, half and half? Half gargoyle and half…?"

His fingers tightened on her throat, and she closed her eyes for a moment, willing him to finish it already. He'd make it quick; he had the strength to do so. Then she wouldn't have to worry about betraying Jessie, or what would happen if the gargoyles left too early, or the tangled mess that lay ahead—because even if they made it through this first attack, they'd need to launch right into the defense of Kingsley.

"What does the heir plan to do with the information once she gets it?" he rasped, his lips close to her ear. "Blackmail my cairn leader? Extort money? Try to send me back from whence I came?"

She felt her brow crease and opened her eyes, finding his glowing orbs dangerously close to her face. His breath washed against her lips, and his body pressed menacingly against her side.

"Jessie called us off," she told him. "She told us not to pursue this further, but she also knows us, so she said whatever we find should be kept between us. She doesn't want to know."

"Lies," he growled, cutting off her air. "You don't think I've noticed how the phoenix haunts my steps? How the puca knows things about me that no mortal in this realm could possibly know? She tracked me down to the hotel bar the other night, did she tell you? She sat right down next to me, as though we'd been friends forever, and tried to pick me apart, piece by piece."

She closed her eyes again as a tear escaped and drifted down her cheek. She put her hand against his chest, feeling his heart beating strongly under her palm.

"Not lying," she mouthed, with no air to push the words out.

His fingers relaxed just slightly, and his brow furrowed in confusion. The image swam from behind her renewed tears.

"Not lying," she said again, the words forming this time. "Think the worst of me—I deserve it. Don't think badly of Jessie. She was thrown into this life, but she is pure and light and good. She consented to finding out what you were at first but changed her mind and called us off. She doesn't know the phoenix is spying. Cyra is doing that as a game, by the way. She thinks it's fun that you're so wily."

"Why would she call you off? What's in it for her?"

"Her dignity? Her sense of right and wrong? I don't know; I'm not her. She rationalized that whatever creatures make you up, it clearly hasn't stopped you from holding a job and securing a cairn. Jessie doesn't want to steal your future from you, Tristan. You tell me, is that something a person like me could make up?"

He pushed back a little, his eyes darting from side to

side. Then his gaze traveled her face, reading her expression, and settled on her lips.

"Why does she care about my future? Why do you think so poorly of yourself?"

"To answer the first, I'll tell you what she told me. That just because we have animosity between us, I shouldn't want to ruin your chance at happiness. You hadn't done anything to deserve that."

"We have animosity?"

"Now? Yes. Before now? No. She didn't know that. She humbled me with the assumption."

He paused for a moment before bringing up his other hand slowly, using his thumb to wipe away her tears. "And the other?"

"You have no idea what kind of monster you've caught," she whispered. "I look at Jessie and know that I never could've turned out like that. I would never have even thought about the possibility that I was ruining an adversary for no good reason. It wouldn't have bothered me. Still doesn't, most of the time. I don't know what it would be like to live in peace. To have the illusion of safety."

"Survival isn't pretty, little one," he whispered. "Being forced to survive doesn't make you a monster."

"Said the big monster to the little one." She smiled up at him as another tear fell. "I've never cried this much in anyone's presence. Not since I was a girl, at least."

"Why?" He wiped another of her tears away. "Why allow me to see your vulnerability?"

She shrugged. "Maybe because you keep putting me in situations where I'm utterly vulnerable. Or maybe because I don't have to stay strong for you. You don't rely on me staying upbeat."

"I don't trust anyone who is happy all the time. It tells me they're hiding something."

She laughed at that.

"I couldn't understand why your mistress pushed herself against my wound in our battle," he said, his confusion still evident. "I thought she made the gash that deep because she wanted to expose me. Only certain parts of my body bleed in a way that expose…what I am."

She breathed out, leaning her head back against the tree. "I don't think you can possibly know how curious I am about your secrets. They are so intriguing. I have so many questions."

"I feel the same sense of intrigue about you, my little deathwatch angel. Or should I call you my little monster?"

"They're both equally true. And no, she didn't mean to expose you. She's incredibly new to magic. I hear she was an absolute terror in the beginning. She has an incredible amount of power and not a lot of control. She messed up, went a little too hard, and then fixed it. It's not all about you, you know."

He dragged his thumb across her jugular, making her shiver, before pulling his hand away. His body remained close, though, dousing her in his heat.

"Why do you…smell like blood?"

Suddenly his hands were everywhere, pulling her shirt so that he could place his hand on her chest, feeling along her stomach and around to her back. Good Lord, why did that touch feel so *good*? Bad sign.

"Hey, what—Stop. No touching." She swatted his hands away.

"This isn't your blood." He pulled her away from the tree and slid his hands along her back, checking her for signs of damage. "Whose blood is this?"

"It's—You're still touching."

He grabbed the hem of her shirt and ripped it over her head, exposing her lacy bra. She didn't get a chance to berate him. He'd already stepped back, pulled his flannel from his wide shoulders, revealing a tight white vest and a whole lot of defined muscle, and then draped it around hers, covering her up again. He helped her put her arms through the sleeves and then tied the bottom ends together so that it cinched at her waist.

"I'm not sure what just happened," she said, looking down at the flannel she was now swimming in. She breathed in his scent, which was all around her now. God, he smelled good.

"Your shirt was ruined. I gave you another." He motioned for her to get walking. "I'll escort you home."

"You were literally just threatening my life, and now we're swapping shirts and you want to escort me home? You are bonkers, bro."

"We seem to start off on the wrong foot whenever we meet."

"Is that what you call grabbing my throat and threatening to kill me?"

"Obviously."

"Great. Well…" She bent down and scooped her shirt up off the ground from where he'd discarded it. "This is evidence I can't just leave lying around."

He took it from her and motioned her forward again.

"No. Give—" She reached for it, but he held it away. She held out her hand. "Give me my shirt. I don't need you blackmailing me."

"Are you going to tell me whose blood it is?"

"No. Give it."

"I'll be able to figure it out. I'll smell it in town. Why did you need to create this much damage?" His voice lowered into a growl. “What did he do to you?”

“I was helping a friend using skills I excel at.”

“Making an enemy bleed?”

She narrowed her eyes and mimicked him. “Obviously.”

He held the shirt up. “I’ll give this back when we reach your house.”

“You’re not walking me home. Are you nuts? I don’t want you knowing where I live. The next time you think I’m plotting against you, you’ll just turn up and kill me in my sleep.”

“What fun would that be?” His tone was dark and silky. “Then I couldn’t watch your pupils dilate when I lean in close or hear your breath hitch when I whisper next to your ear.” His knowing smile was incredibly annoying. “Like that.” He started forward. “I know where you live. When you’re worried about being followed, you need to remember to look up.”

Rolling her eyes at herself, she lurched after him. “What is it with you and the shirt?”

He didn’t answer.

“Why did you follow me?”

“Because I stupidly told you far too much information and then realized you had the resources to dig into my past. I was gaining information in case I needed to silence you.”

"Then what, silence the rest of the crew?"

"If necessary, yes. My leader would've thanked me for it without asking questions. Like you, I have certain skills. Making people disappear"—he held up the shirt—"is a particular talent of mine. Or did you think Nelson personally disappeared those people who went missing?"

She studied him for a moment, and then glanced at the shirt. "Don't kill the guy whose blood that belongs to. Especially if I happened to get the basajaun's blood on there, too. He was just trying not to grab my boobs, I guess, and I took it the wrong way. But honestly, he came out of literally nowhere—"

"Do you always babble when you're aroused?"

"I never do." She arched an eyebrow at him. "I guess you know where you stand now."

His uneven smile softened him in all the right ways. "Touché," he said.

"I have a habit of using information against people. You shouldn't hand me information about yourself."

"I've deduced that, yes. Luckily, I have insurance." He held up the shirt again. "Cross me, and they'll find your shirt next to the dead body."

"Empty threats are beneath you. You did it for him, though, right? Got rid of the production cairn leader who wouldn't meet his demands? Does he know what you are? Is that how he was able to get you to do something that wasn't…on the straight and narrow?"

His smile dwindled. "He knows that I have no birth records. No previous cairn records. I assume you've already deduced that. He thinks that means bad things. His assumptions are based on gargoyle prejudice, but he is, of course, correct. I am not a 'straight and narrow' type of person. We seem to have that in common, you and me. So yes, he uses that as leverage. He assumes that you all know more than you let on. Part of his logic for sending me through Ivy House was because he was hoping I could find something we could use against you."

She laughed. "How lazy do you think we are? Did he try to hack into us, as well?"

"Yes. But he is horribly outclassed."

"He'd never survive in the mage world."

His eyebrow quirked. "I am dying to know more."

"I'll show you mine if you show me yours…"

His gaze raked across her body. "I'll show you mine only after you beg for mercy."

An evil smile curled her lips as they stopped near her glowing porch light, which came on automatically at dusk.

"I don't mind begging," she said silkily, unable to help herself, "*Daddy*."

He sucked in a breath and held it as his pupils dilated. His body hummed with arousal, and electricity practically ignited in the air between them.

"Like that, do you?" She felt the heat from his body and wanted more of it. "Too bad you're not staying around. I'd make you squirm."

"You already do, little one. It'd be easy to return the favor. Why was there a closet of gold bars in that house?"

"It's really anyone's guess. I think the house likes the idea of someone trying to break in and take it."

"And that art. There are some priceless pieces just randomly kept in that room."

"They used to be randomly scattered around the house. Austin's grandma is the one handling all of that."

He shook his head, his gaze tracing her face. "What does the mage mean to you?" he asked, his voice subdued.

"I hope you're not leading up to asking me out, because after two murder attempts, I think I've got the hint to stay away. I only like good boys."

"The mage?" His eyes darkened and his tone dripped with deadly promises if she didn't answer.

Why did that make her smile?

"He's a brother in everything but blood."

"And the gorilla?"

"A FILF."

"What?"

"A friend I'd like to fuck. Just a friend, though. He has some serious trauma in his recent past that he's trying to work through. I'm giving him space to do that."

"And your trauma? Are you trying to work through that, or just ignore it?"

She stared at him, hard. Then reached for her shirt.

"Oops, there goes your good humor. I'll be your FILF, if you'd like." His smile increased his handsomeness, and he knew it.

"We aren't friends, firstly. Friends don't accost and threaten friends. Second, nah, I'll just flag down a random hot dude at the bar, thanks. Shirt, please. It might be salvageable."

"It isn't. Bloodstains. Why haven't you and the weird mage officially joined the Ivy House crew? From what I've seen, you'd be accepted in a minute."

She lowered her hand. His question had taken her by surprise. "Because when this is all over," she said, no traces of humor left, "and the long game is completed, we probably won't be welcome here. We made a pact to do whatever is necessary to take down the Mages' Guild, and that path might require loose morals. They don't need our kind of nightmare tainting their lives, not during peacetime."

He looked at her for a long time, and she opened herself to it. She let him see the parts of her only

Sebastian and his sister had ever truly seen. Or their enemies had seen. The horrors she'd experienced started when she was too young, and they'd just grown and grown until that was all she knew anymore. He'd already guessed at them; he might as well see the truth of it. There was no point in trying to hide—he'd made that plain. If he asked, she would've exposed her whole sordid history, every dark deed and vicious repercussion. Something about him said he'd understand like no one else in her life. But he didn't ask. Maybe he didn't need to.

Instead he nodded and said, almost too quietly for her to hear, "I doubt you're worse than that puca."

"Well." She reached once more for her shirt, being plain stubborn at this point. "That's my night done, I think."

He held the shirt up to punctuate his next words. "I owe you one for this recent…faux pas. The throat grab and threat, not the shirt. Though, in my defense, I couldn't have known your cairn leader would protect me from her staff. Mine certainly wouldn't have."

"Is that what we're calling it? Faux pas?"

"If I pitched you off the roof, then yes, that's what we're calling it. How can I help? What can I do to gain your forgiveness? Make you beg?"

She rolled her eyes and turned toward the house, giving up on the shirt. She knew very well it was ruined, and if his goal was blackmail, he would be hard-pressed to make the allegations stick. The shifter would heal from the injuries she'd dealt by morning, and she'd ensure he didn't rat her out.

But then her reality tumbled into her mind. And she turned around slowly.

She knew her expression was as serious as a heart attack. "What game are we playing here? Because if I ask a favor of you, it wouldn't be on my own behalf."

He sobered as well, seeing that the mood had changed. "I owe you. I meant that. It'll stay between you and me."

She very much doubted she could trust him, but she was also desperate.

"Stall the cairns from leaving. By…a week. I only need a week."

He leaned back onto his heels, assessing her. "Why?"

She shook her head and backed up a step.

He took a step forward, his gaze delving into her. "Why?" he pressed, a little softer. A little more dangerously. Her body tingled.

She ignored it. Shoved it away. She needed to focus now. She needed that cold logic.

She assessed him and knew instantly that there was only one way forward on this.

She spilled the truth. All of it. He was somehow so dialed in with her that he'd know it if she lied, and she needed his help.

After she'd finished, Tristan studied her as he tended to do when his mind was working, maybe assessing threats. Maybe trying to figure out whether she was telling the truth.

"Okay," he said. "I'll stall. What about the battle?"

"What about the battle?"

"Is this one for keeps? Kill or be killed?"

She furrowed her brow. "Kill or the territory will be killed, followed by Austin's brother's territory. The people we hired think we're the bad guys. There is no way to call them off. Not anymore. I don't know if you've forgotten, but real battles are typically dangerous."

"I'll need all the information. I'll want to instigate a warning system, just in case."

"So you'll do it?"

He threw the shirt up and then caught it, still not giving it back. "I would've said yes if you'd just mentioned the battle. But thank you for the blackmail material. I'll have to think on how I can best use it."

He threw her a winning smile before walking away.

Apparently they were playing games after all, and she'd just handed him an ace.

CHAPTER 30

JESSIE

AUSTIN STOPPED THE Bentley in front of his newest and fanciest restaurant—the location of the farewell dinner with the gargoyles and a great spot to give them a good riddance. I only wished it could've been the few days sooner, like they'd initially requested. High-maintenance Gimerel had pushed it back, citing no reason and offering no apologies.

It was not as if it really mattered. Not one of them had reached out to me after the raid. I'd sent invites to come for coffee on a couple of occasions but never received a reply. As far as I was concerned, this whole thing had been pointless, and I couldn't wait to see the back of them.

"Ready?" Austin said, pulling forward again. The valet looked at him in confusion.

"Why, what are you doing?" I asked, turning to look back at the restaurant. "Are we not going to show up to the dinner?"

"We are, I just…don't particularly want to entrust a young kid with this car. I'll park in our spot."

I laughed, running my hand across his thigh. "It'll give us more time before we face the buttheads."

"Did Ulric and Jasper tell you about all the interest they've received at the bar about their jobs? Pay, perks, how we are as leaders…"

"Yeah. Patty, too, I guess. It hasn't resulted in anyone approaching us about joining our crew, though."

"Give it time."

I held my breath for a moment to keep from reminding him that we were already on borrowed time. Surely Momar was going to make a move soon. Being cautious made sense, but he seemed like he was dragging his feet at this point.

Or maybe that was just me projecting. Over the last few days, it had felt like danger was once again bearing down on us. I couldn't shake the feeling that we should batten down the hatches and get ready. The mages hadn't heard of anything, though. It made me wonder if the gargoyles were going to decide to attack or something.

Austin stepped out of the car and came around for me, opening the door and putting out his hand. I hesitated for a moment and then took it, dragging my made-up self into the early-evening air and feeling the heavy weight of the jewels around my neck.

I'd gone gaudy. Super gaudy, actually. I'd put on the most ridiculous set of jewels I owned, huge rubies and diamonds that probably should've been kept in a locked vault somewhere. If I had a crown, I would've worn that, too.

Mr. Tom had thought I was nuts. Patty had been speechless, and my team hadn't known where to look. It was only Naomi who'd taken me in from head to toe, cracked a little smile, and nodded. Time to show Nelson that Gimerel didn't hold a candle to the random wealth Ivy House possessed. Jerk.

My stilettos clicked against the cement, and I slipped my hand into Austin's.

"What would this situation be like with shifters?" I asked as we circled the building.

"You proved dominance in a spectacular fashion. They might not have been happy about it, but they would've acknowledged the superior might of your pack. The others wouldn't have stayed away just to keep from offending an established leader. It's customary to congratulate the winning pack. A custom that opens the doors for alliances or pack friends, whatever the case may be. There are still a lot of politics with shifters, but it seems we are, by and large, a lot more adult about it."

I laughed at his last comment. "Are you calling gargoyles petty?"

He didn't even pause. "Yes. And cowards. The leaders, at any rate. But then, they are all mostly isolated when it comes to trading—something they try to keep within the gargoyle community. Maybe they can't afford to step on toes."

"They are shooting themselves in the foot."

"Yes."

"Has Anthott said anything?" We rounded the next corner and saw the teams standing out front in orderly lines with still wings and hard eyes. Only one member of my team was present—Mr. Tom, waiting for me. "Last I heard, he had gotten cold feet, but hadn't left the territory."

"He's still hanging around. He's watching and waiting, I think, like everyone else."

"I need to do something to shake the fruit loose from this tree."

"We'll figure out something."

Why was everyone around me so positive all of a sudden? Was it because they were trying to balance out my incredible grumpiness?

Mr. Tom stepped up as we got closer. "You look extravagant, miss. Very eye-catching."

I knew "eye-catching" was his way of saying I stuck

out like a sore thumb. Good. There hadn't been any hope of my fitting in. I might as well stand out.

"Are the leaders all tucked inside?" I asked.

"Yes, miss. They've been served their drink of choice and are waiting impatiently for you to arrive."

"And the trucks, are they ready?"

"Ready and waiting, miss."

"Fantastic." I stepped away and onto the red carpet, facing outward to address the crews. I magically increased the volume of my voice. "It has come to my attention that the gargoyle way is to let you all hang out here while the leaders eat and drink inside." I paused for a moment and spread my hands. "But not everyone here is a gargoyle. Shifters would have a big BBQ. But we aren't all shifters. My crew would have a garden party on the Ivy House grass, lately while avoiding the homicidal gnomes and animated dolls. But we aren't at Ivy House. One of the leaders in particular is mighty glad of that."

A smattering of nervous laughter sounded from the gargoyles. Wings fluttered in the Gimerel team.

"So I decided that tonight we should compromise." I lifted my hand, knowing Mr. Tom had the first truck driver on hold on his phone and would give the command.

Sure enough, a food truck pulled around the corner.

"Who is interested in the almighty burger? With this food truck, you have options ranging from gourmet to Plain Jane, like I used to be. Dress it up or dress it down—it is entirely up to you." The next truck rolled around the corner. "More of a taco crowd? We've got you covered. Tacos and burritos and other authentic Mexican street fare with a fine-dining spin. Marinated pork, braised beef—you won't want to miss this."

The next truck pulled through, this one a regular truck with a camper shell, pulling a wood brick oven on a trailer that had originally lived out back and probably shouldn't have been moved. Alas, showmanship.

"A food truck paradise wouldn't be complete without a wood-fire oven. We have Neapolitan-inspired pizzas for you." I waited for them to get settled a little before the next truck pulled into sight. "Did someone say lobster truck? Yes, I think they did. Delicious, buttery lobster rolls, lobster bisque, you name it. But don't forget the crab! My favorite is the herb-crusted crab cake bites dipped in their homemade creamy sauce. Yum."

That truck parked in the nondescript field on the edge of the property. This space didn't have enough room for us to be posh about the situation.

My stomach rumbled as the last food truck rolled through. "Who could forget dessert? Gourmet Frenchbakery-inspired desserts that taste as good as they look."

My team walked out next, dressed down and carrying coolers, pushing an alcohol cart, and bringing out plates and condiments.

"The alcohol and wine selection is unfortunately limited," I said, "but there should be plenty for an unprofessional buzz that you'll try your best to hide when it's time to head back. Please have as much as you want. Of everything. It's all taken care of, and we have more than enough to go around." I paused for a moment, letting the excited murmurs die down. "Thank you for coming, everyone. Really. Despite whatever tomfoolery went on with me and your leaders, I'd like you to know that you are all welcome here, at any time. I don't know your customs yet, I won't abide by some of your ways, but I'm proud to join you on this magical journey. I'm proud to call myself a gargoyle, and I look forward to the battles yet to come, hopefully with you rather than against you. May your trip home be fraught with danger"—laughter was louder now, and more than one fist rose in the air—"and may we someday meet on the field of battle."

I held up a hand in a farewell salute, about to turn around. A loud round of applause stopped me. Feeling the moment, I lowered my hand to my heart and offered them a little bow.

"Right this way, miss." Mr. Tom appeared by my side, ushering me toward the restaurant.

Austin held out his arm for me, and I took it, allowing him to lead us to the door. We were nearly there when he stiffened slightly, slowing.

It took me a moment to pick out the enormous shape standing beside the door, blending into the building. Austin must've felt his presence.

Tristan stepped forward, his suit immaculate, with shiny black lapels, a black dress shirt, and a black tie with white polka dots and matching pocket square.

"Miss Ironheart," Tristan said, offering a bow. "Might I have a word?"

"Uh…yeah, sure." I smoothed the jewels down my front. "We're not going to fight, though, right? This jewelry is too heavy to be running around in. It would probably give me a black eye."

"This is a new suit. I'd rather not ruin it." His smile made his eyes flash.

We stepped away a little, and his wings fluttered uncomfortably.

"My master has tasked me with informing you that he will be filing a list of grievances regarding your failure to properly follow raid protocol. He will also file grievances—as will a couple others, I assume—regarding the failed protocol at the introductory dinner.

You had too much security on hand—the strange vampire and the basajaunak in particular." He paused, holding my gaze, and I knew he hadn't told Nelson about the invisible mages roaming around. The same invisible mages he'd likely seen lurking in the restaurant before coming out to find me. "Some of the leaders will file grievances regarding their introductory reception too, due to the nature of their…gifts."

A heavy weight lodged in my middle. It felt like I was getting in trouble, like I was about to be pulled into the penalty box. Additionally, the system felt rigged. Those men might not like each other, but it felt like they were working together to make sure these grievances pulled me down to the very dredges of their society.

"And this?" I gestured behind me, indicating the food trucks. "I suppose my failure to follow protocol here will result in another list of grievances?"

"For a couple of them, very likely."

"I know I'm supposed to be your enemy, but can you tell me how many of those might stick? Like…is this my undoing in gargoyle society?"

He paused for a moment. "In the short term, very likely. Cairn leaders can be prickly, and you are very new."

Frustration ate at me. "Well. It was a helluva run."

"Will you answer a question for me?"

"Sure, why not."

He squinted a little and adjusted his footing, expanding his chest a little with a breath. His voice was soft, as if he didn't want to be overheard. "In the raid, up in the air, why did you plaster yourself to me? Why did you heal me?"

We'd circled back to the *why* question.

"Because the spell hit you harder than I'd realized, and it would've killed you. Healing is more effective with contact, and I had a battle to get back to."

His gaze was steady. "And the real reason for the contact?"

I studied him for a moment and then glanced around before wrapping us in a protective bubble, making it large enough that Austin would be in it, too. "No one will be able to hear us right now. Listen, long story short, we know there's some sort of something going on with that orange blood you have. You came from somewhere other than an established cairn, and my people have a vague knowledge of where that somewhere might be. That's all I care to know. Hiding your blood absolved me from any fault in outing you."

"I am not your problem, and so you don't care about mine?"

"Is that a trick question? Wouldn't you rather I butt out?"

"Yes. I'm just stating the obvious."

"Right." I felt a grimace drag at my lips. When he phrased it like that, with the tone and harsh look and everything, I felt judged. I felt like I was letting him down. Which was crazy, because he was right—he wasn't my problem. He basically ran my enemy's team.

Still, though, old habits died hard—or would not go away, it seemed—and I found myself explaining.

"Honestly, I probably wouldn't even know what creature you are. That, or I'd be surprised it's real. I'm not saying I don't care." I reached forward and touched his forearm, then quickly pulled back because that was a little too friendly. "I do care, actually. That's why I'm butting out. You seem to want to keep it a mystery, and you have a good reason. I respect that. I won't allow myself or my team to blow your cover and ruin all you've achieved. I especially won't allow that douche leader of yours to find out and turn you away because he's a small-minded dipshit and I really want to punch him directly in the face…" I cleared my throat. "But anyway."

"You protect what's yours."

It wasn't phrased as a question, but felt like one anyway.

"Of course," I said, taking a step back to tell him this chat was wrapping up. "That's my duty."

A grin pulled at his lips. "She was right about you. You're entirely genuine, and you have a good and pure heart. Not at all like the rest of us."

"Was that Niamh? Don't believe her. She's just trying to get your goat."

He shook his head, his gaze finding Austin. "You can help her in there if you show a little of how an alpha does things. There have been a lot of rumors about the shifters, but the leaders don't much believe them." He shrugged. "But it's your show."

As he walked away, he made a circle in the air with his finger. "This was a really nice touch, the food. Tell your filmmaker to splash it all over her network. I'm sure they'll eat it up."

He obviously meant Patty.

"Edgar would've loved the pun," I murmured, watching him reenter the restaurant. "I feel like I missed something, though. Why is he helping us?"

"I don't know," Austin replied. "Nathanial said something similar to me before we left. This dinner isn't going to dig you out of the status hole."

"Definitely not."

"Then would you mind if I took point?" He walked me to the doorway, handsome in his expensive suit. "I've been playing nice, allowing you to try to navigate your people. But now…"

"By all means." I waved him on.

He didn't hesitate, walking into the establishment like the owner he was. The hostess greeted us, her smile professional but her eyes tight.

"Watch yourself, alphas," she murmured. "They haven't had the nicest things to say."

"Thank you, Candace," Austin said, breezing past.

We found them in the center of the room at the table that had been prepared just for them. Two places were left open next to each other, but neither was at the head of the table.

Tristan had taken his place near the door, standing beside Nessa, whom he'd be able to see and hear despite her invisibility potion—and despite the fact that he hadn't taken the potion I'd drunk down in the car. Austin had taken it as well, wanting to be able to hear the mages just in case they had information we needed. That was before we'd found out the gargoyle leaders' positions were plain.

Sebastian stood near the gargoyle leaders, staring down at them with disgust lining his features.

"*Finally*," Nelson said loudly. "She finally shows up to her social funeral. You're done as a gargoyle, little girl. You messed with the wrong group of leaders."

Withor looked positively gleeful. He clearly thought making me a social pariah would discredit any information I had on him. Eram looked equally pleased, never having liked me and now not having to deal with me. Gerard was the only one with a stoic face, unusual for him, and subdued demeanor, as he watched me enter with the solemnity of a man deep in thought.

The raw, primal vehemence Austin channeled so well leaked into the air around him as we neared the table. His power pumped out in waves, heady and vicious. All the eyes at the table widened, their focus quickly zooming to him.

"Yeah, right?" I heard Nessa murmur, clearly to Tristan. He must've had a reaction to the magic as well. Thankfully, it didn't seem aimed at us. "He's been holding back for her sake. He's like…the perfect co-leader. Yay! Now we get to see the alpha come out to play."

"You will stand when the alphas join the table," Austin said, his tone rough and his bearing authoritative. "It's a sign of respect. Or in your case, obedience."

Withor scoffed, the first to recover, arching an eyebrow at Nelson. Nelson shook himself out of his stupor, and then a shaky smile that was probably supposed to be sly curled his lips.

"I think I can speak for everyone when I say"—Nelson lifted his eyebrows, his smile growing, his confidence creeping back—"none of us respect whatever hybrid thing the two of you are trying to do, and we don't owe you any obed—"

With speed that froze Nelson to the spot, Austin pulled his arm from around me and grabbed the other man by the tie. He yanked Nelson up, making the chair shove out from behind him. Nelson's eyes widened and his hands hung lank at his sides.

Rough and slow, Austin said, "I said *stand.*"

The command for the rest of the table was evident. The threat of extreme violence was unmistakable.

Slack-faced, the leaders stumbled out of their chairs, swaying to their feet and half falling onto the table in the process. Once on his feet, Withor grabbed at his own tie, and the others started to look around in concern, as though not quite sure how they'd gotten there.

"Back to your stations," Austin barked, and the guardians who had stepped forward stalled before slinking back to their spots.

Slowly Austin let go of Nelson's tie, backing up.

"Jess?" He pulled the chair out for me and waited until I sat down. After, he took his own seat, pulling in his chair and leaning back again, resting his arm across the back of my chair. "Now you may sit."

"He's good, right?" Nessa murmured. "Scary and exciting at the same time."

The gargoyles slowly took their seats, Nelson clearly unhappy with the situation but not wanting to set Austin off again. He adjusted his tie and tried to cover his newfound obedience by taking a sip of his wine.

"Wine, alphas?" The server who'd waited on us the other night stopped by my side.

"Yes, please," I said. "Whatever they are having." I motioned at the leaders.

"Same, thank you," Austin told him, then turned to the leaders. "We've welcomed you into this territory and given your people an adjustment period to learn how to properly behave. We've allowed you to check out our operations, and when you brought more people into the territory for your play at battle, we allowed it because of your customs. After all that, you still allow your petty insecurities to blind you." He paused for a moment, and silence rang in the room. "I'm not going to tell you how to do your jobs. It's more effective for us to sit back and watch you step into your own graves. One thing I know, however—you'll think back on this trip and know with certainty that you chose the wrong path. We will make sure of it."

He looked over at me then, and I knew him well enough to know that he'd just changed whatever it was he'd set out to do.

"What do you say we go sample from the food

trucks with the others?" he asked me as the server poured us glasses of wine. "We can eat here anytime. We might as well enjoy better company."

I smiled at him and pushed my chair back. "Excellent idea."

Before we left, Austin addressed the leaders one more time. "You've overstayed your welcome. You are now here on our good graces, and my patience has dried up. I'll expect you to leave this territory as soon as possible."

I thought I heard Nessa swear softly, but before I could glance over to see what the matter was, Nelson said, "Gladly," and a strange sort of buzz permeated the restaurant. It sounded like a swarm of bees, but on a much larger scale. Like gargoyle wings when Nathanial was trying to summon his people, but in a chorus.

The leaders all looked in confusion in the direction we were heading.

"What's that—"

"Attack," Tristan said over me urgently, grabbing Nessa's shoulder. "That's our warning system."

"Tristan, sir," someone yelled from the lobby. "We've received notice of an attack!"

"Attack?" I said as my gargoyle flowered power within me. "Who—"

Austin's phone rang as Broken Sue yelled into the

restaurant, “We’ve got mages and mercenaries, sir, crossing the territory in the northeast. Nine mages and two dozen mercenaries. They’re coming in hot.”

“Let’s go, let’s go!” I shouted, yanking off the necklace. “Austin, back your people away until we can get fliers there. Sebastian and Nessa, we need you visible. We’ll fly you in. Nessa, after that, you’ll go on the ground. Sebastian, Ulric will be keeping you airborne. The fliers will take on the magical people so our ground crew can tear up their mercenaries. Let’s get out there!”

CHAPTER 31

JESSIE

THE BUZZING WAS louder outside—three gargoyles in the air were beating their wings fast and shallow enough to make a loud humming sound. It was incredibly handy as a warning system.

Shifters ran toward the parking lot. Broken Sue waited for Austin. They'd drive there and shift when they were close.

"Miss Jessie," Nathanial said as he ran toward me, ripping his shirt off his torso. My team ran behind him, all of them shedding their clothes as well. "You need to call the gargoyles. Don't worry about the leaders, not for this. Do what you were meant to do and join us all together. Bring them into the fight as a unit so that they don't clutter the air on their own."

"Yeah, they'll want to go to battle," Ulric said, out of breath as he discarded his pants. "You'll need to organize them."

I remembered Nathanial telling me the gargoyles would want me to bring the fight to them. I knew in my heart he was right. When called to battle, gargoyles felt excited and eager and giddy with anticipation. They were a battle species, apparently like the basajaunak that had already gathered around us, wanting to do what they were made to do. *Fight.*

"No problem," I said, flicking off my shoes and then shedding my clothes.

Austin grabbed me around the middle and hauled me to him roughly, his hand in my hair and his lips pressed firmly to mine. A car stopped not far away, loaded with shifters waiting for their alpha.

"Stay safe," he told me. "Find the darkness. Don't fear it—I'll never allow you to be lost. Guard what's most precious to me in the world, Jacinta. Guard yourself. I love you."

"I love you," I told him, taking this moment to focus solely on him.

And then we were each going off in opposite directions, him to get to the battle and me to get in the air.

"They will not mess with our home," I said to myself, shifting into my gargoyle form and then launching into the air.

I didn't know why these mages were attacking, or whose mages they were. I'd thought Momar had all his people tied up in anticipation of Kingsley's battle. All I knew was that they'd be sorry for showing up on our doorstep without a larger arsenal. Because I'd bring in these gargoyles, I'd handle the magic, and I would show those useless leaders what it actually meant to be an army of gargoyles.

My roar felt like it came up from my toes. Power boomed from my body, blanketing the whole territory and beyond. I felt Gimerel scattering away from the mages, having no more idea of how to handle magical workers now than they had the day of the raid.

Come to me.

Harder and harder I boomed out my magic, and my wings made a distinct sound that I'd never made before. An urgent sound, not unlike the buzzing from earlier, but much higher-pitched. It carried along my pulses of magic.

Come to me!

The fliers in my crew rose first as the basajaunak stuffed themselves into cars or vans and headed out with the shifters. They stayed just below me. And then more fliers joined us, ignoring their cairn leaders' orders to stay grounded and rising to my call.

The darkness pulled at me, and I welcomed it, using it to boost my summons.

COME TO ME!

In the distance, gargoyles rose into the darkened sky, and the moonlight cast them in haunting shadows. More rose all around me, their wings pumping, their anticipation palpable. I found those with resistance and pushed, working at them, coaxing them with magic.

Not the leaders, though, who were all gathered angrily by the restaurant entrance. I blocked them from feeling the message, wanting them to watch me take their people out from under them. I'd give them back, but not until I gave them a taste of victory.

And then I felt a rock in a turbulent sea. Tristan—his resistance ironclad, his will not at all bending. He needed something a little extra. The gargoyle in him longed to rise, but something within him pushed back. Some dark force would not allow him to go so easily.

It felt a little like Niamh when someone tried to force her into doing something. I wondered if he had a little puca mixed up in him somewhere.

I added a little flourish of magic that could usually entice a person like her. It essentially translated to: *pretty please.*

I had no idea how I heard his dark chuckle. I felt more than saw his deep bow. And then the mighty beast rose into the sky. His wings snapped and his people fell in around him, perfectly organized. A born leader waiting on my command.

The other lead enforcers did the same, if not so perfectly synchronized. They brought their people in around them and waited.

"Okay, let's go, let's go," Sebastian said, starting to run.

In a move we'd practiced many times, Ulric and Jasper swooped down and grabbed the mages. As they rose, Nathanial did the same, holding me so that we could go faster. Tristan followed directly behind and somewhat above my people. Another enforcer was below, and the others fanned out to the sides.

As we cut through the sky, more gargoyles fell in, filling in my ranks. These were the solo guardians, the ones who'd come to check us out. Magic pumped through me, and my heart felt like a battle drum. I felt the distinct desire to connect with everyone in tow. They hadn't spilled blood on my behalf, but they would. I needed to feel their whereabouts and conditions if I was going to be able to protect them in battle.

Through my gargoyle, I extended my magical connection. One and all snatched it up quickly—and one immediately fed me curiosity. Tristan again. He was analyzing each interaction with me, going along with it but still feeling it out.

That didn't matter now. I could see the blasts of light and color up ahead, mages pushing forward a good distance behind a large grouping of mercenaries firing at houses or people on the run.

Anger throbbed within me.

We'd run the last time we heard mages were coming for us. We'd taken the battle elsewhere.

Not this time. This time we were ready.

The shifters were out of their vehicles. Austin's roar went up, a challenge. His shifters followed suit, organizing quickly below us in their heavily practiced formation. The basajaunak flanked their neat rows, hands out and bodies bent forward a little, roaring.

The connections to all the gargoyles were insane, so many flying with me, each now feeding me emotional cues. It was too many. I couldn't compartmentalize them.

Instead I homed in on the lead enforcers, yanking our connections taut and then using magical pulses to communicate. Hopefully they understood. I'd practiced heavily with my crew. These people were strangers. I didn't know how to use this connection to work with them.

Trusting they'd at least pick up visual cues, I leaned forward so Nathanial would lower us in the sky as we reached the shifters. Jasper dove to get Nessa on the ground, and she quickly met up with Edgar.

"This way, Shadow," I barely heard Edgar tell her,

curving away right.

"Why this way?"

"I never know."

Austin glanced up.

Now.

Another magical blast for the gargoyles: *follow me!*

We shot forward with a roar, Nathanial and me in the lead and the others in my crew fanning out in a V. Sebastian took up the rear.

I craned my neck to look behind to see if the new gargoyles were following. To my utter relief, they were. Seamlessly. Organized in a way that Austin would be proud of.

At the lead, following right behind us, was Tristan. He was taking my cues and directing those around him, not just his cairn but all the gargoyles—it did not seem to matter that he hadn't previously worked with them. My God, but he was a helluvan asset. No wonder Nelson hadn't asked any questions about his past.

We were nearly on them when the mages finally looked up.

The first blast came right for me. Nathanial threw me sideways and dove in the other direction. My team knew to split, and as I careened to the side, I half turned back to throw up a shield before the spell smashed into Tristan.

Then I was back and firing, blasting down at the mages with all my power. Austin would handle the mercenaries.

"Lower," Sebastian yelled as Ulric flew him by. "Draw their fire away from the shifters."

I dove with them, quickly caught by Nathanial, my speed increasing drastically. Magic came at us almost immediately, and the mages went from leaning forward to looking up. Hard and complex spells slammed into my shields—these were spells I'd never have the time to pick apart. They didn't have the power to greatly trouble me, though, not with the improved protection spells Sebastian and I had worked up.

The problem was that there were so many of them. Nine to our two. We had to weed some out before the rest of my crew and the gargoyles could take them.

I flung my hands to release me from Nathanial and barreled down into them, taking their fire at close range and reflecting it back. I nearly made it to one of their mages before a spell came at me from the side, knocking me off course. I tumbled through the air and then along the ground, jumping up in time to throw up a shield for Niamh and Mr. Tom, who'd followed right behind me.

Cyra rained down fire in their wakes, scattering the mages but taking a spell for her efforts. Hollace, too, took a hit, and they careened in opposite directions.

Hurt, not dead. They'd be okay.

Niamh's golden hooves beat at the ground a moment before she slammed her horn into the middle of the closest mage. She'd let the others be a distraction. Mr. Tom scratched along another mage, taking a rough shot from a hasty spell.

Grimacing, I launched back into the sky as Ulric flew Sebastian around the mages, allowing him to fire powerful spells at them from right up close. They must've taken potions to help ward away magic, though, because his spells weren't doing much damage.

Gargoyles scattered every which way, not used to this sort of battle. Not used to the pain of these types of spells. They were out of their element, unsure what to do, scared of what was happening even if they didn't want to admit it.

As I flew closer, I grabbed the tethers of our new connections, one and all, focusing as much as I possibly could to pull taut every one. That done, I pumped into them comforting support, courage, and a heady promise of victory. Into the air, I pounded a magical message. *Fight with me! We will win together!*

Working on that but now shifting focus, I swooped back toward the mages as the shifters tore into the mercenaries behind us. Flashes of light blasted from magical guns shot into their ranks. Hollace turned back to them, raining down lightning to cut down the numbers.

Gargoyles once again fell in with Tristan, reorganizing. They dove for the mages, and I hurried to get there first. Spells zipped into the air. Tristan maneuvered better than I'd ever seen, even during the raid. He tilted and dodged, working through the air at an incredible speed. His companions didn't fare so well. One caught a spell center mass, and it knocked him out of the sky.

I threw a catching spell under him to keep him suspended as I got a block up in time to protect two other gargoyles. Tristan reached the mages, but not before one of them hit him in the side with a spell that made him roar in pain. He snatched up the offending mage and, using both of those enormous arms, pulled the guy apart. Literally ripped his body in two like a piece of paper.

Blood splattered everywhere. The mages around him scattered, scared beyond sense. They kept firing spells, though, now directly at him.

I was there, shielding him from damage, no time to attack with any spells of my own.

A spell buzzed right past me, a narrow miss. Tristan turned and grabbed me, firing up into the sky so fast that I might've peed myself a little. He held me as we did a circle, weaving in between the magical attacks and dipping so I could get spells fired off or shields hastily erected at the last moment.

Gargoyles attacked, but not as a cohesive unit. They didn't have a clear idea of what to do. They weren't as fast or agile as Tristan or my crew gargoyles. They didn't know how to engage.

I worked at those connections again, trying to energize. Trying to bring them back together. I panted in fatigue but didn't give up.

Thankfully, my crew was well versed in all of this. They were the saving grace. Ulric took a hit, though, losing his grip on Sebastian. His roar sent a message to our team. *Help!*

Someone needed to grab Sebastian. He could catch himself in a magical net, but then he'd be a sitting duck for the enemy mages.

I flared my hands, frustrated when Tristan didn't recognize the signal I'd established with Nathanial. This time I added a little electricity in the movement and a wiggle, flaring my hands again.

Sebastian fell, utterly composed, trusting that one of us would grab him. He kept firing at the mages, and his spells were starting to get through whatever potion or deterrent they'd taken.

Tristan loosened his grip and then caught on; a shock of alarm coursed through him as he noticed

Sebastian falling. Letting go of me, he sliced through the air, dodging enemy spells and snatching Sebastian up before Jasper or Mr. Tom were able to get there.

A lead enforcer led a group of gargoyles down through the spells with zero fear or hesitation. I flapped my wings as hard as I could, trying to get closer so my defending spells would be more focused. Gargoyle arms closed around me, and I recognized the coloring of one of the cairn enforcers. He picked up speed rapidly, and downward we shot.

My spell covered the others right in time, blocking blasts from three mages, but I didn't have enough juice to reflect the power back at them.

In a moment, it didn't matter.

That little defense was all the gargoyles needed. They closed the distance in record time and dug their claws into the mages. Their wings flapped as they pulled the mages into the sky, making short work of frail bodies. When they were done, they threw the bodies down at the others.

Five mages to go.

One saw the carnage, turned, and ran back toward a street where a line of black cars was parked.

He shouldn't have turned his back on a swarm of gargoyles.

The gargoyle holding me let go and went after him

immediately, easily dodging the spells tossed over the mage's shoulder. The other mages ran in different directions, not used to the aerial onslaught.

Shifters roared behind me as I hammered down spells, taking advantage of the mages' fear and confusion.

Shadows materialized behind one of the mages who had just fired into the sky. Edgar zoomed in behind him with a cheerful "Hi!" He dug his fangs into the startled mage's neck and stayed there as Nessa appeared behind another and peppered his body with her knife blades.

"Jessie, look out!"

I turned in time to see a blast of light coming right for me. My hands were slow in rising, or maybe time had just slowed down. I didn't have the opportunity to say the words to protect myself, or even duck out of the way. Only one thought formed in my brain: *This is gonna hurt.*

I prepared to heal myself as a big body slammed into mine. Tristan. The shot hit him in the side, tearing through his wing and making him grunt in pain. We careened, spiraling quickly—Tristan only had one wing now.

Struggling free, I switched our positioning, holding him as best I could and making a pathetic attempt to fly with him. He was much too heavy for my meager wings.

Choosing a plan B, I began healing him in earnest as I lowered us, made it down, and then helped him get to cover. In a moment, I was rising again. Only two mages were left, and Sebastian hovered over them, held by Jasper, keeping them busy.

I headed that way, once again grabbed by a random gargoyle, and helped Sebastian rain down magic. Our spells were faster and harder than theirs. The mages quailed, sinking down, and then screamed when five gargoyles swooped down to finish them.

Breathing hard, I looked back toward the mercenaries. Then realized there were no more mercenaries. Not any who were left standing.

Ulric's was the first roar of victory. His flying was a little wonky, but he was still in the air. Jasper joined, and then all the gargoyles were roaring, joined in a chorus by shifters and basajaunak.

Tristan rose into the sky again, not quite mended but apparently good enough. He needn't have bothered.

I shifted as soon as I landed, checking the mages just in case one had made it.

"That was a grisly end, huh?" Nessa said with a smile, standing next to a body part I didn't want a closer look at. "And I thought shifters were vicious."

"Shifters *are* vicious," Sebastian said, landing with Jasper.

A loud "*Aaaahhhhh*" drifted from the mercenary area. One of the basajaunak was lifting two disembodied heads into the sky, yelling out his victory. I turned away, my stomach rolling. That was way too much. *Way* too much.

"I think we have a lot of vicious creatures," I murmured, feeling my newly established links with the gargoyles. I'd need to figure out a better way to access through them now that there were so many. It had gotten very confusing during the battle, and I'd missed people. Not that I could've ever covered them all anyway, but it would have helped to have a system.

A few swells of pain caught my notice, and I homed in on them and headed in that direction.

"Miss Jessie," someone called.

I ignored it. They could come to me if it was important.

"Are you okay?" I asked as I reached a hurt gargoyle with a large gash in the side of his leg.

"I'm okay, Ironheart." He grimaced as he took a step away. "I'll be okay." He pointed at the sky. "That felt good, what we did. What we were. Together. That was fun. Dangerous."

I couldn't help a grin. Gargoyles—they did love a good battle.

"Just go sit over there, okay?" I pointed to a little

grassy area. "I need to see how many people need my attention before I can start healing."

"You can heal?"

Why did no one seem to know that?

I sought out the next hurt gargoyle.

"Miss Jessie." Tristan caught up easy with his long strides.

"Yeah? What do you need?"

"What are you—"

"Are you okay?" I asked the next gargoyle, who was badly hurt and barely clinging to consciousness. "Oh, man, okay, lie down. Just right here is fine. I'll help, okay? You're going to be okay."

Where was that healer that I'd sent a summons for in the basajaunak lands? We could sorely use them.

I started healing the gargoyle immediately, turning to Tristan. "Get someone over here to sit with him."

He didn't balk at my order. "Of course," he said quickly.

On I went to the next. Tristan caught up with me again.

"You should be checking in with your people," I told him. "Some of them are hurt. I don't have the energy to heal everyone, so only call me if it's life or death. Otherwise, I'm sure Austin has medical people on the way."

"My second-in-command is seeing to that."

"Ah. Well, what can I do for you?"

Tristan didn't answer me. Instead, he shadowed me as I checked in with the next gargoyle, who was already being seen to by his enforcer, and then the last one, who seemed to be in the worst shape. I set to healing him immediately.

Austin had already worked through his people, sectioning off those who needed medical attention.

"What's the status?" I asked when I caught up with him.

He looked me over briefly, running his thumb along my chin, before glancing over my shoulder at Tristan.

"Thank you," he said. "For taking that magical blast for her."

"She was more valuable to the battlefield than me—simple as that," Tristan replied.

"That kinda cheapens it a little," I grumbled as Austin ran his touch down my arm.

"The darkness?" Austin asked me, peering into my eyes.

I shook my head. "It was fine. I didn't even feel it recede. Throughout the battle it just…felt like *me* this time."

"You must be acclimating to your beast. That's good news." He kissed my forehead. "We have a few wound-ed. They took shots from the magical guns. Nothing that needs your attention, though. Brochan is getting them situated now, and we'll get them home when they're a little further along the healing process."

"How tough were they?" I asked as Mr. Tom walked up. I decided that from now on, all of our cars would have a few muumuus in the trunk, just in case.

"With you covering the mages, the mercenaries were nothing. The pack has really come together. The extra support was the cream. This'll help them feel solid about going up against mages. You?"

I sighed, replaying all the stuff that had gone wrong. "Everyone did great under the circumstances, but I didn't do a great job of keeping track of everyone. We were all over the place, scattering all the time. I haven't worked with a group this large before, and it showed. I didn't do great."

"Pardon my interruption, alphas," Tristan said, "but I disagree. Miss, none of us have had training with mages. It was…eye-opening. They can do a lot of damage in a short amount of time. This was our first time working with each other, too, and taking orders from someone we don't know. Orders in the form of feelings and magical pulses. It was foreign. Exhilarating, but an adjustment. That battle was quick and relatively painless in the grand scheme of things. Your untested leadership was better than I'd expect from an experienced commander in this situation."

I put my hand on my hip and allowed myself a smile, shrugging a little. "Thank you for saying that. I still see all the faults, and I don't like that I missed shielding some of our people, but thank you."

"Hey, guys." Nessa bounded up, a little blood spattered on her face and her smile radiant. "Helluva battle, huh? I think it went well, and look—naked party! There's a lot of really fine backsides here." She winked at Tristan.

"Austin, Jessie." Sebastian walked up, looking relieved. "Crap, sorry. Alpha, I meant. Alphazzz, whatever. Anyway, that battle went best of all. The mages were decent at best, but we handled them well. How'd the situation with the gargoyles go?"

I knew what he was asking. Did this battle change any minds?

Time would tell.

CHAPTER 32

NIAMH

NIAMH SAT ON her porch, rocking slowly back and forth. Her rocks sat in their little pile by her chair, ready in case any tourists might happen by. They'd stopped coming for a while as magical people flooded the area and made Dick and Jane visitors feel like outcasts, but now that news was spreading about Jessie, magical visitors were starting to come for a gawk.

She caught sight of the large shape coming down the sidewalk.

"What's that feller up to, I wonder?" She reached down and grabbed the rock on top.

Gimerel was supposed to have left that morning. They'd hung on for a couple days after the mage battle just in case more were on the way. They'd passed it off as a desire to help Jessie out, but given the gossip in the bar, it seemed their leader was worried about getting attacked on the way out of here.

Their big lead enforcer drew closer, leaving the sidewalk and taking a route through the middle of the street, directly for Ivy House. His glowing, turbulent gaze met hers, a spark of a warning within.

"What is that now, a threat to mind me manners?" she called.

She chuckled a little to herself, let him get that much closer, stood, and threw. Her aim was true, of course. Any fool could throw a rock. The throw was hard, too.

He didn't seem to notice, continuing on. It would clunk him right in the melon.

At the last moment, though, without even looking, his hand came up and snatched the rock out of midair.

That lad sure had a magical boost from whatever part of him wasn't gargoyle. She had been racking her brain, tryin' to figure out what else he could be, but so far coming up blank. Every time she tried to badger him, or manipulate him, or coax him into giving something away, he resisted admirably. He was a hard nut to crack. She was a little in awe, to be honest. She'd never met anyone quite like him.

It was also infuriatin'.

He turned his head to glare at her, pulled his hand out of the sky, and dropped the rock into his slacks pocket.

"Lucky catch, ya bastard," she muttered, and

damned if he didn't smile like he'd heard her. "Ye're gonna have dogs hunting ya if they ever find out what ye are," she called after him as he stepped onto Ivy House soil.

"You're going to be inundated with family if they ever find out where *you* are," he called back as that gobshite Mr. Tom opened the front door.

"Will I, me arse," she said, sitting back down. Her cousins were all scattered to the four winds. They didn't have a care where she was or what she was up to, just like she didn't wish to see them. Though if they did show up at her doorstep, they'd love the basajaunak concoction. That stuff was legendary. Assuming a body could get past the taste.

"Don't mind her," Mr. Tom told the gargoyle. "She has never been housebroken. What can I do for you?"

"I'm here to see the miss, if she's available."

"Right this way, please." Mr. Tom opened the door wider to admit the gargoyle, who was probably here to tell Jess about another list of grievances his wanker of a boss planned to file.

Mr. Tom stood in the doorway after the gargoyle had passed and gave her a dirty look before shutting the door behind him.

After rocking for a while longer, Niamh felt curiosity get the better of her. She wanted to know why that lad had come here alone, and if the alphas would be running the whole cairn out of here when Austin found out they hadn't left.

✧ ✧ ✧

JESSIE

I FELT TRISTAN enter and then Mr. Tom head in my direction.

"What is it?" Naomi asked me. She held her computer, showing me a sample design for the billiard room while we stood in said billiard room. She'd thought it would help with visualization.

The gargoyles were leaving within the next couple of days—they were definitely dragging their feet about it—but the work on Ivy House continued. We had a long way to go.

"Tristan has come to visit. By himself. I have no idea why. Excuse me."

He'd been a huge help in that battle the other day, and when we got back to the restaurant to get our clothes, he'd stopped Nelson from chastising me about taking his gargoyles. Then he'd stopped him from chastising me for endangering his people. Then he'd just removed him from the premises, because Austin had gotten a little worked up about the whole thing. I'd told Tristan that he was welcome here anytime. Maybe he was taking me up on that. Or maybe he'd just come to say goodbye.

"Miss," Mr. Tom started when I met him on the second-story stairs. "Mr.—"

"I know." I passed him, feeling Niamh coming up the walk.

She entered the house just as I was coming down the hall and glancing in the first sitting room, where I'd sensed his presence.

"Good morning," she said, even though it was a little after noon. "Lovely day, isn't it? What's that clown doing here?"

"I'm about to find out."

He sat on the couch holding the bracelet, moving it around in the light.

"Wondering if I replaced some of the real gems with fake ones?" I asked, taking a seat opposite him.

He didn't hurry in his inspection. "I used to think this bracelet was beautiful."

"Not now?"

He looked up before turning and laying it on the table behind him. We hadn't moved it since the raid. I hadn't really thought about it, and Mr. Tom hadn't brought it up.

"Not now, no. I see how hollow the achievement of

protecting it was."

"That wasn't hollow. You lead a fine team. The best team, right? Because no one could best you and get that bracelet?"

"You bested me."

"I also lead a fine team. Or…you know…have a fine team. They just kinda seem to do whatever they want at this point. Sorry about Cyra's addiction to stalking you. She doesn't mean anything by it. She thinks it's a fun game. She couldn't care less about your secrets."

"Who told you she was following me?"

"She usually rats herself out eventually." I crossed my ankles and clasped my hands in my lap.

"Miss." Mr. Tom stepped in the room and bowed. "I was going to ask if you wanted me to make up some snacks or bring in something to drink, but you sprinted away too quickly and made me chase you all the way to the front of the house."

I stared at him for a moment. "And I'm sure Tristan doesn't think less of our professionalism after having heard that."

"Of course not," Mr. Tom replied. "Can I get you something to eat or drink? Espresso, cortado, café au lait?"

I lifted my eyebrows at Tristan.

"No, I'm—"

"Or how about an iced coffee?" Mr. Tom tried. "Something spicy, perhaps? We're nearing the pumpkin spice season. I can nudge it here just a little early. What about a—"

"I've changed my mind," Tristan said. "How about an iced ristretto, ten-shot, with breve, four pumps of caramel, three pumps vanilla, poured, not shaken, with heavy whipping cream on top and three sugars, two mixed in and one on top to make the cream crunchy."

Mr. Tom blinked at him for a moment. "Excellent choice, sir. Coming right up!"

I blinked at him too.

Tristan smiled, his teeth white and straight. "I heard that in the coffee shop the other day. It was so extravagant that it stuck in my mind. I figured it would give him a challenge."

I laughed. "You figured correctly. What can I do for you, Tristan? Or is this a friendly chat?"

He leaned back, his expression turning serious. "I didn't know what to expect when I came to this territory. The setup sounded a little absurd, I will admit. It didn't take me long to see the merit in your mate, though. He has a firm handle on this cairn—pack. But it was you who blindsided me, both at first and during the raid."

I wasn't sure if I should say thank you, so I just kept

quiet, waiting for him to get to the point.

"All the gargoyles coming here heard that you were new to this life and totally inexperienced. Completely green."

I spread my hands. "They'd be right."

"No," he replied, shaking his head, "they wouldn't. Your experience is in actual warfare. Real battles. When you took a stand against those mages, it was clear that you have more experience in your short tenure than my leader has had in his many years. Than any of the living leaders have. We all saw it. We *felt* it, through this new link. Is this link forever?"

"I honestly don't know. The house likes to keep things from me. I'm trying to figure it out, though. You're not trapped. Hopefully."

He shook his head again. "You mistake me. I don't feel trapped. I feel *connected.* In that battle, I felt connected. All my guys did. To you and to each other. It was an amazing feeling. A natural feeling, like we were always meant to have a female bring us together and keep us bonded."

I smiled as my heart swelled a little. It felt good to have done something right with the other gargoyles for once—something that wouldn't immediately result in a grievance being filed against me.

"I've been watching you," he continued. "I've been

watching your crew and your mate. I've thought a lot about it, and if you'll have me, I'd like to join your team."

I froze, immediately repeating that back just in case I hadn't heard him correctly.

Then I thought I'd better make certain anyway.

"What was that?"

"I can start at the bottom and work my way up, if that's how you do things," he said, speaking a little faster now. "Or I can challenge my way into Alpha Steele's pack, if that's the preferred method. Regardless, I'd like to ask for inclusion."

"I…" I gulped, not having expected that, trying to keep my cool and not dance or scream or fist-pump the air. Having him would be a dream come true. He was strong and fierce and a great leader. He also had great respect within the gargoyle community.

There was only one glaring issue. His history.

"Are you safe?" I asked, deciding not to beat around the bush. "Niamh seemed to think you might not be."

"Neither is she," he said without hesitation. "Neither are you. But there is an issue that we do have to discuss. I didn't want to bring it up unless you were seriously thinking about bringing me on."

"Which is?"

"As far as gargoyles are concerned, I don't have any

cairn history. I'm a nobody. Nelson purposely chose to look the other way when I joined his cairn because of my size and strength. Now he holds it over my head, threatening me with exposure that would tarnish my reliability in the gargoyle community."

"Is that a fact?" I said softly, leaning against the armrest, trying to curb my anger.

A smile slowly spread across his face. "You just can't hide that protective instinct, huh?"

"I don't see any reason to. Why would that tarnish your reliability?"

"No previous cairn means no history, and that means no birth status or known stability. I'm a wild card."

"*Were* a wild card, though, right? You've been in his cairn for nearly fifteen years."

"Not very long by gargoyle standards. I took my time deciding to join up."

I wanted to ask why, to ferret out that history he protected so closely, but knew I couldn't. Not after making such a big deal about not caring and not wanting to ruin his future. If I knew what he was, a random creature I hadn't grown up worrying about, I doubted it would mean much to me. Because of that, I might let it slip to the wrong people. To mage kinda people, maybe. If it meant a lot to the magical world at large, that slip might create a problem for him and, given I would be signing on as his protector, for the whole pack.

"So what are you saying?" I asked. "If you leave him and join with us, he'd out you?"

"Yes."

"Which basically just means people would know you have an unknown past?"

"Yes."

"And..." I stalled, thinking I'd missed something. "Why does that affect me?"

"It would greatly lower my status, and in turn, lower yours."

I scoffed. "From what I've heard, my status can't get much lower."

"I wouldn't be able to help your status, then."

I smoothed back my ponytail, suddenly tired of this whole thing. "I honestly don't care. Is that the end of the bad news, then? He won't come with torches and pitchforks and chase you or anything?"

His smile stretched again. "He might've...if it were anywhere but here. He's in no hurry to return to this territory."

"Good. Well, fine, then I guess it's my turn to potentially scare you away. That attack the other day was no fluke. We're attacked all the time."

"Sounds intriguing."

"You'll need to get along with the shifters and take orders from Austin. We co-rule this pack, as you've seen. He's just and fair, but he's strict and doles out harsh punishments if you step over the line."

"He's an incredibly competent leader. He and his pack are an attraction for this territory."

"And now the most serious part. I've drawn the eye of a mage with a magical empire, and our feud has barely even begun. I'm not sure if he sent the attack the other day, but he has a target on the shifters and on me."

I told him about helping Kingsley and that we'd have to eventually venture into the murky depths of the mage world.

"We're going to help Kingsley combat the mage attack. We'll leave almost immediately. Within a couple weeks. It'll be incredibly dangerous, much more so than the other day. *Much* more so."

"You had no idea the attack was coming?"

"None. We were utterly blindsided. Sebastian and Nessa hadn't heard a peep through their network that this was coming. They're currently piecing together who it was and why they might've attacked. I'm damn glad you guys decided to hang around. The timing really helped us out. Not to take pleasure in the situation, since some people got hurt, you included, but…without all of you, we might've lost someone."

"The timing was…quite a coincidence," he said slowly.

I leaned forward, knowing my expression was serious. "I hope you don't think we planned that. Honestly, if I'd known something like that was coming, I wouldn't have allowed any of the cairns to come in the first place. It wouldn't have been the first time I warned potential allies of the danger following us."

"I believe you. I think I speak for a lot of the gargoyles when I say that we got lucky the timing worked out."

"Yeah." I leaned back again. "You guys are crazy. Anyway, life in this territory won't be fun and games. But if you want to join us, we'd love to have you."

"Here we are." Mr. Tom walked in much too quickly, his wings fluttering. "Yes, yes, yes-yes-yes-yes." He stopped near Tristan, leaned over, and held out the tray carrying the coffee. "Here we go. It took a few tries to get it exactly right. I hope you don't mind, but I altered the recipe just slightly. Try it and see if you like it."

He tapped his foot as he waited for Tristan to take a sip, watching every movement. He'd clearly sampled the merchandise.

"Delicious," Tristan said, gliding his tongue across

his upper lip to dislodge some cream. "Many thanks."

"Well." Mr. Tom preened, bent his arm at the elbow, and tilted from side to side for some unknown reason. "Fantastic. I'll just go find some cobwebs to clean. You let me know if you—"

He'd walked out while still talking.

"Ahem…" I held up a finger. "I should probably also warn you that my crew is…well, weird. They're all pretty weird."

"When trying to warn someone away, you might want to lead with that," Tristan said.

NELSON WAS LIVID at Tristan's resignation. He'd threatened to out his murky history, insisted he wouldn't take him back after I inevitably ran my territory into the ground, and promised me he'd make my life a living hell.

The very next day, proof circulated of Nelson's mishandling of his production cairns, embezzlement, abusive behavior, and even the murder of gargoyles who'd stood in the way of his securing better contracts. Nessa and Sebastian had been saving that little nugget for a rainy day, it seemed, and Patty had run with it.

We offered to take over their contracts, offering the production cairns a fair deal with a larger supply-and-demand chain, since we'd branch out into the world at large, not just stay within the gargoyle community. We took on Anthott, as well, who came to see Austin and me shortly after the battle. How that was possible?

Tristan's defection had started a windfall.

A lot of guardians had been circling us, waiting for a nudge to take the risk and join us. Tristan was that nudge. He might've lost status because of his history, an arbitrary thing, but he was known for his battle prowess and levelheadedness. If he thought we were a good bet, a lot of other guardians weren't about to say boo. He brought them on in droves, quickly and effortlessly working with Austin and me on how to best organize and manage them. He'd be Austin's second beta, handling the gargoyles while Broken Sue handled the shifters, taking their orders from Austin and me.

I'd gotten my army.

Not just a gargoyle army, either.

The basajaun secretly going by Phil had turned into a sort of recruiter. He knew which of his people to talk into visiting, usually going for the ones around his and the basandere's age, and once they were here, none of them wanted to leave. The basandere in charge of the wood was changing the feel of it, very slowly but diligently, and they liked the idea of starting fresh in a place with family. They liked the idea of building a wood of their own, that their parents had had no hand in.

Dave had brought two. Nine went to battle. Another ten came out shortly thereafter. We didn't have them all, but we were gaining basajaunak allies.

The other great news was that Mr. Porsche, as Nessa called him, contacted me shortly after leaving. He apologized for the part he'd played at the end and asked if he might visit again. Maybe we could take a ride in the Bentley or have a BBQ at Ivy House.

He also offered his support in our upcoming battle to help Kingsley. Tristan said it was his way of offering his cairn's friendship to us, and a huge step toward building our status.

I didn't care about the status. I was absolutely giddy over his offer of help.

In mere weeks, we would head into Kingsley's territory with real help. With hope.

In mere weeks, we'd head into the battle of our lives.

EPILOGUE

NIAMH

"AH HERE, WE'VE got another one." Niamh reached down next to her as a mousy woman in her late twenties walked along the sidewalk, looking at all the houses she passed. A navy bag crossed her body and hung at her hip, and her grip was tight on the strap. Rectangular glasses with thick black frames sat on her button nose, which was dusted by a smattering of freckles.

When she was close to Niamh's house, she slowed. Her gaze drifted to Ivy House and stuck. She stared up at the huge house.

"Get off with ye, ya bugger," Niamh hollered, throwing the rock. "This inn't some museum."

Her rock landed home, plonking the woman on the head.

"Oh!" The woman staggered into the street.

The blue Porsche Jessie had gotten from that muppet cairn leader zoomed down, swerving to avoid hitting her. She staggered back onto the sidewalk, holding her head and looking at the sky.

She didn't know where the rock had come from.

"Here, lemme give ye another clue," Niamh murmured, grabbing another.

Tristan stepped out of the Porsche, having parked it in the driveway, and looked back at them in time for Niamh to let fly with another rock. It hit the woman again.

"Ow!" she said again, ducking and throwing up her arms. She swiveled to Niamh this time, figuring it out. "Why are you throwing rocks at me?"

"We aren't some kinda circus attraction," Niamh told her, reaching for another rock.

"That's not why I'm here!" She held her arms out in front of her and stepped into the street, not looking for cars.

Brakes squealed. Austin's Jeep slid to a stop as she wandered out in front of it. She glanced at him and startled.

"Oops. Sorry." She didn't head back to the sidewalk, though.

"Are you okay?" Austin stepped down from the Jeep.

"Yes, thank you. That woman is throwing rocks,

though—watch out!"

Niamh sat down smoothly, disappearing the rock into her pocket. No need to get in trouble with the alpha. He could be right cross when a person got him in a bad mood, and with their upcoming departure to go help his brother, tensions were running high.

"She'll stop, don't worry." Austin Steele directed the woman to the sidewalk. "Do you need help getting somewhere?"

"Um, no, I don't think so. I'm headed there, I think. To that house." She pointed at Ivy House.

"Is that right?" He studied her a little harder. "Do you have business with its mistress?"

"I don't know."

His eyebrows climbed. "Why are you going there?"

She paused for a moment, and her tone turned whimsical. "I don't know. I keep getting this feeling like I should go there. So…I'm going to go there."

"A feeling?" He glanced over her at Niamh. "What kind of feeling?"

"Like a…" The woman thought about it for a while. "Like an invitation."

"What is it you do?" Austin asked.

"I'm a healer."

Shivers washed over Niamh. This was the result of the summons Jessie had sent out accidentally in the basajaunak lands.

A body never really knew what to expect with a summons. They could be volatile. They could not work out. One thing they always tended to be, though, was disruptive.

The timing was either great or terrible. They'd all find out together.

THE END

ABOUT THE AUTHOR

K.F. Breene is a Wall Street Journal, USA Today, Washington Post, Amazon Most Sold Charts and #1 Kindle Store bestselling author of paranormal romance, urban fantasy and fantasy novels. With millions of books sold, when she's not penning stories about magic and what goes bump in the night, she's sipping wine and planning shenanigans. She lives in Northern California with her husband, two children, and out of work treadmill.

Sign up for her newsletter to hear about the latest news and receive free bonus content.

www.kfbreene.com

Made in United States
Troutdale, OR
04/08/2024

19044469R00340